TEARS
OF
ALLAH

A Work of Fiction & Music By

Timothy Brannan

Other Books by Timothy Brannan

'74: A Basketball Story
[Also Kindle Edition]

TEACH
[Also Kindle Edition]

Manhattan Spiritual
[Also Kindle Edition]

Adventures in another Paradise
[Also Kindle Edition]

Into the Elephant Grass: A Viet-Nam Fable

Copyright 2012 by Timothy Brannan
ISBN 978-0-9820277-4-5
Published in the United States of America 2012
By Gemini Publishing LLC

Even though this is a work of fiction, it is based on extensive research. I have struggled to be as authentic as possible and to present the story in a balanced well-researched manner.

TEARS OF ALLAH
[The Sound Track]

For the first time, an author has created an original "sound track" as part of a novel. Songs composed and performed by MacPhail, a 21ˢᵗ century one-man band—the author and his synthesizer. Please use the musical queues included beneath chapter headings to play the appropriate selections from the CD or downloads (available separately) or simply play the musical selections on their own.

I
In a Dark Wood

II
Through the Gates

The Prologue
Bellum Sacrum and Jihad

"I am the way, the truth, and the life: no man cometh unto the Father, but by me." *John* 14:6

"And whoever seeks a religion other than Islam, it will not be accepted from him and he will be one of the losers in the Hereafter." *Qur'an* Sura Al-*E-Imran* 3:85

Clermont, France
1095 AD

Odo of Lagery gazed out over the plaza Puy-de-Dôme located in the center of the small village of Clermont on the Ţiretaine River surrounded by the Chaîne des Puys. Clerics and prominent lords from all over France were gathered amidst these volcanic mountains awaiting his address. Odo had, himself, been born a French nobleman in Lagery near Châtillon-sur-Marne. He had benefited greatly from a church education. The monks had taught him well, so well in fact that he had become a priest himself and had ultimately been elected Pope Urban II just seven years earlier.

Now, this most crucial Council of Clermont he had convoked was drawing to an end. He felt sure that he had built a holy fire under this mixed synod of ecclesiastics and laymen of the Catholic Church. They had heard and understood his case for assisting Emperor Alexius I Comnenus against the Seljuk Turks to protect Byzantium. And, on this next-to-last day of the Council, he would add wood to that fire by calling for a crusade not only to help Alexius but to reclaim the Holy City of Jerusalem. He would declare Bellum Sacrum—holy war—against the Muslims who had occupied the Holy Land and were attacking the Eastern Roman Empire. This crusade was necessary, if nothing else, to restore order to the lands he was responsible for, to steer knights toward taking the Holy Land back from the Muslims instead of fighting each other for their provincial lords. And he dared anyone to oppose him.

"The Muslims have occupied Jerusalem since 638," the Pope began. "That is contrary to the law of God." Squinting into the sunlight that drenched the plaza, he could sense the crowd's pent up nervous energy about to erupt like lava once upon a time had spewed from the mountains surrounding them.

"Just this year, Turks and Saracens have massacred more than 3,000 Christians. That is contrary to the law of God and man. The surviving Christians are being treated like animals. That, too, is contrary to the law of God and man." He crushed the air in front of him with his right fist. "Enough is enough!

"Let those who have been accustomed to unjustly wage private warfare against the faithful now go against the infidels and end with victory this war which should have been waged long ago. Let those who, for far too long, have been robbers, now become knights. Let those who have been fighting against their brothers and relatives now fight in a proper way against the Saracens. Let those who have been serving as mercenaries for small pay now obtain their eternal reward. Let those who have been wearing themselves out in both body and soul now work for a double honor.

"For, we must mount Bellum Sacrum—a holy crusade—to recapture Jerusalem from the Muslims and re-establish the Holy City under Christian rule This will be an apocalyptic clash between two cultures, two faiths—Christendom and Islam."

"Bellum Sacrum!" the hundreds of clerics and lords from every corner of France shouted in a chorused response.

"Innocents have been slaughtered. Priests have been slain. Daughters have been forced into prostitution. The cradle of our faith is in the hands of people who are obviously without God."

"Bellum Sacrum!"

"Adhemar of Le Puy, here at my side today, will lead this Crusade. It will set out on the day of the Assumption of Mary, 15 August next. Bellum Sacrum!"

"Bellum Sacrum!"

"There can be no other response! Bellum Sacrum."

"Bellum Sacrum!"

Pope Urban II controlled his facial expression, but he smiled inside. This was the response he needed to keep the knights in check. This was the response he needed to make the infidel Muslims' blood run like wine through the streets of Jerusalem. This was the response he needed to save Christendom.

"As we finish here, today, I want you in the audience—all of you—to come forward and take a ribbon of cloth from the priests around me and tie it to your clothing close to your heart as a symbol of your pledge to take up the cause of the cross and vow to go to the East to rescue your brothers. For he who makes this vow and takes up this cause and sets out on this great journey only for the salvation of his soul and the liberation of the church is remitted in entirety all penance for his sins."

As some in the crowd began to move almost uneasily toward the Pope, a young lad wrapped in a worn, gray hooded cloak skulked about in the far corner shadows of the volcanic stone plaza, partially hidden from view by a giant statue of a local hero Vercingetorix carved from that same dark volcanic rock on which the town was built. The young man didn't know why he was hiding. He was, after all, one of those who had been welcomed at this convocation. He even had blood connections with this place despite his Scottish birth. His ancestors had followed and fought with Vercingctorix. But, not long after this village fell to Julius Caesar in 52 BC despite their best efforts, his ancestors had fled north. Over the next three centuries they gradually made their way, generation by generation, to the north of France, then to Britain and Ireland, ultimately ending up in the highlands of Scotland.

Now, at fourteen, Gwynn Camsron was in France, the home of his ancestors, serving as a squire for the Lord Hughues de Payens, a distant uncle from a very distant part of the family that had not left France in those ancient times.

Today he was on his first mission from his Uncle, to spy on this gathering, to get the sense of the crowd as the Pope spoke and report back to his Uncle what took place. It was an innocuous enough task. Yet, he somehow felt more comfortable hiding from view as the sanguine mob surged forward to claim their pieces of cloth while they chanted along with Pope Urban II: "Bellum Sacrum! Bellum Sacrum! Bellum Sacrum!"

Jerusalem
1118 AD
Hughues de Payens led the determined group of nine knights towards the throne room of King Baudoin I of Jerusalem. André de

Montbard, the uncle of Bernard of Clairvaux followed closely at his right hand. They were all seasoned veterans of the Crusade that had finally avenged the 3,000 murdered Christians and taken the Holy City of Jerusalem back for Christ in a flood of Saracen blood.

"Enter now for your audience with King Baudoin of Jerusalem," a page announced as they reached the opening throne room doors.

As eight of the knights entered, a cocoon of warm sandstone walls and filtered sun light enveloped them. The ninth remained just outside the open doors, hidden behind a huge banner bearing the crest of Baudoin I, King of Jerusalem. The young monarch seemed to almost float in the shimmering light as the knights crossed the room to where he and his aides were seated among a pile of pillows elevated several feet above the polished stone floor on a throne-like perch.

"These nine of us, your majesty, pray for you to hear us," de Payens pleaded as soon as they were within easy earshot. "I say this for myself, Hughues de Payens and for these others: André de Montbard, the uncle of Bernard of Clairvaux; Geoffroi de St Omer, son of Hugh de St Omer; Payen de Montdidier and Achambaud de St-Amand, relatives of the ruling House of Flanders; Geoffroi Bison; and two Cistercian monks Gondemare and Rosal. The ninth knight is not in the room and remains unnamed. When he appears in public, he will always appear hooded and his name will never be spoken. Through his complete anonymity, we hope to protect our new order when all else fails."

The King of all Jerusalem pondered de Payens' words for a moment, glancing ever so stealthily at his primary advisor who nodded ever so slightly. "So be it, then, de Payens. And what is this new order you speak of? What would you have of us today?"

"Now that we have freed our Holy City from the infidels, your grace, we know there will be many who will make pilgrimages to visit here. It is our desire to found an order of warrior monks dedicated to the protection of these pilgrims along the roads from Europe to the Holy Lands and Jerusalem.

"We pledge to take vows of personal poverty and chastity and to supply our own horses, armor, and weapons. All of our property will be held in common for the good of the order and of others."

"Excellent!" The King smiled. "We need just such an order now that we have our Holy City back again!" He stared over at his primary advisor. "Ernoul, we can give these brave and dedicated men quarters for them and their horses in the old Temple of Solomon area, can we not?" Baudoin awaited a nod from Ernoul before he continued. "And, because these knights will be organized as a monastic order, we hereby name you officially as the Order of the Poor Knights of Christ and the Temple of Solomon, and the order is hereby given the right to wear the Cross of Lorraine as its insignia."

"Thank you, your Majesty," de Payens responded.

"Thank you, your Majesty," the other new Knights of the Temple intoned in unison.

"Thank you, your Majesty," the nameless knight whispered in the passage way just outside the doors of the great hall wrapped in the same gray hooded cloak he had worn all those years ago in the plaza Puy-de-Dôme when he was still just a squire.

At Sea
1128 AD

The knight's weathered gray hood engulfed his entire head and face as they were sprayed by the incessant seas splashing across the bow of de Payens' ship while it plowed the ocean toward England and Scotland. Even if somehow the wind should strip away the hood, his face was masked against discovery of his identity. He had served de Payens and the Order for thirty-three years, the last ten years in anonymity as the founding nameless knight, but now was his time to come home, to speak his name once more in public, and to pass on his mask and hood to a new nameless knight. In that way the Order of the Poor Knights of Christ and the Temple of Solomon would always survive, from generation to generation. The line would go on as long as there was time and men to measure it.

"Before your time is done as the nameless knight, Gwynn Camsron, you must help me set up our first two Houses in London and Edinburgh." De Payens spoke the knight's name in a whisper and only because they were completely alone.

"As always, Uncle, you can rely on me to do all that I can in the name of the Order. Only then can I seek out a new nameless one to carry on in my place."

Above them, the stars seemed to hover just out of reach,

gleaming bright and clear like the Order's hopes for the future.

"As you know well, we have been well connected from the start and quickly came to influence the international politics of these Crusades. And, now that we have the power to levy taxes and accept tithing in the areas under our direct control, our ultimate rise to international power seems assured.

"With greater power also come greater threats from enemies past and present." De Payens extracted a golden chain with a roughly pounded Medallion dangling from it. The golden Medallion depicted two knights on one horse. One knight's face was covered by his helmet.

"These growing threats make the nameless knight position even more important than at the beginning. After Pope Honorius II formally recognized us at the recent Council of Troyes, the Order has much to protect.

"Here, my nephew. Wear this and pass it on to be worn by the one you choose to replace you as the nameless knight and those who will follow him." De Payens reached out through the sea spray and under the starry night sky and placed the Medallion around Gwynn's neck.

Bannockburn, Scotland
June 24, 1314 AD

On the morning of St. John the Baptist day, the sunshine gleamed off the burnished arms of the English troops as they exited the vast forest that stretched away towards Falkirk. The troops covered the open country, and the mail of the men-at-arms seemed to make the land glow as if it were in flames. White banners flapped in the wind, and a sea of knights' multi-colored pennons floated above the glittering columns. The English archers, bill men, and spear men advanced under the command of the Earls of Gloucester and Hereford. They were escorted and protected by mailed cavalry. Edward II himself commanded the remainder of the English troops surrounded by a bodyguard of four hundred specially chosen men representing the highest order of English chivalry.

The difficulties of terrain gradually transformed their formation of nine great columns into an enormous, unformed mass of gleaming flashes of armor and clouds of silken banners and colored pennons that floated over them in the soft summer wind.

As the English advanced across the burn like some gigantic amoebae, the Scots knelt before the barefooted and bareheaded Abbott of Inchaffray as he passed among them with a crucifix in his left hand bestowing benediction and absolution with his right.

"These Scots crave mercy!" Edward II cried out as he observed the Scots on their knees at prayer.

"It is the mercy of heaven and not your highness that they seek," replied Sir Humphrey de Umfraville, a Scot on the English side. "For on the field of battle, your highness, they will certainly be victorious or die."

Edward halted his men on the south side of the burn, for they had marched too far in the stifling, midsummer heat and they desperately needed to rest and re-form their ranks before engaging in battle. Each English baron clamored to get at those kneeling, praying Scots. Edward held them back as long as he could. But, as soon as they saw the Scots skirmish line retreating into the New Park, they ordered their trumpets to sound and led their eager young men forward at a gallop, over the burn and up a slow rise towards the trees.

Only two Scots seemed to be waiting for them. One, draped in mail, astride a gray Highland pony, wielded a war-axe. The other hung behind, dressed in white with scarlet crosses covering his breast and his back. His sword was drawn as if to protect the other horseman.

One of the leading English knights, Sir Henry de Bohun, the Earl of Hereford's nephew, recognized the man on the gray horse as the Scots king, Robert the Bruce. Realizing that he had a chance for glory by slaying the Scots king before the battle even began, he put his visor down and lance forward and spurred his horse toward the two. He charged Robert who was out scouting positions with his Templar forces commander, Gwynn Camsron.

Seeing the English knight galloping towards them, lance extended, Gwynn shouted at his commander above the din of the forces on both sides: "Beware, my Liege! The enemy is upon us!"

Robert the Bruce's reaction was not to fall back to a safer position. He knew that to turn now, in front of both armies, especially his specially-trained Scots, would be a sign of cowardice. And, he also held a grudge against de Bohun. For, when Bruce had been on the run in the early days of his reign, Edward I had given his lands in Annandale and Carrick to de Bohun. Later, Edward II had given Bruce's Essex estates to the same family.

"Stand aside, Templar. This is a fight I must take. It is personal." So, instead of retreating or charging, Bruce positioned himself between the charging Bohun and Gwynn Camsron in time to turn his gray palfrey slightly sideways to the charging de Bohun and, at the last second, shift his horse's position to avoid his lance.

As the Englishman galloped by him, his lance missing its mark, Robert raised himself high in his stirrups and, with all his strength, brought down his battle-axe, splitting open de Bohun's helmet and head with a single blow. As de Bohun's bloodied body crumpled to the ground before them, Bruce turned to Gwynn with a grim smile on his face. "Your warning saved me, last of the nameless knights, and I do believe you may have saved this day for the Scots as well."

Bruce leaned further forward and bowed his head slightly in order to remove a gold chain from around his neck. He quickly draped it around the surprised Gwynn's neck. A beaten gold Medallion dangled from the chain depicting two knights astride a single horse.

"This Medallion was recovered from the ashes of the Templars who were burned to death on the eve of 18 March this year on the Isle des Juifs in Paris. I believe it rightfully belongs to you.

"It was formed from gold found under Solomon's temple in Jerusalem. It symbolizes the honor and duty you and your line have served with for all these years, and returning it to you and its rightful place also represents my thanks to you for my life here today and for the Scottish victory to come this day."

"It is my duty and my honor, my liege."

"You and your line must keep the Medallion safe and hidden from view because your enemies are still many and great. But also wear it with pride and live up to the responsibilities that go with it. The time will come when the wearer of the Medallion that now hangs around your neck will be needed."

He turned forward in his saddle and led Gwynn Camsron back to where their men waited, once again kneeling in prayer. As the two reached the combined Highland and Lowland armies, Robert the Bruce held his broken battle axe over his head and screamed: "I haif broken the haft of my gude battle-axe on the enemy's haid!" They leaped to their feet as one, filling the early morning air with their cheers.

Tikrit, Iraq
532 AH
1138 AD

"You must get up from your bed now, my wife." Ayyub's voice was firm, controlled, and just above a whisper as he entered their bedroom. "Shirkuh has killed a man," he explained.

"Your brother's temper will be the death of us all, Ayyub."

"Well, in that regard, I have finally been relieved of my position as Commander of Tikrit."

"Come. Do not be concerned. Come, meet your third son, my husband."

"You must get up from that bed, now, wife. We must flee tonight!"

"And me with your son just born today?"

The night was darker than dark under the new moon. The yellow light from the oil lamps barely illuminated the bedroom enough to see his wife as she spoke from the bed.

"Yes, my wife. I am afraid so."

She cuddled the slight child in the darkness. "Salah-ad-Din Yusuf Ibn Ayyub."

"Yes. Salah-ad-Din Yusuf Ibn Ayyub. As your father, Yusuf, I am obliged to tell you that we must leave tonight for Mosul. Zengi must remember how your father saved his life along the banks of the Tigris."

"I'm sure he will remember my husband. And, there we can start rebuilding our family name."

"Hurry, let us get packed and out of here before we lose the darkness. At first light, Bihruz will give chase, of that I am certain."

"Perhaps he believes he has good reason, my husband. After all, you helped his enemy, Zengi, when he needed a boat to cross the Tigris all those years ago."

"And, he waited patiently for just the right situation to get even for that." He gazed at Righteousness of Faith Joseph, Son of Job swaddled in his mother's arms. "Hurry, wife. I can feel that

Bagdad commander's breath on the back of my neck as we speak."

Adab and Zarf
546 AH
1152 AD

"Mother, I must go to Aleppo . . . . ."

"But, my son, you are barely fourteen."

"But I will be with Uncle Shirkuh serving under Nur-ad-Din."

"And, my son, you are adab, a student of the Koran and of poetry. Not a hot tempered soldier like your uncle."

"So, then, this is a great opportunity, Mother, to learn how to be a soldier."

"You remind me so much of your Father, Yussuf. You seem to share his split interests between religious pursuits, like this Sufi mysticism obsession of his, and the military." She bowed her head just slightly to this young boy who stood before her now and to the man she knew would return someday from Aleppo.

"Perhaps you will learn something new, although I don't think it will be the elegance and refinement of a gentleman because you already seem to possess much Zarf even at your young age. But, I still worry for you, my son."

"I know, Mother, but Uncle promises that the great Nur-ad-Din will honor me with my own igta right away."

"You will have rank, my son?"

"Yes, Mother, and, perhaps, I can begin to make my way in this world beyond study at the madrassa."

"Insha'Allah," she muttered. "God willing."

Damascus, Syria
550 AH
1156 AD

The polo field looked much like a field of battle with all the colorful pennants flying in the breeze and the many horsemen galloping back and forth attacking each other to get a chance at hitting the ball with their mallets. Centuries ago the game had been imported from Persia and employed not just as a sport but as training for cavalry.

"I told my son: 'I shall not object if you play polo once or twice a year, my son, but, even then, six players on each side are quite sufficient. There is no need for a hundred or more on each side as sometimes happens.'"

Nur-ad-Din smiled politely at the story he had heard so many times before. "Such caution would be despised by our young bloods at court." Sitting his royal polo pony, he looked around the field, but his eyes found only one young gentleman he wanted on his side. "Young Salah-ad-Din," he motioned just barely with his left hand as he spoke. "Come, son and nephew of my protectors and friends, the brothers Ayyub and Shirkuh, join us in the match."

At only eighteen, Salah-ad-Din, as the king's personal liaison officer, was never far from his side on the march or at court here in Damascus. Now it seemed the king wanted him close to his side on the polo field as well. "To be asked to ride on the side of the king in a polo match is a sign of high favor, my nephew," Shirkuh urged. "Mount up and get out there before Nur-ad-Din changes his mind."

The Horns of Hattin
583 AH
1187 AD

On July 4, 1187, Salah-ad-Din Yusuf Ibn Ayyub faced the combined forces of Guy of Lusignan, King Consort of Jerusalem and Raymond III of Tripoli. Now the leader of all the Saracens allowed his dark eyes to almost caress the multitude of Allah's soldiers strung out in front of him for as far as he could see. It was he, Righteousness of Faith Joseph, Son of Job who had brought them all together here on this great plain below these magnificent Horns of Hattin, these extinct volcanoes that rose behind them like fecund cones, almost as if they floated in the morning sky. When he spoke to them, he rose in his stirrups and lifted his voice almost as if in morning prayers.

"Today, we cover this plain like the lava from the Horns of Hattin did centuries ago. We now have most of the Kingdom of Jerusalem in our hands. The city of Jerusalem stands before us now. If Allah blesses us by enabling us to drive His enemies out of Jerusalem, we will sweep this plain clean like Allah's lava did so long ago. How fortunate and happy we will be! For Jerusalem has been controlled by the Infidels for ninety-one years. Much time has passed. Many generations have come and gone, while the Franks succeeded in rooting themselves strongly there. Now, Allah has reserved the merit of its recovery for one house, the house of the sons of Ayyub, in order to unite all hearts in Jihad against the Franks!"

In this battle alone Salah-ad-Din's forces largely annihilated the Crusader army in what was a major disaster for the Crusaders and a turning point in the history of the Crusades. He captured Raynald de Chatillon and was personally responsible for his execution in retaliation for previously attacking Muslim pilgrim caravans. Guy of Lusignan was also captured but his life was spared because he had kept his word when his word was given.

That night Salah-ad-Din ordered the execution of all of the Templar and Hospitaller knights. Because of their religious devotion and rigorous training, they were the most feared Crusader soldiers. Seated on a dais before his army, Salah-ad-Din watched as scholars, Sufis, and ascetics carried out the killings.

Damascus
589 AH
1193 AD

Torrential winter rains drenched Salah-ad-Din and his retinue as the Sultan of Egypt and Syria, the unifier of the Muslim world, the leader of the successful Jihad against the Crusaders rode out from Damascus to greet pilgrims returning from Mecca. Salah-ad-Din had, himself, been very concerned that he had not yet made his own pilgrimage to Mecca as his faith required of him. He had been too busy mounting Jihad against those who would wrest control of their lands from them. But, since he had taken back Jerusalem, that failure had weighed heavily on him. So, he felt that the least he could do was honor those who had fulfilled their obligation of faith.

Despite rains that were so heavy the roads had to be cleared of floodwaters before his entourage as they proceeded through the city, throngs of citizens lined the roadways cheering the great Jihad leader and the returning pilgrims. As he greeted the pilgrims, Salah-ad-Din felt shivers shooting through his body and realized that he had left his quarters without the tunic he always wore when out riding this time of year to protect him from the cool air and the rains.

Taking great care to suppress the chills he felt, Salah-ad-Din addressed the pilgrims. "Just as you have done with this pilgrimage, the messengers of Allah will go where they must and do what they must to keep our heritage and our lineage pure and righteous.

"Allah's messengers will appear when the time is right for Islam to rule the world."

Ten days later, the greatest ruler of the Muslim world would be dead from the fever he contracted that day for want of his tunic.

In a Dark Wood

1
Arrival of the Messengers

[Music: "Shards of the Urn"]

"At best, we are no more than a haiku in the mind of god."
What's So Funny About Truth, Love, and Understanding?
(Ethics for the New Age of Extremism), Theo Theodora

"Less than one hour ago, the final one-hundred-mile stretches along the Mexican and Canadian borders were officially sealed off." Ellworth Hayes, INN Washington morning co-anchor turned his buffed bald head toward camera two as directed by the voice in his ear. It didn't seem to matter how much powder or make up the crew applied. His pate still blazed under the television lights. Yet his audience seemed to love it. More than half of his e-mails were from viewers who complimented his glowing head and the "beams" it produced, beams they loyally counted during every telecast. "Beam Counter" web sites proliferated.

"The borders were sealed off as a result of the completion of the remaining two border monitoring stations. Each BMS contains all the latest in high tech detection devices like remote controlled spotter drones capable of firing tranquilizer rounds and dropping tranquilizer bombs. Despite critics from the ACLU to PETA railing against such weapons as inhumane and destructive to endangered species and border crossers, the five-year plan has been completed— and in only three-and-a-half years." Ellworth beamed viewers around the world from Washington, DC to the United States Virgin Islands. He was on a beaming roll today. "Coming in so far ahead of schedule has been attributed to the continued oversight and scrutiny of Florida Democrat Senator Abigail Keayrn, the primary sponsor of the legislation.

"These last two BMS's are just like the hundreds of other such stations already on line as a result of Operation Seal-Off. They are controlled by elite cadres of Border Monitoring Guards highly trained in sophisticated computer systems as well as in police, para-military, and physical skills. Special Forces meets Computer Cop, or something like that."

Ellworth's close shot appeared on, among millions of others, the aging Sanyo 21 inch color television owned by an English teacher at an Anglican preparatory school in St. Thomas, United States Virgin Islands. "You tell them, Worth old buddy. You tell them, man," Gwynn Camsron chuckled half-aloud through his tooth brush. After rinsing his mouth, he eyed the television in his mirror while he trimmed his reddish mustache lightly with the barber scissors he'd bought when he was on R&R in Hong Kong many years before with that same Worth Hayes he now saw in his mirror. Finally, Gwynn stumbled into his Einstein-like uniform of Panama style khaki trousers and loose-fitting white linen shirt, preparing himself for yet another day in American Paradise while his old Vietnam Army buddy Ellworth Hayes continued his one-way conversation with the world.

"The approval of the USA Patriot Act after the nine-eleven terrorist attacks in two thousand one dramatically increased the level of funding for financial investigators at the Treasury Department and gave US regulators greater authority to keep foreign businesses from operating in the United States if they do not cooperate with terrorism investigators."

Ellworth's head beamed again. Often his fans e-mailed him their "Beam Counts" directly, but he also kept an eye on the "Beamer" web sites himself most of which published continuing reports of the number of times during a particular morning news show his baldness reflected light in a way that looked like a beam coming from his head. To date, the largest count ever had been twenty in a single three-hour program. Ellworth unconsciously touched the American Flag pin on the left lapel of his hand tailored blue pin-stripe suit jacket. His sister Dee Dee died in the World Trade Center that day. Some said she took a swan dive from the thirty-third floor while still talking on her cell phone.

"For those of you who have been on Mars or something, here's an INN Special Background Report on Operation Seal-Off. You may remember that the nine-eleven attacks sparked the creation of Operation Greenquest at Treasury. Its mission was to anticipate and disrupt the flow of money to suspected terrorists." He turned slightly and smiled anew into camera one with the news show's signature live shot backdrop of the Washington monument in the foreground and the Capitol at the other end of the Ellipse in the gauzy background.

"Passage of the Homeland Security Act more than a year later provided for a new Department of Homeland Security and for the funding of Operation Seal-Off. Senator Keayrn's controversial Amendment proposed a five-year plan to completely seal off the borders and ports of the United States from the threat of illegal immigration.

"According to Senator Keayrn, Operation Greenquest and Operation Seal-Off combined will force terrorists to become more creative, even reckless, in how they raise funds in the United States and infiltrate our borders to mount attacks against us. According to administration officials, this should also make them easier to spot and track." Ellworth quickly adjusted back to camera two once more as it zoomed in slowly to a full head-and-shoulders shot.

"On another front, we have a breaking news story off the coast of Maine. Our very own co-anchor Jasmine who is supposed to be on vacation up there—has uncovered a story that sounds more like science fiction than science fact. Here, now, is our own Jasmine with a whale of a tale right here on INN, your international news network with more news in more depth than anybody else on television.

"Hello up there in Maine, Jasmine. What's this about an invasion of the pod people?" Ellworth laughed heartily at his own joke.

"Hello down there in Washington, Ellworth," Jasmine's deep but melodic voice responded as the satellite-connected camera on the Maine coast zoomed in slowly on the wind-flushed, softly chiseled face of the New York co-anchor. Her blond hair flowed out behind her in a stiff sea breeze. "Well, I don't know about another *Invasion of the Body Snatchers*, Ellworth, but we do have a dead whale on the beach here in Maine with some kind of pod in its mouth."

Her voice continued as video tape played showing two high school boys walking along the rocky beach. "According to the two sixteen-year-olds in this video, they were on their way to school this morning when they stopped to explore this remote strip of rocky Maine beach—as they often do—looking for shell fish that wash up on shore at high tide and are trapped after the tide recedes. What they discovered, however, wasn't mussels or crabs, Ellworth. What they found was a beached humpback whale with a huge silver-green pod-like object partially visible in its mouth."

Back live, the camera zoomed beyond Jasmine to a close shot of the dead whale with what seemed to be a kind of large gelatinous pod extending from its mouth surrounded by several people in HASMAT suits.

"As we speak, experts—looking a lot like people in space suits, I must admit—are examining the whale and the pod for any possibility of explosives or biological contamination before other environmental and medical personnel begin their investigations into what caused the whale to beach and what the object in its mouth might be and what it might contain. Investigators have told us that the object is not rigid like metal or even hard plastics. It is very pliable and flexible, more like very thick skin. It seems likely that the whale choked to death on it and just drifted into shore." Jasmine shrugged into the camera. "Nobody yet seems to have any idea what this thing is or how it got inside the whale, but everyone is somewhat laughingly referring to the pod as a 'Jonah pod.'"

"Like Jonah and the Whale?"

"Exactly."

"Thanks, Jasmine. So, when can we expect you back in New York?"

"It looks like the vacation is over, Ellworth, so I guess I'll be back at my anchor desk in New York as soon as this whale thing is over. This is Jasmine along the southern coast of Maine. Back to you, Ellworth."

"That's breaking news with my favorite co-anchor—and yours— Jasmine. How did a whale end up on that remote Maine beach? How did that pod end up inside the whale? And, what *is* inside that pod? Stay tuned for further developments on this breaking story right here on INN, your international news network." Ellworth beamed camera two.

"We'll be right back, after we pay a few bills, with more news in more depth than anybody else on television."

2

St. Thomas US Virgin Islands
[Music: "Shards of the Urn"]

"Okay, class." As Gwynn Camsron clicked the off button on the remote to the recently installed forty-six inch flat screen television with his left hand, his right thumb and forefinger unconsciously rubbed the gold Medallion hanging from a thick matching chain around his neck. The television was one of a dozen provided to the school, along with DVD players, by the CEO of Main Street Rum & Liquors, an alumnus of Martyrs and Saints Anglican School. From his own narrow point of view, they were great for showing DVD's of literature that had been translated into film. It seemed so much easier to engage the students about a work of literature if they could see the movie. He had already treated them to James Fenimore Cooper's *The Last of the Mohicans* staring Daniel Day-Lewis. Soon he was going to show them the 1956 Gregory Peck version of *Moby Dick*. He had ordered it off the Internet just a few days ago and was anticipating its arrival.

"Now, we know how INN and the other networks are reporting this whale that washed up on the beach in Maine. But, it's time for us to get back to our topic for today: whales."

Fronds rattled like collapsing dominos on the coconut palms surrounding Martyrs and Saints Anglican School courtyard and playground. He and his students could see them from the windows of this recently renovated upper-level classroom building made of the island standard building material—plastered cinder blocks reinforced with rebar. It faced the island stone school chapel's Danish double entrance as did three other fading yellow cinder block buildings that combined to form the courtyard dotted with lavender bougainvilleas and blood red hibiscus.

"Okay. So to get back to our present topic in English class, let's talk about whales. Or, more specifically, let's talk about the things that Herman Melville did in *Moby Dick* to bring whaling alive." Gwynn had been at this teaching thing for longer now than he could believe. But, he worked hard at keeping it fresh, and the students helped. They were so vital, so open, so strong yet so fragile. "How did Melville make the life of a whaler and whaling itself seem as real to the reader in his day as the networks are making that whale way up in Maine seem to us today?"

The sun sweet trade winds whispered through the open slats of the classroom's metal jalousie windows. Their metal flaps bore the brush strokes of seven generations of volunteer students. This year the brush strokes belonged to his seniors who painted them chalk yellow to match the new yellow paint job on the building. The jalousie painting had been taken on by his seniors as the traditional Senior Class service project. All of the students in his honors English class participated. They were the leaders of the school, the brightest and best the islands had to offer. Next fall they would be off to Harvard, Georgetown, and Stanford, off to Cal Tech and MIT, off to Duke and Davidson, a few even off to McGill or Oxford or Cambridge. And, when one of their teachers also happened to be the Senior Class Advisor, even the best and brightest students tended to participate just a little bit more.

"Keep in mind, Herman Melville didn't have the benefit of so many messengers."

This group of kids was probably the finest class he'd taught since his first year at Martyrs and Saints School in 1972, nearly three years after he'd landed here because of the toss of a coin. He sometimes, in less guarded moments, joked that the Army super spooks had debriefed him so completely that by the time he reached Manila he had no underwear on and only a quarter left in his uniform pocket. He decided that he would toss that quarter to make his decision. Heads it would be St. Thomas. Tails it would be Singapore. He tossed the George Washington quarter into the air and caught it in the palm of his right hand, then quickly slapped it onto his left wrist. When he lifted his hand he revealed old George's profile.

"Remember, class. No radio. No TV. No movies. No cable. No satellite. No Internet. No Facebook. No Twitter. My God," he gasped in mock horror, "how could they even survive?"

The class laughed almost in unison. They were used to being Mr. C's "laugh track."

Once he had reached the islands, he had spent most of what he referred to as his "three lost years" after Vietnam not in St. Thomas but on a small uncharted island near the western tip of the Virgin Island archipelago where he had been conveniently shipwrecked, hiding out from everything and everyone. Once he had recuperated and come to his senses, he had signed onto a charter to St. Thomas as a mate and cook. To his amazement, once he had landed in Charlotte Amalie harbor and had grabbed a copy of the Virgin Islands Daily News, he made only three telephone calls from the public phone at the entrance to Drake's Passage, an alley off of Veterans Drive that edged the harbor, before Veronica Braitwaite had responded with an appointment for an interview. After an hour and fifteen minutes, she had offered him a position teaching English at Martyrs and Saints Anglican School. He had been teaching there ever since.

"Melville relied only on the printed word to convince the reader of the reality, the authenticity of the experiences he portrayed. That's all he had."

Gwynn disappeared into the Caribbean in much the same way his namesake had vanished into the Orkney Islands seven centuries before after the Battle of Bannockburn. Gradually, even the CIA stopped surveilling him on a regular basis just as King Philip IV's progeny had let their efforts to eradicate the Templars wane after Philip's death; and Pope Clement had allowed the *papal bull Pastoralis Praeeminentiae* he had issued on November 22, 1307, instructing all Christian monarchs in Europe to arrest all Templars and seize their assets, also to be basically ignored. Both Gwynns assumed they were no longer considered to be threats. In the Orkneys, his ancestor had lived outside the boundaries of most any intelligence surveillance. However, being in the Caribbean put Gwynn Camsron directly in the eye of the CIA. So he still, occasionally, spotted someone on his tail. He had come to expect that once in a while they would still check in on him just to make sure he really was only working as a teacher of English at a Virgin Islands preparatory school, hard as that might be to believe. He understood. When you saw everything through the prism of the intelligence community, he realized that someone could be a sleeper for a very long time, most of his life even, before he was activated.

"So, how did he focus the reader in *Moby Dick*?"

Armond Braitwaite's hand sprang into the air. His tight-lipped grin indicated that he had an answer. Ashanta Riley glanced sideways with her azure eyes. Armond's hand waved enthusiastically. She smirked. For a change, she had the answer as quickly as Mr. Basketball did. Her hand leaped into a waft of cool Caribbean breeze.

"Yes Ashanta?" He turned toward the sixteen-going-on-twenty-six-year-old caramel-skinned beauty. One of a long line, over the years, of young women who fell in love with him, so each of them thought, for a time.

"Melville uses the chapters on whaling to tell us everything we ever didn't want to know about whaling and then some. But, somehow, it did seem to make the story more real, at least it did to me." Then, in a moment of prescient insecurity, she shrugged. "Oh, I don't know."

"To the contrary, Ashanta, it seems that you, very much, do know." He hesitated. And, she was one of the few who practiced speaking proper English. Gwynn recalled her telling him once over Friday salt fish and callaloo in the cafeteria that she worked so hard on not talking like an islander because she figured being a black woman with blue eyes was going to draw enough attention as it was. He had told her that the attention she would be getting wouldn't necessarily be bad. He had told her that she was beautiful in a special way with her caramel skin and blue eyes and her excellent mind. He had told her how it would be easy to just lime along with her looks and brain if that was what she wanted. He had told her how important it was for her to fall in love with someone nearer to her own age rather than waste such a valuable possession on an old man. And, he seemed to have struck a chord with her, and that chord came up AB—Armond Braitwaite.

"But, once you start thinking and questioning, there's no turning back, Ashanta." There never was any turning back for anyone, was there? Not really. Certainly not for Captain Ahab or Ishmael. Not for Ashanta O'Reilly, and certainly not for Gwynn Camsron.

"And, that, class, will be the subject of the papers you will be writing." He grinned. "Due a week from Friday."

He weathered the obligatory groans before continuing. "Well, I do have what I believe will be a no-groaner for you, this morning. Since the art of whaling plays such a detailed and important role in

Moby Dick, maybe we should take a field trip to see something right here on our very own island . . . well, actually not on the island but in the sea that surrounds our island . . . . Well, the Atlantic Ocean part, that is. Anyone know what I'm talking about?"

Armond Braitwaite's basketball-palming hand shot up again in the back of the room. Due to his six-foot-eight-and-a-half, two hundred and fifteen pound frame, he voluntarily sat on the back row in all his classes. Although he'd been one of five National Merit Scholarship finalists from this class, he was going to Duke on a basketball scholarship. Before Tim Duncan went to Wake Forest back in the nineties, no Virgin Islander would have thought he or she would ever be recruited by the Atlantic Coast Conference. Armond reminded Gwynn of a young and raw Bill Russell on the court. He reminded Gwynn of a young and raw Gwynn Camsron in the class room.

"Anyone, other than Armond—who always has his hand up?"

"Hey, Armond," Daryl Williams laughed. "You sleep wit' your hand up, me son?"

"No, me son." Armond grinned in a way he might have when he was a kid and got caught eating the patés that were supposed to be for guests. "I only keep it up for de rebounds *and* de answers."

The class burst into laughter.

"Okay. Okay. Okay. Since Armond seems to think he knows all the right answers today, guess we might as well let him answer this one. Right, class?"

"Okay, Mr. C."

"Mr. Braitwaite." Gwynn motioned toward the back of the room. "The floor is yours, sir."

The class cheered.

"Whales, Mr. C." He grinned. "Whales."

"And, that, class, is what we've been waiting to hear?"

His students sniggered and mumbled among themselves, not quite sure where all this was leading, but they knew their teacher and class advisor well enough by now to know that it was all leading somewhere, and probably somewhere very interesting and a lot of fun.

"Can you tell your classmates, Armond, what whales have to do with St. Thomas and with a possible field trip for this class that would be relevant to our study of *Moby Dick*? Lay it on us like one of your reverse slam dunks we all dearly love to watch."

The class roared.

"Yes sir. Ah. You see, me sons, we got dese humpback whales dat comes t'rough de channel off Mandahl Point dis time o' year. Okay."

"That's very good, Armond. Of course, the white whale, Moby Dick, was a sperm whale, not a humpback." He paused, then continued in his own version of calypso, honed and polished to near-native perfection from not having been back to the states—or even out of the Caribbean for that matter—since he arrived at Harry S. Truman airport in 1969. When he stepped from the American Airlines 727 onto the roll-up metal stairs that day—a psychologically smashed up casualty of the dark and secret side of the Vietnam war—he was convinced that he had, somehow, walked into a peaceful Casablanca. He fully expected, at any moment, to see Bogart and Bergman peer from around the corrugated fencing that separated the tarmac from the terminal.

"But, a whale be a whale, okay. All 'o we be goin' on dis sailin' trip tomorrow, me sons, to catch a look'at some o' dem whales Armond be talkin' 'bout. Wha' you t'ink?"

"Okay. Okay. Okay, me son!" the class chorused.

"Well," he responded in his normal English. "I just happen to have a sailing partner—a Frenchie named Jean-Lafette Quetel. I'm sure some of you know him or his family. They still grow fresh vegetables and sell them at their little market on the North Side. He was the very first person I met when I came to St. Thomas back in sixty-nine. He was driving a safari bus back in the day and picked me up at the airport. Nowadays, he just happens to serve as a whale counter for an organization sponsored by the federal government and private donations called The Whale Institute. He's willing to take us out tomorrow morning off of Mandahl Point when he does some tracking and counting."

The class clapped and roared even louder than before.

"Okay, calm down or you'll have Braitwaite's mom in here." He chuckled. The class knew he was joking. If anything, he and his classes tended to be the Headmistress's favorites. Yet, their silence was immediate.

"Okay. These are the ground rules. You'll have to bring a permission note from your parents or guardians saying that you can go on this sailing field trip. No permission note, no field trip. And, I'm very serious about this, me sons. The legal liability to the school if you were injured on a field trip you participated in without consent from your parent or guardian is just too great to make any exceptions.

"Let's see. You'll need to dress for boating." He glanced around him at the predominantly dark-skinned students. But, dark-skinned people sunburned, too. He'd seen that in the Nam when a good buddy of his who was a very dark black man sunburned so badly the first week they were in the field together that he had to be medevac'd out of a classified location. "Bathing suits are optional. Sun screen is not, even for those of you sporting the darker natural tans."

The students tittered.

"Be at Red Hook Marina at seven a.m. sharp." He waited for the complaints. After all that was two hours earlier than they normally had to be at school. But there were none.

"Captain Quetel will pick us up there. Look for his sloop, The Mariner. Now, I want you all to keep in mind that Captain Quetel has often confided in me that he believes punctuality is next to godliness. And, believe me, guys and gals, you will regret it if you are late. So, no island time. Captain Quetel will cast off at seven sharp."

"Okay," the class chorused, enthusiastic despite the threat of Captain Quetel's retribution should any of them be late.

"Good. Now let's get back to what this is all about . . . Mr. Melville's use of great detail about whaling and the whaling life in writing *Moby Dick*."

* * * * *

Glistening beneath the sun like a field of emeralds, the Atlantic Ocean chopped about the sloop, Mariner, in low, foamy swells. Jean-Lafette Quetel steered the sloop into the sunrise. As far as anyone on the Mariner could see to port, only Jost Van Dyke Island popped up on the horizon. This time of year, when the early spring trades

29

continually bathed the archipelago, the island was still a brown lump in an emerald sea. To starboard, however, the eastern end of St. Thomas was only a few thousand yards away. It, too, was dry brown just like all the other normally green islands. Just four miles or so across the island, as the pelican flies, the Caribbean Sea stretched out toward St. Croix.

In fifty years as a captain of one kind of boat or another, Jean-Lafette had never been able to see a silver darter's difference between the two bodies of water at this latitude. Both were flat and see-through. Both were emerald green in the depths and an almost white green in the shallows. And, both had been pretty much fished out close into shore. But, only the Atlantic could claim the spectacle they were now pursuing.

The twelve surrounding Martyrs and Saints Anglican School kids lounged from bow to stern in various stages of undress from their school uniforms to bathing suits. As they soaked in the radiant vitality pouring through one of the thinnest areas of the ozone layer, they still waited. They had been waiting since a little after seven bells, off the point at Mandahl, for the whales.

Gwynn straddled the Pilot's jump seat directly behind Jean-Lafette and the wheel he gripped firmly in his two gnarled hands. He continued to scan the sea for a pod of whales which Jean-Lafette felt sure was out there somewhere.

To occupy the students, Captain Quetel fetched a map from his wheel house and motioned for the kids to gather around him. "Crowd in close, kids, and look at dis chart where da whales be comin' from and where dey be goin' to."

"You see, me sons, dese humpback whales be feedin' in da cold wa-ters of Maine and Alaska. Dey be goin' to war-mer wa-ters, like Hawaii and the Caribbean, to birt'. After birt' in winter or early spring, mothers bring deir calves to da rich feedin' grounds o' Stellwagen Bank or other parts of de Gulf o' Maine to feed on little five-inch-long fish called Sand Launce. In da spring, 'bout a hun'red humpbacks doin' dat, okay?

"Dat whale on da TV mos' likely be comin' here jus' like dese ones we might be seein' now."

"Oooooooooooooooooooooo."

"Did'ya catch dat note, Captain?"

"What note, Devon?"

"Ooooooooooooooooooooooo."

"Dere i'tis again. You hear it, Armond? Sounds like it be a long way off. Did'ya hear dat?"

"Ooooooooooooooooooooooo."

"Dat high-pitched t'ing?"

"Yes, mon. Sound like it be I' clo-ser."

"What it does be?"

"Mr. C?"

"Yes, Armond?"

"You be hearing dat noise, too? It be soundin' sort of like a signal or somet'ing."

"A signal?"

"Maybe it's not a signal at all," Ashanta howled. "Maybe, it's the Sirens."

"Dem's signals, me son! Dey blasts and blasts real high like dat."

"No, dem's sin-gers, not sig-nals," Ashanta mocked. "Seriously, don't you remember, in that *Odyssey* book we studied last year?" The young faces surrounding her gaped at her words like they did at the Sirens' songs.

"I remember the teacher saying that some people thought that the Sirens were really whales or porpoises or manatees."

"Ooooooooooooooooooooooo-oh . . . eeeeoooooeeeeoooeeeooo . . . ."

"That sound?"

"Yeah, Mr. C. Dat be it."

"It does be louder now."

"Maybe it's coming from Captain Quetel's underwater listening post. He records all these trips, and he's wired it through his loud speaker system so he can hear what he's recording. Listen closely."

"Ooooooooooooooooooooooo . . . eeeeoooooeeeeoooeeeooo . . . ."

"You mean dat's comin' from undah de sea?"

"That's right, Devon."

"Sounds like da songs belongin' to some o' dem humpback whales we be lookin' for to me!" Captain Quetel bellowed over the crescendo of songs. "Dey gotta be close to hear dem dat strong, me son." He turned down the volume and began talking to the young people again.

"Da whale song be one of de biggest mysteries of de entire animal kingdom. Dey doan have no vocal cords. Dey doan send out no air from deir bodies while dey be singing. So how do dey make dis strange yet beautiful song?"

The kids were uncharacteristically silent, awaiting Captain Quetel's next words while he stepped into the wheel house. Stowing the whale migration map, then checking his sound monitoring equipment, the Captain returned to the deck.

"Some researchers t'ink dat dey sing by moving dese air sacks in deir heads like takin da end of a inflated balloon and letting out da air.

"We doan know if it be a language neither. But, da song it can be broke down like a piece of classical music or somet'ing. Dey sing about 50-60 feet below de surface, for about fifteen minutes or so at a time wit' deir heads pointed down and deir tails pointed up.

"Even more amazin', me sons, is dat on any given day, all da humpbacks in da Pacific be singin one song, and all da humpbacks in da Atlantic and Caribbean be singin deir own song. And, dis years' song be startin' where last years' song be endin'.

"Ever since dis mon, Roger Payne, first he-ard the whale song in 1979 in Hawaii, a song has never repeated."

"Yo! Look to starboard, kids!" Gwynn almost shrieked in his excitement and fell naturally in the familiar calypso of the islands. "Dey be comin' right pas' us!" Captain Quetel turned up the volume on his signal receiver. "Listen how loud dey be singing now, me sons?"

"Ooooooooooooooooooooo-oh . . . Oooooooooooo ooooooo-oh . . . Ooooooooooooooooooooo-oh . . . Ooooo ooooooooooooooo-oh."

"I count eight humps, Cap'n. How 'bout you?"

"Me be countin' eight, too, Gwynn." Captain Quetel wagged his shining bald head. A royal blue captain's hat with gold piping covered the back part of it. The ice blue eyes bulging from his trenched sun-leathered face glowed with incredulity.

"Dere should be twen-ty or more at least, me son, in two pods." His broad lips twisted into a snarl. "Wha'be happ'nin' here?"

"Eeeeoooooeeeeoooeeeooo . . . ooooooooooooooo oooo . . . eeeeooooeeeeooo eeeooo."

"Can we come about and follow them? You know, Cap'n. Get in

closer to them so my students can look at the whales in their natural habitat—close up? No motor; just sail?"

"Me t'ink so, me son. Me t'ink so."

"Kids! We've spotted the pod. Come!"

Captain Quetel shut down the engine he'd been using to give them extra speed as they had tried to get close enough to the pod for the students to really see whales like they had never seen them before, if they had ever seen them before. "Doan be movin' all o' you to one side o' de byoat, now. Watch your heads! We be comin' about!"

"Ooooooooooooooooooooooo-oh . . . Ooooooooooooo ooooooo-oh . . . Ooooooooooo ooooooooo-oh . . . Ooooo ooooooooooooooooo-oh."

"Their songs are already fading again, Jean-Lafette. Hurry, mon. Hurry!"

As Jean-Lafette turned the wheel, the main sail luffed, flapped momentarily, then popped open to the breeze pushing across Drake's Channel. The sheets sang as Gwynn whirled the cranks to haul in those lines until the sail was taut across the wind behind it. The bow of The Mariner plowed westward. Jean-Lafette hit the starter button. The starter whined. The engine sputtered and caught. The sloop drove faster through the emerald swells.

"Eeeeooooeeeeoooeeeooo . . . oooooooooooooooo oooo . . . eeeeooooeeee oooeeeooo."

"Cyan . . . ah . . . can we get up real close, Cap'n Quetel, sir?" Ashanta Riley squealed. Her deep perse eyes seemed to dance nearly out of her head as she leaned over the railing on the starboard side. Spray from the sloop's hull crushing the ocean swells stung her grinning face.

"Spread your barnars out and around dis byoat like I be tellin' you." Quetel waved his arms to indicate the entire sloop. "You all get to see, me sons. You all get to see dem whales close up as your own faces in de mirror, you will." He spat his words into the wake of The Mariner. His fingers gripped the wheel like Seagrape roots and held it steady as the sloop sliced through the emerald mounds toward the rising and submerging humps a few hundred yards ahead of them. At times, they were almost indistinguishable from the two-foot foamy swells of an otherwise rather quiet Atlantic ocean.

"Eeeeooooeeeeoooeeeooo . . . oooooooooooooooo oooo . . .

eeeeooooeeee oooeeeooo."

"Listen up! Captain Quetel is, as you know, an official spotter and counter for The Whale Institute. He tells me that over the past few years there's been an average of fifteen to twenty humpbacks in several pods when they migrate through here."

"But, I be countin' less 'n less o' dem dis year." He tapped his bald head against the wheel. "But dis eight business. Me jus' doan know, me sons. Me jus' doan know."

"Oooooooooooooooooooo-oh . . . Ooooooooo ooooooo-oh . . ."

"What do you guys think? Would Herman Melville—when he was writing Moby Dick—ever have conceived that so many whale species would be in danger of extinction today?"

"Ne-ver!"

"No way, Mr. C."

Gwynn shaded his eyes with both hands to get a better view of the whales as the sloop closed on them from port. "Jesus, Cap'n! Look!"

"Yo, Gwynn? What'cha be seein', me son?"

"Look at the hump on that lead whale, Cap'n." He pointed with his right hand in the direction of the largest hump visible amidst the froth and foam of the pod. "Isn't that something dragging from the whale's hump?"

"Ooooooooooooooooooo . . . . Eeeeooooeeee oooeeeooo."

Captain Quetel shaded his eyes with both hands and stared in the direction Gwynn pointed. At first, he saw nothing. He almost dropped his shade. Then, he saw a glint of sunlight bounce off of the whale's hump. He knew that wasn't right. The whale's hump might glisten in this brilliant sunlight, but it wouldn't reflect the light off so sharply, like the blade of a knife.

"Do you see something?"

"Aye, me son. Somet'ing." He shut the engine. The Mariner slipped without a sound through the sea except for the incessant slash of the hull through bursting swells like a knife cutting through the bubbles in shipping plastic.

"Ooooooooooooooooooo . . . . Eeeeooooeeee oooeeeooo."

The sloop was practically a part of the pod now. Whooshing, sucking sounds surrounded them as the whales blew water from their holes when they surfaced again and again for oxygen.

"Ooooooooooooooooooooo . . . . Eeeeooooeeee oooeeeooo."

Gwynn re-shaded his eyes and returned his gaze to the lead whale, still a few hundred yards in front of The Mariner.

"Ooooooooooooooooooooo . . . . Eeeeooooeeee oooeeeooo."

At times, the sounds seemed like baritone horns. At other times, they reminded Gwynn of elephants trumpeting or hogs rooting.

His kids squealed and pointed at the whales breaching the surface of the ocean with their humps and slashing fluted tails.

"Wake yourself up, Ras . . . and listen." Armond jabbed his lifelong friend Ras Jama Stevenson in the ribs. "Hear dat, me son?" As was often the case, Ras had slept through the entire encounter.

"Wha', me son? Wha' you be talkin', mon?"

"Doan'tit sound like . . . like . . . ."

"Ooooooooooooooooooooo . . . . Eeeeooooeeee oooeeeooo."

"It really does sound like Sirens singing, doesn't it?"

"Dat be it, Ashanta. Dem whales does be singin' to all'o we!"

"Even me, me son?"

"Even you, Ras Sleepy Head. Look, me son. See dem off the bow of the byoat?"

Ras followed the line of Armond's right arm to the end of his exceptionally long index finger. He squinted against the sunlight glistening off the swells in front of them. "OK, me son. I be seein' dem . . . ." He leaped from his napping place and rushed to the side of the boat. "Dis be dem, me son." A huge smile plastered itself across his flat mahogany face. "Iree."

As the lead hump broke the frothing ocean again, Gwynn thought he saw something. "Cap'n, that looks like . . . ."

"Eeeeooooeeeeoooeeeooo . . . ."

"A harpoon, Cap'n?"

Captain Quetel shaded his eyes with his hands. "Could be."

"Ooooooooooooooooooo."

"Could be, for sure. But . . . ."

"But what, Cap'n?"

"Ooooooooooooooooooooo . . . . Eeeeooooeeee oooeeeooo."

"Mary, Mother of God!" Suddenly, Jean-Lafette dropped the shade of his hands and crossed himself with uncharacteristically trembling fingers.

3
Washington, D.C.
[Music: "Shards of the Urn"]

Jagged rose cracks spread across the dark sky over the Potomac toward the Jefferson Memorial and the Ellipse. Through the fourth floor window of a Georgetown townhouse, the darkness was already transforming into a flamingo haze. Beads of sweat from an hour of yoga practice glistened like Bermuda sand over the naked body of Abigail Keayrn, senior senator from Florida. The moisture emphasized a small POW/MIA tattoo at the base of her neck. Meditating in the perfect position on an exercise mat facing the window, her breaths came slowly from the depths of her abdomen.

"As of one hour ago," the schooled baritone voice she recognized as Ellworth Hayes announced as her bedroom television clicked on at the pre-set time of 6:45 AM, "the last hundred-mile stretches of Mexican and Canadian borders were officially sealed off through bringing on-line the final two border monitoring stations containing all the latest in high tech detection devices including spotter drones. These last two stations—like the hundreds of such stations already on line in Operation Seal-Off—are operated by highly trained cadres of Border Monitoring Guards, the Border Guard answer to Special Forces."

The interruption reminded Abbie that she had an interview scheduled with Ellworth later this morning, just before the Senate final vote on her "Save Our Planet" bill.

Meditation was over. It was time to get to work.

* * * * *

The same flamingo haze bathed the interior of an exclusive private dining room at the Watergate where seventeen of the most powerful members of Congress caucused over an early breakfast. Meditation had likely never begun for any of them.

Representative House spoke, in his usual locker room manner, after a long silence. "Every swinging dick around this table has money in his coffers from these so-called pollution interests Keayrn wants to castrate. We've all taken their money, TJ. So what? This is just one of those times we take the frigging money and run! Right, Mr. Speaker?"

Speaker Quinn responded quickly before anyone else had an opportunity to interject his thoughts. "Right you are, House. It's for damn sure that none of us around this table wants Lars Hansen as the next vice president. He's certainly not to be trusted. Then, of course, neither are we."

A chorus of knowing chuckles and agreement swelled around the table.

Senator TJ jumped back into the discussion hurriedly, still hoping to blunt the direction this meeting was going. He still hated being bested by a damned girl. "So, we give the little lady what she wants . . . again," he spat across the white linen table cloth like some kind of challenge. "Do we do that again, gentlemen? Or have we had enough of being manipulated by this damned female upstart who thinks she can be President someday."

"Yes, that's what we do," Speaker Quinn intoned as if he were calling for a vote on the House floor. "If it's a choice between Keayrn and Hansen, what other course do we have? She was sure as hell right about that border protection amendment, now wasn't she, gentlemen?"

"Yeah," House muttered. "And we've all been riding that wave ever since."

"And, what's Hansen ever been right about except about being right?"

A chorus of grumbling acquiescence followed, including Senator TJ's barely audible and still unwilling agreement.

* * * * *

The buzzer behind Senator Keayrn's authentic Jefferson roll-top desk startled her back from the edges of legislative romance embraced in the twelve pages scattered over the open desk: her floor speech on her 'Save Our Planet' legislation. This was, perhaps, the thousandth time that buzzer had sounded since she'd occupied this suite of offices in the Russell Senate Office Building as Chair of the

Energy and Natural Resources Committee. More times than not the buzzer called her attention to some vote or another that she cared little or nothing about. This time was different. The buzzer was announcing the vote on her Committee's bill to, finally, put some real teeth into environmental protection law enforcement, just as her Homeland Security Act amendment had put some real teeth into the enforcement of homeland security by focusing on the borders and coastlines. Strengthening the environmental protection law with substantially tougher enforcement provisions was an important issue that had been relegated to second place by post Nine-Eleven considerations for long enough.

A fifty-two inch sheet screen television hung on the wall just past the far end of an eight-foot long, four-foot-wide, hand-rubbed mahogany early American table that doubled perfectly as her main working desk and conference table. The split screen showed four channels that were covering the up-coming vote on her bill.

"This is Ellworth Hayes, INN, just outside the Senate Chambers where the body is getting ready to vote on Florida Democrat Senator Abigail Keayrn's "Save Our Planet" bill. According to many environmental issues experts, this bill becoming law would be a legislative tour d'force. Its provisions hit offenders where it really hurts according to these experts—in the pocketbook."

Abbie fished her compact from the hand-tanned, hand-stitched llama hide purse given to her by some official of the Peruvian government twenty years ago when she was still a very young congresswoman. She still carried it, after all these years, despite her heavy and committed involvement with environmental issues. PETA would probably stone her as she came down the Capitol steps if they knew. But, the purse was just too full of memories to abandon. And, the llama had been dead a very long time. "Even under threat of a good stoning by PETA," she half-whispered, chuckling to herself. With her left hand, she pulled her raven hair behind her head. Loose, shoulder-length hair just didn't seem to be the order of the day. A tight bun perhaps.

She scrambled in her purse for something to secure her hair with. Finding the hair comb she had used for her morning speech, she twisted her hair into a tight bun. She inserted and secured the comb so that it held the bun of hair in place. Next, she added a touch of powder to keep her cheeks from shining in the television lights. Deep set hazel eyes appeared almost black as she decided she didn't need any liner or mascara.

"In an interview earlier today after her very impassioned floor speech on her 'Save Our Planet' bill with her accompanying amendment, Senator Keayrn, a growing contender in the seemingly open VP nomination race going into the Democratic party convention next month, told this reporter that 'all companies dealing in toxic materials would be required to obtain toxic clean-up insurance to assure payment of costs and fines assessed by EPA against polluters.'

Senator Keayrn's face appeared on the screen: "All revenues generated over and above the actual costs of clean-ups and programs administration, Ellworth, would be deposited in a quasi-governmental fund: The Trust for Environmental Damage Prevention. The purpose of the trust would be to focus funds on projects relating to preventing environmental damage rather than continuing the policy of reactionary mitigation of damage already inflicted upon the environment in some way.

"But, Ellworth, I want every Senator and every citizen to understand that the real purpose behind my Save Our Planet bill is for it to never have to be enforced."

"What do you mean by that, Senator?"

"In other words, I hope that this bill ups the cost of pollution to the point where it is no longer profitable to pollute. That's the only way we'll ever rid this planet of those who pollute in the name of free enterprise."

"Senator, there have been some detractors over the past couple of years. Specifically your most prominent competition for the vice-presidential nomination at the convention this summer—Lars Hansen—beats the drum that terrorism is so important that we really don't have time to waste on such matters as those covered under your bills. What do you say to them, Senator?"

"Well, Ellworth, I hesitate to say this, but I have often been amazed, frankly, at the narrow-mindedness of a few of my colleagues when it comes to environmental issues. I am the number two Democrat on the Intelligence Committee as well. So, I believe I have as clear a vision as anyone regarding the threat of terrorism to our great country. I am on record, for goodness sake, for sponsoring the amendment to our Homeland Security Act that guaranteed border security of the highest caliber. Honestly, I don't see the conflict. I'm sorry if Mr. Hansen and others have trouble entertaining more than one idea at a time, but I don't, and neither do the American people. This false choice business has got to stop. I believe the people of this country understand that both ideas are important, not mutually exclusive. If this bill isn't enacted, we soon may not have anything worth defending against international terrorism because our environment will be so devastated by unchecked corporate pollution in the name of free enterprise."

"Thank you, Senator Keayrn."

"Anytime, Ellworth. And, thank you."

Men thought they had it tough, having to decide between dark pin-stripes or cashmere jackets. But, for a woman to stay on top in a man's world, she had to be far more subtle than that. She had to know when to look business-like tough and when to look business-like soft. When to look casual but not sexy. When to look sexy but not casual. Yet, always maintaining a senatorial aire about her that kept her, seemingly, unapproachable.

"Flavia Smythe, World Video Network, here at the Capitol to find out more about how Senator Abbie Keayrn's 'Save Our Planet' bill—to be voted on in the Senate Chambers in less than three minutes—will save the American taxpayers billions over the next five to ten years in toxic clean-up costs alone, not to mention costs to our clogged federal court system which will be alleviated by an Administrative Hearing system through EPA."

As Abbie closed her purse, she saw herself on all four sections of the screen, close up and appearing very tired as she exited the chambers to talk to the press after her morning speech. Then, WVN, cut to a later part of that interview.

"Flavia, I'll tell you. This is one of those bills that is really quite straight forward if you cut away all of the legalese. If you pollute, then you pay, and you pay the whole bill, no matter how big that bill may be."

"Well, I must say, Senator Keayrn, you certainly make it sound simple, and you've certainly become known as the 'save our planet' senator. And, let's face it, Senator, no matter what happens in a few hours, the name Senator Abigail Keayrn has certainly become a household word, hasn't it?"

The roll would be called on the floor in a matter of minutes. Abbie gathered up the pages of her speech and slipped them into an oxblood vinyl folio. She patted the slick cool material. "For luck."

She pushed her matching Jefferson desk chair back, stood, slipped her purse over her right shoulder, and tucked the folio under her left arm in a series of fluid motions. Almost as an afterthought, she punched the intercom on the Sony telephone/fax complex atop the Early American credenza beneath the double windows against the wall behind her desk. She could see the Capital and the Ellipse from those windows.

"Maureen."

"Yes, Senator."

"I'm off to vote on our bill!"

"Great, Senator Keayrn. I hope your speech this morning worked. We all thought it was fantastic."

"But, you're all biased."

"Well," Maureen giggled. "I guess you could call us that . . . at least. But, we must've gotten a hundred calls in the last few hours—all supportive!"

"That's really great, Maureen. Listen, will you please tell Elle where I am. If she gets back in time, then she may want to come over for the results of the vote. Okay?"

"Yes, ma'am. I'm e-mailing her as we speak, and, if I see her, myself, I'll tell her."

"Thanks, Maureen."

"Oh, Senator?"

"Yes."

"Better take your private exit. There's a pack of reporters out in the hall in front of the office. Maybe you can avoid them that way."

"I'll do my best, Maureen. But, make sure they're still around when I get back . . . provided we win, that is."

"That's cool, Senator. Good luck!"

"Thanks." Abbie punched the intercom off and lunged across the authentic Persian rug that covered nearly all the office floor toward her private doorway into a side hallway. She didn't want to miss this vote.

* * * * *

Abigail Keayrn had been notified that her husband, Sal, was missing in action in Vietnam on July 4, 1969. The telegram was delivered during the annual Keayrn family picnic. Sal was a Navy Seal but was reportedly a member of a Kit Carson team. Beyond that, she knew only that his letters were heavily censored. He was never allowed to call her or her, him. Most of all, the tone of his letters, even with all that censoring, was one of hidden, unspoken things she had not, in all these years, ever been able to quite identify, not even after becoming a member of Congress and having access to all the information available through that office. One thing she did learn was that he could not have been a Kit Carson scout in Vietnam because only Viet-Cong hoi chans who surrendered were assigned as Kit Carson scouts.

Even though she was only twenty-two at the time her husband was classified as missing in action, she became a leader in the POW/MIA movement. Over the next seven years, the movement, under her leadership, was responsible for identifying and bringing home the remains of hundreds of dead MIA's and for the return of hundreds more who were still alive and being held in Vietnam. She was so dedicated that she had a small POW/MIA tattoo placed at the base of her neck that she swore she would not have removed until her husband was found. The tattoo got her on the cover of Ms. Magazine as well as Time and Newsweek.

She gradually attracted the attention of politicos within her own Democrat party. She was beautiful, smart, youthful, the wife of a missing Vietnam veteran, and, thus, a very solid and sympathetic potential candidate. Just what the party needed to defeat the Republican throwback incumbent who had occupied the fifth congressional district seat for nearly twenty years.

Not even the most seasoned of the politicos, however, had counted on Abbie Keayrn's indefatigable campaigning. She proved to be a trooper's trooper, canvassing most of her compact but densely populated urban Florida district door-to-door. The campaign contributions mushroomed. Often she would finish a day's campaigning in the condominiums with two or three thousand dollars in the form of dollar bills and small checks from these everyday folks she touched one-on-one. Abbie won the primary in a close three-way race. Then, in November, she destroyed the opposing incumbent by capturing an astonishing seventy-two percent of the vote. She was off to Washington.

Now, at 55, she worked hard at retaining her youth and health as well as maintaining her power as a senator. She began her day with yoga and meditation, ran most days usually around six thirty or seven in the evening, and worked out with resistance machines several times a week in the Senate gym. Generally, she was in superior shape for a woman at any age and still displayed a natural beauty, a trait she played down as much as possible by her conservative, business-like dress and her prim and proper toilet most of the time as if she were somehow still in a kind of mourning for her husband, Sal, even after all these years.

She was a senior member of the Intelligence Committee and into her fourth year as Chair of the Energy and Natural Resources Committee. She had come into that position when the President took office, and she hoped, now, to have the President take her out of that same position by her becoming his running mate. She had put it all on the line for this vote, today, to "save the planet." If the bill passed, then the first phase of her plan would be complete. She was, now, thanks to those committee hearings and Elle's enthusiastic and inspired public relations, as much a household name as the President or Kleenex. Even if not one voter understood a single word of her bill, that didn't matter. What mattered was that the voters perceived that she was out to save their planet. Thanks to Elle Darby, her very own version of Teddy Sorenson. That the electorate perceived correctly was a fortunate accident.

"We did it, Elle! Seventy-five to twenty-five!" Abbie high-fived her Administrative Assistant who had been waiting for her to come out after the vote had been tallied.

"Killer, Senator Abbie! Just plain killer!" No sooner had their hands slapped than Elle was already returning to the realities of politics. "Now, you desperately need a follow-up issue, something of real significance but within your purview as Chair of the Energy and Natural Resources Committee. Something you can ride right in to the Democratic Convention as the VP front runner, 'cause if there's ever been an open convention year for VP, it's got to be this one."

"That's right. I mean, the President as much as said there'd be an open convention on the VP nomination when he appointed his VP to The Court."

"What else could he have meant by saying that he thought it was only right for the people to choose his new running mate at the convention?"

"Beats me." Abbie shook her head. "You want to talk about this stuff over a nice glass of champagne? I believe that Maureen stashed a few bottles in my refrigerator just for this occasion?" She grimaced. "And, I do have to face the press waiting at the office."

"You're right. There must've been fifteen or so hanging around when I left to come over here. What was that? About fifteen or twenty minutes ago. Maureen was in complete control of the situation as usual."

"She's pumping them full of coffee and feeding them, right?"

"You've got it, Senator. Maureen knows the way to a media person's heart is through the stomach." She smirked playfully. "And, of course, the more we can keep their mouths full the fewer questions they can ask."

"An unintended but perfectly acceptable consequence."

"Let's take the subway."

"Sure."

"That wasn't so bad, Senator Abbie, now was it?" Elle shut the inner office door behind them. There was no one left in the hallway or out front as far as she had been able to tell. The only real evidence that the media swarm had taken over her offices for better than two hours was the recyclable coffee cups and plates and a few finger sandwiches left on the impromptu buffet ala Maureen.

"Not really. We'll be on every network and in every major publication. So, I guess another thirty minutes, a few sandwiches and some coffee, and a few bottles of champagne is a small price to pay for such publicity, right?"

"Absolutely!" She lifted her plastic champagne glass. "To Vpictory!"

Abbie giggled, a little feverish with her success. "To Vpictory!"

The Senator's intercom buzzed. She picked up the telephone and punched the amber blinking button. "Yes?"

"Senator?"

"Maureen?"

"Yes, ma'am."

"Well, I didn't know anyone else was still here."

"There's a sort of unusual call on line two, Senator. Maybe, you ought to take it."

"What's up?"

"It's a man who says he's a prep school teacher in St. Thomas and that he needs to speak with you about an urgent matter. Caller ID displays the correct area code for the United States Virgin Islands."

"What's his name, Maureen?"

Maureen giggled. "He says his name's Kit Carson, Senator. But I ser-i-ous-ly doubt that! The only Kit Carson I ever heard of died back in the 1860's I do believe."

Abbie chuckled. Maureen was right. There was something strange about that name. But, it wasn't what Maureen thought at all. She couldn't imagine why anyone would call her using that name. But, it sure stimulated her curiosity to find out who the person behind the name really was. "Put him on, Maureen. I've got to hear this? Then you get your young self out of this stodgy building and into some new wave or age or whatever disco down in Georgetown or something."

"Yes, ma'am." Maureen giggled again. The line clicked once. "Mr. Carson, the Senator will speak with you now, sir."

"Thank you, Maureen."

The line clicked twice.

"Senator, Mr. Kit Carson is on the line."

"Thanks, Maureen." The line clicked once. Maureen was off and, hopefully, soon gone from here. That poor girl worked far too hard for being so young. Maybe she reminded Abbie a little of herself at age twenty. "Mr. Carson?"

"Senator Keayrn."

"I presume that's not your real name. Is it some kind of sick joke or what?"

"No. No, Senator Keayrn. I mean you no harm at all or any disrespect, but I had to speak with you, and I thought—well, hoped anyway—that you would respond to the name."

"Wha . . . . What? Who are you, really, Mr. Carson?"

"I'm an English teacher on St. Thomas, just like I told Maureen. I served with Sal Keayrn in Vietnam. My name is Gwynn Camsron. Check me out, Senator, until you run into the predictable lock outs even a senator can run into. But, you can get one of your aides to confirm what I'm saying while we're still on the telephone. In the meantime, I hope that I can convince you to come to St. Thomas ASAP to investigate a mystery my students and I uncovered while out whale watching earlier this morning with my best friend, Captain Jean-Lafette Quetel. If you are willing to listen, I have a whale of a tale to tell you ma'am, but I need you to call me back at a different number at a prearranged time using your secure line. You do have one in the office or at home or both, don't you?"

"Yes, I do."

"Then take down this number—(809) XXX-XXXX. That's the Governor's red line. I'll wait for your call at precisely eight p.m. tonight. When the call is answered give them the password 'whales'. Senator, this is a matter not to be taken lightly, I assure you. I would recommend you purge any recording or other record of this conversation immediately because we don't know what we may be dealing with."

"Okay, Mr. Camsron. I don't know why, but for some reason I don't think you're a total crackpot. Maybe because you served with Sal. I don't know. But, I'll make the call. Eight o'clock tonight."

The line went dead. "Well, I'll just be damned!" She slapped down the telephone and turned toward Elle.

"What was that all about, Senator Abbie?"

"Well, my dear LA, that issue you've been dying for us to find may very well have just found us."

"Really? What is it?"

"I don't know yet. I'll probably know something by . . . ." She caught herself. It had been something about his voice . . . an urgency beyond his words . . . a ring of absolute clarity and truth she had seldom heard since Sal was reported missing and almost never in the illustrious body of Congress which she called home.

"Why so secretive, Senator?" She grinned. "Is there more to this Kit Carson phone call than meets the ear?"

"Gwynn Camsron."

"Gwynn What'sron?"

"That's his actual name, Elle," she snorted.

"His actual name. How intriguing, Senator. And what a tongue twister."

"Yes, isn't it? But, I, now, have a long distance telephone date with a possible issue." She smiled. "No more than that."

"Well," she pouted. "I guess you'll tell your alter ego and most trusted assistant and friend all about it when you're ready."

"Yes. When I'm ready."

* * * * *

Somewhere in St. Thomas a telephone rang. Gwynn Camsron had told her it was the Governor's private secured line. Yet, it was hard to believe that the phone on the other end ringing now for the fourth time was, indeed, located inside Government House.

"Good evening, this is Government House secured line one. How may I help you." The female voice was melodic, the words lilting.

"Whales," Abbie rasped.

"Whales? Hold please, Senator Keayrn, for Mr. Gwynn Camsron."

"Whales, Senator Keayrn."

"Whales, Mr. Camsron."

"Thank you for calling, Senator."

"Will Governor Rueben be joining us on the line, Mr. Camsron?"

"Even now, you're still unsure about me?"

"No. Well, maybe. Okay. You know, anyone could answer the phone saying 'This is Government House secure line one.'"

"That's true, of course, and it probably will not help my case much when I tell you that the Governor is not even in this room with me. Just myself and Jean-Lafette Quetel, the captain of the boat we were on when we made our discovery."

"What discovery?"

4
St. Thomas US Virgin Islands
[Music: "Shards of the Urn"]

At dusk, Hotel 1829's hand-laid stone exterior shimmered like a movie set under cream and lemon moonlight. The scent of the sea and the creaking of masts still seemed to permeate the air. The entrance opened into a polished Danish stone atmosphere of drama and romance that lingered from a bygone era. Polished stone walls of the lamp-lit dining room that surrounded Gwynn and Abbie glowed as they sipped Montrachet and relished grilled Caribbean lobster.

"I've never had lobster like this before, only the Maine type. You know, the ones with the big claws." She dipped a small grill-striped piece of the spiny lobster into drawn butter.

As she delicately slipped the morsel into her waiting mouth and moaned with gastronomic ecstasy, Gwynn remembered having the same kind of experience himself the first time he had tasted local lobster. "Well, you see, Senator, it's like this. The Caribbean spiny lobster—the incredibly sweet and tender crustacean you're devouring as I speak—is not actually a lobster at all. It's sort of a cousin to those tasty little morsels known as crayfish up in Cajun country. That's why it's so sweet."

"I just love those spicy crayfish. One of my closest colleagues, Senator Mattie Breaux, was born and raised in New Orleans bayou country. Hurricane Katrina obliterated her family home, along with thousands of others. I worked with her on the restoration project."

"Really? Then, I'm sure she told you that crayfish were not spicy by nature," he teased.

"Oh, don't be silly," she chuckled as she smacked her lips around another small piece of the sweet meat.

"Okay, but I can tell you that this hotel where you are experiencing this gastronomic delight was actually built as a house in 1829 by Alexander Lavalette, a wealthy French sea merchant, for his wife. It was one of the largest homes in Charlotte Amalie. This dining room floor is the original hand painted Moroccan glazed tiles and terra cotta tiles he brought in from Martinique. The kitchen was originally built inside the main house, which was very unusual for that period. Kitchens were nearly always built in separate structures because of the danger from heat and fire. Today, the old kitchen is what now serves as the bar we passed when we first came into the hotel."

"The open courtyard is so beautiful, so West Indian feeling."

"Yes. And, see that staircase on the other side of the courtyard going up to the gallery —the balcony?"

"Yes."

"It's called the 'Welcoming Arms staircase' because the stairs spread out at the base as if to embrace those who ascend them. The upstairs areas now are for hotel guests only.

"I don't know if you noticed when we came in, but standing in front of the hotel, you can still see Alexander Lavalette's initials in the wrought iron of the upstairs balcony. The house became a hotel in 1906. Sometimes I feel like I've been eating here ever since."

"Oh, come on, now," she chuckled. "You're not quite that old are you?"

Gwynn mocked a grimace and held up his hands in surrender.

"Okay, then, old man that you say you are. Now that we've done the obligatory verbal tour of this incredible hotel that seems more like a movie set, let's get down to why you contacted me and lured me down here, anyway." Abbie pouted through the centerpiece spray of fresh cut red and yellow hibiscus in a cut glass bowl. "All you've done so far is hang up on me!" She slugged down her half-full glass of an excellent Montrachet you certainly couldn't find even in your very-much-better-than-average restaurants at home. But, it had been obvious from the moment they entered Hotel 1829 that this was no ordinary place. Clearly, it was also no ordinary evening, even for a United States Senator.

He grinned, a little self-consciously. "I'm really sorry about that, Sen . . . ah . . . Abbie?"

She nodded.

"But, even after all these years, I still have a thing about wire taps and traces, you know, things like that."

"Even over Government House secured lines?"

He nodded and sipped his wine with relish. "Especially over Government House secured lines. After all we are a wholly-owned subsidiary—excuse me, territory—of the United States of America."

"Oh, a full-blown paranoid, huh, Gwynn? Just my luck." She chuckled.

He saluted. "One full-blown paranoid Gwynn Camsron trained and true, although mellowed somewhat by years in academe!" The smile that had smeared over his face like it had been painted on by Dali vanished. "At your service, ma'am." He dropped his salute and regained his smile almost instantaneously.

"So, that's all the more reason for my question, Mr. Paranoid. Why me? Why are you bringing your problem—whatever it really is—to Senator Abigail Keayrn?"

"Well, honestly, I first saw you months ago on C-SPAN chairing the Energy and Natural Resources Committee hearings on your 'Save Our Planet' bill. The way you spoke about saving our rivers and oceans and our endangered sea life and wildlife really got to me.

"It was only after watching the hearings for several days that I realized that Senator Abigail Keayrn was the same person as Sal Keayrn's wife, Abbie."

"So, you really did know Sal?"

"Of course."

"It wasn't just a ploy to get to me?"

"Not on your life, Abbie. Theo Theodora and I met him during Ranger training. He'd been assigned to our new team. We became buddies right away because we were the only ones who were not training to actually become airborne rangers, and the others knew it. They all knew we were different because we were the only ones also training in special warfare and intelligence at the same time. Later, we were shipped to Nam together to become special operations officers." He poked his fork at the untouched lobster on his plate. The fresh parsley garnish lay on top undisturbed. "Our assignment turned out to be a Kit Carson team."

"But, I found out much later—after I first was elected to Congress—that Kit Carson scouts were mostly former VC, not Americans."

"Well, yes, but we looked like a Kit Carson team. We deployed under what appeared to be Kit Carson team orders. As far as our commander knew, we carried out his orders as scouts. But, our mission wasn't really scouting at all. It was ah . . . well . . . ah . . .

most highly classified. Oh sure, we completed the Commander's orders first. We had to in order to keep up the ruse and prevent our commander from becoming suspicious of our activities. But, later, we would change into local civilian clothes to carry out our real orders which were always contained in a black plastic envelope sealed with the command seal of MACV. A team member would pick it out of the garbage behind the mess hall the morning after a dummy grenade was tossed into the hooch we all shared."

"You know?" She nearly touched his hands with her finger tips. "In some ways, you even remind me a little of him."

"No, I don't know." He pulled his hands off the table. "We looked nothing alike. We thought nothing alike. We acted alike, however, in life and death situations. We both avoided them unless there was no other option. Then, we faced such situations with full confidence that we would master the moment, not be mastered by it."

"Sure. I know you are right, Gwynn. But that one shared quality is more important in determining how much one or another person is alike or different than all others, I believe." She smiled.

"You may be more right about that than I care to admit, Abbie."

She nodded as she was rendered speechless by yet another succulent lobster chunk. Well, so far, he'd been right about the lobster. "Crayfish, or by any name, this was by far the sweetest and best lobster I have ever tasted."

"I wrote you a letter just after Sal was declared MIA. I tried to detail all that happened as best I could within the restrictions placed upon me by the military intelligence censors and de-briefers. With all that control, the letter was still heavily redacted before I was even allowed to send it."

"Yes, I received a severely redacted letter from somewhere in Vietnam. The APO was so smudged that I couldn't read it. It said that the letter was being written in the heat of combat by Sal's best friend, First Lieutenant . . . . They blacked out the name all the way through and the entire signature block."

He drew a breath from deep in his chi. It surged up through his lungs, into his throat. "Jesus!" exhaled amidst a coarse whooshing sound as he expelled his breath with great force. "I'm surprised they left in 'First Lieutenant.' No wonder you never called or wrote or anything. I was really bummed out by that for a long, long time, Abbie. You can never know how bad I felt that it was him that was missing and not me. Why not me, for Christ's sake? I didn't have anybody back home. No family. Nothing.

"And, Sal had everything to live for, to go home for. I mean look at you, Abbie" He coughed politely into his open but clasped hands. "Not to be indelicate, Senator, but you look as good or better than the photographs Sal carried with him all those years ago."

"Nonsense. It's just the incredible St. Thomas moonlight and lobster. Speaking of which, you've hardly touched yours."

"Which," he teased. "The moonlight or the lobster?"

"The lobster." She smiled. "Of course."

"Guess I'm not very hungry right now. I've got other things on my mind."

"Then may I?" She tipped her fork toward his plate. "I'm quite used to eating when I have other things on my mind." She grinned.

"Be my guest, Senator. I love to see a woman eat with abandon rather than decorum."

"And I," she began as she pilfered a sizeable chunk of his lobster and placed it on her plate. "I love having the opportunity and the incentive . . . ." She paused to fork another piece from his plate. "To eat with abandon rather than with decorum." She began cutting the chunk into three bite-size pieces on her plate, reconsidered, and lifted the entire piece to her mouth, tearing off a small portion with her teeth.

"It's the islands, mon. It does this to everybody. This island is full of stories about people who came here on vacation and never went home."

"All right, then, Mr. Gwynn Camsron," she mumbled around the savory mouthful of lobster, "mysterious prep school teacher from St. Thomas whose records are too classified for even a senator to access without proper need to know."

"Wait one, Senator. What are you talking about?"

"You don't really think I'd rendezvous in St. Thomas with a complete stranger without having them checked out first, do you?" She waggled her right forefinger at him. "After all, you even suggested it, remember."

Gwynn snorted. "Touché."

"So, tell me. What is it that has you so preoccupied you can't even eat your lobster? Not that I'm complaining about that." She grinned and finished the piece of her host's lobster in one bite.

"Whatever it really is that you lured me out here to tell me about? I mean that phone conversation with you and Mr. Quetel about a large number of whales being missing from the pods that travel through the Caribbean was only designed to titillate my interest enough to get me here. You still haven't shared with me what the *real* discovery was or why it is so important, Mr. Gwynn Camsron?"

"More wine, Mr. Camsron? Madame? A bottle from me to you." Captain Adolpho Sierra presented the bottle.

Gwynn waved away the formal presentation. "Thank you, Captain. I trust your judgment completely." He motioned to pour as the Captain deftly uncorked the fresh bottle. "Please. You and this establishment are among my favorites over the entire Caribbean, and you are my most trusted food and wine advisor and friend."

"Thank you, Mr. Camsron." Captain Sierra smiled warmly. "But you always say that to me when you visit us."

"Forgive me, but that is so true." Gwynn chuckled behind a sunburned but surprisingly delicate right hand. Then, suddenly he stumbled to his feet. "My manners." Gwynn extended his right arm to indicate Abbie. "May I present the honorable United States Senator from Florida, Abigail Keayrn. Senator Keayrn, may I introduce you to Captain Adolpho Sierra of St. Thomas, United States Virgin Islands."

Captain Sierra grasped Abbie's hand for just a moment, almost kissing it, then pulled away. "I am honored, Senator. I have watched you on the television many times."

Abbie nearly blushed under the openness of his gray eyes. "Why I am flattered, Captain."

Gwynn fumbled back into his seat as Captain Sierra poured for Abbie. When he poured for Gwynn, a slow smile invaded the normally expressionless folds of fat which served as his face. "It is my distinct pleasure to serve the two of you tonight." With that pronouncement, he turned on his right heel and marched off to attend his other guests as personally as he attended them.

"So, Gwynn?" She sipped deeply at the new wine in her new

glass. "Mmmmm . . . . Jesus. This is absolutely fantastic, Gwynn! Have you tried it yet?"

"No." He sipped. "Wow. You're right, Abbie. This may be the very best Montrachet I've ever tasted. Gwynn extracted the bottle from the ice bucket.

"Jesus. That is, indeed, mysterious."

"What, Gwynn?" Abbie strained across the table to glimpse the label. "I can't read the label."

"That's because there isn't one."

"That's certainly unusual. I don't think I've ever seen that before, have you?"

"Never. But, how coincidental."

"In what way?"

"Well, my story is sort of like that bottle of Montrachet. You can't really tell what's inside until you taste it."

"So?" Abbie licked her lips playfully. "Give me a glass full, Mr. Gwynn Camsron."

"Of my story or the wine?"

"Both, and do it before Captain Sierra returns and distracts us again."

"Well, as we were counting the whales in the pod, we spotted something that looked like a harpoon lodged in the dorsal fin of the lead whale.

"I remember it like it is just happening.

"Quetel yelled: 'It does be a harpoon right enough, me son! But wid a man's arm all tangled up in its line.'

"Was it an arm or simply atavism?" Gwynn chuckled. "That's what I wanted to know."

"Atavism?"

"That's how Quetel responded."

"So?"

"It's the reappearance of a characteristic in an organism after several generations of absence. Usually this is caused by some chance recombination of genes. It may be referred to as an atavistic variation or, most of us would call it a 'throwback'. It comes from the French *atavisme* and Latin *atavus* for ancestor."

"TMI, Mr. Camsron," she laughed, putting her hands into the air across the table with the palms facing Gwynn. "Too much information."

"Okay," he responded. "I know I have a tendency to give too much detail about nearly everything. But," he continued, "I have heard of whales being sighted with what appeared to be arm-like appendages before. So, I asked Jean-Lafette if he was sure."

"'Mary, Mother of God. Look, me son! It's a arm and it's comin' loose.'

"'We need a gaff or a net or something, Cap'n!' I shouted. 'We need to save that arm!'

"All the time the whales were singing like some kind of accompaniment or musical score to this movie we were playing out. Quetel yelled for me to look in the aft storage compartment for a net with a long handle.

"I quickly moved aft and found the net exactly where he said it would be. With the long wooden handle, one of us would be able to scoop the net into the water and capture the arm that was, by then, bobbing like a giant cork in the wake of the whale.

"Quetel crossed himself again. 'I be bettin' you somet'ing, me son,' he yelled.

"'What's that Cap'n?'

"'Da mon dat fits dat arm me t'inks he be holdin' answers to questions you doan even wan' t'ask.'

"'Got it!' I yelled. I had actually netted the arm and hauled it into the boat. My students were revolted by the shriveled and decaying limb. But, unbelievably, it had a message on it in the form of a prominent tattoo on the inside of the forearm. Five blood red capital letters: YUNUS.

"Well, now you know the beginning with the missing whales and the dismembered arm. Since our discovery, Jean-Lafette and some of my students have done some further investigation. We still don't know what YUNUS represents, but we do have some results from their investigation that will, I presume, become clear over drinks. Jean-Lafette should be here any time now. He is relentlessly on time in a culture that values being very much not on time."

"I woulda swore dat I knew dat whale dey be showing on TV by its flukes. I be swearing it, mon . . . ah, Sen-a-tor," Jean-Lafette Quetel repeated as if he believed Abbie had not heard him the first time. But, as the Captain and whale counter knocked back his fourth Cruzan Gold shot, he seemed to finally realize that he did have her full attention. He leaned forward across the wrought iron table's glass top. The town of Charlotte Amalie twinkled below the 1829 gallery. "You see, Sen-a-tor, da underside of da tail or fluke of a humpback be like our fingerprints. Dere does be dis special pat-tern under da flukes."

"Some of my students," Gwynn interjected, "obtained footage from the networks via the Internet. And, they took a closer look."

"What did your students discover?"

"Armond matched the fluke patterns of the whale that beached itself in Maine with a photograph Jean-Lafette, himself, had taken during an official count of a humpback breaching off of Mandahl Point. That was nearly two years ago."

"So what does this mean that is so important to our national security and the world?"

"The Whale Institute, Abbie. Jean-Lafette sent them a copy. He always sends copies of any fluke photographs he can get as do others all around the world. They have a data base of the flukes and any available information on the whale a particular fluke pattern identifies. They keep data on migrations, sizes of pods, changes in the size of the population overall and in specific regions."

"In other words, they should've already known about this rather quick reduction in the humpback whale population? And, so should we."

"Dere you be, Sen-a-tor!" Jean-Lafette winked and downed another shot. He liked her okay. She seemed pretty smart. Didn't have to lead her every step of the way for her to understand what you had to say. He downed another shot. "Ah, me son, and dere you be."

"I'll make the call first thing in the morning before I visit your students at your school. Over the past couple of years I've tried to get the Institute investigated regarding its accountability in general but to no avail. I couldn't push too hard because Lars Hansen, the CEO of the Institute, is an arch political rival. I should think that this would finally get Justice moving despite the politics of it all."

"We are beginning to think that the disappearance of whales reported by Jean-Lafette coupled with this one now showing up out of nowhere is part of some kind of plot." Gwynn held up his hands in mock surrender. "Oh, I know that this sounds like conspiracy theory mania, Abbie, but . . . ."

"Dere you be, Sen-a-tor! We fear dat somet'ing be ver-y wrong, me son. Ver-y wrong." Another shot slipped down his throat.

The television behind the bar flashed to a news bulletin.

"This is Ellworth Hayes with another INN news flash! It's becoming a veritable epidemic of beached whales. Reports just in from a variety of locations along the east coast tell us that somewhere between fifteen and thirty beached humpback whales have been discovered over the past three days. Most of them look like they have exploded from the inside out. New beached whale sightings seem to be coming in every few hours now. And still there seem to be no explanations forthcoming."

Ellworth beamed camera one as he continued to speak with some urgency. "So far the best we've been able to come up with is a statement from unnamed sources in Senator Abigail Keayrn's office implying that the Senator is out of town on Senate business that might have something to do with these beached whales, according to her office." He paused for effect. "So where is she?"

"Well, really. I'm right here, in good old Saint Thomas checking out the problem, Ellworth," Abbie chuckled under her breath. Then, as if she were suddenly hit with some realization, she burst out: "Damn it! How did he get that information?"

"If you're confused, ladies and gentlemen, all I can say is join the club. But, I promise you that INN will keep digging into this mystery until we find out exactly what's going on and report it to you in more depth than anybody else on television.

"I'm Ellworth Hayes for INN. We'll be right back with more news in more depth than anybody else on television."

5
Aaron's Errand

[Music: Percussion Petroglyph"]

"You shall take in your hand this staff, with which you shall perform the signs." Exodus 4:17

"You've got twenty-four hours to get your young ass to Maui, you poor bastard." Aaron Silver remembered the Assistant AG Hathaway's words as if they were being said now as he pointed the manicured forefinger of his right hand down at some large red lettering on a green roof hundreds of feet below.

"But it's not going to be one big luau, you understand. You'll be investigating the Whale Institute for Senator Keayrn's committee. She wants to know why there's been such a rash of unreported humpback whale disappearances over the past several years, and why it is only now coming to our attention—and not from the Institute."

The green roof covered some sort of shanty-like structure at the edge of an inlet which opened wide to the Pacific Ocean. Even though his mouth was uncomfortably close to the pilot's ear, Aaron still had to shout in order for the pilot to hear him over the whir of the chopper's rotors.

"Wonder what those letters spell out?"

This time the Justice Department investigation requested by Senator Abigail Keayrn directly from St. Thomas was begun immediately. The purpose of the investigation was to explain the disappearance of large numbers of humpback whales in both the Atlantic and the Pacific reported from various sources over the past two years. His boss, Assistant Attorney General for the Environment Paul Hathaway, had refused, for months, to knuckle under to Abbie's pressure to send a Justice Department Investigator to The Whale Institute in the Hawaiian Islands. The institute—mandated with the primary responsibility for counting and tracking whales— was run by Hathaway's friend and Abbie's chief rival for the VP nomination, Lars Hansen. According to what Elle had told him, his boss had only given in when Abbie had called from the Virgin Islands with reports of missing whales and a possible terrorist connection to the recently beached whale in Maine. She had threatened to take Hathaway's reticence and the reason for it to the media. By yesterday afternoon, Aaron was the investigator of record and was on a plane to Maui.

"Only one way to find out, yah," Ace Bien Hoa yelled back over the noise. He belonged to that small "club" of Vietnam pilots who had become lost in the Caribbean and the Pacific, one who, long ago, had taken the name of the base he flew out of in Vietnam—Bien Hoa—rather than keep his own name because he feared being spied upon by the government he had once served with distinction. The former Air Medal for Valor recipient shoved the stick forward. The chopper dropped toward the roof of the shanty on stilts at a craggy edge of south Maui overlooking one of the bays where the humpbacks bred and birthed.

Aaron felt his stomach drop out of his ass as the helicopter groaned in a dive toward the red letters on that green roof. He was beginning to have second thoughts about this assignment after all. But, it was the best case he had been given since joining the department less than two years ago right out of Georgetown Law School. He had been Law Review editor, national Moot Court champion, number one in his class, and sought after by every major law firm in the country. Despite all of the attention, he chose Justice. Every assignment he'd been given at Justice had been carried out efficiently and effectively to completion. He had no real field experience yet, but he believed he deserved this shot. However, he was still surprised. His guess was that it had been his good friend and roommate Elle whom he had to thank for this assignment—for better or for worse, in air sickness and in health . . . if he had any health left after this dive.

"You're okay, bud, yah?" Ace roared as he pulled back sharply on the stick just above the roof. The chopper leveled off.

Aaron struggled to not look green. "Oh, sure." He fought for control of the nausea he felt swelling in his throat. A crippled smile wrinkled his bluish lips. "Lucky for your helicopter that I left my breakfast back in D.C. in a 747 barf bag. At least it wasn't as bad as it could have been without pills."

"Not much on flying, yah?"

His stomach had miraculously returned through his ass into its proper place. "No." Even though it was queasy, he was happy to have it back. "Not really."

The cracking red paint on the roof spelled out:

SMALL CRAFT LANDING

"My idea of flying," he actually laughed, "is a simulation program."

"Don't like flying much, yah?" Ace banked his chopper to the left then began to climb once again toward the dark thunderstorms gathering over the Pacific. The helicopter whirled around one hundred and eighty degrees, away from the ominous blackening thunderstorm, and leveled off again.

"I don't understand why, but I get air sick in both planes and helicopters. It's the only kind of motion sickness I have." He shrugged. "I can ride out a hurricane class storm in a dingy and never even feel queasy. But the minute I get off the ground in an airplane or a helicopter . . . ." He made a face as if he were barfing. "Beats me!" Aaron controlled a laugh. He knew that he would be barfing again if not for those airsick pills Elle had given him at National before he had boarded his flight.

Ace flew his approach from the south and into the wind. The chopper once again dropped through the thick air toward the choppy gray Pacific Ocean and the landing area marked by four red X's. Once the helicopter was down on the pad, Aaron knew that he would feel a lot better.

"Stand down . . . .
Give in . . . .
It doesn't matter what you find, you know.
Stand cool . . . .
And be somebody smooth as silk . . . ."

The old Smashing Pumpkins' *Cherub Rock* blasted like a force field of sound from six Advent speakers driven by a Blau Plunkt Laguna. Bridget Yow steered her open Jeep straight through the scurve only a few hundred yards from the helicopter pad just like her world champion race driver daddy had taught her when he still thought she was a boy and would race Sebring someday. But, Bridget had not become the race driver her daddy had hoped for. Instead, she went to Cal Berkeley and majored in Environmental Science. When she graduated, she already had a job with Green Peace, and, until recently, had served on the crew of a Green Peace ship blockading whalers from migrating whale herds. She had been working for the Whale Institute as a spotter, counter, and tagger for just under three months when Lars Hansen plucked her out of that obscurity to keep an eye on some federal investigator dude from D.C. Hansen emphasized that he wanted her to stay as "close to him as you possibly can" and report directly to him every day on the investigator's activities.

Bridget down-shifted the Jeep and made a sharp turn to the right down a sand rut path. At the end of the narrow road she could see the weathered clapboard shanty with that awful green roof. A stiff figure in a dark suit stood outside the building by the road, waiting, a brief case in its right hand. A travel bag and suit bag sat at the figure's left side.

"That's got to be him," she mumbled beneath the wall of bass booming from her sound system. "Nobody but a Fed would be dressed like that around here."

> "Let me o . . . out.
> Let me out. Let me o . . . out.
> Let me out . . . ."

Aaron recognized the Smashing Pumpkins lyrics exploding from the open Jeep as it pulled up beside him. The female driver slammed on brakes raising a cloud of dust and sand. The fine cloud drifted past him. Tan dust clung to his dark blue suit, long-sleeve white shirt, and navy tie with gray teardrops that were wrinkled and damp from the helicopter trip. With a coat of Hawaiian dust all over him, Aaron was sure that he looked more like a slip figure just removed from its ceramic firing mold than a Justice Department lawyer.

"A veritable 'free spirit', I'll wager," he mumbled.

"Aloha there! If you're talking to yourself, you must be from

D.C. Right?"

"Alo . . . . What?"

"Aloha. Do you talk to yourself much?"

"Aloh . . . no. Actually . . . ." He glanced up at Venus as the young woman jumped from the jeep at the same time that she turned off the ignition.

"Actually? Actually?"

She seemed to prance in slow motion toward him with the surprising grace of a dancer. "Actually, I do." He chuckled half-aloud. She made him very nervous, more nervous than most of the seemingly endless line of women who were attracted to him despite his shyness towards them, especially when she was standing so close to him. He backed up a step.

"Do what?"

"Do . . . uh . . . ah . . . talk to myself a lot." He scooped up his duffel and suit bags in his left hand. His right hand still grasped his brief case.

"Just toss 'em into the back." Her face pinched up. "No. On second thought . . . ." She held up her hand, palm out. "Do you have anything in those bags of yours that remotely resembles casual wear?"

He nodded.

"Good. Then, take that bag into the lua and wash up and change before somebody sees me with you dressed like . . . ." She pointed at him, struggling not to laugh. "Like a . . . ."

"Like an FBI agent or something?"

"That's it!" She snapped her fingers. "Like an FBI agent or something. Nobody'd ever trust me around here again."

"And, is that important to you, Ms. . . . ."

"Yow. Bridget Yow." She hung her head almost like a pout and extended her slender hand. "And, no, it's only important to my job."

"Aaron Silver. Justice Department." He dropped the brief case and grasped her hand in his. "Pleased to meet you, Bridget."

"Me, too, Aaron." She allowed him to hold their handshake for a few moments.

Aaron released her hand at the first pressure of her pulling away. "And, what's a lua?"

"The bathroom. It's in the main terminal building there." She pointed toward a small stone and wood building just beyond the shanty.

Aaron slipped his brief case and suit bag into the back of the jeep, scooped up his duffel and headed for the shanty.

"Rest Rooms are straight back from the front door. You can't miss 'em!" Bridget's perpetual-pout lips grinned. Well, she figured if she was going to have to play babysitter to some Fed anyway, then, at the least, she was going to have a little fun. And, he was sort of cute under that suit of his and all that Kapalua dust.

The Whale Institute

Aaron was startled from his narcoleptic-like state by several quick blasts from a steam engine whistle as an old locomotive chugged by them on the small gauge tracks nearly paralleling the highway on the driver's side. "What the hell is that? Did I wake up in Disney World or what?"

"No, FBI boy. That's the Lahaina, Kaanapali & Pacific Railroad or what we call the Sugar Cane Train. "

"The Sugar Cane Train, huh? The real thing?"

"Well, sort of and not really."

"What do you mean, sort of and not really?"

"It's sort of the real deal because some dude back in 1969—Mac McKelvy, I think was his name—rebuilt the old railroad for, like, six miles or something between Lahaina Town and Puukolii. He wanted to recreate the old days when the train hauled field workers and the raw sugar cane they harvested for milling. It's sort of not the real thing because the train itself is made of metal rather than wood which was the standard building material for railroad cars in the early days of the railroad. It's been a great tourist attraction or visitor attraction." She shrugged. "Visitors—that's the PC thing to call tourists these days."

The Whale Institute's business offices shared a portion of a long pier jutting out into the Pacific from the harbor in Lahaina Town with a lighthouse that still blinked at ships and passing whales in the night.

The original lighthouse had been a 9-foot wooden tower built in

1840 to aid navigation for the many whaling vessels that came to the harbor. It was the first lighthouse in Hawaii and predated any lighthouse on the United States Pacific Coast. The light was provided by whale oil and was kept burning by a Hawaiian caretaker. The height was increased to 26 feet in 1866. It was rebuilt as a concrete structure in 1905.

The Institute originally chose the site because it was one of the islands' best locations for land bound whale counting. However, over the years, harbor traffic had increased so significantly that the Institute's counters had found it necessary to venture further and further and further away from the clutter of town business in order to count the humpbacks accurately. So, they moved the entire operation except for their business offices to a hidden beach area nearby.

Bridget steered the jeep off of Honoapiilani Highway onto a packed dirt access road to Puamana Beach Park. Once she drove past the deserted beach, picnic tables, and portable toilets, she steered the jeep through a wide gap in the stand of Palms and cacti that defined the boundary between the park and the open beach beyond. A rutted gravel road that was on no map zigzagged its way up the coast line toward the institute research and residences complex. Because of the protected location, even though the complex was located just outside of town it was completely isolated. Another jeep pulled in behind them from among the palms and cacti that choked the narrow cracked cement road.

Within moments after their arrival, Lars Hansen, CEO and President of the quasi-governmental institute, alighted from the following jeep and hurried into the reception building lobby. As he caught up with them, he extended his right hand. "Lars Hansen, Mr. Silver. Aloha."

He shook Aaron's hand until Aaron was sure it would fall off. "I've just been on the phone with the AG Paul Hathaway, and I assured him that we would accommodate you in every way possible during your investigation." He paused.

"Does that mean there might be some way in which you would not be willing to accommodate my investigation?"

"Indeed not. Only, sometimes a thing may be beyond one's ability to make the appropriate decision. That is all. To that end, I have assigned Bridget, here, exclusively to set you up in your cottage and act as your personal 'guide'. Perhaps you would like to go to the cottage and settle in now. I know you must be exhausted. It's a long trip from DC to Maui. The five hour time difference this time of year takes some getting used to."

Bridget interrupted. "It's a really cool little house, Aaron, directly on the beach. You can actually see Lahaina Harbor from your kitchen windows."

"Sounds like you know the house pretty well."

"I guess I should. I stayed there for a few weeks when I first came on board—until my employee's cottage was ready for me to move in."

"Cool."

"Oh, and, there's an almost new CD player—a gift from one of the Institute's patrons."

"I bought an assortment of CDs myself—classical, new wave, contemporary jazz, even old standards like Sinatra," Hansen interrupted. Then he paused to observe this youthful investigator more closely. They were always the worst kind, the young. They were always out to prove something, to get ahead. What had Hathaway sent him, anyway? "Of course, if you prefer that noise your X generation or gen Y or whatever it is you call it these days passes for music . . . ."

"*We* don't call it anything, Mr. Hansen," Aaron interrupted. "Others like you seem to come up with those kinds of names. Not us."

Hansen huffed and cleared his throat, obviously not used to being talked to in such a manner. "At any rate, young man, if you do prefer those types of music, then I'm sure that your attaché during your visit, Ms. Yow, will be able to accommodate you." He stared at Bridget, nodding.

She giggled uncomfortably. Her sea-like eyes darted a glance at Aaron. He hadn't flinched. "Cool," she muttered.

"What's that, Ms. Yow?"

"Oh, cool. I've got some discs I'm sure Aaron will like. Not much on MP3's though. The music quality just isn't there regardless of the so-called convenience."

"So," Aaron mused, "that's why the big speakers and cd player in the jeep instead of an Ipod?"

Bridgette grinned in response.

"Well, why don't you take Mr. Silver to his guest bungalow at the far end of the beach, Ms. Yow?" His brow, thick with hair which seemed to be experiencing some kind of genetic creep toward his equally thick eyebrows, furrowed. Then, his narrow lips, suddenly twisted into his version of an understanding smile. "You can help Mr. Silver . . . Aaron . . . get settled in . . . and you can both 'cool it' for the rest of the day. Show him a little aloha, Ms. Yow. Let him get to know what the island is like. It's a very interesting and beautiful place."

* * * * *

The first day of his investigation Aaron ran up against Haver. As he recalled from one undergraduate English class or another, the word was Scot for "talking nonsense." And, Albert Haver, Office Manager for the Whale Institute and campaign manager for his boss, Lars Hansen, was definitely living up to his name. Because that was precisely what he was doing. In Gaelic. In English. In Washington American Bureaucratize. No matter what the language, the office manager was talking nonsense.

"Nearly everything was put in fireproof storage over on the Big Island. After the move, we didn't have enough space here on the pier in the few small offices we had left to keep it all. Years and years of files." Albert's six-three skeleton twisted at the left side of his horn rims. "It'll take a few days."

"Correspondence and ledgers from last month?"

"If we can find 'em at all, what with the move and all after we landed the new location on the beach . . . on a long term lease . . . which I helped negotiate, I might add."

"You not only might, but you did, Mr. Haver. Now, if you would only be as forthcoming with your office records as you are with your personal anecdotes."

"Look, Sliver!"

"Silver, Mr. Non . . . . Mr. Haver. Silver."

"Silver. Sliver," he snarled. "What's the difference? Anyway you say it or spell it, the name comes out a pain in my ass, now doesn't it, Mr. Sil . . . ver? And, I got too much to do to be this bothered by some political hack from the Justice Department. You savvy?"

Aaron didn't flinch. His eyes became green lasers into Haver's center. It was time to use Aaron's rod. "I am conducting . . ." he almost whispered in controlled, well-enunciated words. "I am conducting a bone fide Justice Department investigation with full subpoena and even indictment powers if necessary, Mr. Haver. So, I suggest that you begin to show some signs of cooperation with my requests and a little respect, not for me personally, but for me as a lawful investigator for the United States of America. If you are not capable of that, sir, then I will have more lawyers on your ass by tomorrow night than you have whales in your Institute whale logs."

Aaron fought with a smirk. It definitely felt good to whack such an asshole for all he was verbally worth with the rod of the federal government and watch the blows do their damage.

"You have until noon tomorrow, Mr. Haver, to comply with the requests I have given you today. Do I make myself completely clear, sir?"

The fingers of Albert Haver's left hand automatically began twisting his glass frames. His pasty face seemed to glow a rose like color underneath the skin. His Adam's apple bobbed and weaved like a caged fighter with words he dared not utter. He pivoted on his oxblood wingtip heels away from this Sliver of a nightmare, leaving his back and the rear of his dull brown crew cut for it to stare at. "Good afternoon to you, sir!" somehow growled and hissed up through his larynx.

"Good afternoon to you, too, Mr. Haver. I so look forward to our meeting here, tomorrow at . . . ." He chuckled to himself. He could hardly believe, himself, that he was actually going to say it. "High noon."

Washington, DC

"This *is* a secured line, Elle, right?"

"Yes, Aaron. Listen, roomy, you're at a random phone booth miles away from the Institute. Our line at this end is completely secured. Don't worry."

"I didn't want to use my cell. They can be tapped easily."

"Please, Mr. Silver. Aaron. You can speak freely."

"Thank you, Senator Keayrn. I thought you were still in St.

Thomas."

"I am. Your clever roommate patched me in. Mr. Camsron will drive me to the airport tomorrow. I'm just glad to see that Hathaway responded so quickly."

"You can say that again, Senator. I was on a plane to Maui almost before I knew what I was on a plane for."

"What have you got, roomy?"

"Listen, it's all pretty vague at this point. It seems as if a significant number of the Institute's staff is disenchanted with the way things are being run. Some even have vague suspicions that Lars Hansen and his board of directors are involved in something not quite on the up-and-up."

"Anything concrete, Mr. Silver? It's going to be difficult for me to do much unless . . . ."

"I understand the politics of the situation, Senator Keayrn, and I can appreciate your position."

"But?" Elle transitioned for her friend and roommate.

"Yes. But." He cleared his throat. "Sorry. All I can tell you now is that my instincts—combined with the staff complaints and some telephone records linking the Institute's 'contribution' program to companies of dubious origin—lead me to the conclusion that this could be something pretty big. Some of these connections may be even a little scary. I'll know better in the next day or so, Senator. I sort of have to tread a bit softly even though this is a legitimate investigation. I mean, this dude, Haver . . . ."

"Haver?"

"Yes, ma'am. Haver."

"That means nonsense, or something like that, in Scottish, doesn't it?"

"Yes, ma'am, it does. And, that's exactly what I'm getting from this dude, Al Haver. He's the Office Manager, but he's also the big boss's campaign manager.

"Like I said, Senator Keayrn, I can't be sure of anything until I dig a little deeper with Bridget's help. But, I, personally, would bet the farm on this one!"

"Good. That may not be concrete, but Elle says your instincts are good, so . . . ."

"So, you be careful, Aaron. Don't get your cute buns into any

---

real trouble, you hear me?"

"I hear you, Elle, and I'll try to obey."

"I'm serious, Aaron. Half of the women in D.C. would go into mourning if anything happened to you. You just don't seem to realize it. So, just don't take any unnecessary chances, okay?"

"Listen to your roommate, Mr. Silver. We want you hurting the bad guys. Okay? We don't want you hurt."

"Okay, Elle. Senator."

"I'm getting off, now, Mr. Silver. I'm sure you and Elle must have personal roommate kinds of things to talk about. Thank you, again."

"Thank you, Senator."

"For putting you in harms way?"

"No, ma'am. For giving me this chance. I think it's going to make my career at Justice."

"I hope so, Mr. . . . ah . . . Aaron. I do hope it will prove career-making for both of us. Good bye." She flipped off the speaker phone, leaving Elle alone on a regular telephone with Aaron.

"Okay, Aaron, what about this Bridget girl?"

"She's the woman who met me at the Kapalua Airport. Lars assigned her to be my, shall we say, 'babysitter.'"

"Yes. So how is Bridget involved in your investigation?"

"Well, Bridget's been able to get to the people who work here better than I can. That's how I know enough despite that Haver dude to make some predictions. And, she's set up a meet tomorrow night with some of the more courageous employees at one of the local clubs. Cool, huh?"

"Yeah, cool." Elle sighed. "I don't want to seem like a mother or anything, Aaron, but please be careful."

"You know, Elle, I think that Bridget and I have sort of become . . . ah . . . sort of friendly."

"Oh, Aaron, that's cool, sweetie. But, that's even more reason to be careful. You've only known her for a couple of days, now. No matter how you feel." She giggled. "Or how your loins feel, you still can't really be sure of her motives, yet. After all, she does work for Larsen."

"Yes. I know that, Elle. But, damn it, I just know that she's all right. She is so cool!"

"Believe me, Aaron, sweetie, I'll be happier for you than you are for yourself, if this all works out. Just listen to your roomy and be very wary of this relationship until you, both of you, get out of there in one piece. Okay?"

"Okay. It won't be as easy as trying to stay out of trouble, though, Elle." He chuckled. "I can guarantee you that."

"Just promise me that you'll do your best, okay?"

"Okay."

"Keep in close touch."

"I'll call as soon as I have something."

"Take care, sweetie."

"I will. Bye."

"Bye."

* * * * *

Abbie picked up her cell and dialed a number she had not dialed in awhile, Sergio Manny's direct private line. But, to assuage her feelings of guilt and responsibility for young Aaron Silver she had to make this call because she feared that she had put his young life in jeopardy and that there was not a lot that she could do about it except make this call and ask Serge to make some calls of his own and a few inquiries. The rest would be up to Aaron.

Serge was always a comfort to talk to in times like these, although he'd deny it to the death, because he felt that kind of sensitivity undercut his tough-as-nails Director of the FBI image.

"Yes. Hello." The fact that she was puzzled at someone other than Serge answering the phone transparently transferred to her voice. "This is Senator Keayrn. Is he in?"

"Oh, my, yes, Senator. He's just stepped away to the little boy's room. This is Sara Metcalf, his secretary. I don't know if you remember me or not, but I met you . . . ."

"At his daughter's wedding reception. What was that? About three years ago, now?"

"Yes, ma'am. I'm pleased that you remember, Senator. We're all so proud to know you, ma'am. But, don't let on to the Chief that I said so."

"No problem, Sara. How's that husband of yours . . . Ted? I

heard through the grapevine that he'd been very ill. I do hope he's improved."

"Yes, ma'am. Ted's doing fine, now, Senator. He's been home . . . out of the hospital, you know, for about six months now. The doctors all seem to think he can go back to work once he's regained his strength. His heart's fine. As he says, it was just his brain that sort of got a little uppity." She chuckled. "That's what my Ted calls a major stroke, Senator. His brain getting a little uppity."

Abbie couldn't help but laugh herself at that. "Well, I'm sure he'll be fine. He seemed to be a tough man."

"Oh, you're right there, Senator. Ted's no pushover . . . ." She gulped. "Uupps! Here comes the Chief, Senator Keayrn. I'll put him on right away . . . . Chief. Senator Keayrn on the line for you, sir."

"And, it sounds like you've been giving her an earful, too, Sara," Sergio Manny gruffed out through thick purplish lips that smoked far too many cigars. The smile that twitched there belied a lighter intent than the words and their delivery seemed to indicate on the surface. Just one of the many reasons he had built a reputation for inscrutability over his nearly eight years as the Director of the Federal Bureau of Investigation . . . the realization of a life-long dream.

Sara mock pouted. "She's just so nice, sir, and easy to talk to."

"How the hell do you think she got where she is, you poor old secretary, you?" he howled.

"Now, Mr. Director, sir," Sara admonished with a giggle. "FBI Director's cannot have nor display a sense of humor. That's the regulation, sir. You know that." She, too, was howling.

He snatched the telephone. "Sorry, Senator. We're just a little punchy here, tonight. Sara and I and about ten others have been working on a pretty big case which, of course, I can't talk about. You were lucky to catch me at this number this late at night, you know."

"Hello, Serge. It's good to talk to you as well," she chuckled. "I'd have tried the house, my dear . . . just not until morning . . . ." She shrugged at the telephone as if it were a person. "Anyway, I know you never sleep, you old reprobate."

"Seldom, anyway. So to what do I owe this honor of a phone call after weeks of silence and missing your niece's baby shower."

"I'm truly sorry about Bett's shower. She did receive my gift, didn't she?"

"She said she did, but I don't remember what it was."

"I not only don't remember, Serge, but I also never knew. Elle bought something for me." She fought a laugh. "I've just been so damned busy with this bill of mine."

"Congrats, by the way."

"Thanks, Serge."

"I know you worked your ass off for it, honey. You deserved the win." He paused and lit a hand rolled Havana cigar. "How do you think it'll affect your VP chances?"

"Don't know, for sure. But, the exposure was just great. As all the news people are saying, if nothing else, I've become a household word. Thanks to Elle. And, that should count for something at the convention, don't you think?"

"Certainly seems that it would have a lot to do with what goes on in July, my dear."

"We surely hope so, Serge. We sure do."

"So what's on your mind, Senator?"

"Well. I need a little special help on the QT?"

"What kind of special help?"

"There's this young man . . . an investigator for the Justice Department as a matter of fact under Assistant AG Paul Hathaway in Environmental Law."

"I know who you mean."

"This young man, Aaron Silver, has been assigned to do some investigative work for me on this disappearance of whales business. I don't know if you've been reading about it lately or not?"

"Your sister mentioned it, but I haven't any first-hand knowledge."

"Anyway, he's out in Maui conducting an in-depth investigation of the Whale Institute due to the fact that these whale disappearances were never reported by the Institute, and one of its primary reasons for existence is the monitoring of the various whale populations."

"And, I guess, it doesn't make things any easier to have that idiot Larsen out there as the CEO, huh?"

"Yes. It does make things politically volatile. And, that makes me nervous for Aaron."

"So, what do you really want from me, Senator Sister-In-Law?"

"I want you to surreptitiously investigate a woman by the name of Bridget Yow. She has worked for the Institute for the past several months. Before that, she was with Green Peace. Larsen has assigned her to 'babysit' Aaron, and I'm concerned about who she really is and whether or not he can trust her."

"She's offered to help him?"

"Yes."

"Standard operating procedure would be to take the help with open eyes."

"I understand, but I have reason to believe, after a conversation with him earlier tonight that his eyes may be a bit clouded with infatuation."

"Oh, I see. Well, I can have it for you by tomorrow p.m. at the latest."

"Great. Get the information to Elle, please Serge."

"So, this whale thing is the new big issue the politician needs to ride the crest of a wave of super public opinion into the convention with, right?"

"Well, yes. Sure. But, Serge, this is an issue which could be very important to the environmental agenda I believe in so strongly . . . regardless of politics. You know that."

"Yes, my dear. I do know that."

"Tomorrow, then?"

"Yes, I'll have the information for Elle personally."

"Serge, you are such a dear. If you weren't happily married to Sweeney, I think I'd make you marry me."

"I appreciate the compliment from my favorite senator and second favorite woman. But, I could never compete with the ghost of Sal Keayrn, my dear."

"Maybe. Maybe, you're right, Serge."

"Don't worry too much about it, dear. We all lug ghosts of one sort or another around with us, now don't we?"

"I suppose so."

"Yeah. And, Abbie, you know you can count on that report being there same as if you were there to receive it."

"I know. Thanks brother-in-law. I owe you."

"Well, when you become VP, I'll start collecting. How about

that?" he belly laughed.

"Sounds fair enough. Give my love to Sweeney and to Bett. Rub her stomach for me."

"Sure thing, dear. And, how's the weather down there in American Paradise?"

"Pretty darned nice, actually, even though I'm not getting much of a chance to enjoy it."

"See you soon, I hope."

"Soon as I get back we'll try to work something out. Love you all, Serge. Bye."

Three nights later, Elle had no sooner gotten off the phone with Abbie than the phone rang again. "Jesus, I guess this must be my night for late phone calls." She snatched up the ringing telephone. "Hello."

"Hi, Elle."

"Aaron. Is that you? You sound stressed, very stressed."

"Probably because I am, Elle. I need to talk with your Senator in a setting of absolute secrecy and privacy.

"What's this all about?"

"Can't. Not on the phone. But, we're booked on the first flight out in the morning . . . six-thirty or seven . . . something like that. Should be in D.C. in time for lunch."

"No. You can't take that chance, Aaron. If any of what you suspect is true, you are both in imminent danger. Call that number I gave you before you left. The Marshals will make sure that you get to a safe house. Aaron, please do what I'm telling you, okay?"

"Yeah. Okay. I've got to go, now, roomy. I'm being followed. Bridget, too."

"Bridget's okay, by the way."

"Oh?"

"The Senator ran a check on her through the Bureau. They didn't have much on her except that she was a Green Peace activist with a few arrests. You know. The usual."

"So you ran a check and found out what I already knew. That's no help, roomy."

"Don't be such a smart ass, smart ass!"

"Cool. Then what else?"

"Grab your ass cheeks, sweet cheeks?"

"Grabbing."

"She's working undercover for Green Peace. Her whole purpose for being at the Institute is to find out what's going on. Her mission is very similar to yours."

"Cool! You see. I told you she was very cool, didn't I?"

"You did." She whispered into the telephone receiver, a breathless happiness for her favorite person in the whole world nearly robbing her of her own breath. "Now get off the phone with me and make that call!"

"Just as soon as I find Bridget."

"What do you mean? Where is she?"

"Not sure, roomy, but I'm afraid Larsen and his goons might have grabbed her already when she went back to the cottage to grab more information we've collected."

"Then you'd better get on with it and find her fast."

"Roger and out."

"Goodnight," Elle chuckled. She could just see him giving her one of his left-handed salutes as he spoke.

"Goodnight. And, thanks, Elle. We'll be okay. But, just in case, I'm dropping an envelope full of surprises into the mail for you as soon as we get off the phone."

Lahaina Town

Aaron Silver's own mother would not have recognized him as he slipped from the shadows of a cluster of six public telephones at the back of the Lanai ferry landing. His normally child-like face was matted with two days of thick, black beard growth. The gray eyes, which normally seemed to be lasers, gawked through cataracts of sleeplessness at the sunshine of a new morning on Maui. He had not slept since he and Bridget had met with five Whale Institute employees in a local club the night before.

The breakfast he had just wolfed down at Whalers' Inn had been the first food he had eaten as well. Aaron clutched a manila envelope under his jacket. They already had Bridget. He was pretty damned sure of that when he could not raise her on her cell phone. And, they might soon have him. He wasn't as sure of that. They had separated after the meeting. That way, hopefully, Hansen wouldn't find both of them. One thing he was very sure of. He was determined that they would not get their hands on the evidence passed to them last night.

Damn! He only hoped that the two dollars and seventy cents postage would get the evidence to Elle. With no return address, the post office would have to ask her to pay any additional postage, wouldn't they?

He kept a van that was disembarking from the ferry between him and the street as he walked briskly toward a postal drop box he had spotted earlier only a few yards from the ferry vehicle ramp. Aaron glanced around. No one seemed to be paying any attention to him yet he still would like to have been on that ferry when it pulled out for Lanai. But, he had business to take care of. "First item of business first," he muttered to himself as he slipped the large envelop into the drop box then strode off as rapidly as he felt he could get away with without attracting attention.

For his second item of business, he had to find Bridget.

6

Diamonds, Drugs, and Dhimmi

[Music: "Gwynn Lost"]

"Unavoidably, now, it is us or them. It is our world view versus their world view. Western Modernist or Islamic Fundamentalist. Fraternity of Greed versus Cult of Death."

What's So Funny About Truth, Love, and Understanding?
(Ethics for the New Age of Extremism), Theo Theodora

"You seem to have stayed in pretty good shape for a school teacher, LT," Theo Theodora huffed as they toweled off from their showers and dressed after sparring at Gwynn's favorite gym—a dojo facing the downtown market square off Main Street just a couple of blocks from the major tourist traffic. Even on days when as many as eight to ten ships might stop in Charlotte Amalie harbor, few tourists ventured this far away from the area commonly known as "Main Street."

"You, too, for a writer." Gwynn retorted. "But, I guess one can never predict when the old skills might come in handy."

"Or be necessary, LT." Theo grinned and tapped Gwynn's left bicep with his loosely clenched right fist in a mock punch.

"Yeah. Guess it's something like one of those oldie but goodie rock 'n roll bands. They may have found their thrill on Blueberry Hill, but most of them haven't performed since. They keep practicing, though, in anticipation of the day they will be asked to perform again."

"And, that's us, all right, LT. To be sure. Just a different kind of band waiting for our invitation."

As the steam from the showers began to dissipate, Gwynn still could not clear away the fuzziness and create a clear picture as to why his old Army buddy had surprised him at the dojo this Saturday morning of all mornings. In fact, he had almost decided to forego the dojo because he had to drop Abbie off at the airport by eight.

Discipline by repetition prevailed, however, and he found himself at the dojo warming up when Theodore Theodora sneaked up on him and threw him to the mat with a "Hi, LT. Long time, no see." He grinned down at Gwynn. "I see that attack from behind is still your big weakness."

Theo had become an instant terrorism expert when he published his book, *What's So Funny About Peace, Love, & Understanding (Ethics for the New Age of Extremism)*. Within two weeks after the book hit the bookstores, he appeared on nearly every major news and talk show on radio, satellite, network television, and cable as well as being featured on web sites, chat rooms, and blogs of various religious and political persuasions and the continuing topic on Facebook, Twitter, and every other social media outlet in existence. He relentlessly explained to America that his work expounded from a belligerently logical two premise point of departure. His first premise was that the inexorable extreme of activism is the annihilation of everyone else. His second, that the irresistible extreme of passivism is the annihilation of self. Both sides in the terrorist fight, he asserted, ultimately would be forced to come to some synthesis from these two antithetical realizations in order to survive.

Theo had even appeared on the Golf Channel where he shared an anecdote from his college days in the sixties. He and some college friends had become enamored of groups like the Weathermen. So, they decided to commit their own existential act of revolution. What did they plan to do? Well, blow up a golf course, of course. Gwynn was just happy that Theo did not name him as one of the co-conspirators. His students would never have let him live that down.

Gwynn had read the book. In fact, he had read practically everything Theo had written over the years. He might have even described himself as a fan of sorts, and he definitely believed that Theo's basic assumptions in his latest book were correct. Gwynn felt that he could say that for at least two reasons. One, they had shared experiences at the most visceral levels. He had seen and experienced much of the same stuff of life and death that Theo had on various assignments with their so-called Kit Carson team. Theo had been his second in command, his "junior" Lieutenant from their days together at Princeton. Along with Gwynn, he had joined the Army right out of college and with Gwynn always in the lead they built their very unique intelligence operations field team. He had come to trust Theo then, and he believed that he would be able to count on Theo even now.

Two, he had also studied Islam extensively in order to be able to teach his students accurately about the religion and the culture related to it. So, he understood where Theo was coming from with his significantly un-PC view that the goals of Islam were no different from those of so-called radical Islam or the terrorists. It didn't make them good or evil. It just made them what they were.

"And, after all these years, what brings an attack from the rear by Mr. Hot Shot World Famous Writer and newly anointed terrorism expert in my humble American Paradise dojo?" He guffawed. "How long has it been now, Theo?"

"Hard to believe, I know, LT, tumbling around on this mat like a couple of kids, but it's been closer to forty years than to thirty. We're getting to be a couple of old farts, you and me."

"And, after all these years, you still call me LT?"

"Old habits die hard, LT." He grinned. "Especially, good ones."

"Yeah. It was you, me, Worth, Sal, and Lincoln against all odds."

"That's for sure, LT. That's for sure."

"You know, it was easy enough for me to follow what happened to you and Worth. Both of you have been so much in the public eye. But I never found a trail on Sal after he went MIA. After awhile, I just assumed that, absent any Hansel and Gretel trail, he either seriously did not want to be found or was actually dead. Either way, it was beyond me. So, I let it go."

Theo did not respond. Rather, he allowed for a silence to break the conversation so, hopefully, he could redirect it. Now was definitely not the time to talk about that. "Anyway, LT, I'm sure you're wondering why I'm here . . . now. Well, the reason I'm here is that I talked with one of your students yesterday morning— Armond, I believe his name was. Armond Braitwaite."

"You talked to Armond yesterday?"

"That's right, LT. He called my office, pestering my staff about the possibility of terrorism connections to the beached whales over the past few days."

"Oh, man, I'm so sorry, Theo."

"It's okay, LT. Armond claimed to be conducting research for an honors senior project at Martyrs and Saints High School in St. Thomas. He said he wanted to talk to us, to me, because I was supposed to be the terrorism expert of all terrorism experts.

"He was very persistent and finally got our attention when he informed us that while on a whale counting trip, he and some others had discovered a dismembered arm attached to a whale with the word YUNUS in red capital letters tattooed on it.

"Once I talked with him myself—he's very impressive and you should be very proud of him—I found out that he was a student of none other than the late Gwynn Camsron."

"The late Gwynn Camsron. Yeah, Theo. That's really clever. Just right for a wrighter like you."

"Oh, man, you're doing that writer spelled w r i g h t e r thing, aren't you?"

"You remember."

"Then I realized that, living or dead, you might unintentionally be getting involved in all this and thought it was important that we talk. I asked Armond where to find you on a Saturday morning. He seemed excited that I wanted to talk to you in person and pretty sure this place was where you would be. So, I took a charter late night flight, and here I am. I figured, if nothing else, it was a good excuse to spend some time in America's Paradise and share some salt fish or stew goat and Cruzan with an old friend."

"Involved in all what, Theo?"

"Unlike you, LT, I didn't drop off the face of the earth when I left the team. I've kept up my community contacts. Part of my work, you know."

"I didn't have to, Theo. They kept up with me, day and night for years."

"Guess they feared you might start a coup or something, huh? Any one of us could've, you know."

"I know, but . . . ."

"But, you were the only one to go into hiding in the Caribbean."

"I know, but it's the Caribbean, for god's sake? Are you kidding me?"

"Jesus, LT. The Caribbean has been a smoldering hotbed of

Communism for a lot of years, and the CIA refers to it as our 'front yard.' That translates to: we have a smoldering hotbed of Communism in our front yard. What better place for a, shall we say, social reformer with eyes on the US, to set up shop?"

"That's why all the surveillance over the years? Christ! They were worried about me going rogue? Don't the idiots know that if I wanted to plan anything, I'd do it as if they were watching me twenty-four/seven even if I thought they were not. They'd never get a whiff." Gwynn swallowed hard before he continued. He did not like where he was going with this. But, he seriously had no choice but to ask it. "That's not why you're here, is it Theo?"

"What do you mean, LT?"

"To get a whiff?"

"Oh, come on, LT. This is me, your go to guy from the team of teams. I took an oath, just like you, and, to this day, I stand by that oath to back my teammates no matter what, just like I'm sure you do. So I'm here for exactly the reasons I told you.

"Look, I know you guys have to be aware of it even down here. Back home there is this war going on now, LT. For lack of a better term, it's usually referred to as the War on Terror. And the growing belief in the intelligence community is that if someone is going to plan Jihad against the old US of A, what better place to do it than down here in this laid back, out-of-the-way location still hot with Communists after all these years.

"All that aside, LT, there is an exceptional amount of Jihad-related chatter being picked up all over the world just recently. A growing percentage of that chatter has to do with your lovely little Caribbean and an organization that has recently appeared from out of nowhere called—you guessed it—YUNUS. Actually, YUNUS Apparatus. So, I just didn't want you to go out there and, perhaps, unwittingly get yourself or young Armond or someone else killed by this new YUNUS Apparatus bunch."

"Why, Theo, I didn't know you still cared," Gwynn chuckled.

Laughing with him, Theo responded. "Let's get out of here and go find some of that famous salt fish, stew goat, and red peas-and-rice I've heard so much about . . . and lots of Cruzan rum with lime."

"I'm not driving." He chuckled.

"Still laughing at your own jokes, are you?"

"Old habits are hard to break."

"Well, I know just the place on Back Street. It's only a few blocks walk. Then, you can fill me in on all this. I have a feeling there's a great deal I will need to know."

"Like it or not, LT, we may have finally received our invitation to perform again."

OTHER EXCERPTS FROM

What's So Funny About Truth, Love, and Understanding? (Ethics for the New Age of Extremism)

The opening paragraph of *What's So Funny About Peace, Love, & Understanding? (Ethics for the New Age of Extremism)* informs the reader that the phrase is also the title of a song written by Nick Lowe and performed by Elvis Costello then continues: "The song seems to reflect a yearning for values that have somehow been lost. In fact, in this New Age of Extremism, we must realize finally that, whether we like it or not, survival is the biological imperative of the species. It's what drives our chemistry and our electricity. That same imperative must, by reasonable inference, extend to our families and our country and what we represent. In these pages, I hope to convince you that peace, love, and understanding are not to be laughed at and have not gone anywhere. They've just been temporarily supplanted at the top of our list by the primary biological imperative, the drive to survive.

"Unavoidably, now, it is us or them. It is our world view versus their world view. Western Modernist or Islamic Fundamentalist. Fraternity of Greed versus Cult of Death.

"As the should-have-been-famous Professor of Literature, Max Halperin, used to say, 'You pays your money and you takes your choice.'"

Further along in Theo's work, he relied on the story of Jonah and the whale to provide a more religious and philosophical context for his assertions.

"And, God said to Jonah: 'Arise, go unto Nineveh, that great city, and preach unto it the preaching that I bid thee' (The *Bible*, Jonah 3:2). In the corresponding book of Yunus (Sura 10:13), The

Qur'an tells us that 'Many a generation we have annihilated before you when they transgressed. Their messengers went to them with clear proofs, but they refused to believe. We thus requite the guilty people.' Are we to expect the coming of a new Jonah or Yunus who will destroy the unbelievers?"

At a later place in the work, Theo writes about the origination of the term 'Tears of Allah.' "At one point in his life of preaching Allah's word, the prophet Muhammad seemed to lose his way. He could no longer find the God for which he was a Messenger. In his dismay, he climbed to the top of a mountain to seek solitude. In his solitude, he wept, and his tears formed diamonds. He was astonished because he knew that human tears could not create such a miracle. Only the divinity within him could have made the miracle possible. His were tears of Allah.

"On October 10, 2001—centuries after Muhammad's miracle of the Tears of Allah and less than a month after the nine-eleven attacks—Al-Qaeda released the following statement: 'Jihad for the sake of Allah today is an obligation on every Muslim in this land. Carrying out terrorism against the oppressors is one of the tenets of our religion.'

"For this effort, Al-Qaeda reportedly forged a new weapon. This new weapon is also called Tears of Allah. But this Tears of Allah is not diamonds. It is liquid heroin, so strong that its formula requires 50 kilograms of opium to produce one liter. Their plan, according to international intelligence sources, is to introduce this powerful new form of heroin into the water systems throughout the United States at the appropriate time to promote further and more complete addiction among addicts and confusion, disorientation and, hopefully, death to the other infidels. They call it the water of truth."

* * * * *

As the two old friends talked, Sandy's Back Street Café was just beginning to fill up with lunch customers, mostly locals and a few adventurous tourists.

"The Muslims, they have a way of speaking and writing, a way of saying things, so that they can later deny or at least avoid what they said or what was written previously. Just take a look at the

Qur'an, LT. A perfect example is the Sura that talks about telling lies. I forget the Sura number, but instead of saying 'Thou shalt not lie,' the *Qur'an* says: "Truly Allah guides not one who transgresses and lies.' How obtuse is that?"

"Pretty much, I'd say. And, I remember a few years back when I was researching Islam for my class. They wanted to know more about it after nine-eleven, so they came to me."

"And, of course, you responded?"

"What else was a teacher to do? Anyway, I also discovered this indirectness of language. I thought it was, perhaps a result of translation. Then I began to hear more Muslims speaking in English, many even as their native tongue, and I could still hear it—this around-end kind of talk."

"That's the point, LT. That's just the point!" Theo stabbed the air with the fingers of his right hand.

"Interesting, Theo. Very interesting, but don't we get the same thing from our own leaders out of DC?"

"Sure we do. They all lie. They all cheat. They all steal. They all manipulate others to their own ends. Jesus, LT, you know that as well as I do even if you have cloistered yourself here in this seaside monastery for more than a quarter century."

"Yeah, Theo. Of course I do. I can never forget that, together, we used to do the very same things for God and Country."

Theo nodded. "We did."

"The difference, Theo?"

"The difference, if there is any at all, is we can at least marry who we want."

"Or not," Gwynn interrupted.

"Or not." He chuckled openly. "And we can say what we want and do what we want because there's no 'speech police' or 'behavior police' breathing down our necks to make sure we do exactly what they want you to do the way they want you to do it."

"Not much of a difference?"

"No," he shook his head, "not much, that is true."

"But enough to make all the difference."

"Yes, that is also true," he nodded. "I guess it just depends on whether you want to think for yourself and do for yourself or have others think and do for you. Both are legitimate choices, I guess."

"And, we're talking about whom at this point?"

Theo chuckled. "Yeah, I guess that's no different than our discussions about the villagers in Vietnam. The argument gets pretty damned circular, doesn't it, LT?"

Gwynn chuckled also, a slow and thoughtful kind of chuckle as he nodded his head.

"And, to get back to the whole Tears of Allah thing, LT, the public doesn't know it yet, but both diamonds and that new drug called "Tears of Allah' are just some of what investigators have found inside the pod that was lodged in that first beached whale's mouth. You know, the one in Maine?"

"Really. I hadn't heard that yet, Theo."

"Well, it hasn't hit the news yet. As I indicated before, LT, I do still have some very special connections. And, because of my accepted expertise in things terror related, I was just recently asked to take a look at a terrorist manual that was located in the Tobago Cays in the Grenadines after it had been posted on the Internet several months ago. The title and content of this manual certainly seem to indicate a possible connection to this dismembered arm with the YUNUS tattoo on it that your young man referred to. This could indicate a conspiracy designed to bring down our civilization as we know it."

Theo extracted a thick sheaf of copy pages from the slim oxblood leather folio he had picked up from his rental car before they walked to the restaurant. He dropped them onto the table in front of Gwynn.

"Just take a glance at these copies I made for you, LT. Just take a look at the frigging first page. The language certainly seems uncharacteristically straightforward, much less obtuse or, as you put it, 'around-end.'"

In the name of Allah, the merciful and compassionate

Salaam Alaykum. Peace be upon you.

In the name of Allah, the merciful and compassionate and under the name of Yunus, peace be upon him. The confrontation that we are training for with the Great Satan regime does not know Socratic debates, Platonic ideals, nor Aristotelian diplomacy. But it knows the dialogue of bullets, the ideals of assassination, bombing, and destruction, and the diplomacy of the cannon and machine-gun. Islamic governments have never and will never be established through peaceful solutions. They are established, as they always have been, by pen and gun, by word and bullet, by tongue and teeth.

Soon, the power of Allah will be unleashed upon the world through this group, the Leader's own special elite organization: Allah's spearhead, Allah's spear shaft, and Allah's spearmen— the YUNUS Apparatus.

"This could turn out just like I wrote it in my book, LT." With that, Theo began to quote from his book.

"Is there any doubt that the time has come to deal or be dealt? That this is an age to feel or be felt? That this is a period to fill or be filled? 'To everything there is a season, and this is the season to kill or be killed. It is the time of the messengers. It is the season of the Tears of Allah."

It had not changed in nearly forty years. Theo still seemed to be waiting for applause. Despite his trustworthiness, he had always liked the applause. Gwynn flipped through the pages quickly, spotting a number of items he would look at carefully once he made it home.

"You know, Theo, I just put Abbie Keayrn—Senator Keayrn— on a plane this morning before I stopped at the dojo."

"Senator Keayrn? Sal's wife?"

"Yeah. I called her when we spotted the problem with the missing whales that Armond called your office about."

"Well, LT, I suggest you get her back down here ASAP! With her heavyweight status on Energy and Intelligence policy, she can put a real, much-needed spotlight on this whole thing down here."

"San-dy, me-son! Tell de kit-chen we be needin' salt fish, stew goat, and some peas and rice. But, most im-por-tant, a bottle of Cru-zan Gold Re-serve, two glass-es, and some lime slic-es, please.

T'anks."

"You've really got that island Calypso stuff down, LT."

"After almost forty years, I would hope so. But, if you ask any Virgin Islander they'll tell you that I still don't have it right." Gwynn waved at the owner who doubled as the bartender and host as he extracted his cell phone from his pants pocket. It was a reluctant capitulation to the brave new world of instant international communications as well as being a gift from his seniors. They had determined that Mr. C simply had to be dragged, kicking and screaming, into that new world. They determined the best way was to give him a cell phone. He was far too polite not to, then, use it, because he would not want to insult his seniors who collectively could no longer abide his unwillingness to embrace the world as it really was, not as he somehow remembered it. And, he had to admit it was somewhat amazing. He had just selected the number from a list of all the numbers he ever used and entered it with one press of a "speed dial" key. Already Abbie was answering.

"Keayrn."

"Abbie?"

"Well, hi there, Mr. Camsron."

"Where are you?"

"In a taxi on the way to my office from Reagan. Where are you?"

"Sandy's for lunch with an old friend."

"I very much enjoyed our visit even under the circumstances, and I want you to know, Gwynn, that my staff is already putting things into motion to find out what the hell is going on with these whales . . . ."

"Abbie."

"And that YUNUS arm thing."

"Abigail. Senator. I need you to turn that taxi around and go back to the airport."

"But I only just got back?"

"I know, but something's come up, and I have to go down to a small island chain in the Grenadines called the Tobago Cays. I think I might be able to find the man who belongs to the arm down there."

"Then, don't you dare go without me, Gwynn Camsron! You just wait until I get there, you hear me?"

"Yes, Senator, I hear you."

* * * * *

The *Tortola End* had been crafted from the ruins of a sugar plantation at the edge of the sea on the west end of that British Virgin Island for which it was named. A chorus of coki tree frogs seemed to envelop the alfresco restaurant in high-pitched croaking sounds that were so much a part of the milieu they soon seemed to become background white noise almost like a kind of silence. The Chef and owner Martin Boom was a Tortolan who had learned his culinary art from a string of French Chefs aboard a dozen different cruise ships. When Chef Martin came home to open his restaurant, he set his standards as the best West Indian cuisine prepared in the most elegant French manner. Diners came from everywhere to this enchanted place. Yachts anchored just off shore. Even windsurfers occasionally found their way to the small beach. And, the St. Thomas ferry made a quick, unscheduled drop off before stopping at Road Town when passengers requested the stop.

Abbie had just arrived from St. Thomas on the last ferry as the bus boys lit the storm lanterns at each table and the tiki torches surrounding the open-air dining area. Shadows of the host and wine Captain, waiters and waitresses, bus boys and diners stretched and collapsed like black holes in rhythm with the flickers of the torches and the lanterns along the mortared stone walls of the building that held the inside dining area and the kitchen.

"No matter how often I come here I am always amazed at how, once the sun goes down and these torches and lanterns are all lit, it's like the same kind of magic as the lighting on a stage."

Abbie nodded absently as she settled into her wicker chair barely acknowledging the shadows of reality flickering up against the wall while Gwynn poured her some sauvignon blanc. They had been out of Montrachet.

"Just one of the penalties we pay," the Captain, himself originally from London, had explained with some humor in his voice, "for living out here in the middle of the ocean in this bloody paradise of ours."

"In other words, your wine shipment is late." Gwynn had retorted.

"Very late, sir."

"So sorry I'm running late, but the flight was delayed. The taxi from the airport to the hotel was late. I left the hotel late. The ferry was late. I'm just one big l . . . a . . . t . . . e."

"I get the idea, Senator. You're just another Lewis Carroll character who is late through no fault of your own. Just like the Montrachet the restaurant doesn't have because their shipment is late. Whatever. You and the Montrachet—both white rabbits, each in your own way. It's okay. Have some of this surprising sauvignon blanc and relax. I've taken the liberty of ordering the house special for both of us. I recall how taken you were with our lobster, and this is a way of eating local lobster that is truly unique to this restaurant—West Indian Lobster in Red Curry Sauce Francais. It's like lobster in a creamy béchamel-style sauce spiced with lots of red curry and Caribbean lime. Goes great with the wine.

"And, you'll need to eat hearty, my dear Senator, because we're gonna have to eat our own cooking in the galley while we're at sea. That may not prove fatal, but we will both definitely need all the energy we can muster over the next few days."

"And why is that?"

"Well, you see, that would be because we will definitely be working hard, Senator. I've got a major lead that my kids generated. One of them actually had the balls—excuse, me—the nerve to contact Theo Theodora. The information we have actually came directly from him."

"That self-styled terrorism expert?"

"One in the same, although he'd probably take great exception to your implications by the use of 'self-styled' to describe his expertise. He takes great pride in his depth of knowledge and accuracy in all things. And, believe me, I know that all too well."

"Oh, really? And how's that?"

The dark shadows on the wall seemed to stabilize gradually as the flames from the torches and the table lanterns alternately sputtered and flared in the breeze blowing up from Africa.

"Well, quite by chance, we roomed together our freshman year at Princeton and by choice for the remaining three years. Along with me, Theo helped organize the team your husband also served on in Vietnam. He was actually my second in command. Got to know him pretty damned well back then, and it seems that after all these years, he hasn't changed much at all. He was always a great tactics guy, probably because he's paranoid as a loon and was even back then.

"Theo suggested to me at Sandy's yesterday that your influence with the Energy and Intelligence committees was very important to us being taken seriously. He also thought it would be equally important for you to accompany me down-island to check it out first hand, so we'd have some kind of official verification of whatever we might find." Gwynn hesitated for a moment. "Very honestly, Senator. Abbie. This expedition could be extremely dangerous."

"I think I can deal with that. I've been to Afghanistan, Pakistan, Iraq, lots of other hot spots around the world."

"Okay." He reached across the table with the sheaf of papers in his hand that Theo had given him in Sandy's. "As long as you understand and are willing to go along regardless. So, tonight, read this document, please. Theo believed it was important enough to fly down here overnight to get it to me."

"Okay."

"Okay. So, anyway, assuming that we are actually going, I've been able to arrange the use of the Governor's yacht. In fact, the Governor would like a few minutes with you before we cast off."

"Fine. I've met with Governor Rueben a number of times before. He's quite charming, if memory serves."

"Oh, yes. Juan was charming even when he was one of my students." Gwynn rolled his shoulders and threw his arms into the air. "Especially when it comes to beautiful women.'

"So that's how you know the Governor well enough to borrow his yacht. You were his English teacher."

"More than that, if the truth be known. You might say I was his personal mentor. Without my help, he probably would never have gotten into Columbia. You know, back in those days, a Princeton grad's recommendation still meant something, even at Columbia." He shrugged. "And, if Juan hadn't graduated from Columbia with a degree in political science, he likely would never have had the temerity to become a politician and ultimately run for and be elected Governor.

"So, here we sit in Plato's cave where if it were not for the people who are being illuminated in the torch and lantern light, there would be no shadows on the wall tonight. You might say, then, that I was the light that shined on Juan that caused him to cast his shadow on the wall which is what we perceive as reality."

"Now that's a lot of academic something or other but it sounds more like philosophy than literature."

"Perhaps it is, my dear Senator. Perhaps it is."

7
The YUNUS Apparatus
[Music: "Gwynn Lost"]

Abbie turned off her Blackberry and plugged it into the wall socket to recharge while she slept. The Marina suite overlooked Charlotte Amalie harbor. Lights on the boats and ships glowed in the very dark night like stars in some kind of subterranean sky. On the rattan glass-top table in front of her lay the file Gwynn had made her promise to read before she decided on whether to go with him or not. But, it did not really matter what the file's contents revealed. She already knew she was going. She believed that she had little or no choice in the matter. She was obliged as a United States Senator to see this through regardless of the possible personal consequences.

She opened the manila envelope and extracted a copy of the computer printout of a recently discovered terrorist training manual. She was at a complete loss to understand how a writer or journalist like Theo with no official government standing whatsoever would know about, and even possess, documents such as this before a member of the Senate Intelligence Committee had them. Yet, it was clear as day when she opened the folder and glanced at the cover page that Theo Theodora had gained possession of a copy of a highly sensitive document before she even knew it existed. He even had the document long enough to write a few notes on the pages as he had read them. Near the top of the Transmittal Sheet, she read a typed statement presumably made by the CIA translator. Just below, what seemed to be Theo's handwritten notes added after the copy was made because the handwriting was actually in ballpoint pen rather than being part of the copy.

Abbie sipped at the lemon grass tea she had ordered from room service while she glanced down the cover page, then began flipping through the pages quickly. However, some items and phrases attracted her attention to the point that she finally stopped and returned to the cover page. Then, she began again, perusing each page very carefully, one at a time, with continually increasing existential dread.

EYES ONLY

"This manual was located by a combined Interpol and CIA operation during the search of a reported *al Qaeda* member's shanty on a small otherwise uninhabited island in the Grenadines. The shack was used primarily as a listening outpost as well as an Internet transmitter station. The manual was found in a computer file called "Yunus." The file contained both Arabic and English versions of the manual. The following is an English-only transcription of the manual."

No mention of the fact that Yunus is the Arabic Jonah. Jonah was swallowed by a whale. After a while in the belly of that whale, God saved him and sent him to the people of Nineveh as his messenger. I would say that there's some real symbolism here. Something is definitely afoot, as old Sherlock might put it.

* * * GOVERNMENT TRANSLATION FOLLOWS * * *

TRANSMITTAL SHEET

Property of the guest house.

IT IS FORBIDDEN TO REMOVE THIS DOCUMENT FROM THE
HOUSE WITHOUT PERMISSION

The

YUNUS Apparatus

Manual for Warriors *

[Emblem description: For some reason, no actual drawing was provided with this copy of the manual.]

A drawing of a black-turbaned fighter riding a humpback whale, his sword piercing a globe from the Middle East to the United States with blood dripping from its tip to form the word YUNUS in bold red letters wrapped around the bottom half of the emblem.

Islam is superior to all human conditions and earthly religions

The Leader presents this humble effort to those young Muslim men who are pure, believing, and fighting for the cause of Allah. It is his contribution toward paving the road that leads to majestic Allah and establishes a World Caliphate, The United States of Islam, according to the prophecy.

*Author's Note: Substantially based on *The Manchester Manual*, found by Manchester Police, 2000.

COVER

DECLARATION OF JIHAD
BY
THE LEADER

"ALLAH'S SPEAR"

In the name of Allah, the merciful and compassionate

Salaam Alaykum. Peace be upon you.

In the name of Allah, the merciful and compassionate and under the name of Yunus, peace be upon him. The confrontation that we are training for with the Great Satan regime does not know Socratic debates, Platonic ideals, nor Aristotelian diplomacy. But it knows the dialogue of bullets, the ideals of assassination, bombing, and destruction, and the diplomacy of the cannon and machine-gun. Islamic governments have never and will never be established through peaceful solutions. They are established, as they always have been, by pen and gun, by word and bullet, by tongue and teeth.

Soon, the power of Allah will be unleashed upon the world through this group, the Leader's own special elite organization: Allah's spearhead, Allah's spear shaft, and Allah's spearmen— the YUNUS Apparatus.

In the name of Allah, the merciful and compassionate.

We, the YUNUS Apparatus, pledge and covenant: To be the destruction of the Godless, Great Satan regime, To make *their* women widows and *their* children orphans, To make *them* desire death and hate appointments and prestige, To retaliate against every dog who touched a Sister even with a bad word, and To slaughter *them* like lambs so the rivers of the world flow with their blood.

In the name of Allah, the merciful and compassionate

Thanks be to Allah. We thank Him, turn to Him, ask His forgiveness, and seek refuge in Him from our wicked souls and bad deeds. Whomever Allah enlightens will not be misguided, and the deceiver will never be guided.

The Leader declares that there is no God but Allah alone; He has no partners. The Leader also declares that Muhammad, may Allah bless and keep Him, is Allah's servant and prophet.

[*Qur'anic* verses]
"*O ye* who believe! Fear Allah as He should be feared, and die not except in a state of Islam."

"*O* mankind! Fear your guardian lord who created you from a single person. Created, out of it, his mate, and from them twain scattered seeds of countless men and women; fear Allah, through whom ye demand your mutual rights, and be heedful of the wombs that bore you for Allah ever watches over you."

"O ye who believe! Fear Allah, and make your utterance straight forward: That He may make your conduct whole and sound and forgive you your sins. He that obeys Allah and His messenger has already attained the great victory."

The most truthful saying is the book of Allah and the best guidance is that of Muhammad, may Allah bless and keep Him.

The worst thing is to introduce something new. Every novelty is an act of heresy, and each heresy is a deception. Deception at every level is the brink upon which the world stands, and we have Allah's spear in our hands.

We are Allah's spear.

In the name of Allah, the merciful and compassionate

In our past, martyrs have been killed, women have been widowed, children have been orphaned, men have been handcuffed and imprisoned, harlots' heads have been crowned as chaste women's heads were shaved, atrocities have been inflicted on the innocent, gifts have been given to the wicked, and virgins have been raped on the altar of prostitution, and we have been powerless, without our Nation of Islam.

After the fall of our orthodox caliphates and expelling the colonialists, apostate rulers took over the Nation of Islam. They jailed thousands of the Islamic Movement youth in gloomy detention centers that were equipped with the most modern torture devices and manned with experts in oppression and torture.

But the rulers did not stop there. They began to openly erect crusader centers, societies, and organizations like Masonic Lodges, Lions and Rotary clubs, and foreign schools. They used every means at their disposal to produce and seduce a generation that did not know anything except what they want, did not talk about anything except what interests them, did not live except according to their own way, and did not dress except in their own style of clothes.

They also tried to fragment and eradicate our Muslim identity. As part of that effort, they spread godless and atheistic views among the youth, claiming that socialism and democracy and communism were compatible with, in fact came from, Islam.

Their goal was to produce a wasted Islamic generation that would do everything that is western and produce rulers, ministers, leaders, physicians, engineers, businessmen, politicians, journalists, and information specialists who look, think, and act western.

[*Qur'anic* verse:] "And Allah's enemies plotted and planned, and Allah too planned, and the best of planners is Allah."

However, majestic Allah turned their deception back on them through the YUNUS Apparatus. Many who were raised in this manner have been awakened from their sleep now and are continuing to return to Allah, regretting and repenting. What better way for Allah's warrior to strike than as one who looks and acts like all those around him?

These young men returning to Allah realize that Islam is not just performing rituals. It is a complete system: Religion and government, worship and Jihad, ethics and dealing with people, and the *Qur'an* and the sword.

The Nation of Islam became the Nation of Ignorance as a result of its divergence from Allah's course and His righteous law for all places and times. This state of ignorance has come about as a result of Islam's children's love for this world, their fear of death, and their abandonment of Jihad. Unbelief is still the same. It pushed Abou Jahl, may Allah curse him, and

Kureish's valiant infidels to battle the prophet, Allah bless and keep him, and to torture his companions—may Allah's grace be on them. It is the same unbelief that drove Sadat, Hosni Mubarak, Gadhafi, Hafez Assad, Saleh, Fahed, Ahmadinejad. None deserves our support or service. Allah's curse be upon the unbelieving leaders, and all the apostate rulers who torture, kill, imprison, and torment Muslims.

We cannot resist this state of ignorance unless we unite and be true to our religion. Without that, the establishment of religion would be a dream or illusion that is impossible to achieve or even imagine its achievement. Sheik Ibn Taimia—may Allah have mercy on him—said, "The interests of all Adam's children would not be realized in the present life, nor in the next, except through assembly, cooperation, and mutual assistance. Cooperation is for achieving their interests and mutual assistance is for overcoming their adversities. That is why it has been said, 'man is civilized by nature. Therefore, if they unite there will be favorable matters that they do, and corrupting matters to avoid. They will be obedient to the commandment of those goals and avoidant of those immoralities. It is necessary that all Adam's children obey."

Governing the affairs of the people is one of the greatest religious obligations. In fact, without it, religion and world affairs could not be established. The interests of Adam's children would not be achieved except together. When they come together, it is necessary to have a leader. Allah's prophet, Allah bless and keep him, even said, 'If three people come together, let them pick a leader.'

Since Allah has obligated us to do good and avoid the unlawful, that would not be done except through laws and enforcement of laws. Likewise, the rest of what He obligated us with would not be accomplished except by force and lordship, be it Jihad, justice, pilgrimage, assembly, holidays, support of the oppressed, or the establishment of boundaries.

These young men returning to Allah realize that an Islamic government will never be established except by the bomb and rifle. Islam does not coincide or make a truce with unbelief, but rather confronts it. The confrontation that Islam calls for with these godless and apostate regimes, does not know Socratic debates, Platonic ideals nor Aristotelian diplomacy. But it knows the dialogue of bullets, the ideals of assassination, bombing, and destruction, and the diplomacy of the cannon and machine-gun. The young and dedicated have come to this text and these premises to prepare themselves for the greatest sacrifice and gift a Submissive can provide. His life for Jihad, as commanded by the majestic Allah's order in the holy *Qur'an*.

Are you one of these? Are you a YUNUS Warrior?

In the name of Allah, the merciful and compassionate

[*Qur'anic* verse:] "Against them make ready your strength to the utmost of your power, including steeds of war, to strike terror into the hearts of the enemies of Allah and your enemies, and others besides whom ye may not know, but whom Allah doth know."

Indeed, if you are not sure that your answer is YES to the question above, then you should stop reading, put down this manual, and walk away. No one will ever contact you again. However, it is most important that you understand that if you cannot say YES without any reservations, then you MUST stop reading NOW!

\# \# \# \# \# \# \# \# \# \# \# \# \# \# \# \# \# \# \# \#

\# \# \# \# \# \# \# \# \# \# \# \# \# \# \# \# \# \# \#

IF YOU CANNOT SAY "YES"

YOU MUST STOP READING AT THIS POINT!

FAILURE TO STOP NOW COULD MEAN YOUR

DEATH!

\# \# \# \# \# \# \# \# \# \# \# \# \# \# \# \# \# \# \# \#

\# \# \# \# \# \# \# \# \# \# \# \# \# \# \# \# \# \#

Senator Abigail Keayrn averted her eyes and involuntarily stopped reading. Should she heed such a seemingly ridiculous and unenforceable statement made by a bunch of true believer fanatics? Or should she do her duty as a United States Senator and read on, on pain of death? Her chin quivered ever so slightly as she returned her eyes to the page.

FIRST LESSON
PRINCIPLES OF MILITARY ORGANIZATION

THE PRIMARY MISSION OF THE YUNUS APPARATUS:

TO OVERTHROW THE GODLESS REGIMES AND REPLACE THEM WITH A NEW CALIPHATE, THE UNITED STATES OF ISLAM

Other missions:

1. Gathering information about the enemy, the land, the installations, and the neighbors.

2. Kidnapping enemy personnel, documents, secrets, and arms.

3. Assassinating enemy personnel as well as foreign tourists.

4. Freeing the brothers who are captured by the enemy.

5. Spreading rumors and writing statements inciting people against the enemy.

6. Destroying places of amusement, immorality, and sin; not a vital target.

7. Blasting and destroying the embassies and attacking vital economic centers.

8. Blasting and destroying bridges leading into and out of the cities.

Military Organization has three main principles without which it cannot be established:

1. Military Organization (commander and advisory council),

2. The soldiers or warriors (individual members), and

3. A clearly defined strategy.

MILITARY ORGANIZATION REQUIREMENTS:

The Military Organization dictates a number of requirements to assist it in confrontation and endurance. These are: 1. Forged documents and counterfeit currency, 2. Apartments and hiding places, 3. Communication means, 4. Transportation means, 5. Information, 6. Arms and ammunition, 7. Transport Missions Required of the Military Organization.

IMPORTANCE OF THE MILITARY ORGANIZATION:

1. Removal of those personalities that block the call's path. [A different handwriting.] Military and civilian intellectuals and thinkers for the state.

2. Proper utilization of the individuals' unused capabilities.

3. Precision in performing tasks, and using collective views on completing a job from all aspects, not just one.

4. Controlling the work and not fragmenting it or deviating from it.

5. Achieving long-term goals such as the establishment of an Islamic state and short-term goals such as operations against enemy individuals and sectors.

6. Establishing the conditions for possible confrontation with the regressive regimes and their persistence.

7. Achieving discipline in secrecy and through tasks.

SECOND LESSON
NECESSARY QUALIFICATIONS *AND* CHARACTERISTICS FOR YUNUS APPARATUS WARRIORS

1. Islam: The warrior must be Muslim. How can an unbeliever—someone from a revealed religion (Christian, Jew)—or a secular person, a communist, etc. protect Islam and Muslims and defend their goals and secrets when he does not believe in Islam?

(The Israeli Army requires that a fighter be of the Jewish religion.)

2. Commitment to the YUNUS Apparatus Ideology: This commitment frees the warriors from having to concern themselves with such conceptual problems.

3. Maturity: The warrior must be able to face hard and continuous work in dangerous conditions. This requires a great deal of psychological, mental, and intellectual fitness, not usually found in a minor.

4. Sacrifice: The warrior must be willing to do the work and undergo martyrdom for the purpose of achieving the goal and establishing the religion of majestic Allah on earth.

5. Listening and Obedience: In the military, this is known today as discipline. It is expressed by how the warrior obeys the orders given to him. That is what our religion urges. The Glorious says,

"O ye who believe! Obey Allah and obey the messenger and those charged with authority among you."

6. Keeping Secrets and Concealing Information: Secrecy must be used, even with the closest people, for "deceiving the enemy is not easy," Allah says, "even though their plots were such as to shake the hills!"

[*Qur'anic* verse] Allah's messenger, God bless and keep him, says, "Seek Allah's help in doing your affairs in secrecy."

It was said in the proverbs, "The hearts of freemen are the tombs of secrets" and "Muslims' secrecy is faithfulness, and talking about it is faithlessness." Muhammad, Allah bless and keep him, used to keep secrets related to his work from the closest people, even from his wife A'isha, may Allah's grace be upon her."

7. Free of Illness: The Apparatus warrior must fulfill this important requirement. Allah says, "There is no blame for those who are infirm, or ill, or who have no resources to spend."

8. Patience: The warrior should have plenty of patience for enduring afflictions if he is overcome by the enemy. He should not abandon this great path and sell himself and his religion to the enemy for his freedom. He should be patient in performing his mission, even if it lasts a long time.

9. Tranquility and "Unflappability": The warrior should have a calm personality that allows him to endure psychological traumas such as those involving bloodshed, murder, arrest, imprisonment, and reverse psychological traumas such as killing one or all of his own comrades. He must be able to carry out the mission.

10. Intelligence and Insight: When the prophet, Allah bless and keep him, sent Hazifa Ben Al-Yaman to spy on the polytheists and sat among them, Abou Soufian said, "Let each one of you look at his companion." Hazifa said to his companion, 'Who are you?" The companion replied, "So-and-so son of so-and-so."

In World War I, the German spy, Julius Seelber managed to enter Britain and work as a mail examiner due to the many languages he had mastered. From the letters, he obtained important information and sent it to the Germans. One of the letters that he checked was from a lady who had written to her brother's friend in the fleet. She mentioned that her brother used to live with her until he was transferred to a secret project that involved commercial ships. When Seelber read that letter, he went to meet that young woman and blamed her for her loose tongue in talking about military secrets. He, skillfully, managed to draw out of her that her brother worked in a secret project for arming old commercial ships. These ships were to be used as decoys in the submarine war in such a way that they could come close to the submarines, as they appeared innocent. Suddenly, cannonballs would be fired from the ships' hidden cannons on top of the ships, which would destroy the submarines.

Forty-eight hours later that secret was handed to the Germans.

11. Caution and Prudence: In his battle against the king of Tomedia, the Roman general Speer sent Lilius, one of his top commanders, as an emissary to discuss truce between the two armies. He was accompanied by some of the General's finest officers, disguised as slaves. In reality, he had sent them to learn about the Tomedians' ability to fight. During that mission, one of the king's officers, Sifax, pointed to one of the slaves and yelled, "That slave is a Roman officer. When I met him in a neighboring city, he was wearing a Roman uniform." At that point, Lilius used a clever trick and managed to divert the attention of the Tomedians by turning to the disguised officer and quickly slapping him on the face a number of times. He reprimanded him for wearing a Roman officer's uniform when he was a slave and for claiming a status that he did not deserve.

The officer accepted the slaps quietly. He bowed his head in humility and shame, as slaves do. Thus, Sifax's men thought that the officer was really a slave because they could not imagine that a Roman officer would accept these hits without defending himself. King Sifax prepared a big feast for Lilius and his entourage and placed them in a house far away from his camp so they could not learn about his fortifications.

To overcome this setback, the Romans conjured another clever trick on top of the first one. They freed one of their horses and started chasing him in and around the camp. After they learned about the extent of the fortifications they caught the horse and, as planned, managed to abort their mission about the truce agreement. Shortly after their return, the Roman general attacked King Sifax's camp and burned the fortifications.

12. Truthfulness and Counsel: The Commander of the faithful, Omar Ibn Al-Khattab, may Allah be pleased with him, asserted that this characteristic was vital in those who gather information and work as spies against the Muslims' enemies. Omar sent a letter to Saad Ibn Abou Wakkas, may Allah be pleased with him, saying, "If you step foot on your enemies' land, get spies on them. Choose those whom you count on for their truthfulness and advice, whether from your own kind or inhabitants of that land. Liars' accounts would not benefit you, even if some of them were true; the deceiver is a spy against you and not for you.

13. Ability to Observe and Analyze: The Israeli Mossad received news that some Palestinians were going to attack an Israeli El Al airplane. That plane was going to Rome with Golda Meir — Allah's curse upon her—the Prime Minister at the time, on board. The Palestinians had managed to use a clever trick that allowed them to wait for the arrival of the plane without being questioned by anyone. They had beaten a man who sold potatoes, kidnapped him, and hidden him. They made two holes in the top of that peddler's cart and placed two tubes next to the chimney through which two Russian-made "Strella"[PH] missiles could be launched. The Mossad officers traveled the airport back and forth looking for something that would lead them to the Palestinians. One officer passed the potato cart twice without noticing anything. On his third time, he noticed three chimneys, but only one of them was working with smoke coming out of it. He quickly steered toward the cart and hit it hard. The cart overturned, and the Palestinians were captured.

14. Ability to Act, Change Positions, and Conceal Oneself:

a. An excellent example is what Noaim Ibn Masoud had done in his mission to cause agitation among the tribes of Koraish and the Jews of Koreitha. He would control his reactions with each group and managed to skillfully play his role. Without showing signs of inconsistency, he would show his interest and zeal towards the Jews one time and show his concern about the Koraish at another.

b. In 1960, a car driven by an American colonel collided with a truck. The colonel lost consciousness, and while unconscious at the hospital, he started speaking Russian fluently. It was later discovered that the colonel was a Soviet spy who was planted in the United States. He had fought in Korea in order to conceal his true identity and to gather information and critical secrets. If not for the collision, no one would have suspected or confronted him.

Our own Leader was a hero in the American war waged against the Vietnamese people. Now, he will show us the way to the new Caliphate, the United States of Islam.

Abbie again broke off from reading. This time the effort was like trying to tear loose from the source of an electrical charge surging through her body. Quaking uncontrollably from the inside out like someone in the throes of the hard chills of break bone fever, she crumpled across the table, spilling the remains of her lemon grass tea, her head buried in her arms under pages of the *YUNUS Apparatus Manual for Warriors*.

8
Caribbean Waters
[Music: "Gwynn Lost"]

Abbie was even more unnerved after she stayed up most of the night completing the thirteen lessons in the *YUNUS Apparatus Manual for Warriors*. And, she was still shaken after a brief meeting the next morning with Governor Juan Rueben over coffee at the Red Hook Marina, although she was certain that he never suspected. Juan Rueben was not the only one who could be charming. And, her specialty, over the years, was charming under pressure.

Despite all, she found herself hustling along the dock toward the Governor's motor yacht, somehow optimistic about her and Gwynn embarking upon a search for a one-armed sailor that Gwynn's students had somehow mystically conjured as a recuperating patient in a small hospital in the Grenadines. In that respect, his students somewhat reminded her of Elle and her own staff back in Washington. They were always coming up with information that just seemed to appear on the Internet or something. She had told Elle more than once that she wasn't even going to ask how they did it. She just assumed it was a generational thing. The students' discovery combined with Theo's find of the *YUNUS Apparatus Manual for Warriors*, also in the Grenadines, seemed to point directly to that area as the hot spot for their investigation.

She spied Gwynn languishing in a deck chair on the yacht. "Ahoy on deck. Permission to come aboard," she chuckled.

"Yo. Come aboard." He jumped to and helped her board. "Now, that you're here, let's go find us a one-armed sailor, Senator."

"I'm ready. I've already met with Governor Rueben. He sends his best to his mentor and friend and wishes us great success on our adventure and a safe return. He says for you to get his boat back in one piece."

"I'll bet he did," Gwynn laughed.

"He's just as charming as I remembered . . . in that special Latin sort of way, you know?

"Oh, yes. Juan is a great and charming guy, and he is truly as decent and well-meaning a guy as you'll find anywhere."

"Can we talk about this mysterious trip for a minute?"

"Sure." He paused. "Did you read the document I gave you last night? And, by the way, I really enjoyed our dinner and the ferry trip back. It took a little doing to get Lincoln Varlak to stop his ferry on his way back to St. John and St. Thomas just to pick us up."

"Don't tell me!" She held up both her hands between them, palms toward Gwynn. "I know. Lincoln Varlak was a student of yours too."

Gwynn's lips tightened, but he remained silent.

Abbie began to giggle. "He was, wasn't he?"

"Okay," Gwynn relented. "Okay. He was."

"Okay," Abbie interrupted. "The answer is, yes. I read the document, and it scared the hell out of me almost to the point of making me physically ill. But, I got through it, and I'll get through this trip, too, no matter what."

"Then, you're sure you want to take this chance with your life, Abbie? Senator? I mean, if we run into these guys, they're serious about their holy mission. They will not show us any compassion or mercy. We could very well die at their hands. You understand that and you're sure about doing this?"

"Yes, I understand." Her lips trembled slightly at first and then firmed into a look of true determination. "And, I'm even more certain than I was before I read that damned document. I'm not going to let people like that take over my country. Not if I can help it."

"Okay, then. Let's get to the wheelhouse and get this boat on course for the Tobago Cays."

"So, what's so special about this old sailor that your kids uncovered?"

"The reason he's in the recovery home facility is he's recuperating from losing his left arm. Right?"

"Right."

"And the arm we found was a left arm. Right?"

"Right."

"So . . . ." He shrugged as if the rest were obvious. "How many people are going to be in the hospital in the Caribbean missing an entire left arm that was pulled out of the shoulder socket?"

"I see your point. Don't we need to get moving, then, Mr. Camsron?" she teased. "I mean, time is a-wasting, isn't it?"

"Hey, Abbie. Cool out, mon. Take it easy." He chuckled. "Dis be de Car-ib-bean, me-son."

"But, my time is important. Your time is important. Everybody's time is important. It's really all we've got." Suddenly her face clouded. "And I think we're running out of it!"

"Exactly my point." He grinned at the perplexity lines in her face. "In other words, if time is so important and in such short supply, then shouldn't we slow down enough to enjoy it before it passes us by? If somehow this ends up being the end of our time, then shouldn't we at least savor what we have left of it before it's gone?"

"I never thought about it quite like that before, you know? I mean, in DC and in the Senate time is like a slave driver rather than something that ought to be relished."

"*Carpe diem quam minimum credula postero.* Up on your Latin, Senator?"

"Not really, not all that much."

"It's from Horace's Odes. It roughly translates: Seize the day, for tomorrow you may die."

"Ridiculously appropriate, you might say."

"Yeah. You might say."

The Brown Pelican plowed Pilsbury Sound's mixture of Caribbean and Atlantic waters between Red Hook and the entrance to Drake's Passage on the other side of St. John at better than four knots per hour. Gwynn was at the wheel. Abbie poured drinks behind him. The boat could do better than seven knots per hour but cruised comfortably at three-and-a-half to four.

"Didn't you ever, in all these years you've been down here, want to do something important?"

"I guess I've wanted basically to leave no footprint behind."

"But, Gwynn, there aren't any 'no foot print' options around that I know of, and I'm chair of the United States Senate Energy and Natural Resources Committee. Probably haven't been since the early American Indian. If ever."

"And, now," Gwynn chuckled, almost nervously, "we approach

the essential human conflict, do we not?"

"And, what, pray tell, is that?"

"To print or not to print, that is the bare foot of it all."

Abbie snorted trying to hold back the laughter.

Gwynn slammed another shot of Cruzan Gold Reserve. The rum burned like honey sun internalized. "But, it's really not a funny subject, you know?" He sucked hard on a thick lime slice.

"I know." Her lips moved into neutral position as she sipped at her shot glass brimming with the exotic amber of pirates and scoundrels.

"I mean, I am aware that there are times when I live a little bit on the edge of reality. I freely admit that. But, just because there are no 'no footprint' ways of life left, that doesn't prevent me from still believing in making one's way through the forest without trampling a lichen or breaking a twig or crossing the open beach without disturbing the sand.

"But, anyway, all that aside, I believe that I already *do* something important, Abbie. I teach kids about literature and life to the limits of my knowledge and experience. And, I learn a lot from that process myself. Kids, themselves, are super teachers, you know?"

"No. I didn't know." She grinned. "But I am learning."

"But, most of all, I see these kids." He beamed in his own way. "My kids going off to become lawyers, doctors, teachers, scientists. Now, if I am obligated somehow to leave footprints, those are the kind I want to leave."

"Even politicians, so I was told back at the Red Hook Dock?" She smiled softly, apologetically. "Listen, I'm sorry. I didn't mean that what you do isn't important."

"I know. I understand. You meant *really* important like Juan Rueben, for example." His voice lowered so much that she could hardly hear him above the drone of the twin inboard engines and the tearing of the sea beneath them. "Or you." He touched her right cheek. Her skin glowed in the morning sunlight as if his touch had somehow ignited it.

"The governor's driver told me that both he and Juan were students of yours back in seventy-six?" She caressed his fingers and his palm with the sun-warmed curves of her face. She could feel the ends of her raven hair brushing the back of his hand. Suddenly, she felt compelled to pull away, to distance herself from the magic of this scenario. It wasn't real after all. It was more like a scene in a movie than shadows on the walls of Plato's cave or the *Tortola End*.

Gwynn smiled. "Oh yes. My bicentennial class. We had an absolute blast that year studying all kinds of unusual literature. Diaries, letters, memoirs. And we watched all of the *Adams Chronicles*."

"So Juan Rueben really was one of your students at Martyrs and Saints?"

He grinned, now. "You guessed it yesterday. How else do you think that a mere school teacher like me would be able to grab the Governor's personal motor yacht on a moment's notice?"

She huffed playfully, adjusting the straps of her one-piece bathing suit. "And, all the while, I thought it was because of me!"

"Sorry, Senator."

"That's okay, Mr. Camsron." She glanced down her slender body. "The sun's awfully hot already. Think I'll go below and change into something more 'sunfortable'."

"Cool, mon."

"Yes, that's what I'd like to be. Cool . . . mon."

"Soon as we hit the other side of Pilsbury Sound and enter Drake's Passage, we'll probably pick up a lot more breeze coming from down island. Where we are now, the breezes are sometimes blocked a little by St. John and Tortola—we'll pass right by *Tortola End* to port—and other down islands."

"Down islands?"

"Yes. The islands further down the archipelago toward South America."

"I've been with the committee all these years, yet I never heard them referred to that way?"

"It's pretty much a local expression, I guess."

"I guess that's why I never heard it before?"

"These are your first trips to the islands, then?"

"I'm afraid so."

"Well, let me tell you something, Abbie. We have another local expression that pretty much is our motto to live by."

She grinned. "Oh, and what's that?"

"You've got to take the lime with the sugar."

"Whatever does that mean? Take the sour with the sweet?"

"Something like that." He paused. "But, you can infer from it something even more important, I think."

"What's that?"

"Take advantage of opportunities when they are presented."

"But aren't we all—in our own ways—opportunists anyway?"

"Absolutely. I'm convinced that's what survival is all about, grabbing opportunity by the throat. It's just that you don't always recognize opportunity as opportunity. Sometimes we see it as a barrier or a trap."

"When it's coming up limes instead of sugar?"

"Exactly."

"You're such a smart ass, aren't you?"

"I've been told as much by many but never by anyone quite like you." An almost embarrassed grin flittered across his lips.

"Be back in a few." Abbie leaped to her feet and bolted for the hatchway.

"Make sure you put on lots and lots of that SPF thirty stuff. It's in the head. Otherwise, sweet Senator, you will grill up like that lobster you love so much, okay?"

"Aye, Captain." She mock saluted as she disappeared down the hatchway.

"Look here, Abbie. This is truly amazing!" Gwynn shouted as he pointed at the 64 inch flat screen television in the Salon. They had anchored in a sheltered cove off a very small island just south of Guadeloupe. "It's INN way out here in the middle of the ocean—well sea, actually."

"The Lies We Believe That Will Get Us Killed. That's the new book by Theo Theodora—the prophet who makes a profit. It's coming out next Christmas, Theo, is that right?"

"That is if there *is* a next Christmas, Worth."

Abbie walked into the Salon, still applying aloe vera to her sunburned face. "Hey, that's your Theo, isn't it, Gwynn?"

"So it is. The boy sure works fast."

"Quite, Theo." Ellworth was, himself, quietly irritated with his former comrade-in-arms' apparent delusion that somehow the USA would be taken over by the Muslims in what will amount to an armed invasion. "If there is a Christmas," he mimicked in a mocking kind of way. "What kind of Nostradamus crap is that?"

Theo visibly ignored his old friend's pique. This kind of air-time was too valuable to allow Worth to spoil it for him with personal banter and politically correct sidesteps. However, Theo covered his face in mock embarrassment. He just couldn't resist a little comeback. "Are we really allowed to say crap on network television, Worth?"

Ellworth nodded and, in doing so, set off beam alerts around the globe.

"Anyway, I see that I have you speechless for once, so I'll just wade in here about the new book. Okay?

Ellworth nodded again.

"The first lie to worry about is the one that claims radical Islam is a perversion of Islam rather than accepting that Islam is Islam. And it's really all in a name here. I mean, Islam means submission in Arabic for goodness sake. That is not what one would call a neutral kind of name for a religion.

"The second lie is its corollary, that Islam is a peaceful religion. It is not. It is premised upon everyone being Muslim. And, I'm sorry, man, but any time we're talking about everybody having to be the same on anything, it's not going to be peaceful getting there!

"The third lie, torture does not work. Of course it works if the various techniques are skillfully employed and the appropriate types of questions are asked and the responses verified. One of the reasons that the apologists for our enemies have made such a big deal of torture is precisely because it *does* work.

"The threat of violence or pain is even more effective than the pain or violence itself. But only if the person being interrogated actually believes that the threats of violence and pain will be carried out.

"The true irony that comes with the apologists' entreaties to do away with torture is that the enemy prisoners will then easily be prepared for what we will do and confident in their knowledge of what we will not do. Thus they are not intimidated by threats of pain and violence because they know we will not make good on those threats.

"That's where we are in this new age. The enemy doesn't believe we will inflict the pain and violence necessary to intimidate them into talking. So, we are, then, forced in the future to actually do the very things that the apologists argue against because we're doing what they want now.

"Fourth, the combining of church and state works. The very notion of church and state together seems oxymoronic on some theoretical level or another.

"And, Fifth, religious tolerance means we must discriminate against all other religions because one religion has been discriminated against. That's not it at all. Let's get this straight from the start. Religious tolerance is not even guaranteed by the constitution. Religious freedom is.

"And religious freedom does not mean bending over backwards to give one religious faction special powers, protections, and freedoms over and above other religions simply because it seems to be less well-tolerated than others. So, Muslims, for example, have the right, the freedom to be Muslims. That's protected by the constitution. They do not, however, have the right or expectation of protection regarding being tolerated by others beyond enforcement of the laws. Being treated with tolerance by others is something one must earn, like friendship. One earns that friendship, that place of tolerance, by being a trustworthy friend, a reliable neighbor, a good citizen."

"Theo, you are so like the prophet of doom who keeps surfacing throughout life much in the same way a device in one of your books might repeatedly assert itself in order to emphasize some point you wish to make. You just simply fascinate us all with the creativity of your theories."

"Thank you so much Worth for your insight and for having the good judgment to have me on your show again and on such short notice." He chuckled almost as an afterthought. "And, I do look forward to your special tonight on this whole beached whales thing."

"And, thank you, Theo Theodora, my colleague and friend. I'm sure your interest in my special tonight couldn't be so self-serving as to have anything to do with the fact that you will be making a special guest appearance on that show tonight as well, I do believe.

"That's right Worth. We'll be looking at the possibilities of any terrorist connections to those beached baleens."

"For now, this is Ellworth Hayes on behalf of all the INN crew and staff, good evening everyone. And, stay tuned to INN, the network with more news in more depth than anybody else on television."

"What's the deal with this mysterious Medallion you wear around your neck, Gwynn?" She sipped a Cruzan Gold Reserve and coke with lime as she turned to him on the ottoman. "It looks like some kind of antique or something." The television was off. The stereo was off. The only sounds other than their voices and the occasional creaking and cracking of the Brown Pelican were the low, soft waves lapping against its hull. "I mean, there were times today when the sun hit the gold just right so that it actually seemed to be generating some kind of energy or something."

"Nooo . . . ." He shook his head emphatically. "Nothing like that. It's just a family heirloom from my dad's side of the family. He was killed in a head-on collision with a sixteen wheeler when I was twelve. His will instructed me to always wear the Medallion around my neck for "good luck." Gwynn shrugged. "So, what else was a twelve-year-old boy to do? I put it on, and I have never taken it off except when x-rays required it or when I go snorkeling or scuba diving so as not to attract barracuda. In Vietnam, I wrapped it in duct tape along with my dog tags so that they wouldn't make any noise."

She caressed the gold circle, staring at the two knights riding a single horse. A battle helmet visor covered the rear knight's face. "What do all these words etched in the space around the edges mean? Do you know?"

"They are four Latin words: *Decus, Fidelitus, Probitus, Virtus.* Translated they mean Honor, Loyalty, Honesty, and Valor.

Abbie continued to touch the Medallion almost reverently. "Jesus, and possessing such an icon as this and wearing it every day didn't ever make you think that it might actually be something special beyond just as a family good luck piece?"

"I never said that. My god, Abbie, when I was a kid, especially before my Father was killed, there were always the stories at Christmas about my ancestors also named Gwynn and the Poor Knights of Christ and the Temple of Solomon or Knights Templar as you might know them and my direct ancestor Young Man Phelps of Cams Ron Burn who, according to family legend, was one of the first people to actually discover the new world. There is a pretty cool story attached, if you really want to hear it."

She nodded vigorously and held out her glass. "More Cruzan, then the story."

After he had filled her glass with shaved ice and rum with a touch of coke and a twist of lime, he settled into the sofa.

"A long, long time ago in a galaxy far, far away . . . ."

They both began to laugh at the *Star Wars* take-off.

"Seriously, a long time ago, back in eleven eighteen, a young man from the Clan Camsron called Gwynn of the Highlands was one of the original nine knights who formed the Knights Templar. He held a very special position referred to as the Unnamed Knight.

"When he was only fourteen, his family had sent him off to France where he served as a squire for his distant Uncle, Lord Hughues de Payens. The plan was that he would return to the Highlands ready to take over the Clan leadership when the time came.

"But that was not the way it turned out. Instead, Gwynn of the Highlands was the beginning of the first and only Clan ever to be named for a first name or given name rather than a surname. Over the centuries it would become known as the Clan of Gwynn."

"What's the Clan of Gwynn?"

"Interestingly, it is basically a clan of one. The only member of the clan is the Unnamed Knight who holds possession of the Medallion first presented to Gwynn of the Highlands ten years after he had been picked, by his Uncle Hughues, to be the initial Unnamed Knight."

"What did he do?"

"The Unnamed Knight was the new Order's hedge against their potential and actual enemies. Since he was never seen in public without his face being covered and since his name was never spoken in public or to anyone outside of the Order, he was almost invisible to their enemies. If the Templars were ever destroyed, he would be the one who might remain unknown and able to keep the Order's stories, secrets, and treasure from those who would destroy it all."

The Medallion passed from Gwynn to Gwynn over the generations until Gwynn V's identity was somehow discovered and he was burned at the stake by the King of France in thirteen fourteen along with Grand Master Jacques de Molay. He had picked his successor, a young lad from the Clan CamsRon, who was already leading Templars in the fight for Scottish independence along side Robert the Bruce, King of Scots. He had not, however, been able to transfer the Medallion as required. Some agents in Paris, who were familiar with the situation and who were friendly both to the Templars and to Robert the Bruce, discovered the Medallion on the charred body of Gwynn V. They recovered it and sent it to Robert the Bruce. At the Battle of Bannockburn was the first opportunity he had to present it to the new Gwynn, and so it seemed, the last Gwynn, because the Templars had been disbanded and destroyed except for those that escaped."

"So, that's how this Medallion got its name?"

"Yes, that's it. And, he passed it on to his nephew Young Man Phelps, and it has come down the generations to me attended by all of the legends and stories and the onus of honor and responsibility that was attached to it for all those years. Most people discount those old stories anymore.

"However, when I was about to graduate Princeton and go into the Army, the elected leader of the Camsron Clan approached me about the Medallion of Bannockburn as it was called from that day forward—named after that famous battle in which the last of my namesakes, Gwynn VI, was a hero. The leader tried to make me understand what it meant to the Clan for the Medallion to have surfaced after many, many years of being missing.

"Like all too many on this earth, those Clan types were much too fixated on the past and the dead and not enough so on the present and the living. I, on the other hand, chose to live in the present as best I could and tend to the living as best I could. Perhaps it has been my payback for all the killing during the war. I don't know. But, that was why teaching in one of the last outposts of the modernized world seemed exactly perfect for me, and I have never abandoned that tack. I have tried very hard to help the living. In this case, the living happen to be my kids at Martyrs and Saints.

"With that plan, I was able to get as far away from all of that Clan malarkey as I possibly could and still occupy the same planet with those people.

"So, I left them to their superstitions. But, I never had any valid reason to believe that the Medallion was seriously anything more than what my father said it was: A family good luck piece with a great story behind it. Of course, I do recall with some irony, that my Father was wearing the Medallion when a sixteen wheeler flattened his 2-month-old XKD Jag.

"As far as I was concerned, that collision reduced the value of the Medallion to a few lines in my Father's will: 'To my son, Gwynn, I bequeath, as is my historical responsibility, the family good luck piece—the golden Medallion of Bannockburn—which I wear around my neck. Wear it always, my son, and protect it with your honor and your life, and pass it on to your first born son when you die.'"

"So, you just walked away from that incredibly rich family heritage?"

"I guess I did at that. But, the idea that some Medallion hanging around my neck somehow made me the next Gwynn in the Clan of Gwynn and the leader of the Camsron Clan because my father was from some line of nameless Templar knights was simply more than I was willing to consider . . . at least until now."

"What's so different for you now, Gwynn?"

"All this stuff sort of falling into my life. The whales, the tattooed arm, the *YUNUS Apparatus Manual for Warriors*—all that. I never believed in coincidences, but this has been some kind of huge coincidental convergence so far. And, now, this voyage with you to find the answers to the questions prompted by all these coincidences. I guess, now it does sort of seem like I have been singled out for something, just like the old stories I learned at my Uncle's feet foretold."

9
Gwynn Lost

[Music: "Gwynn Lost"]

"Mr. Stotkos. Please, tell us why you are in hiding?"

Gwynn and Abbie sat in palm rattan style Captain's chairs facing the narrow cot of the one-armed sailor. Based on what the kid's had learned through the International Red Cross, only one person in the entire Caribbean had been recently treated for a severed left arm. Their reports said it was a male somewhere in the Grenadines' Tobago Cays at a facility called the Hospital of the Grenadines. The hospital administrator explained to them that he, personally, had discharged a man resembling the students' description, only months ago and had since lost contact with him. Along with that went any hope of payment for his considerable hospital bill. It was not, then, an easy task for Armond Braitwaite and Ashanta Riley to convince the administrator that it was in the best interest of the entire world for him to provide whatever information he could about his former patient.

Finally, he admitted that a one-armed Greek sailor had been recommended by the Hospital of the Grenadines as a priority candidate for their group recuperation facility. There seemed to be no file entry or paperwork regarding the dispensation of that recommendation. However, the administrator assured Armond that it was strongly rumored that he was in hiding in a small native recuperation community on an even smaller island, so isolated that the community only had limited generator power and practically no modern infrastructure.

The students had ultimately tracked him down through a newly formed organization called the Caribbean Medical Alliance. It kept track of patients and resources throughout the Caribbean, matching them as best they could based upon necessity and with the utmost confidentiality. The Chief Operating Physician of the alliance, Gabrielle Ottley, assured the students that the Hospital of the Grenadines knew exactly where the patient was. They were just being cautious in protecting him from the wrong kinds of inquiries.

"The administrator there gave you just enough to lead you somewhere else, to me for example, but not directly to the patient." Doctor Ottley, on the other hand, admitted that her willingness to share the secret information of the sailor's whereabouts with the students was only because they were Martyrs and Saints students of her high school mentor, Gwynn Camsron.

The Trades from off the African coast wafted through half-opened, split palm jalousies. Everything about the long-term residency building was palm made. The building was constructed from split palm planks. The open places between the palm planks were filled with a kind of palm putty. Light sockets and limited electrical outlets were attached to thick electric wires running completely exposed along the palm plank walls. Fronds were thatched expertly into an extremely tight weave and smeared with coconut oil to create rain resilient, if not actually waterproof, roofing. The building was as much an icon of the construction skills of the past when the coconut palm provided food, shelter, energy, and clothing to the Caribbean as it was an anachronism.

"Zhe people Stotkos work for when lose arm, zhey after Stotkos because Stotkos jump ship at secret port. Hide wizh locals. Locals take Stotkos to hospital next island. Zhey hide Stotkos here. Zhey afraid ship people come for Stotkos because Stotkos know too much what zhey do."

"Well, Mr. Stotkos. Do you know too much?"

He just barely nodded.

"Then, tell me what you know that these people are afraid of." Her expression was one of pity and concern. "Maybe, just maybe, I can help you."

"What you say, Mr. Stotkos? You help the Senator out, and we'll help you out. Okay?"

"Okay. Okay." The wizened old sailor settled himself at the edge of the white sheets of his hospital bed and summoned all of his Greekness to tell his story as the warriors and sailors that were his ancestors told their tales. He cleared his throat.

Gwynn started the mini tape recorder. "We're ready." To him, Stotkos was like Coleridge's Ancient Mariner or his poor old drunken Uncle Ian.

"Stotkos work net and harpoon on one of ten ships. Zhey capture whales. Not kill. Capture in great nets. When nets full, ships tow to secret port here in Grenadines. Zhen ship out again. Stotkos never zee whales no more. But Stotkos hear zhings.

"One day, a rogue whale jump nets. Stotkos hurl harpoon. Harpoon hit hump. Whale shoot into air, dive for bottom. Harpoon line sing and stretch tight. Suddenly, line slack. Stotkos pull in with one hand and reel in wizh ozher. Stotkos grab last of line wizh left hand. Whale shoot from sea like missile. Maybe hundred yards from ship. Line snap tight around Stotkos' arm. Whale splash into sea and dive for bottom again. Stotkos see arm tear out of shoulder. At first, Stotkos feel no pain, but Stotkos scream anyway. Line snap. Whale drag Stotkos' arm splash into zea. "Zhen, pain come. And blood. Stotkos lucky not bleed to death." He looked at his empty left shoulder socket scarred over completely from the emergency hot knife cauterization by his first mate. "Maybe."

"The tattoo on your arm spelled out YUNUS in red capital letters."

Stotkos nodded absently. "Stotkos hear stories about zhe Yunus. Zhey be terrorists over zhe world. Zhey brand you if you work for zhem and you are not Muslim. You are what zhey call Dhimmi—protected unbelievers. Zhey treat you like slave, but zhey pay very good before zhey kill you."

Suddenly Stotkos grasped Gwynn's shoulder with his only hand. "I don't know what else, Madame Senator, sir. I can't know no more." His eyes darted about glazed over with fear as if he expected his persurers to emerge from the shadows and kill him. "You gotta zee zhrough zhe eye of zhe whale."

"What did Stotkos mean? He 'can't know any more', and we have to 'see through the eye of the whale?'"

"I'm not sure, but my guess is that the 'can't know any more' thing has to do with whatever self-preservation he believes he still has to do. He doesn't want anybody thinking that he gave away the whole plot or plan or whatever it is that he is still too afraid to talk about."

"You're probably right about that, Gwynn. And, what's that old saying? 'You can see the universe in the eye of a whale.'"

"Yeah, but the only whale eyes I know about around here are off a nearby small uncharted landmass called Whale Island. The inhabitants call it that because it has always been a stopping off place along the annual migratory route of the humpback whale. A place where I spent nearly two years recuperating after a shipwreck."

"When was that, Gwynn?"

"Nineteen seventy. Not long after I hit the Caribbean. I was crewing on a ketch. We were taking it from St. Thomas to Barbados for an owner.

"There were four of us. Me, the Captain, the first mate, and a cook. The Captain was worried about pirates for some reason I never discovered, so he had hired me as a sort of mercenary I guess you'd call it. I was like special security for the trip, an insurance policy against the possibility of a pirate attack. He was so preoccupied with the pirates, I guess, that he ran head on into a huge reef during a tropical storm that sure seemed more like a hurricane when you were in it. They were all forward in the wheel house with the Captain eating when the boat hit the reef. I was on watch, aft. They were all killed, and, when their bodies eventually washed up on the island, I buried them.

"Auntie Gotlieb swore that a humpback whale risked grounding to nose me ashore at sunrise as she walked the beach and chanted her morning mas in the Cove of Whales where the humpbacks gathered every year.

"Auntie's words had been the community voice for the people of Whale Island ever since anyone there could remember. And, she shared all she knew about her island and the sea and the whales with that nearly-dead shipwrecked and waterlogged American she had nursed back to health. The American she called Gwynn Lost."

Whale Island
Tabago Cays, Grenadines

Whale Island was a cluster of fecund spires rising up to a thousand feet out of the Caribbean like crystals silhouetted against the blood sun setting behind it. One of the dots on a map that represented the Grenadines. In that sense it was charted.

"It's absolutely enchanting, Gwynn. I've never seen anything like it before." She pressed her shoulders inward as she released a deep sigh. "I'm at a loss. It's like a, ah, like a, like a cathedral made from crystals of the very sea itself. You know?"

He bowed his head. Tears squeezed through his tightly closed eyelids. "It *was* a cathedral. A cathedral of nature. It was an island world much like the world reflected in the residence hall where we found Stotkos. Natural. Of the land." Gwynn's voice crumbled into the sounds of the engines. "I don't know what it's been turned into."

Auntie Gotlieb looked like she was a hundred years old when Gwynn first caught sight of her sitting in front of her coconut palm roofed hut. And, for all he knew, she could have been, but he never would have expected her to look it.

When she saw him, Auntie put her fragile arms around his neck, sobbing and hugging him as if she would crush him into her heart if she could. "Me Gwynn Lost come back now to see Auntie after all dese years. Never t'ought me be seein' him ev-er a-gain."

Gwynn forced back the tears as he eased gradually away from Auntie's desperate grasp. "Auntie, let me introduce my friend, United States Senator Abigail Keayrn. She came all the way from Washington, DC in the United States to see you, Auntie."

Abbie extended her hand. "It is so nice to meet you, Auntie. Gwynn has told me all about how you saved his life all those years ago."

Auntie grabbed her hand with the withered, knotted fingers of both her hands. "Meetin' friend of Gwynn Lost good, too, Missy Sen-a-tor."

"We're here to find out what's going on, Auntie."

"Why so, me son?"

"We heard some things. And, look at you. You look like an old soupsop. This place looks like death warmed over too. What is going on here?"

"Da changes in dese lit-tle islands be comin' from da death of all da coral and o'der sea life in dese Caribbean wa-ters. Too much whales. Too much whales. And, 'cause o' dem, everyt'ing be dyin', and dem mens doan' care none 'bout it."

"What are you talking about, Auntie? Whales? That's part of why we're here."

"Do you know da story of Jonah and da whale, dear?"

"Sure," Abigail responded.

"But do you also know da story of Yunus and da Whale?"

"No, can't say as I've ever heard of Yunus and the Whale."

"Yunus, Auntie?"

"Yes, me son, Gwynn Lost. Yunus."

"Isn't that the *Qur'an's* version of Jonah?"

"Yes. Dat does be what dem mens calls Sura number ten."

Auntie's black eyes stared out across the bay that had been her front yard for more years than most could remember. As they sipped some of her famed lemon grass tea with lime and her own recipe for coconut milk sweetener, she spoke to Gwynn and Abbie in a faraway hushed voice as if she were in a trance as she recited what she knew of Sura number ten.

"Many a gen-er-a-tion we have 'nihilated afore you when dey transgressed. Deir messengers went to dem wid clear proofs, but dey refus-ed to believe. We dus re-quite de guilty people." Auntie's black eyes welled with tears as she reached out and held each of them by the arm with one of her shaking hands. "Please, Sen-a-tor, Gwynn Lost. Dem mens be sayin' dat all o' we is de guilty people. Please help us. Please doan' let dem re-quite we."

As Gwynn and Abbie returned to the docks and readied to board the Brown Pelican for the night, Abbie asked him a question that had bothered her the entire time they visited with Auntie Gotlieb. "Why didn't you ask Auntie Gotlieb about the *YUNUS Apparatus Manual for Warriors*?"

"I didn't need to. She told me all I needed to know to confirm that something strange is going on around here—something strange and very probably terrorism-related, and it's something that has even got Auntie Gotlieb too scared to fight." Gwynn offered Abbie his arm and helped her board the Brown Pelican. "That's something I never thought I'd see. But, you could see it in her eyes. Hear it in her voice. Couldn't you?"

"Yes. Even though I don't know her at all, I could sense it. Yes."

"All the more reason not to tell her any more than necessary, for her own good."

Two middle-eastern sailors disembarked their respective boats just a few slips down from them and passed by Gwynn who was now making sure that the yacht's lines to the dock pilings were secure.

"Allahu akbar. God is great," one of the sailors whispered with a heavy accent as they passed each other.

Gwynn wondered almost absent-mindedly why the man would say something in both Arabic and English.

The second sailor responded: "Allahu akbar. God is great."

They slapped hands.

"Gwynn! Watch out behind you!"

At the sound of Abbie's voice, Gwynn attempted to turn, but a third sailor had slipped up behind him. He slammed a needle into Gwynn's neck before Gwynn could make a move. Whatever was in that syringe paralyzed him instantly.

"Damn it!" The old attack from behind trick.

The other two sailors quickly boarded the Brown Pelican and pursued Abbie who was trying to escape by locking herself below decks.

10
Adhan, the Call to Prayer

[Music: "New Soldiers of Allah"]

Allahu Akbar, Allahu Akbar.
Allahu Akbar, Allahu Akbar.
Ash-hadu alla ilaha illa-llah.
Ash-hadu alla ilaha illa-llah.
Ash-hadu anna
Muhammadar-Rasulullah.
Ash-hadu anna
Muhammadar-Rasulullah.
Hayya 'ala-s-Salah, Hayya 'ala-s-Salah.
Hayya 'ala-l-falah, Hayya 'ala-l-falah.
As-Salatu khairun min an-naum, As-Salatu khairun
min an-naum.
Allahu Akbar, Allahu Akbar.
La ilaha illa-llah

The Words of the Adhan echoed in the room for the eighteenth time since he had been brought to this place.

> Allah is the Greatest, Allah is the Greatest.
> Allah is the Greatest, Allah is the Greatest.
> I bear witness that there is none worthy of worship but Allah.
> I bear witness that there is none worthy of worship but Allah.
> I bear witness that Muhammad is the Messenger of Allah
> I bear witness that Muhammad is the Messenger of Allah
> Hasten to the Prayer, hasten to the Prayer.
> Hasten to real success, hasten to real success
> Prayer is better than sleep, Prayer is better than sleep.
> Allah is the Greatest, Allah is the Greatest.

There is none worthy of worship but Allah.

He felt very sure of that count, but that was about all he was really sure of. He knew that Islamic prayers were fixed at the same general time period each day. He remembered reading in his research that Islamic prayer times were traditionally set according to the movement of the sun, not to the time on a clock. Even now, this was how Muslims observed the five formal prayers each day. Because of the rotation of the earth, the revolution of the earth around the sun, the tilt of the earth, the various latitudes of the earth's locations, daylight savings time, and other contingencies, the times for these prayers changed from day to day depending on location.

Their prayers began before dawn with the Fajr in remembrance of God. But, he couldn't be sure how many times the morning prayer line 'Prayer is better than sleep' had been repeated. It was only said at Fajr. If he could only remember that, he would have been able to know how many mornings he had been captive.

Around noon, the Dhuhr prayers were performed to remember Allah and seek His guidance.

Asr came in the late afternoon when people were usually busy wrapping up the day's work, getting kids home from school, or whatever. It was viewed as an important time to take a few minutes to remember Allah and the greater meaning of their lives.

Just after the sun set, Muslims remembered Allah again as the day began to come to a close with Maghrib.

Before retiring for the night, Isha'a was said to remember Allah's presence as well as to seek His guidance, mercy, and forgiveness.

Recalling these facts helped Gwynn focus. The focus helped him keep track of time passing. It seemed like he had only been in the small room for twenty or thirty hours. But he was not nearly as confident of his hour count as he was of his call to prayer count. Yet, relying on his Adhan count exclusively seemed to indicate that he had been there for at least three full days, not twenty to thirty hours. This would probably be the fourth morning because he had been brought here in the afternoon, just before Maghrib. For sure, he was no more than a couple of hours off either way. That meant a four-hour window of error at most. Not enough to make any real difference until his time in captivity became weeks.

They—whoever *they* were—had made one huge mistake, however. They had left him alone with recorded calls to prayer and silence. The calls to prayer and darkness. The calls to prayer and no food or water. The calls to prayer and nothingness. So, their first mistake was in not knowing that he was one of the few who had actually read *Being and Nothingness*. He was one of the few who would actually do such a thing as count the calls to prayer to prevent himself from falling under their spell of existing outside of time.

Not one person had entered his room except to bring him food and water at random intervals or communicated with him in any way. Yet, being alone was something he had faced many times. More often than not he had embraced it in the way one embraces nourishment. Perhaps not being alone was something of significantly more importance to people whose Friday prayer could not even be said without others present and participating than it was to someone like himself who often seemed to grow stronger through separation from others.

What if they were shortening the intervals between calls to prayer in a graduated fashion? To confuse him? But, how would his captors know that he understood anything about the timing of their prayers? He felt his forehead skin wrinkle in concentration. Could they actually be affecting his count somewhat, no matter how disciplined he was? After all, he was drugged, and he sure as hell wasn't the same type of disciplined being he had once been. Yet, he also knew that he needed to maintain his focus. He must develop a plan to save Abbie and escape from wherever it was that they had been taken.

He could hear another prayerful voice. It sounded far off at first. Gradually, he was able to pinpoint it to just across the hall. It was a real person's voice, not a recording. This new voice was delivering a supplication before wudu or cleansing with water and Salat Ul Fajr:

"Allahumma rabba hadhihi-d-da'awati-t-tammati wa-s-Salati-l-qa'imati, ati Muhammadan il-wasilata wa-l-fadilata wa-d-darajata-r-rafi'ati wa-b'ath-hu maqamam mahmudan illadhi wa'adtahu.

"0 Allah, Lord of this most perfect call, and of the Prayer that is about to be established, grant to Muhammad the favor of nearness to

You and excellence and a place of distinction, and exalt him to a position of glory that You have promised him."

Salat Ul Fajr

The Salat Ul Fajr was the pre-dawn prayer that began The Leader's day with the remembrance of God. It was the first of the five prayers he observed each day along with his Muslim brothers around the world. In Muslim communities, people were reminded of the daily prayer times throughout the day by the Adhan, the Islamic call to prayer. No Adhan was available in the middle of the Caribbean. But a web site on the Internet provided the times for prayer and even a recorded call to prayer was broadcast that was played throughout the compound. That was what Gwynn had been hearing for what seemed days now.

"Sallallaahu 'alaihi wa sallam.

"I make wudu in the name of Allah as the Prophet did."

Before the first prayers of the day, the Submitter must cleanse his body from head to toe so that he will be worthy of submitting his prayers to Allah. Whenever, the Submitter breaks the wudu, he must perform the ritual again, washing hands, nose, mouth, face, beard, arms and elbows, head and ears, turban, feet and ankles three times each.

"*Subhaanakallaahumma wa bihamdika ashhadu anlaa ilaaha illa anta astaghfiruka wa atoobu ilaika.*

"I declare You free from all defects my Lord and all praise belongs to You and I bear witness that there is none worthy of worship except You. I seek Your forgiveness and I turn to You.

"Allahumma-gh fir-lee dhan-bee wawass si'lee fi dari wa bariklee fi rizq.

"O Allah Forgive my sins, make my home accommodating and grant me abundance in my livelihood."

The new live voice continued. "The Prophet, may Allah bless him and grant him peace, asked: 'Does any one of you have water?' They answered: 'No.' So he extended his hand, and water flowed from between his fingers as he said: 'Make wudu in the name of Allah.'"

Even though he was in another room, Gwynn could hear the

man's hands dipping into fresh water as the sun's rose petal like rays crept up over the edge of the earth.

"Al-Miqdaam ibn Ma'd Yakrib said: 'I came to the Prophet with water for wudu, then He washed His face three times, then washed His forearms three times, then washed His mouth and nose three times, then wiped His head and ears — their outsides and insides — and washed each of His feet three times.'"

All Gwynn could see through the slightly ajar door were the emerging shadows on the walls of the room across the narrow hallway of men seated on the floor evoking a strange kind of connection with his memory of the shadows on the walls of the Tortola End. He could, however, hear the one man's voice chanting above all the others. There was something about that voice.

"Allahummaj 'al-ni minat-tow-wa beena waj-alni minal muta-tah-hireen."

Gwynn thought he knew what that meant. "I testify that there is no deity except Allah; He is One and has no partner. And I testify that Muhammad is His servant and apostle."

He again lost consciousness.

Salat Ul Dhuhr

Gwynn's head still felt like it was the size of a satellite and maybe even as far away. His ears rang with the music of the spheres and the sound of noon time prayers. Abbie's smile seemed to appear out of nowhere and gobble him up, back into interstellar space.

He was beginning to recall more clearly what had happened. He'd been blindsided. That was all there was to it. He still knew his craft cold. And, he had kept current. That was not the problem. The problem was in the doing. Knowing what to do as well as he ever did, maybe even better, made him feel he could still execute as well as he ever did or better. That confidence had proved to be misplaced. Now he was captive and, he presumed, so was Abbie.

Blurs began to transform into near shapes with star showers streaming through them. Somewhere deep inside his consciousness he realized his reactions, his feelings, his sensations were all creatures of whatever drug had been slammed into his neck and whatever was in the gruel and water they were occasionally feeding him. Some good drugs, he managed to quip to himself. The spheres grew more distant and their music less insistent as he struggled for focus. Showers of light became luminous shadows behind the forming shape of a bearded man wearing an Arabian style tunic and a black turban.

His squinting eyes locked onto the dark brown eyes that smoldered inside the head covering that draped around the bearded one's face. My god, it is Muhammad himself, Gwynn nearly laughed out loud. He struggled to lift his arms, to touch the bearded face with his hands, but he could not. His arms seemed to be strapped to whatever he was lying on, some kind of mat on the dirt floor.

"How can this be?"

"How can what be?" Muhammad responded.

"My god!" This man was not Muhammad. He was . . . . "Sal?"

"But, how could you possibly recognize me?"

"Your voice at first," Gwynn gurgled without hesitation, "when I could hear you praying. Now, it's your eyes. It's all in the eyes." His mind stumbled. "You never forget a person's eyes, Sal."

"Saladin, my old friend, not Sal. It has always been thus."

"What do you mean? 'It has always been thus?'"

"Although you knew me only as Sal Keayrn, my real name is Saladin Keayrn Muhammad. You knew me only by my Mother's family name, but my Arab family goes back more than three thousand years, my old friend. Then, my Father's family lived in Babylon. The men were scholars. Later many became military leaders as well including the great Salah-ad-Din himself. That is some kind of difficult inertia to overcome, my old friend, even if I had been so inclined, and I certainly was not. I revere my family and their legacy to me through my Father who created the original 'secret apparatus' army for the old Brotherhood and my Mother who, upon his execution and while I was still in her womb, dedicated me as a Messenger of Allah."

"I never knew, even during our dances with death together, that you were anyone other than Sal Keayrn from Boston via Dublin," Gwynn interrupted. "Abbie—your wife—never knew you were anything but the dark Mick," he continued involuntarily chuckling as if to himself, not to anyone in the room that still seemed like a black hole with him and his MIA partner illuminated in the center by the noon sun streaming in through the lone partially opened door. "Remember, how you told me she called you her dark Mick? So, neither your wife nor your best friend really knew who you were. Why was that, Sal-a-mander?"

"Clever insults will not encourage the rekindling of our friendship, my old friend. Of that I can assure you."

"And even less-than-clever threats will fail to discourage me from slitting your throat if you've harmed the Senator in any way . . . and I mean any way. Do you understand my meaning?"

"The Senator, as you refer to *my* wife, has in no way been harmed."

"Where is she, then? I want to see for myself."

"Your old war buddy's word is not good enough for you anymore?"

"Not on your life! My old war buddy, it seems, does not and never did exist. And, the man before me now can lie with impunity, can't he Sal? Can't he? Can't you?"

Saladin smiled in a condescending manner.

"So, tell me where she is, Sal. Take me to her or bring her here. Or, are you afraid of what I might see?"

"Afraid? Afraid of what? Of you? Even if I were foolish enough to have a friend whom I feared, I do not fear my prisoners. And, you are my prisoner, my old friend. But, insulted I am. Insulted that you would think otherwise of me."

"The 'otherwise' I am thinking of you right now you probably wouldn't want to hear. You know, the old you'd-kill-your-own-wife-in-the-name-of-Allah-the-slayer-of-infidels type of 'otherwise.' After all, a United States Senator—especially a female—is a perfect example of all that is corrupt about us. Isn't she?"

"According to our law, she is still my wife. She is mine to do with as I please. That does not change with time."

"No one can do with another as they please, no matter what your religion tells you, Sal. And, that doesn't change with time either."

"That's almost funny coming from you, Gwynn, the ultimate infidel. If I remember correctly, you don't believe in Allah or in any other god for that matter. How was it you used to put it? 'Even if there was a god, I don't see how it makes any difference if I believe in it or not.'"

"That's pretty close. And after nearly three years of killing and more than thirty years of teaching literature to high school kids, I still pretty much believe the same thing."

"Of course you never knew, but after we would talk about such things, I felt so unclean that I felt compelled to make wudu. Of course, I could not because that would have given me away now wouldn't it? Can you imagine an Irish Muslim making wudu in the middle of the jungles of Vietnam in 1969?"

As he turned and walked toward the light that streamed through the open door, Saladin Keayrn shouted to someone in the hallway, "Bring the prisoner some solid food and some fresh water. And, no more drugs. We don't want him dying on us before we are ready."

Salat Ul Asr

Whale Cove recessed deeply into the shoreline of the small island creating a huge lagoon-like area. The mouth of the cove was narrow. Thick growths of Sea Grape trees overlapped and interlaced, nearly hiding the bay from view to those who approached by sea. Dozens of humpback whales and calves frolicked within the confines of the cove. Gwynn noted that the water was not as transparent as it usually was in coral protected bays. He could still see the whales under the water but they appeared to be more like outlines or smudges.

Sal's cadre of what seemed to be hundreds of warriors and support staff scurried about, busy wrapping up their day's work. It would soon be time for them to halt their efforts to take a few minutes to remember Allah and the greater meaning of their lives with Salat Ul Asr.

"In studying these whales, we found out many things that are helpful to our cause of building the ultimate army. Instead of a 'secret apparatus' military force like my Father developed for the old Brotherhood, I have created the 'YUNUS Apparatus' for the New Brotherhood."

"It appears, you see, that humpback whales navigate by combining a large number of sensors available to them. You know, like water temperature, memory, the currents, the tides, and depth. But, their primary tool is what we call bio magnetic navigation.

"We know, for example, that tuna, pigeons, and starlings—among others—make use of biomagnetic navigation. That is they find their way around the planet by sensing the Earth's magnetic field and using it like a map, and, based on our experiments, it seems that whales do as well. We found bio magnetite, in the brains of our humpback whales which we have bred here on Whale Island for the past ten years much like the whales in the Arabian Sea near Oman.

"But, we now have enough of them."

"Enough of them for what?"

Two calves breached near the shore.

"Suffice it to say, we have developed ways to control that navigational tool so that we can now pretty much pilot a whale to where we want it to go. The only problem is that the navigator must be in very close proximity to the whale. So we have developed an entire technology around placing a living person inside a whale with the navigational and communications tools to guide a whale to a particular destination and to keep in touch with the strategic headquarters and tactical commands in America as they go as well as all of the basic tools needed by an invading soldier. This has become the basis for our new 'YUNUS Apparatus' army. Our forces believe so strongly in what they are doing that they continue to volunteer in huge numbers as YUNUS warriors even though the threat of dying inside one of these whales is still very high.

"But, these are humpbacks, right?"

"That is correct."

"Humpbacks are baleen whales, and because of the way they are made with all those plates for filtering the catch they gulp in, they can't really swallow something the size of a human being, can they?"

"Using humpbacks was important to our plan because of their predictable migration paths that put them in the right places. So, we experimented, my old friend, with just that idea, and we discovered that we could accomplish our goal by artificially dilating the esophagus and slowly force-feeding the pod. We have also tried surgically implanting a pod, but it requires too much recovery time on the part of the whale. Some even died.

"The southwest monsoon system in the Arabian Sea drives one of the five largest upwelling systems in the world. During the peak monsoon months of July and August sea-surface temperatures drop to sixteen or seventeen degrees Celsius. This creates high nutrient levels in the upwelling systems resulting in accelerated productivity of phytoplankton blooms. This phenomenon has been accepted for many years now as the method by which enough food could be produced to permit whales to reside year-round in the tropical Arabian Sea. Yet no one had tried it.

"We believed we could replicate that here. And we have, my friend." Sal patted Gwynn's left shoulder with a cupped right hand. "We have.

"Our scientists developed an approach to mimic the Arabian Sea environment in such a way as to provide the same kind of year-round habitat for humpbacks as they have off the shores of Oman.

"We captured whales on the high seas and brought them here to become a part of our great experiment to develop an extended pod of humpbacks that could live year-round in one place. Then we could build a large enough population and test out our theories about using them to transport men and materials.

"Despite the crowded conditions in the cove, the humpbacks appear to be not only surviving, but thriving and even multiplying. The project has been such a success thus far that we are now in a position to infiltrate America using these whales piloted by our YUNUS warriors." He smirked. "Jonahs to you, my old friend."

He finally paused, waving his right arm to indicate the expanse of the cove as whales breached and swam on their backs with both flippers in the air or raised their flippers or tail flukes out of the water, then slapping them on the surface in tail lobbing or flipper slapping.

"Messengers of Allah, my old friend. Messengers of Allah."

"Oh, so that's why the water's so clouded?"

Allahu Akbar, Allahu Akbar.
Allahu Akbar, Allahu Akbar.
Ash-hadu alla ilaha illa-llah.
Ash-hadu alla ilaha illa-llah.
Ash-hadu anna
Muhammadar-Rasulullah.
Ash-hadu anna

Muhammadar-Rasulullah.
Hayya 'ala-s-Salah, Hayya 'ala-s-Salah.
Hayya 'ala-l-falah, Hayya 'ala-l-falah.
As-Salatu khairun min an-naum, As-Salatu khairun
min an-naum.
Allahu Akbar, Allahu Akbar.
La ilaha illa-llah

Ignoring Gwynn's sarcasm, Sal responded. "We must return to quarters, now, my old friend. It is time to pray."

Salat Ul Maghrib

The red light of the set sun had finally faded from the sky in the west, leaving a darkness that was still somehow infused with subtle reddish light.

"You are all alike," Saladin Keayrn muttered, wagging his head in near disbelief at his own words while he poured dark tea from a small metal pot that sat on the floor between them. He filled two glasses that looked more like shot glasses than tea cups.

"You care nothing for your heritage, for history, for destiny. You ignore it even when it hangs around your neck like that Medallion you have worn ever since I have known you. A symbol of the Unnamed Knight, the one who is supposed to save everyone, to save everything when all else fails. Yet, you don't even know its significance. Or you refuse to believe. I remember asking you about it one night back in Vietnam. All you told me was that it was a keepsake, a family heirloom passed down from generation to generation that your father willed to you as a good luck piece when he died. Typical of your kind."

He offered Gwynn one of the glasses and took the other one in his right hand. "Be careful. It is quite hot."

"Didn't you learn anything from our failures, Sal?"

"What do you mean? What am I to learn from you or from your history?"

"I'm not all that sure, but what I do know is that the Clan of Gwynn, the Unnamed Kbnight, resides in me whether I like it or not just as the blood of Salah-ad-Din resides in you. How foolish either of us would be to deny this moment. I mean, here we are. Me and my long lost friend Sal Keayrn, better known as Saladin, the son of Saladin Muhammad, faced off like two gunfighters at the OK Corral. And, you seem hell bent on meticulously repeating every mistake of the past. Only this time you guys are the ones who are the invaders. Call it Bellum Sacrum or call it Jihad, it's all the same fraud."

"No, you are wrong. There is one that is not a fraud. Only Jihad, only the way of Salah-ad-Din, defender of Allah, is true and righteous. He captured your relic of the so-called True Cross. He beheaded your so-called elite knights. He took back your so-called Holy City, Jerusalem, and unified and transformed the Muslim world.

"Allah says, 'Not equal are the companions of the fire and the companions of the garden,' and the prophet says, 'Islam is supreme and there is nothing above it. Others fight for worldly gains and lowly and inferior goals. Islam fights so the word of Allah can become supreme.'"

"Then that's why we've been at each other's throats for the past eight hundred years?"

"No, my old friend. We've been at each other's throats as you put it for all these centuries because one of us is right and one of us is wrong." Saladin smiled a grim, thin smile that barely concealed his contempt. "But you have been unwilling to capitulate."

"So, because you think that you and Allah are right and everybody else is wrong, you're going to invade what you perceive to be the stronghold of the infidel by hiding in the bellies of whales like Jonah?"

"Because we are born to serve Allah."

"And, here all these years I've been under the delusion that we are born to survive and reproduce and hopefully make a better world. Whom one chooses to serve is a separate and far less fundamental question than why one is born."

"Mere sophistry, my old friend. Survival. Reproduction. Making a better world. All only to serve Allah, my old friend. Only to serve Allah."

They sipped at their now tepid tea for a long while. Absent any artificial light, the darkening evening seemed to absorb the small room and the two men with it.

"Speaking of serving Allah, Sal. After all this time and all this talk we haven't even talked about your book."

"My book?"

"Yes. I read your book, Sal. The *YUNUS Apparatus Manual for Warriors*. I assume you are The Leader."

Sal bowed his head ever so slightly in a sign of humility barely visible in the lightless room. "Many do call me that, my old friend."

"Then it is your book?"

"Yes. It is my book." He paused. "And you read it?"

"Cover to cover."

"Imagine that. And, how did you ever get a copy? It is very secret, for our training purposes only."

"Not for you to know, but one thing I know for sure, though. Reading it scared the hell out of Abbie."

"My wife read the manual also?"

"She did."

"I'm surprised that she didn't say anything to me about that."

"Probably because she was so afraid and disgusted afterwards."

"Then, she did not understand."

"Then, neither did I. So, enlighten *me*, Sal."

"Enlighten you? How?"

"I could see that you used every single bit of knowledge you learned in our work in Vietnam in writing the manual. The detail in every aspect of being an insurgent was unmistakable. The thought control techniques employed were well chosen and well played. I was particularly impressed by the Tenth Lesson: What is not to be printed or written down."

"Yes, one of my best lessons if viewed in all its simplistic complexity."

"'What is not to be printed or written down is not to be printed or written down. It is obvious that what should not be permitted to be printed or written down cannot be herein published nor can the rules by which this is determined. This will be a verbal only lesson. No notes are to be taken in any form.'"

"I am honored that you could quote from my book from your memory. A memory that is still nothing short of miraculous, my old friend. "

You know, Sal, I can see how you believed in all that stuff they taught us at spook school. It made sense. But do you actually believe all that crap about the spear of Allah and Islam being superior to all other human conditions and earthly religions? Or are you just using all this to get what you want, whatever that is? World domination perhaps?"

Sal smirked. "That would be a typical reaction from your kind, my old friend. You who could never submit to anything bigger than yourself certainly would find it difficult to understand how someone could believe in something as great as Islam."

He paused and his smirk faded to a sad smile as he shook his head, then took the last sip of his now cool tea. "But, yes, I do believe, as you put it, 'all that crap' because it is not crap, my old friend. It is the true way of life, the only way of life. The time will come when you will have to submit or die."

"You see, Sal, that's my biggest problem here. If I have to submit or die, then I am left with no choice at all. I could never live with such a choice as my only choice. I will never submit. Every double helix in my old Scot body rebels at the idea."

Salat Ul Isha'a

A single candle illuminated the darkness from the center of Gwynn's cell-like room. He sat, once again, on a woven palm leaf mat facing west. Sal also sat on the dirt floor on a mat facing east. The candle was situated half way between them as the Ul Isha'a prayer time was half way between sunset and sunrise. Their shadows stretched across the floor and up the walls in rhythm with the flickering of the candle's flame as it danced in the night breezes that slipped down the hallway of the ruined stone masoned building and through the half-opened door.

"We disagree in fundamental ways, Sal. For example, the *Qur'an* promotes public prayer. In fact, Friday special prayer cannot properly be said alone. But, the New Testament tells us to go into our closets to pray. What a contrast, huh?

"That is the great battle, Sal, isn't it? The individual versus the collective?"

"I don't understand your distinction between individuals and the collective. In Islam the individual is the collective and the collective is the individual." Saladin wagged his head in frustrated disbelief. "You must come into the arms of Allah, my old friend. Then, you will not concern yourself with such meaningless Aristotelian shadow debates. Allah provides all the answers as well as all the questions. Join me. Join us. Join powerful groups of students and professionals that form our political and social base for the invasion and takeover that we have patiently built for years. So many are daily saying the words and willingly submitting to the power and control of the Messengers of Allah.

"Within days, the humpbacks will complete the deposits of their cargoes of diamonds, drugs, and YUNUS Apparatus warriors. Our new YUNUS Apparatus army will be complete. Our invasion, planned over the past ten years, will be launched. With you at my side we would be even more invincible!"

"And, here I thought invincible was invincible."

"All you have to do is say the words with conviction, *'La ilaha illa Allah, Muhammadur rasoolu Alla.'*

"This means: 'There is no true god but Allah, and Muhammad is the Messenger of Allah.' Once you have said these words you immediately convert to Islam and become a Muslim.

"Say the words, Gwynn.

"Please, come into the arms of Allah, my old friend. Otherwise, they will very soon crush you."

For the next several days, Sal visited him twice daily, just after Fajr and just after Asr. They continued to debate long and heatedly. He seemed genuinely concerned that should he not be able to convert his old friend, he would surely have to kill him. Gwynn almost felt sorry for him for that.

"Americans seem more interested in the two PC's than in anything else."

"The two PC's?"

"Yes. Pay Check and Political Correctness." His accompanying laugh was somewhere between a sneer and a horse laugh.

"I'm sorry, Sal. I do not follow you."

"Oh, sure you do. You just don't want to admit that your own people are so obsessed with being politically correct that they have made themselves vulnerable to their enemies. They will defend an ashram or a mosque when accused of terrorist activities rather than risk being seen as anti-Muslim. So much to our advantage. We count on this type of behavior in our planning. They are so afraid they won't be able to pay the bills for their avarice and their obsession for things that they will not do anything to possibly damage their ability to get that paycheck. We also count on this in our planning."

Gwynn began to feel grateful to Sal for this kind of dialogue. Not in some Stockholm Syndrome kind of way but, quite the opposite, for forcing him to face up to his past, his Clan history and what it all meant in the here-and-now. He had to face the fact that he *was* the Gwynn that Robert the Bruce had predicted would be called upon someday. And, whether he liked it or not, whether he believed it or not didn't really matter all that much. It was what was. For both him and Sal, it was no longer a matter of belief. The inevitable clash was simply a matter of momentum and had been since the eleventh century.

"What, Sal? No more drugs? No more mind games? No real torture?"

"You have nothing that I want, my old friend. But, even if you did, I am confident that you still know how to combat such tactics."

"So the drugs and solitary and all that was just your normal Middle Eastern Muslim hospitality?"

Sal remained silent and forbearing at the insult.

"No. I can answer that for you, *my* old friend. I do have something you want more than anything."

"And what would that be?"

"My soul." He swept his arms around to indicate the small sand floor room and everything in it. "Otherwise why all this? All the drama? Why this Arthur Koestler *Darkness at Noon* kind of charade where you try to convince me that I belong to a corrupt and evil society that must be cleansed and that only you and your Islam and your Allah can do that. But, I'm not buying, Sal. And, believe me, I know that you are not wrong about a lot of your criticism. But also believe me that your way of dealing with the problems is not the right way as far as I am concerned. And, I know how to combat that too."

"You are mistaken. I only need to keep you caged up until I can fly off to DC and give the signal for the final Jihad to begin." His eyes almost took on a glow as he continued. "Within days after that, the YUNUS Apparatus will execute our most sophisticated plan which we have been developing piece by piece ever since I went missing in action.

"We'll drug them, then scare them—the unbelievers, the Dhimmi. Then we will lull them with the media so we can control them. And, we will keep everyday life so much the same that they will never know the difference," he spat. "Then we will be in control of America the once beautiful and the home of the once brave." He held his right hand up for continued silence.

"And, you're probably going to ask me why in the world am I telling you all this about my planning. That is the last thing one does when confronting one's enemy. But, I would have to answer you that I don't really care at this point what you know because it is just simply too late to stop us. Unless you can kill me right now, within days, my old friend, the United States of America will become the United States of Islam." Saladin's last sentence skidded to a stop as he leaped to his feet, knocking the candle over and abruptly left the room.

The next day, the seventh day of his captivity, the recorded call to prayer for Salat Ul Fajr did not echo throughout the compound at sunrise. Sal did not visit after morning and afternoon prayer times. A couple of local islanders brought him his meals rather than Sal's Muslim cadre, and the food was no longer Middle Eastern Halal. It was West Indian.

McLean, Virginia

Roaring toward DC and the Virginia farm lands beyond at near terminal velocity, Saladin Keayrn realized that a few practice jumps might have been useful. After all, he had not performed a halo jump since Vietnam, even though he had continued to sky dive when he could. The jolt of the chute opening after free falling for close to 20,000 feet was significantly fiercer than he remembered.

As he floated toward a recently plowed field near McLean, Virginia, snatches of his last conversation with Gwynn seemed to force themselves into his thoughts.

"Gwynn, I know that you have lived here in the Caribbean ever since Nam. So, I take it for granted that you've been a little sheltered from much of what has been going on in the world out there to say the least."

"How do you know?"

"From what you tell me and what I have garnered from various intelligence sources. People have been keeping an eye on you all these years."

"I know that."

"But do you know how badly America has fallen over those years? Ever since Vietnam, the USA has become progressively more and more the home, not of the brave, but of the coward. We knew as far back as when we served together that the time would be coming when it would be right for us to take over because the Americans would not fight back."

"Like so many others, Sal, you mistake a reluctance to fight for an unwillingness to fight. You mistake democracy for dhimini. Americans will never sit still for that!"

"Oh, I believe they will, my old friend. I believe they will because they only care about being politically correct and receiving their paychecks . . . ."

"Your two PC's?"

"No, **your** two PC's, my old friend."

His boots hit the plowed field, also much harder than he had remembered, jarring his entire body and shattering his train of thought. He gathered his chute and stashed it in a stand of oaks at the edge of the field, then made his way toward the pre-arranged safe house set up by YUNUS Apparatus sleepers. There he knew he could make contact with the secret YUNUS network throughout the country including those who waited patiently to take charge of the new government. He would also be able to obtain the clothing, explosives, and other assistance he needed to set up The Leader's signal, the special sign that would put his plan in motion.

Whale Island

The antiquated flying goose churned up the aqua sea on the southern coast of Whale Island. Theo Theodora guided the rented seaplane toward the seemingly deserted docking area just off of the entrance to the hidden Whale Cove. Jean-Lafette Quetel's gnarled fingers nearly punched holes in the leather of the co-pilot's seat. He had never been in a seaplane before. Until today, he had been very happy with boats being boats and planes being planes. And, he would be very pleased when that reality returned to his life.

"Sure dis be da right place, Mr. T'eo? Doan' look like nobody be here, me-son. Nobody, dat is, but da Brown Pelican, Mr. T'eo."

Theo glanced in the direction of Jean-Lafette's pointing hand. The Brown Pelican was the only other craft of any sort tied up at the dock. "That is what my intel says, Quetel."

"Okay, me-son. We be checking it'out." The left pontoon of the plane bumped against the moorings. Jean-Lafette opened the door and hopped off the plane onto the weathered wooden pier. He grabbed a couple of lines and secured the pontoon as Theo cut the engines. This he was familiar with. It was the same as with a boat.

"Grab those two Glocks out of my brief case, Quetel. And the extra clips. Just because the place looks deserted doesn't mean it is."

Jean-Lafette quickly pulled the weapons from a battered leather briefcase stowed behind the pilot's seat and checked the two nine millimeters to make sure they were locked and loaded and ready to use if necessary.

"So, you're a little more familiar with hand guns than you are with airboats, Quetel?"

"Right ya be, Mr. T'eo. I, too, spent my time in da military way back in da day."

Once ashore, they searched frantically for Abbie and Gwynn. What they found was deserted Quonset hut after deserted Quonset hut and empty crumbling stone building after empty collapsing stone building with signs of laboratories, dormitories, and offices operating there until very recently. There was, however, absolutely no evidence that anyone still inhabited the compound.

After nearly an hour of careful, cautious searching, they finally found Gwynn performing Thai Chi in his captive's quarters.

"We thought we'd have to fight our way in and back out to the seaplane, LT," Theo offered, almost as an explanation for the weapons he and Jean-Lafette were carrying. "But here we are and there doesn't seem to be anyone around except you."

"About time you guys got here!" Gwynn quipped. "I was just

about to lose track of what day it is."

"By the way, LT. What day is it?"

"Doan' make it hard on da boy, Mr. T'eo. Let's see can we find de Sen-a-tor now."

As they continued to search the complex for any sign of Abbie, they discovered a DVD in the security room and played it while the three of them watched. The video showed a woman covered in a black Afghan chadri walking along the beach at Whale Cove. Whales frolicked in the background as one by one a crowd of men began to gather around her, cutting her off from the sea.

The first stone seemed to be thrown in slow motion as Gwynn stared, transfixed, awaiting the impact. When the smooth white throwing stone hit her skull, Gwynn winced when he heard the crack. A hail of stones followed so rapidly that he could no longer differentiate the sounds of individual stones hitting her body now crumpled and bleeding on the white sand.

Gwynn almost lost his balance for a moment as he reached out to the woman in the video, hoping against hope that if he could only touch her maybe he could save her. A part of him understood how irrational that was. Another part of him did not care. Tears drizzled down his cheeks, and he did not attempt to dry them or hide them. He wore them like badges of honor for a member of the team. "That's Abbie," he wept. "How could he do that to his own wife?"

"How can you be sure, LT? I mean, that chadri the woman's wearing covers everything but her eyes."

Gwynn reversed the disc and replayed the beginning. Within a few seconds, the camera shooting the incident zoomed in to a close shot of the woman as she turned toward the camera just as a cadre man hurled the first stone. He paused the disc. Her eyes were frozen on the screen of the monitor. "Those eyes, Theo. Look at those hazel eyes. They are seeking help, mercy, something other than what she knows is to come. And, Theo, Jean-Lafette, those hazel eyes belong to Senator Abigail Keayrn."

"You've got to stop Sal, LT. You know that, don't you?"

"Yes, hell, I know that, Theo."

"Have any idea where the man be at, me-son?"

"Yes, I think I actually do, Jean-Lafette." He turned toward Theo, staring directly into his eyes. "What I don't have any idea about is why you didn't think, just maybe, it would be a good idea for me to know that Sal Keayrn was the person I was after? One of our own. One very dangerous 'mother'."

"Okay, LT. I will admit I made an error in judgment."

"Correction, Junior. You made a HUMONGUS error in judgment! A FATAL error in judgment!"

"All right, a humongus and fatal error in judgment, LT. I know I really screwed up here, but it's all working out." He gunned the seaplane engines as Jean-Lafette untied the mooring lines and jumped aboard.

"Except for the Senator. I don't think it's working out so well for her, now is it, Junior."

Theo averted his eyes as images from the video disc they had found flashed in his mind. He realized that for Gwynn to call him Junior, his old Vietnam nickname because he was second in command of the field team, he had to be angry as all hell at some kind of sub atomic particle level or something. "I am truly, truly sorry for that LT." He tried hard to wipe the images of the woman in a black Afghan chadri being stoned to death on the beach by concentrating on the take off. "I would do anything if I could make that right again." He glanced over his left shoulder at Jean-Lafette. "Get to the Brown Pelican and take her home, Quetel."

"Right, ya be, Mr. T'eo!" Jean-Lafette dropped from the airboat cabin back to the dock and sprinted toward the Governor's motor yacht without looking back.

"Seal the door, LT." Theo heard the door lock snap shut. "Let's di di mau!" He gunned the engines again and steered the seaplane toward the open sea. A long silver blue plume of water blossomed from its wake. "It's a long way from here to DC!"

Washington, DC

"This is INN breaking news." The sixty-four inch television seemed to stretch and swell in size in the Watergate ballroom as video footage of a coastal area buffeted by rough seas filled the screen. Slickered rescuers pulled two bodies from the breaking waves. Members of Washington's elite froze, some with salmon mousse canapés almost touching parted lips, others in mid-swallow of Moet Chandon or Cristal, and still others with nearly-spoken words on their tongues like hors d'oeuvres.

"Just a short time ago, the bodies of Department of Justice Investigator Aaron Silver and a female employee of The Whale Institute, Bridget Yow, were recovered after they had been reported as washed overboard in an unexpected storm which blew up while they were aboard a Whale Institute vessel looking for a large pod of whales that had been reported off the coast of Maui.

"We don't know for sure yet. But, according to Executive Director of The Whale Institute Lars Hansen—who was aboard the vessel when the two young people were washed overboard—a tragic accident."

"Ellworth. Excuse me. Jasmine in New York."

"Yes, Jasmine?"

"I have Gerald Hathaway, Assistant Attorney General and administrative Chief of the Environmental Section, on the telephone."

"Great, Jasmine. Let's hear what he has to say."

"I have with me via videophone, the Assistant Attorney General, Gerald Hathaway, who was Investigator Aaron Silver's boss. Mr. Hathaway. Thank you for talking with us under these difficult circumstances. Our sympathies go out to Mr. Silver's family and friends as well as to you and the agency."

"Thank you, Jasmine. Aaron Silver was a fine young man who was just beginning to build a great career here at Justice." Hathaway rolled his balding gray head as he spoke. "It seems that poor Aaron and the young woman from the Whale Institute who had been acting as his guide and assistant during his stay met with a terrible, terrible accident."

"That's what has been reported, Mr. Assistant Attorney General, but do you have any further details?"

"Well, Jasmine, according to Lars Hansen, Executive Director of the Whale Institute." He struggled to get the words out. "It seems that what transpired was that Mr. Silver—Aaron—became sea sick.

"The Whale Institute vessel was out to view a particularly large pod of humpback whales that had been spotted earlier in the morning by a small plane flying over the islands. Anyway, Ms. Yow—Bridget Yow—rushed forward to help him. The seas were particularly rough and the winds were high from a sudden gale that had blown up. That was probably what made Aaron sick. Just as she reached Aaron, a series of waves washed over the bow sweeping them overboard into the sea." He seemed to hold back tears as he cut off his sentence.

"And, this tragedy would never have happened if Senator Abigail Keayrn hadn't insisted on and, in fact, intimidated my boss, the Attorney General into sending an investigator out there for no apparent reason except her own political gain. That investigator was young Aaron Silver."

"I know this has been painful. Thank you for talking with us this evening Assistant Attorney General Gerald Hathaway.

"We're still attempting to reach Senator Keayrn for her comments on this tragic incident. Two young people drowned off the coast of Maui during a Department of Justice investigation. As soon as we are able to locate Senator Keayrn, we'll bring that interview to you live.

"This is Jasmine for INN news."

* * * * *

"Good evening, once again. This is Ellworth Hayes, and we have an INN Breaking News Alert. Just moments ago, our own Jasmine brought you an exclusive interview with Assistant Attorney General Gerald Hathaway regarding the drowning of one of his staff members. We believe, now, that INN's co-anchor has finally been able to locate Senator Abigail Keayrn for her comments on his death and a response to allegations from the Assistant Attorney General that she was responsible for Silver's death by drowning while on a Whale watching expedition off of Maui. We take you to Jasmine and an exclusive video phone interview in the Russell Building offices of Senator Abbie Keayrn, Democrat from Florida.

The screen went black. Then a very close shot of Elle Darby's face appeared. "Jasmine, I'm sorry to have to inform you that our office has received as yet unconfirmed reports that Abbie—ah, Senator Abigail Keayrn—has been killed while on a fact-finding mission in the Grenadines. It is so terribly ironic that this news should come at the same time as the news about the tragic deaths of Aaron Silver and Bridget Yow. Not only was he investigating the Whale Institute at Senator Keayrn's request, but, on a more personal note, he was my roommate. So, as you can imagine, the past several hours have been terribly trying.

"Beyond that, Jasmine, Aaron Silver's preliminary reports

indicated that he was on to something about the disappearance of a large number of humpback whales over the past several years never reported by the Whale Institute. The Senator believed they might be some of the same whales that have recently been washing up on our beaches. She also believed this to be, possibly, part of a major terrorist plot being put into play from the Caribbean. And, Jasmine, it was something big enough that Aaron Silver, Bridget Yow, and Senator Abigail Keayrn are all now dead because of it!"

Tears burned at the edges of her eyes.

"And, I'm going to find out what happened to them, no matter what it takes or who gets in the way." She paused, brushing tears from her flushed cheeks.

"Thank you for allowing me this opportunity to speak to Assistant Attorney General Hathaway's ludicrous and insensitive allegations. However, I will not dignify his allegations with a response. Suffice it to say, there's something very suspicious about the Assistant AG's explanation, since Aaron Silver has never been sea sick a day in his life. Air sick, yes. Sea sick, never! Quirky but true.

"And, finally, this office will have no further comment until there has been a full follow-up investigation to determine whether the Senator died accidentally or was killed, very possibly we think by Islamic terrorists planning to invade this country."

"Thank you, Elle Darby, Chief of Staff for Senator Abigail Keayrn, Democrat from Florida. Our hearts here at INN go out to you and the rest of Senator Keayrn's staff, friends, and family at this time."

"Thank you, Jasmine."

* * * * *

"Well, I guess we're finally rid of that damned girl, at least, Mr. President Designate Hansen." Senator T.J. clicked off the flat screen television mounted on the wall directly opposite his desk—a desk that had been used by Senator Everett Dirksen when he was Republican minority leader back in the sixties. T.J. now held the position of Ranking Member of the Committee on Homeland Security and Governmental Affairs. But, he was very much ready for a change, as much so as old Ev Dirksen was ready for it during the vote for cloture on the filibuster against the Civil Rights Act when he said that there was "no force so powerful as an idea whose time has come."

The senator waved his left hand in a manner indicating he wanted Larson Hansen to close the door behind him. He agreed absolutely and completely with the late Senator for whom this building that contained his offices was named. And this new idea whose time had come was more powerful than anything since old Ev's days in the Senate.

"Is that so, Mr. Vice President Designate? Is that so?" He eased the door shut.

"Yes, sir. I've been told on good authority that The Leader had her stoned to death in the Grenadines when she and that coward Camsron tried to stop him."

"Yes, Camsron escaped and fled without any concern for her life, so I understand."

"That's what I hear, too, sir. That's absolutely right. And, The Leader?"

"The Leader is eternal and invincible. He meets with me every day via satellite, and I can assure you that he plans to give the unmistakable signal tonight at the Washington Monument to begin the takeover. Then, all of our sleepers throughout the country, even in the highest levels of corporate America, and obviously among our most powerful leadership, will awaken."

11
The Bust of Balzac

[Music: "The Essential Human Conflict"]

The manila envelope arrived addressed to Elle Darby in Aaron's meticulous handwriting. Elle's hands trembled under the weight of the envelope. Tears scalded her usually tough sienna eyes. Her fingers fumbled with the metal clasp, then tore off the gummed flap. She sucked in a very deep breath and held it as if it were the last breath she would ever be able to draw. As she finally exhaled very slowly, she separated the top of the envelope and looked inside, then dumped the contents onto the coffee table in front of her.

"If only Abbie were here," she muttered. "But, at least someone can finally see what Aaron gave his life for."

She sifted through the items as if she hoped somehow to get a "vibe" or something simply from touching the objects themselves. Three mini-cassette tapes that she had no way of playing. Four computer flash drives that she quickly glanced at on her laptop contained a myriad of documents linking the Whale Institute directly to likely whale-nappers and smugglers through contributions from a global non-profit, Submission Whale Research, and many other non-profits all eventually traceable back to SWR. Contributions to the Institute all began around the same time period when whales began to disappear without a trace. Also, Hawaii Office of Elections and Federal Elections Commission fund raising reports showed that Lars Hansen CEO of the Institute and a super pac Hansen for a New America had received a major portion of their contributions from those same interests when Hansen had entered the early Presidential primaries after the President had appointed his VP to the Supreme Court in an unprecedented move. In a memo from Hansen to Institute Senior Staff obviously designed to address the issue of his candidacy, he stated that these were not attempts at running against the sitting President for the Presidential nomination. Instead, these primaries would prove how popular a choice he would make for the number two spot.

Some hand-scratched daily log entries that seemed to create a kind of "things to do" list.

1.   Immerse the people in the water of truth. YUNUS to deliver Tears of Allah into water supplies nationwide within twenty-four hours after The Leader's signal.

No one is God but Allah. Allahu Akbar!

2.   Then, smash the Balzac plaster on loan from the Musee d'Orsay in Paris. It epitomizes the decline into total sin and arrogance by the west. Even to this day it still provokes the public's displeasure because of the association with an erected phallus and the fact that the critics claimed that the hand of Rodin worked not as the hand of a sculptor works but as if the Hand of God was his own hand.

No one is God but Allah. Allahu Akbar!

3.   Next, shred the canvas of *The Tower of Babel, 1563* by Pieter Bruegel the Elder on loan from Kunsthistorisches Museum Vienna. The painting was originally supposed to demonstrate the dangers of human pride. Instead, Bruegel treated the subject of the construction of the Tower of Babel as it was, according to the *Bible,* a tower built by humanity to reach heaven.

No one is God but Allah. Allahu Akbar!

4.   Then, pour the acid onto *Mending the Nets.* In one great moment, we will dissolve the fishing village of Cullercoats, England that Winslow Homer believed conveyed the notion of the importance of skills acquired through generations of families at work. Mending, along with dividing the catch and distributing the fish at market, occupied the fisherwomens' time for most of the day. Just because it is their work.

No one is God but Allah. Allahu Akbar!

5.   And, slash the Pollock into shreds. Any Pollock. All Pollocks. The drunken god of pollycock.

No one is God but Allah. Allahu Akbar!

Through their art they defile us and they insult Allah.

No one is God but Allah. Allahu Akbar!

A paperclip attached pages of rambling handwritten notes on plain stationery to an 8"x10" black-and-white glossy of The Buddhas of Bamyan.

"There is only one way to control the Dhimmi until we can convert or eliminate them. We will destroy everything they have made in every way possible just as we smashed the two idols that had been carved into the side of a cliff in the Bamyan valley in the Hazarajat region of central Afghanistan during the sixth century."

The notes continued.

"They hewed the main bodies of the two statues directly from the sandstone cliffs. The artisans created details in mud mixed with straw coated with stucco and painted them to enhance the expressions of the faces, hands, and folds of the robes. They constructed lower parts of the statues' arms from the same mud-straw mix.

"And, the Taliban dynamited them on orders from leader Mullah Mohammed Omar.

"I, The Leader, was there when we destroyed them because they were built by the people and they represented the people and their culture both which we could not allow.

"One after another the icons of self-indulgent, unenlightened, infidel cultures will fall under the saber of the avenging Messengers live on international television. The same cleansing will take place all across the country once I, The Leader, have given the unmistakable signal to begin.

"The next blood drawn will not be simply plaster, paints, and canvas. It will be the infidels, the kuffar themselves, who will finally bleed.

"No one is God but Allah. Allahu Akbar!"

Copies of several typed pages copied from some larger document that seemed to be related to training of Jihad warriors were rolled up with a couple of rubber bands.

THIRTEENTH LESSON

TEAM WORK
PRISONS AND DETENTION CENTERS

IF AN INDICTMENT IS ISSUED AND THE TRIAL BEGINS, THE
WARRIOR HAS TO PAY ATTENTION TO THE FOLLOWING:

1. At the beginning of the trial, once more the warriors must
insist on proving that torture was inflicted on them by security
or police investigators before the judge.

2. Complain to the court of mistreatment while in prison.

3. Make arrangements for the warrior's defense with the
attorney, whether he was retained by the warrior's family or
court-appointed.

4. The warrior has to do his best to know the names of the state
security officers who participated in his torture and mention
their names to the judge. [These names may be obtained from
warriors who had to deal with those officers in previous cases.]

5. Some warriors may tell and may be lured by the police and
security investigators to testify against other warriors
[i.e.affirmation witness], either by not keeping them together in
the same prison during the trials, or by letting them talk to the
media. In this case, they have to be treated gently, and should be
offered good advice, good treatment, and pray that Allah may
guide them.

6. During the trial, the court has to be notified of any mistreatment of the warriors inside the prison.

7. It is possible to resort to a hunger strike, but it is a tactic that *can* either succeed or fail.

8. Take advantage of visits to communicate with warriors outside prison and exchange information that may be helpful to them in their work outside prison [according to what occurred during the investigations]. The importance of mastering the art of hiding messages is self-evident here.

9. When the warriors are transported from and to the prison [on their way to the court] they should shout Islamic slogans out loud from inside the prison cars to impress upon the people and their family the need to support Islam.

10. Inside the prison, the warrior should not accept any work that may belittle or demean him or his fellow warriors, such as the cleaning of the prison bathrooms or hallways.

11. The warriors should create an Islamic program for themselves inside the prison, as well as recreational and educational ones, etc.

12. The warrior in prison should be a role model in selflessness. Warriors should also pay attention to each other's needs and should help each other and unite vis a vis the prison officers.

13. The warriors must take advantage of their presence in prison for obeying and worshipping Allah and memorizing the

Qur'an. This is in addition to all guidelines and procedures that were contained in the lesson on interrogation and investigation.

Lastly, each of us has to understand that we don't achieve victory against our enemies through these actions and security procedures. Rather, victory is achieved by obeying Almighty and Glorious Allah. Every warrior has to be careful not to commit sins and every one of us has to do his best in obeying Almighty Allah, who said in his Holy Book: "We will, without doubt, help Our Messengers and those who believe in this world's life and the Day when the Witnesses will stand forth."

May Allah guide the YUNUS APPARATUS.

DEDICATION

To this pure Muslim youth, the believer, the mujahid for Allah's sake.

I present this modest effort as a contribution from me to pave the way that will lead to Almighty Allah and to establish a true Caliphate along the lines of the prophet.

The prophet, may Allah bless him and grant him peace, said, "Let the prophecy that Allah wants to be in you, yet Allah may remove it if He so wills, and then there will be a Caliphate according to the prophet's instruction, if Allah so wills it.

"He will also remove that Caliphate if He so wills, and you will have a disobedient king if Allah so wills it. Once again, if Allah so wills, He will remove the disobedient king, and you will have an oppressive king. Finally, if Allah so wills, He will remove the oppressive king, and you will have a Caliphate according to the prophet's instruction."

THE IMPORTANCE OF TEAM WORK:

1. Team work is the only translation of Allah's command, as well as that of the prophet, to unite and not to disunite. Almighty Allah says, "And hold fast, all together, by the Rope which Allah stretches out for you, and be not divided among yourselves." In *Asahih Muslim*, it was reported by Abu Horairah, may Allah look kindly upon him, that the prophet, may Allah's peace and greetings be upon him, said: "Allah approves three things for you and disapproves three things: He approves that you worship him, that you do not disbelieve in Him, and that you hold fast, all together, by the Rope which Allah provides, and be not divided among yourselves. He disapproves of three: gossip, asking too much for help, and squandering money."

2. Abandoning "team work" for individual and haphazard work means disobeying the orders of Allah and the prophet and falling victim to disunity.

3. Team work is conducive to cooperation in righteousness and piety.

4. Upholding religion, which Allah has ordered us by His saying, "Uphold religion," will necessarily require an all out confrontation against all our enemies, who want to recreate darkness. In addition, it is imperative to stand against darkness in all arenas: the media, education, religious

guidance, and counseling, as well as others. This will make it necessary for us to move on numerous fields so as to enable the Islamic movement to confront ignorance and achieve victory against it in the battle to uphold religion.

All these vital goals cannot be adequately achieved without organized team work. Therefore, team work becomes a necessity, in accordance with the fundamental rule: "Duty cannot be accomplished without it, and it is a requirement." This way, team work is achieved through mustering and organizing the ranks, while putting The Leader before them, and the right man in the right place, making plans for action, organizing work, and obtaining facets of power.

The Leader.

IN THE NAME OF THE LEADER, MAY ALLAH GUIDE HIM, IN THE NAME OF THE PROPHET, MAY ALLAH BLESS HIM AND GRANT HIM PEACE IN THE NAME OF ALLAH, THE MERCIFUL AND COMPASSIONATE.

Finally, a crumpled sheet of lined notebook paper that had been flattened out and folded in half. On one side, Aaron had scribbled: "Why in the world would Hansen have such stuff in his files at all, even hidden away?" The other side of the torn page held a crude cartoon-like drawing in Aaron's hand of what appeared to be bull's horns and July 4 written between the horns.

Elle suddenly became aware that she was trembling as if she were chilled from the inside out. She knew she had to get this material to someone who could make sense of it all and do so right away. This seemed like some kind of blueprint of a plot to destroy the country. Abbie's brother-in-law was a phone call away. She picked up her phone and began to dial the Director of the FBI's private line with shaking fingers.

12
Eclipse on the Ellipse

[Music: "The Essential Human Conflict"]

"Back away everyone!" Gwynn shouted as he thrashed his way through the throng that had been gathering for hours around the Washington Monument behind a security line of Capitol Hill and District of Columbia Police. "Get back!"

"If you've just tuned in," Ellworth Hayes whispered into his microphone, "this is Ellworth Hayes." He stared directly into the depths of Camera Two even though he could see on the monitor to his right that the picture being telecast was not of him but of a man yelling at the crowd to back away from the Monument. Then he received his cue in his ear.

"Hello, America and the world. The images you are seeing on your television screens are being shot in the crowd that has been gathering for nearly an hour now as word circulated that there was an unidentified man in a robe standing under the Washington Monument and shouting in a mixture of English and Arabic. One by one, the world's news organizations have set up shop, yet, to this point in time, no one seems sure of what his rants mean. Both the DC and Capitol Hill Police have suggested that the yet-to-be-identified man seems to be threatening to blow up the Washington Monument.

"The Monument was designed by architect Robert Mills. Construction began in 1848 but was interrupted by the American Civil War, so it was not completed until 1884. It was formally dedicated in 1885 on February 22, Washington's Birthday. At that time, it was the tallest structure on the planet and cost almost two million dollars to build, a huge sum in those days. It would be about forty-two million in today's dollars.

"Tonight, it seems that an unidentified man in a hooded robe is threatening to blow it up. All we can do is continue to bring you the coverage in more depth than anyone else on television. We are all waiting to see how this will play itself out in the shadows on the Ellipse on this night before the Fourth of July."

As Camera Two flashed ready to go live, the monitor zoomed in on the face of the man yelling at the crowd. "Back away! Please back up everyone! This man is serious."

"My God!" Ellworth went limp, almost fainting. "My God! That's Gwynn Camsron!" Suddenly, his director queued him in his ear piece that he was live. Suddenly, he realized that the monitor picture had changed to a close up of his face without his realizing it. "Ladies and Gentlemen, it seems . . . ." He gulped to gain some control. He was still very lightheaded. But, after all, he was live in front of hundreds of millions of people around the world. He had to maintain some decorum. "It seems, to my absolute shock and astonishment, I actually know the man you just saw yelling for the crowd to get back. He is an old Vietnam War buddy of mine, Gwynn Camsron. We were on the same special operations team in Vietnam and served together for nearly three years."

Gwynn turned toward the hooded man on the other side of the police line. "This man is here to kill history, not people! So, if you leave now, you will be safe. Isn't that right, Sal?" he yelled from just behind the police line. "Isn't that right Saladin Kearyn Muhammad?"

"Sal Keayrn? Muhammad? This is becoming stranger by the moment, even more *Twilight Zone*-like than all those whales landing on our beaches recently. The unidentified man in the hooded robe, it seems, may be another of our old Vietnam War teammates, Sal Keayrn. Until now, he was listed as MIA in 1969 and declared dead just a few years ago. He was the husband of the late Senator Abigail Kearyn whom we just reported died while on an investigative trip to the Caribbean. Is there some connection here that we don't know about yet?"

"Get back, sir," the policeman directly in front of Gwynn instructed.

"But, officer, I'm trying to save lives here. I know this man. We served together in Vietnam. I used to be his commanding officer, and I can assure you he is deadly serious about blowing up this Momument. Maybe I can talk some sense into him."

"PTSD or Gulf Syndrome? Something like that?"

"Something like that. Please, officer, let me try."

The officer rattled off something incoherent to Gwynn into his shoulder mounted communication device. "Copy that," he responded to what seemed to be only static to Gwynn. "Okay, pal. You got your chance. But, headquarters says you've got to stay behind the line here."

The moon glowed through a rip in the clouds above the capitol. Its golden light cascaded over the Ellipse much like the light on a stage. Only, Gwynn was no longer a part of the audience. He was now directly on stage, and he could no longer avoid his role by slipping off into the night to go fight some war. This *was* the war.

"Sal! Listen to me, man," Gwynn shouted past the police officer in front of him. "You don't really want to do this."

As a result of the moonlight, the shadow of Saladin Keayrn, the only son of Saladin Muhammad, danced behind him as straight as the spire he stood beneath. The moonlight spilled down from the peak over the entire obelisk creating what seemed to be a giant golden needle reaching skyward in the bright lights that illuminated the Washington Monument at night. As he paced about seemingly agitated, his off-white hooded tunic, dyed gold by the moonlight, seemed to blend into the Monument giving him an intermittent invisibility. But, even when he seemed to disappear, the shadow he cast upon the Monument remained.

Ellworth still seemed to be stunned by the turn of events and rambled on as if he were just half-consciously relating a story to someone there in the studio with him. "I can't figure out why Sal Keayrn is there, threatening the Monument. I mean, we served together in some pretty difficult circumstances in Vietnam. Basically, we did the Army's dirty work so to speak. He was a great soldier. A trusted team member. Then, on a mission north of—I guess I can say it by now—the DMZ, he went missing during an unintended fire fight with a scout squad of North Vietnamese regulars. We just accidently ran into each other. Sal was never heard from again.

"His wife and widow Abigail Keayrn became a leader in the MIA/POW movement in the seventies and rose to prominence, first in the United States Congress and then in the Senate. Until her reported death, Senator Keayrn was on track to become the President's running mate in the upcoming election.

"Now, she is dead, and her dead husband is alive. Talk about irony heaped upon irony."

Saladin's left hand held the detonator. The wudu cleansed fingers of his open right hand reached toward the heavens. "There is no God but Allah, and Muhammad is his Messenger." Saladin's voice projected out over the mall as if he were a muezzin summoning the people to prayer from a mosque's minaret. His voice almost seemed to be electronically amplified. "There is no God but Allah, and I, too, am His Messenger."

Television cameras from all over the United States and around the world whirred as the shadow's words spewed into the microphones and camera lenses closing in on his face, a face that was nearly invisible within the confines of the hood covering his head and the ever-present black turban. "In the name of Allah the merciful and compassionate."

Without warning or expectation, tear gas canisters began exploding around them permeating the air with a dense but transluscent foggy gas. Even the officers manning the police line were taken by surprise. They had not been equipped with gas masks and began to disburse involuntarily as many of them were overcome by the fumes.

INN's cameras focused on thousands of people fleeing almost as if they were choreographed. Saladin and the Monument seemed to disappear momentarily in the tear gas fog.

Both Gwynn and Sal knew how to control their reactions. Each had made it through the Army's special tear gas training without his mask. Even if it had been nearly forty years ago, you didn't forget stuff like that. Their watering, burning eyes penetrated the gas fog and locked for a moment. They could hear each other breathing. Their voices seemed to be the only sounds on the Ellipse just like they used to in the old days in the jungles. It was almost like hearing the other's voice inside one's head telepathically rather than hearing spoken words through one's ears—the language of shadows.

"You really sure you want to do this, Sal?"

In response, Sal waved the detonator in his left hand above his head. The tear gas had been bad enough, but the overt threat of actually being blown to hell and back triggered the human impulse for self-preservation of the men and women from around the world who had continued to cover the story. Finally they fled, leaving all their equipment behind and their cameras still shooting. Even the last remnants of the police line seemed to disappear into the fleeing mass. For a moment, television screens around the world went black.

"Sorry for that brief interruption," Ellworth Hayes whispered as if he were within a few feet of the scene rather than safely inside the INN Washington studios. "What you are all seeing on your television screens right now is being broadcast live over an INN satellite link via several different INN cameras abandoned due to the imminent threat of a suicide bomber at the Washington Monument.

"That means we are technically no longer live at the Monument, because there is a delay of a few seconds in order to give our great director and staff a chance to edit in the best shots as we go and to correct the aspect of the pictures so you will see the video properly rather than at odd angles or upside down which is how the pictures are coming in to us. We apologize in advance that due to the angles of our cameras that are still functioning we may see only what appear to be more like silhouettes than actual pictures of the people.

"It appears that a man whom we, exclusively, have identified as Sal Keayrn, Vietnam War veteran—supposedly deceased—is threatening to blow up the Washington Monument. A second man, whom we have also, exclusively, identified as Gwynn Camsron another Vietnam War teammate of Sal Keayrn—and of mine—is attempting to talk him out of it. Let's tune in to what we can still see and hear."

"It's not too late, you know, Sal. We can still get out of this mess."

"How did you even get here, Gwynn?"

"It wasn't easy, Sal. You remember Theo, don't you? He and a friend from St. Thomas helped me escape."

"I made a big mistake not killing you then."

"Yeah, Sal, you did. You should've killed me when you had the chance. That was always the way, wasn't it? Leave no living enemies behind. Did that in some way conflict with our oaths to each other?"

"Yes, but I had truly hoped, my old friend, that you would change your mind and embrace Allah. I guess I still haven't learned that lesson well enough. I still can't bring myself to violate our vow to protect our teammates no matter what. Everyone else has fled. So, I'm going to offer you thirty seconds."

"Thirty seconds. Is that all I get, Sal?"

"That's all you're ever going to get from me, my old friend. Once I press this little red button, I will become history. So, that thirty seconds will have to count for all you believe I owe you for what you consider to be my betrayal.

"That will make it midnight. It will be July 4—Independence Day in America." He paused as his face contorted into a mask of anger. "But it is also the anniversary of the great Salah ad-Din's victory against the Crusaders at the Horns of Hattin." As he spoke those words, his face transformed into a vessel of pride and rapture. "It will be my final Salat Ul Isha'a.

"In thirty seconds, there will be no turning back. In thirty seconds, a new order of all things will begin like it did at Hattin. In thirty seconds, Islam will rule the world as the *Qur'an* says it should."

"Come on, Sal. Look at you. Look at me. Look at us. Look around you, man. Witness what religion has wrought." But, the timbre of Sal's voice made Gwynn realize that even a former Kit Carson teammate's words were futile at this stage. No one, probably not even Sal himself, could shake his resolve now. Final action was nearly upon them as the bell at St. Anthony's Cathedral began tolling in a new day.

"Do you remember our team motto, Gwynn?"

"Better to be Falstaff than dead."

"That's right! A rather erudite motto for a bunch of super killers, wouldn't you say?"

"I would say but practical nonetheless."

Saladin's left thumb prepared to depress the detonator. "So, di di mau, Falstaff. Run for what's left of your super killer life!"

Gwynn the Falstaffian, knew without any doubt that Sal meant it, so he was up to full speed within a few steps. For a brief moment, he actually thought about how fortunate he was that he still kept in shape and ran nearly every day, as he put it, even at his age. As he continued to sprint away from ground zero, he could almost hear the detonator being pushed by the left hand thumb of a person he once thought he could always trust to watch his back.

"My God!" Ellworth Hayes gasped in front of the entire world. "Sal's going to do it. He's really going to . . . ."

The sound of the explosion interrupted Ellworth Hayes and nearly erased Saladin Keayrn's final words, the words he hurled into the air like grenades. The blast ignited charges that had been planted around the inside walls of the monument by a YUNUS Apparatus support team that had been working as grounds keepers at the park for months. Yet the almost melodic screams that were Saladin Keayrn's final words in Arabic escaped the tear gas fog and the ear-splitting explosion. They soared skyward hovering over the Ellipse like a chant. The dust cloud from the explosion blotted out the golden glow of the moon and, with it, all the shadows.

"Good God! Did you feel that?" Ellworth's response to the earthquake-like tremors was automatic and uncensored. It was genuine and personal. Almost immediately realizing his lapse, he faced his world-wide audience once again with composure. "We just felt the reverberations of that explosion here at our studios, and we are located several blocks away." Ellworth jerked his head from side to side looking for some guidance from one of his producers or directors as to what Sal's last words might have been. "There goes the tallest stone obelisk on earth. There goes the greatest symbol of our revolution, of our democracy. There goes the live shot that serves as our backdrop every day on INN Morning News."

"What?" Gwynn glanced around him, confused, disoriented, surprised that he was still alive, that the force of the explosion had not at least knocked him to the ground. He felt the warmth of his own blood dribbling from his ears. "What did he say?" His head was ringing so loudly he almost couldn't hear his own question.

Sal's words seemed to bounce back toward earth off of that sky heavy with dust. It mixed with those words chiseled in stone as the monument honoring the first President of the United States of America began to crumble. As if in slow motion, marble, granite, and sandstone chunks collapsed and tumbled into what appeared to be the Inferno itself. One of the chunks bore the inscription: *Laus Deo*. "Praise be to God."

"Did anyone hear what he said?" Suddenly, Gwynn realized that he was the only person still standing. Everyone around him still hugged the ground or huddled under a park bench or any cover they could find, even each other, shielding their heads from the force of the explosion with their arms and hands.

"Allahu akbar!" The sound of the words crept from under a tattered gray cloak lump beneath a bench to his left. The outline of an ancient face peered from the shadows of the loose hood. "The martyr, may Allah be pleased with him, shouted, 'God is great!'"

"Allahu akbar!" Saladin's words continued to reverberate among the final crashes of the crumbling Monument. "Allahu akbar! Allahu akbar!"

"And, so it begins," Gwynn muttered, rubbing the Medallion that hung around his neck with his right thumb and forefinger and staring at the pit of hell sprawled out over the Ellipse. "And, so it begins."

Through The Gates

"Lasciate ogne speranza, voi ch'intrate"

13

[Music: "The Ache" (0-2:05)]

Journeys always seemed to begin with entering a dark wood or sailing some wine-dark sea. American naturalist and journalist, Chace Durante's journey began with flying into Glasgow aboard an International Charter Jets Gulfstream 550 GV. The luxury jet had been privately chartered out of Richmond, Virginia by Appears Global, Incorporated—an international media conglomerate of newspapers, magazines, radio and television stations, and Internet sites that practically blanketed the globe. From Glasgow, Chace Durante took Scotrain to the town furthest north in Scotland, Scrabster, the jumping off point for the Orkney Islands. Orkneyjar. Seal Islands. However one styled it, those islands were becoming a focal point for investigations concerning an unexplained and continuing decrease in the population of Harbor Seals. It had become an environmentalist hobby horse over the past several years. The islands were also experiencing one of the worst economic downturns on the planet. Since the ascendancy of the United States of Islam, their American tourism had just about dried up. He was there to take a look for *Neo Geo*, the Caliphate approved replacement for *National Geographic*.

Chace over-nighted at the Ferry Inn in Scrabster. He wanted to find out if anyone knew or had ever heard of a woman called the Wise Woman of Hoy. She was rumored to be some kind of seer or something who had her own special theory about the disappearance of the seals, one that did not comport with the scientific ones. That was his one intriguing lead. After overnight turned into several days of inquiries, especially with the area newspapers like *The Inverness Courier*, *The Caithness Courier*, and *The John O'Groats Journal*, Chace ran across a reporter at *O'Groats* who remembered an interview he did as a first-year reporter for *The Orcadian*.

Miles "Virgil" Kirk had been assigned a human interest story on a really old woman who was supposed to be some kind of witch or something. She had a name that was steeped in tradition and magic. But, it was not the Wise Woman of Hoy. As far as anyone knew, the Wise Woman of Hoy was only a character out of Norse mythology.

The woman Virgil had interviewed four years earlier had, at that time, lived in Stromness, and she was actually called the Seeress of Stromness by all who knew her. His recollection was that she believed the sudden disappearance of so many seals was due to Finfolk magic emanating from a small island north of Mainland. His series of three major articles on Orkney traditions and magic entitled: "The Legacy of the Old Man and the Wise Woman" had won him a Scottish Press Award and the nickname "Virgil" from his colleagues. Although opportunities in Glasgow and Edinburgh had immediately presented themselves, he chose Scrabster. That way he could move up a bit in salary and prestige yet keep his Orkney Islands beat which he really liked. It was home. And, he was comfortable with the provincial roads hugging Thurso Bay or Scrabster Bay, depending upon which town you came from. Highway A9 gave him easy access to everything in the area he needed for work, from the Ferry Landing further north, which was the gateway to his beat, to Thurso slightly south where his actual office was located. Also, he did not have the same kind of pressure to live up to his nickname that he would have at the larger papers. Around here, his colleagues viewed his nickname almost as some sort of a complimentary joke, not at all with the kind of serious portent he was sure would have attached itself had he opted for the big cities and the big money. But, that had been four years ago. A great deal can, and does, change during that amount of time.

"I don't know if she still lives there or if she's even still alive," Virgil continued over the phone. "She was pretty old when I interviewed her. Well over one hundred as I recall. But I do have an address and directions in my notes here at work somewhere. I'll track them down and make copies of what I have for you, if you'd like. And, I can include my contact info, maps, directions, whatever I have in the files. You can pick them up here at the office tomorrow and still have time to make the ferry to Stromness. Hopefully, that will help you on your journey."

"Thank you, Virgil. That's very kind of you."

"If you need anything else, please just give me a jangle on the cell. Whatever I can do to help you with your investigation, I'll be happy to do, Mr. Durante. Since the new Caliphate took control, we don't actually see many Americans at all anymore, especially ones wanting to see our seals. Even when we did," he chuckled, "your Americans mostly seem to prefer it warm and sunny anyway. No offense, Mr. Durante, but we're a bit hardier breed up here. Norse and Scot right along side one another, very often in the same body. You'll, no doubt, find that out for yourself, especially when you get out there in the midst of the Orkneys."

"That is probably truer than you could ever know."

"And, who knows, maybe you'll remember me when *Neo Geo* is looking for new people. I'm thinking it's finally time to be expanding my horizons, if you know what I mean."

"Yes, I think I do," Chace Durante replied. "I'll drop by in the morning, early. Thank you very much." Chace paused for a moment before hanging up. "What the hell, Virgil. Why not come on up here to the Ferry Inn, if you've a mind to, and we'll have some food and some drinks at Popeye's—on me, well, on the company. And, that'll save me a trip."

"That sounds great, but I would recommend The Captain's Galley instead. It's been named top seafood restaurant in the UK by Scotsman newspaper. And the food is simply to die for."

"We'll do that then. Not die, but dine at The Captain's Galley. How's seven thirty?"

"Eight's better for me. It's going to be a rough day."

"Eight it is, then, at The Captain's Galley."

14
Seeress of Stromness

[Music: "The Ache" (2:07-4:24)]

Even in July, the salty morning air had a bite to it. Most of the nearly eight miles of water called Pentland Firth was already behind the passenger ferry MV Hamnavoe. Virgil Kirk had been right about The Captain's Galley. The food was superior. But the "Trio" was not to die for. It was, most definitely, to *live* for, because if you died for it then you would never have the pleasure of eating it. Flame grilled halibut, sea bass, and John Dory with extra virgin olive oil, fork crushed new potatoes, and sweet pepper sauce vierge.

The blustery breezes stung his nostrils and chilled his face in spite of the reddish gray beard he had allowed to grow since the Caliphate take over. As the ferry cruised by the western coast of Hoy, the first island they passed, Chace Durante was stunned by the red sandstone four hundred and forty-nine foot sea stack known as the Old Man of Hoy. It stood on a plinth of igneous Basalt rock, close to Rackwick Bay on the west coast of the island. The stack had formed as the rocky shores and steep sea cliffs of the headland gradually eroded under the continual force of the sea crashing against the rock from three sides. The force of the water weakened cracks in the headland, causing sections to collapse, forming a free-standing stack. Sometimes even small islands formed from this phenomenon. This time, in this place, it was merely nature's sculpture.

Just as his guide, Virgil, had suggested in his newspaper series, the Old Man was something like an Orkney Islands Statue of Liberty. As he stared at the towering hulk that did somehow resemble a man, he imagined what it must have been like to witness that uncompromising series of natural events resulting in the emergence of the Old Man, as one chunk after another of red stone cracked away in time-lapse motion and plummeted into the crashing waves below.

Virgil's articles also showed maps drawn between 1600 and 1750. This area appeared as a headland with no traces of a sea stack.

By 1817, landscape painter, William Daniell, sketched the sea stack as a somewhat wider column than it was now with a smaller top section and an arch at the base. Experts agreed that the stack may not get much older, as there were strong geological indications that it could soon collapse.

The Statue of Liberty, he realized, was not a present from nature. Rather, it was a present from the people of France to the people of the United States of America to celebrate its centennial. Frédéric Auguste Bartholdi, not the forces of pounding seas, sculpted the one hundred and fifty-one foot statue. With the pedestal and foundation, it stood three hundred and five feet tall. Officially titled "Liberty Enlightening the World," the statue was dedicated on October 28, 1886.

Old Man was just about 400 years old, but it was giving way faster than ever to erosion. No one could be sure if it would last another fifty or one hundred or two hundred years before ultimately collapsing into the sea. Not unlike civilizations generally, he mused. Seemingly including his own country once represented by Lady Liberty.

The Statue of Liberty on the other hand was about half as old, yet it would see only one more New Year's Eve. The new Caliphate had scheduled its implosion for the next July 4 to celebrate the first "official" anniversary of the United States of Islam.

According to his own sources inside the new Caliphate, their plan was to have the entire security council of the United Nations in attendance while the New York Philharmonic played the 1812 Overture with fireworks blazing and exploding in the night sky. As the finale, the Statue of Liberty would implode on command. Such public displays of physical destruction of the monuments and symbols Americans still held so dearly even in, maybe especially in, their new found occupation was designed to have the same kind of debilitating effect on them as the destruction itself had on the objects being destroyed. At this point, the Caliphate faced only world-wide apathy. With world-wide diplomatic acceptance, the old United States of America would be smashed like the Statue of Liberty.

Unlike the Statue of Liberty's poetic invitation in "The New Colossus" by Emma Lazarus:

"Give me your tired, your poor,

Your huddled masses yearning to breathe free,
The wretched refuse of your teeming shore.
Send these, the homeless, tempest-tossed to me,
I lift my lamp beside the golden door!"

the Old Man seemed to be saying, "Welcome to the Orkney Islands, Orkneyjar, islands of the seals. Please give us your willing suspension of disbelief, for this is the world of Finfolk and fairies, of folklore and myth." Those, too, were Virgil's words in the lead to his first article.

Chace Durante still was not quite sure how he got here or why. However, thanks to Virgil, he was, at least, well aware of *where* he was when he finally jumped from the ferry onto the dock in the harbor of the second largest town on the largest of the Orkney Islands, Mainland.

He was also well aware that he needed to maintain this cover as Chace Durante. That was crucial to the credibility of his research trip which seemed to be well-timed. It was still the middle of the Harbor seal birthing season.

He certainly did not want anyone to suspect that he was actually Gwynn Camsron late of the USVI where he had taught English at Martyrs and Saints Anglican School since converted into a madrassa. He was also the same man who was wanted for "attempting to interfere with acts of martyrdom" when he tried to talk his Vietnam war buddy, Sal Keayrn, out of blowing up the Washington Monument. So, even if he had not been a wanted man, a fugitive, Public Enemy Number One to the new Caliphate, he would still be unemployed. Therefore, he needed a job.

The position of Unnamed Knight to the Rescue had been, seemingly, still his for the taking. So, he took it. However, it was the quick realization that he still needed money to fund his own job and to keep the infant Nine movement developing that seriously and rapidly spurred his interest in locating the Vault of the Unnamed Knight if it actually existed. Until then, that legend had been simply a part of the old story telling stuff which had been, because of the death of his father, the purview of his Uncle Ian. But, when Ian would get snookered on Christmas or New Years Eves, he would rattle on about the secrets of the Unnamed Knights and the Clan of

Gwynn and how he knew there was more to the tales than what was in the stories handed down from generation to generation. There was, he swore, a place where all the secrets and treasures were hidden. He just didn't know enough to find it himself. Once or twice he had even sputtered that he did know *how* to find out, *how* to get enough information, yet he never followed up, and he wasn't quite sure why not.

"If you ever want to chase down your past, lad, just you go to the last daughter of the Wise Woman of Hoy." He would sputter a bit and then always add: "Me boy," and break down laughing. "The Wise Woman of Hoy, me boy," he would splutter again. "The Wise Woman of Hoy palloy, me boy, me boy." He would continue to laugh and splutter until he could no longer laugh or splutter. Then Uncle Ian would have another wee bit and deteriorate into post fun morbidity.

He could not help but wonder what it must have been like for Gwynn of the Highlands, the first Unnamed Knight, when he made his first trip to these islands and for Gwynn VI, the last Gwynn, with a price on his head, when he fled to the safe harbor of these islands after all freedom had been so close but suddenly seemed so lost. A time when the world was so completely controlled that no one noticed the unrelenting fundamental changes taking place. A time, it seems, not unlike today when everyone seemed to be drinking deeply of the "Water of Truth."

"Uncle Ian said it time and again, Theo. If I ever wanted to know the clan secrets, I had to look for the Wise Woman of Hoy."

"Yeah, but even you admitted that the old man was plastered when he told you things like that, LT. In fact, you were usually plastered when you said things like that to me. Are you sure you're not plastered now, LT?"

"No. Stop it, Theo. Regardless of all that, now that I really need to know everything, there seems to be no Wise Woman of Hoy anywhere to be found except in some Viking myths. But, there is this Seeress of Stromness woman. Like Madame Sosostris. Madame thrice blessed."

"Too esoteric. Too literary. Nobody reads Eliot anymore, LT. They read yours truly Theo Theodora, so they have somebody to hate." He suddenly erupted in laughter. "Or they read the *Qur'an*.

Even in English, it would be considered better reading than *The Wasteland* or *The Love Song of J. Alfred Prufrock* or even Theo Theodora."

"I'm sure you're more right than I will ever be willing to admit, Theo."

"Probably, LT. So, what else is new?"

"Certainly not your predictable double entendre," Gwynn muttered into his fifth throwaway satellite phone in less than a week, "or anything here in Stromness." As they talked, Gwynn wandered through the center of the village along a single main street that twisted and turned for more than a mile along the shore of a nearly circular Hamnavoe Bay. The islands of Outer Holm and Inner Holm sheltered it from the Scapa Flow.

"I have to say, though, that there is nowhere I have ever been that is quite like this Stromness place," he continued. "It's absolutely breathtaking up here in a kind of otherworldly sort of way, and it definitely is where the evidence leads me in my search for the Wise Woman of Hoy. But, this is definitely not Hoy. The town looks out on Hoy Bay and the hills of Hoy just beyond. Can you imagine it, Theo? A world in which the Wise Woman of Hoy is not in Hoy at all. She's, instead, a hundred and eight or so and hiding out near this small town on Mainland Island, the biggest one of these little islands off the northern coast, masquerading as the Seeress of Stromness. I just can't imagine why no one—like my Father or Ian—ever told me. And, my god, it's breathtaking up here. Did I say that before?"

"Yes, LT, you did," Theo chuckled. "And my guess is they thought you were still too young, and they both died before you were old enough. I believe that happens often in families."

"Whatever." The answer Theo gave was more right than wrong, he imagined. "But, that didn't make it any less irritating. Sort of like this main street name just changing again for the fifth time since I left the Ferry Master's office. Damn, Theo! I'm getting lost in a town with only one main street."

"But, LT, if nothing's changed, then it ought to be easy enough to find your way around," Theo chuckled. "And, you said it had a bunch of little side streets and wharves and stuff like that. Nearly every single house or shop seems to have a small wharf behind it, is how you put it. Very picturesque, I would guess. You should get a lot of good photos on your cell phone anyway."

"Yes, very picturesque. Remind me to phone you my photos on the run before I have to throw it away. However, my guess is that, aside from the name of this street, not much else has changed here over the past fifty years or so. Oh, they've got Internet and satellite TV and all the rest of our modern technology. I mean, we can even talk over these cell phones from out here in the middle of nowhere. But it still feels like nothing's changed. I really don't know how to explain it.

"According to what Ferry Master MacCharon told me, the town has grown north in more recent years. That development created a need for an alternative road so that most traffic could avoid the main street. A by-pass, Theo. A freaking business by-pass in these remote and still wild Islands.

"I'm looking for the street that will take me to Outer Town Road. That will take me out of town. I'll call you later after I've had my visit with this Seeress of Stromness. It's going to be a long hike— five or six miles at least."

He was glad that he had taken a bit of late morning breakfast at the invitation of the Ferry Master before embarking on this little walkabout of his. Not only had MacCharon provided him with some great pastries and strong black tea but he also had been a great store of information and an entertaining story teller in his own right.

"The name Stromness, lad," Master MacCharon began in his Orkney style Scottish accent, "comes from the Norse, Straumrnes, or Point of Land by Hoy Sound. Stromness first appears in records as the village name in 1544."

"That could explain the discrepancy between what I have been told over the years about a Wise Woman of Hoy and finding, instead, a Seeress from a place with a name that means a point of land by Hoy Sound."

Ignoring his interruption, the Ferry Master continued. "In sixteen seventy the Hudson's Bay Company chose Stromness as the first and last port of call for their ships en route to and from Canada. Unlike our town today, Stromness was still a very small village of just thirteen houses. This led to a boom, however, that marks the real start of the Stromness you see today, lad.

"The Hudson's Bay Company reported Orcadians to be 'more

sober than the Irish and prepared to work for less than the English.'
They offered annual wages of around fifteen pounds for laborers and
twenty-five pounds for tradesmen in their Canadian settlements at a
time when the annual salary of the Stromness schoolmaster was less
than ten pounds.

"Little wonder that those from Stromness saw much more of the
world than most. That seemed to make them more willing to shed
the old and the past and embrace the new and the future without
really changing who they were and how they lived all that much.
And many, having made their fortunes with the Company, returned
to Stromness to build a home. By seventeen ninety-four, the village
had grown to a settlement of two hundred and twenty-two houses, of
which about one hundred and thirty had slate roofs. That was a sure
sign of wealth in those days.

"Later years saw fishing also growing in importance, and
Stromness became the center from which the lighthouses around
Orkney were manned and maintained. It is also recorded that in the
eighteen twenties, about ten percent of the entire local population
was employed making straw hats. Stromness acquired a legal
distillery in eighteen seventeen." He winked. "Earlier it had had a
number of illegal ones, but what started out as the Man o' Hoy
Distillery only survived until nineteen twenty-seven.

"Our Stromness today is a bustling and charming town as you
shall see. The narrow passages and roads and the private wharves on
the shore side are fascinating, as is the maze of steep streets and
paths that lead up the hillside.

"The main harbor and its quays are now found towards the
northern end of the center of the town and benefit from access by a
new road along the shore that keeps traffic out of the north end of
Stromness. This is a busy and interesting place, as well as one that
gives the best views of Stromness itself. The harbor is also the
terminal for the passenger-only ferry that connects Stromness with
Graemsay and the north end of Hoy, if you have any need of going
there.

"Stromness is now home to a number of businesses serving the
needs of divers wanting to explore the remains of the German fleet
that was scuttled in Scapa Flow in 1919. This draws together the
town's strong nautical past with the modern tourist industry in a way

that helps build further on Stromness's very attractive atmosphere." He lowered his head ever so slightly. "But, since this new caliphate thing in the States, all that kind of tourist business has been way down."

"The Seeress of Stromness, Ferry Master MacCharon? You said you knew something about her?"

"What is this fascination with her, lad? She is just some crazy ancient Spae-wife nobody listens to anymore, if they ever did."

"Spae-wife? I haven't heard that term before. What is that?"

"According to our legends, a Spae-wife is a woman who possesses the supernatural wisdom and some of the supernatural powers of a witch but without any of a witch's mean spirit. These women supposedly originated on a small invisible holy island as a result of the mating of a she-wolf and a Finman. They became known for their skills in medicine and surgery, in dreams, in foresight and second-sight, and in forestalling the evil influence of black witchcraft. Such women were looked upon with a kind of holy respect. Over time, the Spae-wife became an indispensable member of each community primarily called upon for healing, childbirth, charms, protection from evil, and, what seems to be your old lady's specialty, seeing the future. Throughout Orkney the Spae-wife was generally well thought of in her local community but was also treated with an awed kind of respect that, in many cases, probably bordered on fear."

The Ferry Master paused and sipped at his now-tepid tea, allowing all he had said to sink in to Mister Chace Durante's brain before he made his most important pronouncement. "Well, lad, I guess it must be very hard after having that kind of power over people to get used to the idea that the communities have put you behind them and nobody pays you no mind no more."

"That may be true, but I have an old address. A reporter, Virgil Kirk, gave it to me."

MacCharon nodded. "Yes, I remember him. He was with *The Orcadian* a while back."

"That's the one. He's with *O'Groat* now."

"Good for he."

"Look, Ferry Master, I just want to know if she is even still alive. This Spae-wife, as you call her. If so, is the address still good? If not, how can I find her?"

"Now calm yourself there, Mr. Durante. I'd be surprised if I can even remember where she lives." MacCharon seemed genuinely perplexed as he leaned across the captain's table and the formal tea spread upon it. "Here, give me a look at that folder you got there. Maybe something there will jog my memory a bit."

He shoved the manila envelope containing Virgil's folder toward the Ferry Master. "Here then, take your look because this is really important, ah, to the story I'm working for *Neo Geo*."

He shuffled through the file quickly as he talked. "I don't understand. I can put you in touch with the best seamen around. They can tell you more about the Harbor seals in five minutes than that old hag would ever be able to tell you."

"But, she *is* the story, Ferry Master MacCharon. And, that's what I'm looking for, you understand. A great story for our world-wide readership. And, you would, of course, be our cited source for locating her."

"Well, last I heard she was still alive. Many different people have related stories to me about how she has finally gone completely daft. But, she's still living at the same place in the same little cottage she's always lived in and her mother before her. That's the location you've got in your folder here, and it seems to be the right one. Far as I know there's no phone out there still." He reinserted all the materials into the folder and handed it back across the table to his guest from America. "Also, I might add, your guide Virgil's directions are quite accurate."

"Thank you, Ferry Master MacCharon. And, thank you so very much for the sumptuous tea. I feel like I could walk all day."

"Well, that's good, for you may have to." Ferry Master MacCharon grinned. "It's more than just a wee walk to the Temples of the Sun and Moon."

* * * * *

He walked east along Outer Town Road until it became A965, then on to the intersection with B9055 toward The Stones of Stenness and The Ring of Brodgar located on an isthmus known as The Ness of Brodgar between the saltwater Loch of Stenness and the freshwater Loch of Harray. Staring out across the heath like plain, his view of the twenty seven remaining stones of The Ring of Brodgar was unobstructed. Originally there had been sixty stones that sketched a perfect circle with a diameter of one hundred and four meters. Off to his left stood The Stones of Stenness—only four standing stones scarred, gray, and moldering with age—rose from an unbroken bed of heather to define that ellipse. The feelings that flooded him were primal and defied description or definition. The sense of all those who had come before him overwhelmed him in the moment.

The Seeress of Stromness lived roughly nine miles east of the main part of the town that bore the same name, in a one-room cottage on the side of Loch of Harray where the Neolithic village of Skara Brae was located. Some even joked that the Seeress' cottage was actually part of the original Kara Brae. Out of one window, she could see the Temple of the Sun or The Ring of Brodgar. The other window looked out over the Temple of the Moon or The Stones of Stenness.

When he finally found her, she was sitting in her rocker on the small front porch of the cottage as she often did in the mid afternoon when, on a clear day, she could see those two sources of her power at the same time. When he introduced himself, she nodded knowingly and invited him in as if she had been expecting him. As she prepared afternoon tea for them, she informed him of her lineage.

"I knew your Father and your Uncle."

"I was not aware of that, Seeress. Please, tell me more."

"First, I must tell you of my lineage. It is part of the necessary ritual of things." She told him that she was named after her Mother and her Mother's Mother, and her Mother's Mother's Mother, and so on back nearly twenty generations to the wife chosen by Gwynn VI in the thirteen hundreds.

"According to the legends, that very first Seeress was, herself, rumored to be the daughter of a she-wolf and a Finman, a Finfolk princess who needed a mortal husband in order to protect her from growing old and repulsive like the Finwives of her people who did not find human husbands. When she discovered Gwynn, shipwrecked on an Eynhallow Island beach, the first seeress took it as a sign that he was fated to be her human husband. For Gwynn, their union reinforced the magic that protected the Medallion and the secret location of the Vault of the Unnamed Knight. She lived with the last Gwynn near the site of the kirk which, as legend tells it, was the cairn marking the location of a vault that housed all the secrets and wealth protected by the Unnamed Knight.

"The place you search for has been uninhabited since eighteen and fifty-one when disease and death raged among the four families still living there back in those days. Most people believed that the well had been polluted because it lay below a midden, a very old kind of landfill for disposing of shite and such. So, the experts of the time thought the disease was typhoid. Finally, when there seemed to be no other choice, what remained of the four families evacuated the island.

"The island's name is Eynhallow or Eyin Helga in Old Norse. However you say the words, the meaning is the same: Holy Island. On that island sit the ruins of a small piled stone constructed church dating back to the twelfth century. It was used as a house from the fifteen hundreds until the evacuation of the island in eighteen and fifty-one. When the owner of the land took the roof off to make it uninhabitable, he discovered that one of the buildings underneath the roof was actually an old kirk. A church. That find supported the belief of many that a monastery was once present on the island, perhaps even prior to the church being built. Some still believe that, in early Norse times, a Celtic church may have been built. Indeed, the very name of the island suggests the idea of some kind of supernatural or religious sanctuary," the Seeress continued as she served the steeped opaque amber tea she had prepared along with some sweet crackers.

"Your Father, Garn, he knew it all. He knew what even Ian didn't know. Your Father, he came here more than one time I can assure you, young man."

Young man. Gwynn knew he was going to like the way this woman saw things, this Seeress of Stromness. "Why would neither my Father nor Ian tell me about you?"

"I don't know the answer to that. But, I do know that your father said that he wanted to know the final thing, but he would never go there."

"Go where?"

"To the island. To Eynhallow."

"Why Eynhallow?"

"Because that is where the old kirk stands. Because that is where all the secrets are buried. Because that is where all the magic lives. Because that is where the future begins."

"And, you would know about this because you are a seeress, right?"

"I understand your doubt, young man. But, my ancestors and I have, over the centuries, possessed what you might call a 'gift' or a 'curse' depending on how you see it. Sometimes we see things, have visions or dreams, hear whispers that come true. Some folks say we came from Eynhallow, that we're what is left of the magical Finfolk who, in ancient times, came to the island during the summer months. After all, it's still the home of all that's magical in this life. And, at one hundred and eight, I am the last of that long, long line of daughters of the she-wolf. The lineage stops with me because I had no daughters and no nieces. No one else is left. So, Gwynn Camsron, Gwynn VII, gaze now upon the Temple of the Sun and The Temple of the Moon as the day finishes. Feel their magic and hear me well for the stories and prophecies die with me."

15

Guidman o' Thorodale
(A Tale told by the Seeress of Stromness)
[Music: "The Ache" (4:24-end)]

"Orkney's Finfolk were nomadic. In winter they lived in their beloved undersea kingdom of Finfolkaheem. When summer arrived, they moved to the magical, invisible island of Hildaland—meaning Hidden Land. It is possible that Hildaland was made up of a number of islands that, over time, came to be thought of as just one. That one is the uninhabited island between Rousay and the Orkney Mainland, the island of Eynhallow.

"Through the magic of the Finfolk, Hildaland was kept hidden from mortal eyes, though the shores of this earthly paradise were often glimpsed by travelling Orcadians.

"From the various tales that come to us today, it seems that Hildaland was surrounded by a magical bank of fog that enveloped unwary travelers and shifted them from the mortal world to the world of the Finfolk for no matter how brief a time. Some vowed that the island rose suddenly from the depths of the sea. Others said it was simply invisible and usually could not be seen by mortal man, except when they would occasionally run aground on it.

"However it was hidden, Hildaland was generally believed to be a beautiful green island of glistening streams and fertile fields. There, the sun always shone with rich fields of corn and barley growing in the warm breeze, while wandering herds of cattle grew fat.

"Not half a day away, the Mainland parish of Evie was the home port of The Goodman of Thorodale. He had a wife who bore him three sons. Alas, she died young, so he soon married another. The bonniest lass in Evie, he dearly loved the girl.

"One day, they were down on the ebb. Thorodale sat on a rock to tie his shoestring. Suddenly he was startled by his wife's screams. Thorodale turned and saw what looked like the shadow of a man dragging his wife roughly towards a boat. By the time Thorodale waded into the water's edge, the shadow man and his captive were

190

rowing out to sea. Long before Thorodale reached his own small boat, the shadowy Finman had vanished by using Finfolk sorcery to make his vessels invisible and propel it faster than flying. Thorodale knelt in the ebb and roared like a lion that he would have his revenge on the Finfolk and protect human kind.

"Many a long night and day thereafter Thorodale thought about his vengeance, but he could see no way this could be done. Then one day he was fishing at slack tide, near the middle of the Eynhallow Sound between Rousay and Evie, when he heard a female voice singing. He recognized the voice as belonging to his lost wife, though he could not see her.

"Goodman, grieve no more for me,
For me again you'll never see;
If you would have of vengeance joy
Go ask the wise Spae-wife of Hoy."

"Thorodale returned to shore and, staff in hand, took his silver in a stocking and set off for the island of Hoy.

"What passed between him and the Spae-wife called the Wise Woman of Hoy was not recorded as far as anyone in our lineage knows. We can be certain, however, about much of what she must have told him, because of what he did after he left Hoy. We know that she told him how to get the power of seeing Hildaland, the home of the Finfolk. We know that she told him how he was to act when he saw the hidden isle; and we know that she told him that nothing could punish the Finfolk more than taking any part of their Hildaland from them.

"For nine moons after he returned home, Thorodale went nine times on his bare knees around the great Odin Stone of Stenness at midnight when the moon was full.

"For nine moons, at full moon, he looked through the hole in the Odin Stone and wished that he might gain the power of seeing Hildaland.

"And, after doing this for nine months on the days when the moon was full, he bought a great quantity of salt. He filled a meal chest with salt, and set three large straw baskets beside it.

"His three sons were now near grown young men, so Thorodale

explained to them what they should do when he gave the word.

"Then one beautiful summer morning, just after sunrise, Thorodale looked out on the sea and in the middle of Eynhallow Sound he saw a pretty little island where land was never seen before.

"Without taking his eyes from the island, Thorodale roared out to his three sons in the house: 'Fill the baskets and make for the boat.'

"Down came the sons carrying the baskets of salt, which they set in the boat. The four men jumped in and Thorodale ordered them to row straight for the new island.

"The sons were perplexed at their father's instructions for only he could see the magical island. Quickly, the boat was surrounded by whales.

"Suddenly a great monster of a whale raised its head right in the boat's course, opening a mouth huge enough to swallow men and boat at a single gulp.

"But Thorodale bade his sons bend to the oars and he rose to his feet in the bow. Then, right into the terrible jaws, he threw a double handful of salt. Instantly the monster vanished. You see, the creature was only an apparition, a trick of the Finfolk's sorcery. The salt, a consecrated substance, destroyed their evil magic.

"As their boat entered what was left of the fog near Hildaland, two most beautiful mermaids stood waist-deep in water near the shore, their long golden hair fluttering over their white shoulders. So melodious was their song that it went straight to the hearts of the rowers, causing the young men to stop rowing.

"But Thorodale, without turning his head or taking his eyes off the magical island, kicked the two sons nearest him. 'Mend your stroke, boys!'

"Then he cried to the mermaids: "Begone, ye unholy limmers! Here's yer warning!"

"At that he hurled a cross made of twisted tangles on each of them. The mermaids plunged beneath the waves with pitiful shrieks just as the bow of the boat touched the enchanted shore.

"But on the beach awaiting them was a huge and horrible monster. Its tusks were as long as a man's two arms, its feet as broad as quern stones, and with blazing eyes it spat fire from its mouth. Seemingly ignoring the threat of this unholy beast, Thorodale leaped boldly onto the land and threw a handful of salt between the creature's eyes. With a terrible growl, the monster vanished but in its place stood a tall and mighty man. The man was dark and scowling and in his hand he held a drawn sword.

"'Go back!' he roared. 'Go back you human thief! You that come to rob the Finfolk's land. Begone! Or by my father's head, I'll defile Hildaland with your foul blood.'

"When the three sons heard that, they trembled and begged their father to return to the boat and make their way back home.

"Thorodale ignored his sons' pleas and kept his eyes on the Finman.

"Without warning, the Finman made a sudden thrust at Thorodale's breast with his glistening sword. Thorodale sprang lightly to the side as if he expected the blow, and with a flick of his wrist threw a cross into the face of the dark stranger.

"The cross was made of a sticky grass called 'cloggirs' and when it struck the face of the Finman it clung tightly and would not fall off.

"With a howl the dark man turned and fled, roaring as he ran with pain, grief, and fury.

"The Finman was afraid to pull the cross from his face because to touch it with his hand should have caused him even more pain— the blessed symbols are agony to those under the Devil's rule!

"At that point, Thorodale was sure that he was the very Finman that had dragged his young wife away from the beach. Turning to his cowering sons, Thorodale roared at them: "Come oot o' dat ye duffers! Bring da salt ashore!"

"The three sons came on shore, each bearing a big basket of salt. Their Father lined them up and bade them walk abreast around the island, each son scattering salt as he went. And when they began sowing the salt there arose a terrible alarm among the Finfolk on the island and their animals.

"Out of the houses and byres, down to the sea they all ran, helter-skelter like a flock of sheep with mad dogs at their heels. The Finmen roared, the mermaids screamed, and the cattle bellowed as every last mother's son of them and every hair of their beasts took to the sea, never again to set foot on the island. Their homes, steadings and their crops too, all vanished.

"Satisfied, Thorodale cut nine crosses on the turf of the island

and his three sons went three times around Hildaland sowing nine rings of salt in all.

"And that is how the Goodman of Thorodale took revenge on the Finfolk and restored the vanishing island to the mortal world."

The Seeress seemed more like an ancient woman now than she had before she told the tale of the lion-like Thorodale. "Buffeted by wind and wave, our holy island once was an otherworldly place of sea-monsters and magic, appearing and disappearing out of the shifting mists until mortal man finally claimed it by clearing the Finfolk's Hildaland of all enchantment and laying it bare to the sight of man and heaven. Then the mortals called it Eynhallow—the Holy Isle—and a kirk was raised there."

Darkening dregs was all that was left of their evening tea. Her hotch-potch had long since begun to simmer, gradually filling the hut with the mingling odors of cabbage, celery, carrots, onions, and turnips. "And, then, they abandoned her. Because of all this history, you will not readily or easily see what you seek on the island once made visible by Thorodale. You cannot see it but it is there, hidden as if by magic.

"You must penetrate the shelter of the stones of sand that point upwards toward the sky. Therein lies the pathway to the vault in easy sight of the eye. What seems to be water is stone. By what is stone and seems to be water, the way is shown.

"What you need to know and understand is as much in these things I tell you over this evening tea as it is in what you may find in the vault or cairn at the kirk."

The Seeress continued to stare out the small windows of her cottage that looked directly at The Ring of Brodgar and The Stones of Stenness—The Temple of the Sun and The Temple of the Moon—in the distance, and she began to sing in an off-key, broken voice that weighed of the ages, a voice that in its very distastefulness was magically melodious, even beautiful.

"Eynhallow fair, Eynhallow free
Eynhallow sits in the middle o' the sea
A roaring roost on every side,
Eynhallow sits in the middle o' the tide."

16
Vanishing Island
Eynhallow, Orkney Islands, Scotland
[Music: "Orkneyjar"]

Jo Ben's *Description of Orkney* written in 1529 included the following:

> "Eynhallow, as it were, the Holy Island, and very small. It is of old times related that here, if the standing corn be cut down, after the setting of the sun, unexpectedly there is a flowing of blood from the stalks of the grain; also it is said that if a horse is fastened, after sun-down it will easily get loose and wander anywhere during the night. Here you may discern the futitious [sic] and fabulous traditions of these people."

The sea swelled and crashed over the lower deck of the MV Thorodale, a double decked angling rig Gwynn Camsron had chartered out of Evie still using his Chace Durante cover. Angling was off partly due to the changes in world politics that the crew of the Thorodale did not care about in the least. They simply needed the business, even if it was from some crackpot American who wanted to see the seals on Eynhallow. He could hardly see where the waves were coming from because of the thick mists eddying and swirling around the island in the way he imagined it might have been back in the ancient days before the Goodman of Thorodale had broken the Finfolk spell of invisibility.

For the moment, the holy island was invisible again to the eyes of mortals like themselves but not to their technology. A storm had swooped in on them from the north-west so fast that it caught them unawares as they were approaching the southern coast of their destination. Although they couldn't see the land right in front of them, Captain Flett saw it on the boat radar displays in the wheelhouse in time enough to drop anchor and hope for the best.

"Captain? Flett is an old Orkney name, isn't it?"

"That it is, Mr. Durante. That it is."

It was as if Chace Durante had turned on the "talk" switch when he asked about the family name, for suddenly the taciturn Captain could not stop talking.

"Some folks think our name came from the Old Norse word *flagth* meaning witch. Back in those times, the name was seen as a bit derogatory, as you might imagine, so it was probably given by the ruling Norse to some troublesome family descended from earlier Pictish settlers. Looking about at me and mine, I'd say that would be about right." He flashed a low-keyed smile. "However, a man name of Gregor Lamb, the leading expert in Orkney family names, uncovered some information that showed the Flett name probably originated in the parish of Firth, back on Mainland, the last of a line related to a Norse nobleman named Kolbein Hruga. The first actual mention of the name in Orkney dates to a report of the murder of one Thorkell Flett in 1137. That makes our surname the oldest in all of Orkney."

"So, your family comes from the Eynhallow Fletts, then?"

While they began to make preparations for going ashore, thick black clouds raced overhead blotting out the morning sun that they had hoped was blessing their trip when they left Evie just before sunrise. Thunder roared around them and lightning flashed like exploding Tesla coils creating a flashing luminous mist. It was as if the very air itself was iridescent. Yet, nothing seemed to deter Captain Flett.

"That's right. The earliest record of Fletts on Eynhallow dates to sixteen ninety-nine," he continued. "One George Flett was listed as an indweller in Eynhallow. Land records from seventeen fifty show that a George Flett rented half of the Island. Court records from seventeen seventy-six—about the same time as your revolution— reveal that a John and George Flett were summoned by their landlord to appear before the Sheriff of Orkney for failing to pay their rent for seventeen seventy-four and seventeen seventy-five. Finally, more land records show that, in seventeen ninety, a George Flett and a John Flett each rented one-quarter of the island. It was on this island that James Flett was born in eighteen twenty-four. It seems quite likely, then, that the Flett Family inhabited Eynhallow for well over one hundred years before they were forced to leave because of an outbreak of typhus in eighteen fifty-one.

"Today, Flett is the fourth most common surname in these islands. But, you're right, Mr. Durante. It's the Eynhallow Fletts that we hail from."

Chace Durante could barely hear the Captain's words over the ferocious roosts of water racing between the two larger islands of Rousay and Mainland that somewhat sheltered Eynhallow, not so much like a wall or barrier of any kind as it was like an embrace. Within that embrace of such powerful tidal surges nestled this single gem, the once-invisible holy island and, with it, all of its reputed magic.

He watched from the wheelhouse, while Captain Flett and his sons lowered the Thorodale's pontoon-style dinghy into the completely unpredictable waters of Eynhallow Sound. The lamb-like cries from new pups on a beach full of Harbor Seals almost sounded for a moment like pipes in the wind. His eyes lifted from the bouncing orange and black dinghy that looked like two rockets held together with a rubberized raft. They squinted into the wind, peering toward the beach. There, he could see through the luminous mist enough to make out a mix of light gray, silver, and brown seals with dark spots or white rings. Each languished in his or her single spot from which they did not move until they delivered their pups, completed their haul-outs or were put in some danger that they could not scare off with a sneeze, snort, growl, or hiss. They were also not to be touched by another while they lingered in their spots. Then they were gone.

Other gaps of clarity in the glowing mist also revealed three very large dark dorsal fins slicing the waves between them and the shore. At first sight, he thought they were sharks.

"Orcas landward!" Captain Flett shouted at his two mates. "Keep a sharp lookout now, and hold the dinghy ready to go soon as this storm passes and them orcas vacate the area."

"*If* they leave, you mean, don't you, Captain?" the older mate everyone called Red shouted back.

"That's true, Captain. It's pup season for the selkies, you know. And, the orcas love them seal pups."

He recalled, as he listened to the crew's chatter, that one of the primary theories for the sudden decline in seal population was due to over killing of the Harbor Seals and especially their pups by Orcas.

That was pretty much what everybody else thought as well. That was not, however, what the Seeress thought.

"Yes, Boy. That I know as well as you or your brother there," Captain Flett threw back at his younger mate, his son of seventeen. Red was nearly twenty. It wouldn't be all that many years until the MV Thorodale would belong to the two of them and his youngest at only fourteen. Galen's interests seemed to lie in the Galley, and unless he was absolutely needed above decks, in the Galley was pretty much where he stayed. Only one could be the Captain, though, and that was going to be a genuine problem some day between The Boy and Red. The Boy was leaping ahead of Red in just about every way. He could find the fish better, catch the fish better, work with the anglers that leased their boat better. But, if you wanted to keep the rig running, Red did that better than just about anybody in or around Evie. He kept the aging hulk's twin engines humming.

Overhead, Fulmar Petrels circled, waiting for the storm to clear enough so they could resume flying low over the waves like Albatrosses in search of brunch, hoping to find some small fish, squid, or crustaceans, even ships' garbage. They darted about as the heavy clouds whizzed past them, finally exposing the late morning sun. The birds and wildlife were all around him. It was not like he had to go searching them out. They were everywhere he looked in these islands. So, he did not really understand why he was suddenly so much more aware of the Fulmars or of the several Osprey also circling above, all in search of a meal. Gwynn could only assume it was some kind of Animal Planet or National Geographic kind of moment—getting ready to land on the pebbly beach of an island that had been uninhabited by humans for nearly two hundred years, now a refuge for all manner of sea birds and seals, a place even for Orcas to feed on straying Harbor Seal pups.

Of course in these days of the new Caliphate, the United States of Islam, there was no more Animal Planet or National Geographic. In fact there was no television at all in the way it used to be. Now whatever media was still allowed in what used to be America presented a new and unified vision through the permeating prism of Islamic censorship yet mimicking the trusted, accepted media approach from the past. *Neo Geo* was, of course, a part of that mimicking prism.

Gwynn thought it strange that, for all the nearly instantaneous changes with the instituting of the new Caliphate, people in other parts of the world—like here in the Orkneys—still thought of Americans as Americans in the old way, not the new. He was not even sure if the rest of the world actually understood that, in just a few short weeks, there was emerging a new Caliphate American. He wondered how long it would take for the world to achieve that realization. He wondered if he could be a part of preventing that awareness from ever being necessary.

He remembered from his cover research, that Harbor Seals were the least vocal of all pinnipeds. They usually made noises only when they felt threatened. So he could only believe that the chorus of snorts, hisses, growls, and sneezes coming from the beach was a result of the seals being aware of the Orcas so close off shore or of them and their vessel.

The dingy almost beached by itself amidst the shimmering mists that hugged the shoreline. Stepping onto that sand was like stepping into another dimension of existence. As Gwynn penetrated what remained of the luminescent mists to stand by the skeletal remains of two old houses just off the beach, he could see the Eynhallow kirk clearly a few thousand yards away. Everything looked just as the Seeress had described it to him.

When he finally reached the ruins, he immediately began investigating the piles upon piles of grayish sand stones individual craftsmen—each with his own tale to tell—had painstakingly chipped and shaved and stacked or arched like sandstone tiles to create the complex that they still outlined in great detail. Certain sections of the ruins reminded Gwynn of mastodon-like monsters turned to stone by Medusa's hair or Ansel Adams style high contrast photographs with deep dark shadows and shades that seemed to actually carve the dry stone tiles that remained standing into new shapes from old matter.

The external walls and several of the rooms were nearly in tact except for not having roofs. Dr. Raymond Lamb, a former Orkney archaeologist, believed that church construction began around 1150. The Eynhallow Kirk was built from local stone. So, any red sandstone must have been imported from Kirkwall. The St Magnus Cathedral there was built with the same type of sandstone. Gwynn leaned down and picked up a large shard of red sandstone that had obviously been a structural part of the complex at one time.

"Those fragments remain an enigma to this day."

"I'm sorry. These looked like the fragments I have shorn against my own ruin." Gwynn blurted out the semi-joke involuntarily as the Finfolk like specter's voice fractured his reverie, a kind of self-indulgent swoon that irrationally obliterates all else momentarily. Gwynn's problem was that he had felt, in some undefinable way, enchanted from the time he stepped out of the dinghy from the Thorodale onto the undisturbed sand and pebble beach just above where the seals were hauled-out, still surrounded by mist that glowed intermittently from explosions of lightning. "I was told that no one lived here."

"That is correct. 'No one' does not live here. I do."

The specter's hooded robe was soiled with dark spots from the sand and dirt of the island. It reminded Gwynn of a leopard's skin. He could just barely make out the specter's dialect. It markedly differed from most Scottish pronunciation he had been exposed to and even from the dialect he had been hearing in other parts of the Orkneys. Although he had been in the islands for three days, he was not getting used to it yet. And, now, this Eynhallow dialect seemed even more obscure, more ancient somehow. It would take some additional getting used to. He would have to pay very close attention to what was being said.

"I keep an eye on the birds and the seals for the Queen and I watch out for the kirk here, too. I guess you might call me the Caretaker of Eynhallow, you might at that. Or just Flagg. That, too, would do."

Gwynn believed that he had, now, finally located the place that held the rumored Vault of the Unnamed Knight. It should be somewhere inside this strange, almost Stonehenge-like pile of dry stone and deep shadows that was built as a church back in the twelfth century. He could sense a kind of connection with The Circle of Brodgar and The Stones of Stenness.

But, the angler crew was back on the boat as far as he knew waiting for him to signal that he was ready to come back aboard. They wanted no part of the island themselves. And, the Seeress had told him that the island had been free of humans since the middle eighteen hundreds. That was confirmed by the Internet, and he had read about one incident back in 1990 in one of the more local papers. It was still talked about according to Captain Flett. The locals called it the Eynhallow riddle. He was not really sure, himself, what to call it.

"On Saturday, July 14, 1990, an outing, organized by the Orkney Heritage Society and the Royal Society for the Protection of Birds, landed a number of ferry passengers on the uninhabited island of Eynhallow for a short visit. As usual the crew counted the number of passengers upon disembarking. Eighty-eight visitors stepped from the boat and onto the soil of the once magical island. According to the evidence from the crew, only 86 returned.

"These two missing passengers sparked off a massive air and sea search. Men from the local police and coastguard scoured the island as well as the coastlines of the islands nearby.

"To no avail. In the air a helicopter dispatched by the Shetland Coastguard swept the area with their heat-sensing equipment but nothing was found.

"Needless to say the whole incident was blamed on the ferry crew miscounting the number of passengers but at the time the Chief Inspector of the Kirkwall Police was not so sure. 'We have corroborative statements from the crew Members. It's a strange one,' he said.

"The Eynhallow incident had some of the older Orcadian folk murmuring about the old ways and whether the missing "tourists" might actually be none other than Finmen returning to their ancient home.

"Others sat together and discussed whether the missing passengers had perhaps been stolen away by the sea dwellers, for as they knew already, a Finwife was destined to grow old and repulsive unless she could obtain a human husband. The husband did not necessarily have to be a willing partner.

"The mystery was never solved.

"But whatever happened, the Eynhallow incident served to prove that although it may seem that the people of Orkney have been swamped by the modern magic of television, radio, cinema and video, the islands' ancient lore remains—bubbling just beneath the surface of everyday life. There, it is remembered and revered, and, to a certain extent, still feared."

So, Gwynn was quite surprised to encounter another human being on the island. The man in the spotted robe motioned toward him with his right hand outstretched, just short of touching him.

"And, sir, if you don't mind my asking, what's that about your neck?"

"It's an old family heirloom." Gwynn reflexively touched it with his right forefinger and thumb. "A Medallion."

"And, who might you be, then, sir? Your name that is, if you don't mind my asking."

"Clan name is Camsron. Gwynn Camsron. Some say, Flagg, that I am Gwynn VII, if you ever heard any of those stories."

"You don't say, now, do you?"

"I guess I do say, at that."

"Then, we've been waiting for you."

"Waiting for me, Flagg?"

"So the story goes, when the time was right, a new Gwynn would arise. No longer a caretaker of the Medallion but a leader, a wielder of the Medallion's power for the good of mankind. We have been awaiting a man named Gwynn who possesses the key."

"The key?"

"Yes. The Medallion you wear around your neck, sir, I do believe." The Caretaker of Eynhallow pointed a bony finger at Gwynn's neck. "That looks like the key to enter the vault right there around your neck, you might say, Mr. Camsron. All that, and your name being Gwynn, I'd say presented itself as a potentially very significant day for this holy island and for you, sir, I should say."

"Then, I have some questions for you, if *you* don't mind my asking."

"Certainly, sir. I will be most happy to give you whatever answers I am able to provide."

"Thank you, Flagg."

"You be most welcome, sir."

"OK, then, how long have you been here?"

"On this island, you mean?"

"Yes, Flagg. On this island."

The Caretaker of Eynhallow glanced about him. For as far as the eye could see there was not a hill of any size, not a tree, only low shrubs and heather covering the land like thick purplish green cloth down to the pebbles and the sand of the beaches that bordered Eynhallow Sound. "I guess I have always been here, Mr. Gwynn Camsron, Gwynn VII, waiting for you."

"That doesn't tell me very much, now does it, Flagg?"

Flagg lowered his head slightly but did not respond.

"So, since you don't want to answer that question with a straight answer, then maybe you can tell me how the builders of this small church knew about this symbol."

"Why don't you let me show you, sir." Flagg pointed toward the dark shadows defining an entrance into the crypt-like church complex through a Romanesque stone archway. "This entire complex was designed and built as a cairn itself, a cairn of all cairns—a holy place marking the spot where lay a very special underground vault although no one else knows that. It is special in that it was made like a tomb, carved out of one piece of red sandstone and is accessible only by a member of the Clan of Gwynn bearing the Medallion that matches the vault's keystone design." He paused.

"An intriguing mystery surrounds the red sandstone fragments that lie in a number of the kirk's outbuildings. Just like the piece you hold in your hands.

"It is thought these stones were first discovered during the 19th century clearance of the site, but their purpose remains unknown outside these shores.

"They do, however, have a distinct resemblance to the stonework found in the St Magnus Cathedral in Kirkwall. But, the Eynhallow Kirk is made from local stone so the red sandstone, like what was used in the cathedral, must have been imported for some special reason again unknown away from these shores.

"The red sandstone was originally designed to point the way to the Vault of the Unnamed Knight. Most of it came from the shards the stone masons created as they carved out the vault from one huge solid block of red sandstone."

As they entered into the shade of the first arch, the words of the Seeress echoed in his head. "You must penetrate the shelter of the stones of sand that point upwards toward the sky. Therein lays the pathway to the vault in easy sight of the eye. What seems to be water is stone. By what is stone and seems to be water, the way is shown."

Gwynn could not help but notice how the flagstones strung along to the next arch a hundred feet away looked like a stream of water sluicing through the grass. Pointing at the flagstones strung out in front of them like some kind of runes, he nearly smiled. "To me, well, that certainly looks more like a stream there than it looks like a pathway to a vault, now doesn't it?"

As they crossed into the realm of the arches, he observed scattered runes carved into the wider stones that made up the bases of the arches. He knew that the word, rune, came from an early Anglo-Saxon word meaning secret or mystery. These ancient characters were used in all kinds of Teutonic, Anglo-Saxon, and Scandinavian inscriptions. Usually the markings were a combination of perpendicular, oblique, and a few curved lines. The runes had been quickly adapted to carving on wood and stone by around three hundred BC. The first six runic signs were for *f, u, th, o (a), r, c (k),* hence the name *Futhorc* for the runic alphabets. There were two alphabets, one of sixteen signs and the other of twenty-four. They were used extensively throughout Northern Europe, Iceland, England, Ireland, and Scotland until the establishment of Christianity. For some reason, Christians saw runic inscriptions as messages of evil, even worse, pagan. So, from then on, the use of runes was reviled as a pagan practice. In Scandinavia their use persisted even after the Middle Ages where they were used for manuscripts as well as inscriptions.

Gwynn had no idea what any of the symbols, words, or phrases meant. He was no expert in ancient languages. He had just brushed up a little on certain things for this journey. One of them happened to be a spotty background on runes. And, he did sense something, energy of some sort that was almost electric. It was similar to the special effects in movies when some symbol or artifact glows after the right someone reaches out and touches it.

"Gwynn of the Highlands—the very first Gwynn—came here himself in 1148 with his newly chosen Gwynn II and made the original impression of the Medallion. Gwynn gave only the Master Builder custody of the impression. 'From time to time,' he instructed the Master Builder and his craftsmen, 'other Gwynns may come themselves, or their representatives or proxies may come, to deposit items into the vault you will build that can only be opened by the

Medallion being placed into the impression on the vault's keystone.' And, with each new Gwynn, the old and the new Gwynns—if humanly possible—would make their way to the kirk on Eynhallow to transfer the Medallion. I have the original impression made by Gwynn of the Highlands. It normally resides in a secret collection that comes with the vault. But, I just happen to have it with me this morning, sir. I will be happy to show it to you."

"Thank you, Flagg. Let's have a look. I'd really like to get this all settled once and for all."

"Very good, sir. Then, I must make sure that your Medallion matches up with the original before I can actually take you to the exact location of the vault. Gwynn of the Highlands warned me . . . ah, warned the Master Builder charged with crafting the church vault that it might actually be possible for someone to have a Medallion that works on the keystone even though it may not be the original Medallion. Only the wax impression can authenticate the Medallion. He never said how that might be, but that was what he said . . . or, at least, that is how the story goes."

The Caretaker of Eynhallow pulled out something wrapped in a cloth made of an old woven fiber that Gwynn could not even identify. "Place your Medallion in here, sir." Flagg actually grinned as he opened the cloth, exposing a wax impression encased in stone of what looked to be the same as the Medallion Gwynn wore around his neck.

Gwynn reached behind his neck and unclasped the gold chain. He caressed the Medallion as he reached forward to place it inside the wax impression.

"Perhaps, sir?" Flagg interrupted Gwynn's movements. "Perhaps you would allow me. The impression was first made in the year 1148 from the original Medallion before it was even named as the Medallion of Bannockburn. It is very delicate from all the years of waiting."

"Be my guest."

The Medallion was a perfect fit.

Once Flagg was convinced that Gwynn was the one he had been waiting for, Gwynn did not need the Seeress' clues in riddles, because Flagg guided him directly to the keystone. And, sure enough, just as Flagg had told him, shards of the red sandstone were imbedded along a path directly to the keystone. It seemed to be the same kind of red sandstone he had seen lying around on the ground where they entered the ruins. He had brought a chunk with them. When they reached the keystone, Gwynn placed it carefully on the mound of stones in front of the entrance to the vault, adding his stone to the cairn of centuries. Gwynn inserted the Medallion into the keystone impression. He tried to push or pull the stone. Nothing happened. Then, he pushed harder and he heard something grind and shift. He kept pushing and slowly a small doorway opened up to a narrow passageway leading into a chambered cairn. This was not the usual Orcadian piled stone construction but the rare cut-out-of-stone construction usually reserved for high level burial tombs.

Flagg held back. His spotted cloak almost glowed in the late morning light as the sun suddenly broke through. "I cannot proceed with you any further, Mr. Camsron, sir. No one but you is permitted past this entrance."

"Are you certain? After all you've been here as the Custodian low these many years, how many you will not say. Don't you have a desire to see what's inside?"

"Yes, I do, sir. But I cannot. I would betray the trust granted to me. This is your place, Mr. Camsron, sir. No one else's."

"All right, then. But, I guess you could find some torches and lanterns, candles, whatever you might have in case I need the light."

"I can do that, sir, and I can offer you some history that may prepare you in some way for what you may or may not find inside the vault."

"Sure. Why not? I've gotten this far. I can wait a bit longer so you can tell me your tale."

"It begins with the death of the last Gwynn and his successor Young Man Phelps of Cams Ron Burn. Young Man Phelps was only sixteen when he made the trip from Jarl William's court in Rosylnn to the island of Eynhallow at the written request of the most famous of his Clan, Gwynn VI, the man referred to with great reverence as 'the last Gwynn.' He was dying and pleaded with him to 'come and visit with a dying old man in his last days, Young Man Phelps. It be your duty.'

"And it certainly was his duty. The old man was, after all, his mother's brother. He was still revered even by the Jarl himself. So off Phelps went on the week long journey to the island of Eynhallow to be with his Uncle—whom he had met but once as a child when he had given him his own sword —at his death.

"'Young Man Phelps, you must keep this Medallion safe until the coming of the next Gwynn. For now, you are the one and only guardian of the Medallion of Bannockburn. It is your sacred trust. Accept this Medallion, Young Man Phelps of Cams Ron Burn, and with it all the glory and all the stories, all the secrets and all the riches of the Clan of Gwynn, the line of the Unnamed Knights." Gwynn reached out and clasped the chain around his successor's neck. No sooner had he released his grasp on the chain than he fell face down onto the stone table between them, dead.

"So, when Young Man Phelps CamsRon left Eynhallow, the smoke from his Uncle's pyre still curled into the morning air. He took with him the Medallion and the myth. He took them away from the protection and control of the enchanted island and out into the day to day real world of survival, power, and riches which increased the chances that such a powerful sword could end up in the wrong hands, and even in the wrong hands it was still a powerful sword.

The way the Seeress had related the story to him as she pondered the leaves in her evening tea cup was that "Young Man Phelps endeavored through his friendship with Henry Sinclair to put his stone on that cairn by joining Henry in exploring Green Land and the new world in search of the lost Templar Fleet. However, as far as anyone knows, Young Man Phelps was lost with all hands off the coast of La'Merika as he battled and destroyed what he hoped would be the last dragon—the Knight of the Crimson Dragon—in order to save his own people as well as a people he had never even seen except as small figures scurrying along the ridgeline just slightly inland from the shore of the new land he had come to find beyond the Green Land.

"So, why have you not come before?" she had asked.

"I never believed any of this, of the stories, at least not until recently."

"And why are you here now?"

"To save the world." Gwynn shrugged. "If I can."

"And, if you cannot?"

"To place a stone on the cairn."

"You'll be needing that light, sir?" The voice of the man in the soil-spotted robe bounced off the infinite variety of angles created by the piled stones of the small church giving it an otherworldly almost megaphone like quality not unlike the sound of the muezzin's voice when calling Muslims to prayer.

"I don't think so, Flagg." Gwynn peered further into the dimness of the cairn. "At least not just yet. For some reason it seems awfully light in there for a tomb, that's what this looks like to me. A tomb."

"To my knowledge, Mr. Camsron, many have visited here but no one is buried here except, possibly, the last Gwynn."

"I guess I'll have to take your word on that, Flagg."

"Aye, sir."

"I'll be back shortly. See if you can round up some of those torches or lanterns or whatever just in case."

As he stepped inside the doorway into a narrow entry passage to the vault carved out of solid red sandstone, he was immediately intercepted by a puzzling verse scratched into the wall. This inscription was not in runes, so he could read it easily. There was, however, a single rune beneath the verses as if it were an attribution or signature.

> No matter when in time
> You finally read this rhyme
> It will mean the same
> Regardless of any claim.
> What lies within this tomb
> Is new life in the bloom,
> The corpus of the trust
> To do whatever you must
> To keep what you be given
> And save the world we live in
> With the power of the Medallion
> From always being driven
> By the destroyers of heaven.

* * * * *

"Well, LT, you've certainly lived up to your alias."

"What do you mean by that, Theo?"

"You know Chace means hunter, and you sure as hell brought home the bacon."

"Theo, Theo, Theo. Now that's a mixed metaphor, or something far worse, if I ever heard one."

"What do *you* mean by *that*?"

"You basically said that I'm acting like a hunter by bringing home butchered and processed meat from a domestically grown animal? That smacks more of farmer to me."

Theo laughed. "Guess you got me there, LT."

"And, you know, I think we need to *get* Lincoln Walks Alone Black, too."

"Yeah, someone with his international finance experience and his numismatics obsession could be *very* helpful in tracking down some of the stuff you found in the vault."

"You're probably right there. And all that antiquities stuff he likes. Some fascinating questions about banking and finance that go back into antiquity being posed by some of the documents in this vault."

"I mean didn't you say something about Florins and some kind of records of a bank account in some bank in Florence?"

"Yes, there's both."

"Both?"

"Yes. Both. One thousand seemingly original fiorino d'oro coins from 1252 AD and a document recording 10,000 Florins in a bank account with Banca Monte dei Paschi di Siena. I believe that's the oldest surviving bank in the world as we speak. The statement of account is dated 1472, the year the bank was founded by the Magistrate of the city state of Siena, Italy. It has to have value as a document from that period even if it is not legally enforceable. The account is described in the documents as, and I quote, 'an account in perpetuity.' Can you imagine how much that would be worth today with over seven hundred years of interest?"

"Probably millions. Maybe even hundreds of millions."

"At least, and there must be a dozen or more accounts and warrants and deeds. I mean, according to some of this stuff, the island of Eynhallow actually belongs to me by virtue of a deed to "Gwynn Camsron better known as Gwynn VI or the last Gwynn" as "payment in full for all services to the crown both previous and to come." It's dated 1328 and signed by the King of Norway.'"

"Well, at least, Linc can find out if we've got anything other than a handful of collectible coins and some very old more or less legally worthless documents or what."

"I know he was fascinated with my Medallion from the time we first met."

"Yeah, what was it he called it? Some fancy word for medals and coins and such?"

"Exonumia at first sight, I believe is how he puts it when he tells the story." Gwynn nearly giggled into the cell phone. "I don't know how this translates across the Atlantic via some satellite or another, but my hands are still trembling, and I'm practically giddy right now at this find, at the scope of this find. My god, Theo, I am stunned at the bluntness of the question it raises about everything. If this was true—something no one in their right minds really believed was true; I didn't believe it was true—then what else is actually true that only mad men willingly admit to?"

The Numismatist

17
The Great Horned Owl

[Music: "Lincoln 'Walks Alone' Black"]

In Lincoln "Walks Alone" Black's mind, the "hoo hoo-oo hoo hoo" of a male Great Horned Owl would forever echo off the pines, poplars, and sourwoods that surrounded his great grandfather Isaac Black as he made his way on horseback along a dry stream bed leading, he hoped, to the top of the mountain. Lincoln had heard the story so many times that it seemed to be his own memories that were stored in his mind and seemingly in the various owl objects he had gathered together in his office over the years rather than memories someone had imparted to him.

Lincoln caressed a Great Horned Owl coin—a silver Canadian fifty cent piece—designed by Quebec artist Jean-Luc Grondin. He could, at a glance, see a display of a dozen of the coins he had bought years before in one of the mahogany display cabinets that lined most of the open space along the walls of his office. But, just for luck, he always kept this one coin on his desk, within easy reach, so that, at any time, he could reach out and put his hands on something tangible that reminded him of the tortured history of his family and what they had to overcome simply for him to be behind this desk, holding this coin.

The moon had been full and the air was clear on that night so long ago. The horse could see well. So could Isaac. And, the great nocturnal bird of prey the Cherokees called an uguuk, followed him, its great yellow eyes unblinking in the moonlight. It saw well, too. As long as there was enough moonlight to travel by, Isaac was determined to keep going. He could not quit on himself now. Branches broke off to his right. Crickets chirruped.

The swamps of his South Carolina had been scary enough what with the slave chasers after him and all. They said he killed a man with his bare fists, and maybe he did. But the white bastard was gonna cut off his balls with a Bowie knife for supposedly looking at the so-called gentleman's sister. As he loaded their wagon with supplies from Tabor's General Cash Store, he caught her staring at him out of the corner of his eye. He purposely avoided looking in her direction at all. Then, he heard her yelling to her brother, "That boy there! He was staring at me in a very bad way! I could tell!" They were on him before she had even finished the sentence. So, what was he supposed to do? Spread his legs and say, "Yes, massa. I did what she say, massa. Go ahead, massa. Cut my balls off, massa."

These mountains, though. They were wild as any swamp and a lot more difficult if you didn't know them well. And, he didn't. He knew the Carolina Low Country and its swamps. Until he ran, he had never seen land rise so high as a small building. But, food and game were plentiful if you knew the signs. The animals weren't starting to thin out with civilization like back east . . . back home. Hell, it was home, too. His mommy and daddy raised him in their slave quarters shanty on that cotton plantation. They had taken black as their last name when Massa Gutherie allowed them to marry as a part of his slave reform policy. He had the idea that nurturing the concept of family among his slaves would make them happier and create for him a continuous supply of slaves. Not a new idea, by any means, but it was new to Massa Gutherie.

And, it was Massa Gutherie's half-brother, Duke Hatteras, who he struck in self-defense four days before. When the bastard raked his knife toward Isaac's crotch, Isaac landed a right fist the size of a sledge head directly against Duke's left temple. He was sure he felt the blood vessel burst. Duke's knife barely sliced the top of Issac's right thigh as he toppled in a gentlemanly heap on the dry dirt of Main Street. Blood oozed from his slack, purple lips. His eyes which only moments before had burned with the passion of castrating a nigger now stared through a cloud at the top of his head.

"Get that nigger!" Sister Hatteras screamed, waving her milky-skinned, delicate-boned hands at Isaac. "He's gone and killed my Duke!"

Isaac remembered bolting for the nearest horse, a sorrel mare belonging to some drifter who had tied up only a few moments before while he shopped in Tabor's General Cash Store. He had the reins untied and was in the saddle with his boot heels digging into the sorrel's sides before anyone could really move. He remembered shots and the sounds of bullets over his head as the mare galloped off in a cloud of red dust which helped disguise his getaway. He also remembered heading straight for the swamps because he knew them like the back of his hand. If he could lose the slave chasers that were sure to come after him for the bounty anywhere, then it would be in those swamps. Once out of there, he'd head for the mountains. A couple of days into the mountains and they'd never find him.

From where the sound of the branches cracking came, a possum's eyes leered at him from behind the trunk of an oak that must have been a hundred or more years old by its size and the thickness of its bark. He slid the drifter's rifle from its saddle case without a sound. There would be meat tonight for him or the uguuk.

When the moon set behind the tops of the mountains that surrounded him, he made camp and cooked the possum on a make shift spit over a roaring fire. He had to keep the fire up to keep away the coons and bears and foxes. Some said that even wolves and mountain lions prowled these hills. After eating, he changed the poultice on his wound. The cut was already scabbing up despite the small breaks in the scab from so much riding. It would be healed soon . . . another two or three days. He tied the fresh poultice in place with clean strips of sheet he had stolen off of a clothes line just before he entered the swamps back in South Carolina. Beyond his ring of fire light he thought he heard something in the brush. It was more of a hint of a sound than a real sound. Then there was what seemed like a Great Horned Owl call just outside the circle. Maybe it was the owl come to claim a raw share of the possum he had left for it on a poplar branch at the edge of the clearing.

Branches cracked. Brush crushed beneath something, and a dark slender figure seemed to catapult into his circle of light, landing on its knees. Isaac's rifle already pointed directly at the figure before it could stumble back to its feet.

"Please . . . . Please . . . help me!"

It was a female voice with a quality he had not heard before and some kind of accent as if English was not her native tongue.

"White men . . . come . . . after me!" She stumbled to her knees again directly in front of his bed roll and stared down the barrel of his rifle. Her face was soft caramel in the fire light. Tears flooded her cheeks. "Please . . . dark man . . . help me!"

Now he could make out the fringed doe skin ceremonial dress

she clutched around her like a blanket or a robe. She was an Indian of some kind. "Here, ma'am." He placed his rifle at the head of his bed roll. "Sit here by the fire and wrap this here blanket around you." He held his bed roll blanket out to her as he stood.

"No . . . no time! White men out there." She flapped her arms and hands towards the darkness beyond the fire. Muscles and nerves spasmed all over her face and neck as she fought for some kind of control over her terror. "They come to take me away . . . ."

The sound of twigs snapping in the darkness was muffled by the leafy forest floor. The wrong birds called out to each other. He thought there were three, possibly four. "How many white men?" he whispered, picking up the rifle he had just laid down. Then, he checked his pistol. It was fully loaded. The stranger whose horse he had stolen back in South Carolina to make his getaway had been very generous, leaving a rifle and a six-shooter both slung over his saddle.

"Three," she whispered. "Three devils."

"Trust me?"

"I must."

"Then lay down here as if you were sleeping and let them come to you."

"Yes." She huddled against his saddle, wrapped in his blanket. "I wait."

By the time she responded, Isaac was in the shadows behind her. He could almost feel the Indian girl shivering inside his blanket while he waited for the white devils to come. Just like any other animals, they would come for their prey.

They slipped from the shadows one at a time. Two came around the side of the fire to Isaac's left. One approached from his right. Isaac saw their bearded faces aglow in the fire light as they sneaked up on the girl. Isaac isolated the one on his right. He slipped his knife from his belt, aimed, and let fly. The knife he had owned since his father gave it to him when he was twelve years old as a reward for learning to read and write his name and numbers struck the stalker in the heart.

"Jed? What was that noise, Jed?" one of the men on the left called out when he heard what sounded like a body falling to the ground. Both men looked about when Jed did not answer. The Great

Horned Owl that had shadowed Isaac for so long dove and swooped through the clearing causing both men to cower.

Isaac aimed his one-shot rifle at the chest of the man who spoke as he raised up out of his crouch and squeezed the trigger. Powder flashed. The butt of the rifle slammed against his shoulder. A moment later the target fell to the ground just like that damned possum had, a lead ball through his skull. The third devil turned to run. Isaac dropped the rifle into the brush. He unholstered his pistol and quick fired three shots at the fleeing white stalker who had now become the prey. He snatched up his rifle and bolted into the clearing to make sure they were all dead. Couldn't let nobody go back with no stories that might lead the slave chasers to him.

"You alright, ma'am? You okay?"

The Indian woman peeked from under the blanket. "I am okay." Her lips, blue from fear, twitched in something approximating a smile. "Thank you for saving my life."

"It's okay." Isaac mumbled as he checked the three bodies. They were all dead. That meant he had three to bury. And he'd have to bury them deep so the animals wouldn't dig them up

"My father great chief of Cherokee. He reward you well if I am returned to my village. Those men captured me from near my village while I did the wash for my wedding day."

"Sure. Sure. Everybody's daddy's a great chief or something." He chuckled. "Right now, though, I got to bury these white devils deep so's the animals won't dig them up and leave signs for others to question."

She stood and dropped the blanket from around her. Her black hair shimmered in the fire light. "Then you take me to my village?"

He leaned down to her face. Her high cheeks were golden red in the glow of the dying fire. Her black eyes glistened like hard coal. His fingers reached out as if they had a mind of their own, their tips just brushing her left cheek. She trembled. His fingers quivered. Maybe she was telling the truth.

"I show you the way."

"Yeah, okay. We eat some possum, sleep here tonight, and I'll take you to your village with first light, princess."

"I am Daughter of the Dawn, first born of Chief Walks Alone

and his woman, Doe Child.

The sun was just coming up over the eastern ridge of the valley they were moving toward.

"Is this not a beautiful dawn?"

"Yeah." Isaac reined in the sorrel that walked behind him carrying his Cherokee Indian princess. "It is, but . . . ." The mare stopped and began nibbling at a patch of scrub grass that had struggled up somehow through the leaf meal forest floor.

She pouted down at him. "But what, Isaac Darkman?"

"But . . . ." He stared out from the shadows of the great virgin oaks and spruces and firs strung across the valley pink with sunrise promise. "But not as beautiful as the one who bears its name."

"You are a most unusual man, Isaac. You kill with the skill of a warrior, but you speak to me with the tongue of a poet." She dismounted into his waiting arms. Her lips parted just inches from his as she spoke. "Which one is really you, Isaac Darkman? Which one is you?"

18
Lincoln "Walks Alone" Black
[Music: "Lincoln 'Walks Alone' Black"]

The great grandson of Isaac Darkman had also made a beeline for the Great Smoky Mountains when he was finally discharged from the Army after two tours in Vietnam as a "Travel Agent." His "front" job was finance officer, the only black man in the entire MACV personnel complex who was not an enlisted man. He knew well that he could thank baseball for that. His secret job was to actually make all arrangements necessary for certain very secret off-the-books special operations missions. The minute he was discharged, Lincoln "Walks Alone" Black headed for the lodge of Chief Light Step, his godfather and his grandmother's brother, a direct descendent of Daughter of the Dawn's brother who succeeded Chief Walks Alone for whom Lincoln was named. He wasn't running from slave chasers like his great grandfather, Isaac Black, but he was running from death—the memories of death, the sounds of death, the smell of death, sending people to their death. And, so far, he had not been able to run fast enough to outdistance the stench. Even though he had never seen a day of combat, he'd been through the TET Chinese New Year offensive. He had seen the destruction of bombs in cyclo taxis, children blown apart in the streets. He had held that one small girl with the black marbles for eyes in his arms at Tranh Hung Dao circle. Smoldering pieces of a Lambretta open-air bus spread around her like a circle of metal monuments rising from the flames. When he moved his hand to touch her face, to reassure her that everything would, still, no matter what, be all right, he realized that her eyes did not flutter, did not move. His hand stopped, moved back over her eyes. No. She was not seeing his hand. She was not seeing anything. She was, in fact, dead. But, he could not accept that. Not in his arms. Not in the arms of the great grandson of Isaac who had saved the life of a Cherokee princess. So, he tried to revive her with CPR but to no avail. He finally forced a Cahn Saht to take a look. He looked at Lincoln as if he were insane. "She dead, you American fool," the Vietnamese policeman spat at him. "She dead!"

Lincoln had spent a good part of his youth in these hills, yet they still awed him beyond belief each time he returned. Even after the Asian mountains and jungles, even after the destruction, even after the ruination of young men, and even after the deaths which were sometimes more blessed than continuing to live.

The story from his youth told to him time and time again by his daddy and granddaddy folded through his consciousness as he flipped his fly rod far ahead of him into the current, letting it drift a few yards before he reclaimed it from the hip-deep icy stream that swirled over shallow rapids just beyond the ridge from Light Step's lodge and cast it back into the frothing stream. Patience, persistence, and concentration were essential to catching trout . . . or courting a woman if you're a black man like his great grandfather wooing a Cherokee princess who was already promised to another.

When Isaac returned Daughter of the Dawn to her village, her Father, Chief Walks Alone honored him with a great celebration. Chief Walks Alone promised him anything he wanted. Isaac did not hesitate. He asked for Daughter of the Dawn to be his wife. The Chief told him that he "must first become brave of Cherokee. Then, since she is already promised to another, you must fight her betrothed in mortal combat. The winner gets my daughter."

"The horror, Light Step. The horror of what one human being is willing to do to another is too great for any person to have to hump." Lincoln scooped the last thick flakes of rainbow trout off of his plate with his fingers. The fishing had been good. He caught a dozen and Light Step grilled them to perfection over a wide flat cooking fire in front of his lodge.

"I cannot know your feelings, my son, but I understand your words." Light Step pulled on the stem of his red clay pipe and passed it to his godson. "I can only say to you that what we must carry we will carry. It's only a matter, then, of with what honor do we carry what we must carry. Remember the horror your great grandfather, Isaac, husband of my grandfather's sister experienced when he had to face Daughter of the Dawn's betrothed in mortal combat? He beat his opponent fairly but walked away without killing him. To Isaac, it was the honorable thing to do. But, the circle of warriors closed on him and would not let him free from the circle until he had smashed the skull of Dancing Deer with his tomahawk because that was their way. From that day forward, every time your great grandfather saw hhis wife she would remind him of Dancing Deer who, by his own standards, he had murdered in cold blood. He carried that horror with him to his grave."

From the earliest memories of his childhood, the Cherokee part of Lincoln "Walks Alone" Black had also yearned to be in the forests, fishing, hunting, and trapping . . . living off of the land and leaving no footprints. He spent as much of his summers as his family could allow with his godfather in the Smokey Mountains. But being sharecroppers, they needed him home to work the farm as much as possible. So, when he was home, he and his Granddaddy spent hours together roaming the woods that surrounded their small cotton farm where his grandparents raised him and his two younger sisters. The same farm where they had raised their son, his daddy, and the same farm where their son, his daddy, married their mommy and raised him and his two sisters, Beatrice and Lucia. The same farm where his daddy was lynched for raping a fourteen-year-old white girl who had really been beaten and raped by the banker's son . . . and everybody knew it. The same farm where his mommy was raped and bludgeoned to death after his daddy had strangled in the noose dangling from a limb on the giant pecan tree by the front door of the house. The same farm that they all picked cotton for. He remembered how the points of the cotton pods stung as they pierced beneath his fingernails even when his fingers were numb. Occasionally, drops of blood would ooze onto the pods as he continued to pluck fluffy balls from their pods and toss them, stained with his blood, into the waiting burlap bag cinched to his waist with bailing twine. He knew he could not stop or the boss would say he was injured and not pay him for the day. So, like the others, he picked on, even when it made gripping a bat or fielding ground balls and line drives difficult. He and his sisters would never save enough to pay off the farm by just growing their own cotton. They had to work others' fields as well. They needed the cash. That was how his Grandmama Mary kept them going.

It was the same farm where smoke cloaked the barnyard the night his fate was set. He always remembered with some relief that, at least, Grandmama Mary had been away visiting Aunt Bessie near Atlanta the night the sparks shot from a cross that flamed up like fireworks exploding on the Fourth of July. Cinders stung Lincoln's skin like the cotton pods once stung his fingertips as they drifted towards the dark loamy soil of the Black farm. Tears of sorrow stung his eyes.

"Your Daddy and Granddaddy found out what happens when one of you gets outta his place, boy. Your momma too!"

"All you got is this here piece of dirt you call a farm, nigger. Now you own it, so you say, you think you're some kinda big ass nigger, don't 'cha? Well, if you plan to keep it, you better start acting right or you just might wake up one morning dead, nigger."

Even as he sat now in his stuffed swivel chair behind the enormous mahogany trunk slice desk that was given to him by the World CEO of International Investments and Futures, one of his three largest clients, with literally millions in the bank, Lincoln could still feel every spark as it burned into the skin of his memory. He could still hear every word as if those Klansmen were taunting him right now in this very room.

"Only way we know to get rid of you niggers once and for all is to kill off you bucks and screw your women 'til all they can have is white babies . . . ." The laugh that erupted from Walter Debury's throat was hideous beneath his Grand Clud hood. The gaggle of white-cloaked and hooded men who sat astride their tractors behind their leader joined him. The laughter curdled in the night air. But, the whole time, he kept thinking about that kid at the baseball game in Greensboro when they were twelve. He had been white, too.

"Walter. My God, man. We went to school together, Walter. We played on the same baseball team in high school. We won the state championship together! What's happened to you, brother?"

"I ain't your goddamned brother, nigger!" The Grand Clud spat tobacco juice out of his mouth hole. "I'm your better!" He swept his flowing white robes back toward those behind him. "And so are them!" Walter ignited his John Deere engine, keeping his shotgun leveled at Lincoln and his two sisters who were frozen in place by his side like alabaster sculptures. Yet they trembled. "And you'd best be remembering that fact of life, boy!"

The others of the hooded mob started their tractors too and began to trail out of the barnyard behind Walter Debury, the great Grand Clud of the Ku Klux Klan, down the tractor path past their cotton to county road 2999. It was there, at the county road, that the rest of the world was supposed to begin. Not in their own barnyards. Those bastards had gone too far. Coming onto his land and threatening him and his poor frightened sisters. And why?

"Are they gonna rape us, Lincoln?"

"Like they did mamma?" Lucia echoed her older sister.

"I honestly don't know, girls." As the last tractor's tail lights were lost in the darkness beyond the burning cross, Linc turned to those two alabaster statues and hugged their shaking bodies back from their medusa sleep. "So, you best get on into the house and lock and bolt the doors and windows just in case. Beatrice, you get out Granddaddy's old Winchester and the bullets. It's in that old chest Grandmama keeps in her bedroom. You know how to use it. I taught you, remember?"

She nodded.

"So load it and wait for me. Don't let anybody but me into the house, you hear me? Beatrice?"

"Yes, Lincoln. I hear you."

"Anybody else tries to get in, you shoot 'em! You got that!"

"Yes, Lincoln ."

"Shoot 'em until they fall down, Beatrice." He slammed his right fist into his thigh. "Until they don't get back up!

"And if they get up, shoot the bastards again!" He felt the tears nearly spewing from his eyes. They burned like lava, those tears of disappointment, those tears of betrayal.

Beatrice hugged her younger sister, Lucia, to her breast and hung her head. Plaits rolled across her caramel shoulders like woven wool. Linc touched her chin with strong but sensitive fingers. "Get your chin up, girl. We got us some fighting to do!"

But, he knew better. He was still just a boy, not even graduated yet. So, he did what was practical, what was smart and, yes, what was safe for all of them. He talked Grandma Mary into selling the farm as soon as they could and for a lot less than it was worth. She and the sisters, Beatrice and Lucia, moved in with their Aunt Bessie in Atlanta. He, on the other hand, finally accepted the baseball scholarship that UNC had offered him two years before he had even graduated high school. He and Grandmama Mary signed the letter of intent before she went to Atlanta, and he took it straight to Chapel

Hill.

Lincoln Black reeled forward in his chair nearly out of control for a couple of seconds as the chirping of the telephone startled him. Being out of control for any amount of time was something he avoided at all costs. Had he dozed off for a moment? With the one to three hours of sleep he got a night, it certainly wouldn't have surprised him. He buried his head in his hands. No matter how hard he massaged his temples with his fingertips, the price he had paid for that fight he did not take on so many years ago would never go away. Sure, he got his revenge, in a way. He had become an NCAA All-American baseball player who had a college degree which most of the Klan mob did not. He was a war veteran which none of the Klan mob was. He had become disgustingly successful and celebrated for that success in a way that none of those good old boys could avoid knowing about it. And, he had saved his sisters from what would have been rape and sure death. Then, ironically, they survived only to become Muslim women who lived under Sha'ria law that allowed rape and even death to women when and where necessary as determined by men.

"Black here."

"I hope it's not that bad, Linc."

"Theo?"

"Yes, Linc. It is I."

"What's happening, my brother?"

"A whole lot, my brother, and I need a whole lot of a favor from you, Lincoln 'Walks Alone' Black. "

"That's one of the things I liked about you the first we met at MACV HQ way back in our Vietnam days. You never did like to waste time. Get right to the point. That's your modus operendi, right?"

"It's for Gwynn."

"For Gwynn? If it's for Gwynn, you name it."

"But, it could be very risky, even dangerous, and it may not be so easy."

"So what's new in that, my brother?"

"Nothing, I guess. Seems like everything's hard these days. So why not this?"

19

Beyond the Little League World Series

[Music: "Lincoln 'Walks Alone' Black"]

The first time Lincoln Walks Alone Black had met Gwynn Camsron was in the southeast regional play-offs to determine who would go to the Little League World Series in Williamsport in the summer of 1955. His team represented South Carolina, and he was, as far as he knew, the only negro boy in the entire play-offs. Negro was still the term in use in those days and boy was still the appropriate word to use when referring to a male who had not yet reached majority regardless of his race. Some sports reporters around the country got ahold of that fact and began calling him the Jackie Robinson of Little League Baseball. A local follow-up to those stories had been published in the morning sports section of the Greensboro paper. That kind of press back in those times really put a lot of heat on because it didn't happen very often. He would never forget that night. It would be the first thing, of all memories, to cross his mind at death. He was certain of that. At twelve years old, Gwynn Camsron had taught him something about courage.

Those were the days, back in the fifties, before daylight savings time was being observed in most of the south and certainly not in North Carolina where God's time was the only time recognized by the state legislature. This game, held in Greensboro, was scheduled for six-forty-five on a very muggy August evening. So, the game would have to be played under the lights because it was already dark by six.

The field manager put the lights on at five-thirty. The diamond magically began to smolder in the growing darkness. He remembered beginning to warm up by lobbing a few to his catcher, Freddie "The Throw." "The Throw" could pick a guy off stealing second while still in his crouch. The stands at the local baseball stadium began to fill with spectators. Lincoln would always remember those cold chills that shot through his arms first, then the rest of his body as, in the darkening night, a chant began to grow from fragments:

"NO NIG-GERS!"

"NO NIG-GERS!"

"NO NIG-GERS!"

Gradually, as he continued to warm up, the chant became more organized and finally it echoed across the diamond in ragged unison:

"GO HOME JACKIE! GO HOME!"

"GO HOME JACKIE! GO HOME!"

"GO HOME JACKIE! GO HOME!"

He recalled staring over at the dugout to see what Coach Sams would tell him to do. He had felt uprooted like when the gardener yanks a nearly-mature carrot up just enough to traumatize the carrot and its root system to make it grow more rapidly but not enough to pull it out of the ground to harvest.

"How's the arm, Linc, baby?" Coach Sams had barked at him, trying to take his mind off the rhubarb from the crowd.

"Real good, Coach." He yelled in order to be heard. "Real good . . . except . . . ." He sort of shrugged generally towards the chants from the stands. One part of the crowd would yell one thing. Then the other would respond.

"NO NIG-GERS!"

"GO HOME JACKIE! GO HOME!"

"NO NIG-GERS!"

"GO HOME JACKIE! GO HOME!"

"NO NIG-GERS!"

"GO HOME JACKIE! GO HOME! "

"I know you can handle the pitching, son, but do you think you can handle *that*?" He shouted back across the noise of the crowd. He ground his fingernails into the splintery undersurface of the visiting team dugout bench in order to keep himself there. He knew that if he came out onto the field and seemed to be, in any way, protecting young Lincoln, he would only incite the crowd further. But he reached out to the boy with his eyes and his heart and hoped he would sense it. "What about it, son?"

"I'd really like to try it, Coach. I just want to see . . . . I *need* to see . . . ."

"Then, go for it, son. All I can say is we're all darned proud of you, son. We're all with you. So, go on out there and pitch your heart out, son, for yourself and for your team. Good luck." Coach Sams jerked his cap off, then slapped it right back on his balding head. "Okay, Throw! Get Lincoln ready!"

"Right, Coach Sams."

Linc began his warm ups in earnest. The crowd sensed that he was going to be the starting pitcher. Their chant rained down on him as he began to reach the first level of his pre-games. Rhythm . . . accuracy . . . control . . . . No smoke, yet. That's what his Father had taught him, and he had once pitched on the same team with Satchel Page in the Negro League.

"NO NIG-GERS JACKIE! GO HOME!"

"NO NIG-GERS JACKIE! GO HOME! "

"NO NIG-GERS JACKIE! GO HOME!"

A few spectators began filtering hesitantly onto the playing field, almost as if they didn't know what else to do as an encore.

"CALL THE GAME! CALL THE GAME! CALL THE GAME!"

"Ladies and gentlemen. Please. May I have your attention, please!" Gwynn Camsron seemed to find himself yelling into the mic that had been wired out to the pitcher's mound for the pre-game ceremonies when the NAACP had planned to congratulate the Little League for being "years ahead of everyone else by allowing a young Negro boy to participate for the first time."

Years later, Gwynn confessed to Linc that he was "sort of in a trance." He didn't seem to be in control once he saw those fans invading their baseball field and bringing with them their stupid hatred. He told Linc that something within him snapped, and the next thing he knew he was shouting into that microphone.

"Please, can I have your attention, please. Just for a moment. Please."

Somehow the crowd that had begun mobbing the field halted. The center field American Flag that had been flapping in the humid night breeze seemed to freeze in place.

"Thanks. Thank you all. Listen. Look, I don't know you folks. I don't know the players on the Rocksville team. I don't even know this player who is the target of all your heckling tonight. What I do know is that I'm an athlete . . . a baseball player. And I've always been proud of that! But tonight you make me want to crawl into a hole and just die of shame." Gwynn had tugged at his cap, then yanked it off his head as tears of that shame burned his eyes, and threw it to the ground with all the force he could muster. "You make me so ashamed to be a human being much less a baseball player."

Lincoln remembered that moment always with tears in his eyes. And, he never lost the irony of that night in the ballpark under the lights getting ready to play America's pass time. The irony was that, in Gwynn Camsron's moment of shame, Lincoln felt what may have been the greatest pride he would ever feel in his life and it was for the action of another, not himself.

A copy of the *ANA Journal* lay on his desk, opened to an article on ancient coins. *The Numismatist* most recent issue held his place. It, coincidentally, contained an article specifically on the original Italian currency that became the first currency of the western world in the middle ages, the fiorino d'oro. When he was not making money for his clients in the world of international finance, he was researching ancient coinage and other methods of exchange, and he collected as much of it as he could find and afford. His numismatic collections were numerous and huge when compared to his Great Horned Owl collection. He couldn't keep track himself anymore, so like many things in life, he delegated the responsibility of keeping a record of his collections and their contents to one of his most responsible and fastidious assistants.

The new Caliphate had, so far, left his kind alone. His kind meaning black and affluent and educated as well as being a professional in the financial markets. The general sense, it seemed, was that if one was a person of color one probably had more feelings against the old United States of America than one had for it. They would be perfect converts if given the time and opportunity to make such a decision. And, the new government appreciated, so it seemed, that the international economic market had to continue despite the cataclysmic changes in the United States of America, now the United States of Islam.

Linc firmly believed that he could also trace his compulsion for ancient coins and medals back to that same night and that same person. It was after the game was finally cancelled by the police that he went up to Gwynn and personally thanked him for what he had done. He remembered Gwynn being almost embarrassed. It was then that Lincoln remembered seeing the Medallion for the first time and being immediately enchanted by it. "What is that?" he had asked, pointing at the gold circle that dangled around Gwynn's neck, exposed when he opened the top buttons of his uniform to cool off.

"It's just a good luck piece my Father left me in his will."

"Oh, your Daddy's dead?"

"In a car crash a couple of weeks ago."

"Hey, I'm real sorry about that. Gosh, that must make it awful tough to be here." He remembered sticking out his hand, then, suddenly, without thinking. "My name is Lincoln Black." Then he blurted out, "My Cherokee name is Walks Alone," which he never told anybody. "And I lost my Daddy too. A lot more than a couple of weeks ago though. And, it wasn't in no car wreck."

Gwynn shook his hand firmly. "Gwynn Camsron. I'm sorry about your Father, too." He leaned forward while they were still shaking hands and whispered. "My medal. It's called The Medallion of Bannockburn. It's an ancient Scottish relic. Supposedly it means that I'm some kind of knight or something." And Lincoln remembered vividly that Gwynn winked, right there in the midst of all that insanity on that hot, August night. "Just an old wives tale, you know."

"Huh!" Linc grunted. "Old wives tale is it? Doesn't look like that now from the inside of that vault or cairn or whatever it's called, does it 'Sir' Gwynn Camsron." He picked up the American Numismatic Association's journal and prepared to speed read the first article of his research on the many and varied items Gwynn had found in the Vault of the Unnamed Knight. Original fiorino d'oro coins comprised just one of the more intriguing items. He knew he would have a great deal of reading to do, and he couldn't delegate this. It was far too sensitive. So, he didn't know how often he found himself thanking John F. Kennedy and Evelyn Woods for the speed reading thing, but he felt sure it wasn't often enough.

Suddenly it dawned on him that he could easily check out what Wikipedia had on the coin on-line. He was still getting accustomed to all that was really available to him via the Internet. Sometimes that source proved interesting because of the slant taken by whoever provided the content on a particular item or the arguments that often ensued over the facts involving an item or even the URL's embedded within the content linking to related items. The Wikipedia entry began:

The Italian florin was a coin struck from 1252 to 1523 with no significant change in its design or metal content standard. It had 54 grains of gold (3.5g). The "fiorino d'oro" of the Republic of Florence was the first European gold coin struck in sufficient quantities to play a significant commercial role since the seventh century. As many Florentine banks were international supercompanies with branches across Europe, the florin quickly became the dominant trade coin of Western Europe for large scale transactions, replacing silver bars in multiples of the mark (a weight unit equal to eight ounces).

In the fourteenth century, a hundred and fifty European states and local coin issuing authorities made their own copies of the florin. The most important of these was the Hungarian forint because the Kingdom of Hungary was a major source of gold mined in Europe (until the New World began to contribute to the supply in the sixteenth and seventeenth centuries, most of the gold used in Europe came from Africa).

The design of the original Florentine florins was the distinctive fleur de lis badge of the city on one side and on the other a standing facing figure of St. John the Baptist wearing a hair shirt. On other countries' florins, first the inscriptions were changed (from "Florentia" around the fleur, and the name of the saint on the other), then local heraldic devices were substituted for the fleur de lis, many resembling the Virgin Mary.

He called up a new window and went to the American Numismatic Association web page. There he selected the on-line publication and called up the new article in *The Numismatist* on-line at the same time he had the journal article in front of him.

The *Numismatic News* was also on-line, so Linc popped up another search window and grabbed that web page as well. Being a member in good standing in both the American Numismatic Association and NGC Collectors Society had its advantages when he wanted to get a fast start on research.

He then set up a third search window strictly to conduct other searches and immediately typed in Dutch East India Company. "First joint-stock company founded in 20 March 1602. Dominated spice trade for the next two centuries. Finally went bankrupt in 17 March 1798. Minted duit in 1735 by VOC *Vergaan Onder Corruptie* (referring to the acronym VOC) which translates as 'Perished By Corruption'. The VOC became bankrupt and was formally dissolved in 1800, its possessions and the debt being taken over by the government of the Dutch Batavian Republic. The VOC's territories became the Dutch East Indies and were expanded over the course of the 19th century to include the whole of the Indonesian archipelago, and in the 20th century would form Indonesia."

Linc shifted his silver rimmed glasses down on his nose slightly so that when he looked into the computer screen he would be actually looking through the lenses rather than over them. He had tried contacts off and on over the years but found them troublesome and not worth the daily bother. Glasses he just had to keep clean which he did fastidiously. In fact, that was far better for him. After all, he could not go around cleaning his contacts right in front of people when he became a little nervous. With glasses, he could.

He was, in fact, meticulous and fastidious about everything from his condominium to his dress. He always looked so neat and clean and perfectly groomed with his close cropped silver hair and beard that many often confused him with a Muslim, a confusion that was perhaps understandable to some extent given the current circumstances but was, nonetheless, intolerable to him. He would always respond that Muslims were not the only people who liked to be clean. It was just that they were the only ones who chose to make a damned religion out of it.

He had worked all his life with the NAACP for equal rights for everybody, but now they were transforming into a black Muslim type organization, becoming exclusive rather than inclusive. He wanted nothing to do with that. He agreed with his friend and client, Theo Theodora, that Islam was, by design, exclusive to all other faiths or thought. That, in his mind, did not promote the notion of equal rights which had been the driving force behind the NAACP since its inception. So, he had resigned as President of his local chapter which had been his position unchallenged for more than twenty-five years.

"Well, Lincoln 'Walks Alone' Black, you just have to excuse these poor folks from Greensboro for being so ignorant. I mean they don't even know how to spell Negro, now do they?"

Linc remembered quickly picking up on where his new friend Gwynn seemed to be going. "And, they don't know how to say it either." Diffuse a tense situation with humor. That was what they would learn to call it in later life.

At the time, they simply laughed and sort of hugged without touching like boys might back then, long before hugging became the hip thing to do. Even now he wondered what some of those folks must have thought seeing those two boys—one Negro and one white—hugging it up and laughing it up just after all that terrible mess and the game being cancelled because of them. It would always be their fault to those folks that nobody represented their region in Williamsport that year. Two coming of age boys in America standing up for what was right. It was their South African train. It was also their Birmingham. Their Selma. Their Philadelphia. Even though those events had not yet taken place. It was their profiles in courage. And, make no mistake about it, a body might get sidetracked. A body might run into a detour. A body might simply lose his or her way. But, you could never ever take that away from someone once they had it. If you ever did try, however, you would be doing so at your peril.

20
Theo's Hideaway

[Music: "Lincoln 'Walks Alone' Black"]

Lincoln was surprised how similar his life had once again become to his great grandfather Isaac's life. Isaac had been on the run from slave hunters in the Great Smoky Mountains on a stolen horse. Lincoln had once been on the run from his past in those same mountains with what he felt like at the time was a stolen life. Now he was on the run from the Caliphate as he guided his Cadillac through a series of S-curves along Skyline Drive that slithered along the eastern side of the Shenandoah Valley like a cement snake. This time, nothing stolen.

In early August, Route 11 would be humming with the largest yard sale in the world. That is, if the new powers that be would allow it to go on. He had not heard any news or rumors that it would not, so he assumed it would. He kept up with such things or at least his assistants did, and they informed him daily. The Internet still made that easy to do even with the intrusive government scrutiny of the Caliphate. You never knew when you might run across a coin or Medallion or document that made that particular trip to the Route 11 yard sale worthwhile. That was his excuse, anyway. But, what really happened was that he had found many of his owls at such sales. Probably too many. One of them dangled from his rearview mirror— a painted ceramic Great Horned Owl head he had actually picked up at the Route 11 event several years earlier.

Despite the fact that those same powers-that-be were now after him, he had to admit that they were a savvy enough bunch to pretty much leave people alone unless they had to come down on them—as an example or something. He was, unfortunately, rapidly turning into one of those 'or somethings' himself.

Theo's Hideaway was somewhere off Highway 250 near Staunton. He wasn't exactly sure where, but it was located underground in the middle of the northern Blue Ridge range. Theo had told him to look for the sign. He would know it when he saw it, Theo assured him.

Well, he certainly hoped that he would, because his jeopardy due to his resignation as NAACP President and the comments he made afterwards as well as his recent research and financial transactions had been drawing the attention of what he referred to as the Perfection Police. He was under constant surveillance until finally he escaped into these Virginia mountains as they were actually coming to arrest him. He had to laugh a little that it took them so many months to finally get enough on him to come after him directly. He also had to laugh because he was pretty sure he had lost them early on before it even looked like he was going to make a run for it, before they could secretly apprehend him.

Forty miles along Highway 250, the sign made itself unmistakably clear to him. On both sides of the road stood giant plastic owls with hand printed signs attached to them, reading:

Theo's Hideaway
Owls only

A hand drawn arrow below the words pointed left. The entrance to a two-wheel path was barely visible in the brush and brambles that claimed the forests at the edges of Highway 250. No sooner had he made that turn into the brush than he heard a truck pull up behind him stopping on the highway. What he couldn't see but could surmise, knowing Theo as he did, was that the occupants of the truck picked up both owls and signs and immediately drove off heading further east. No more than two minutes along this cart path and his Ebony Cadillac was scared and scratched.

"Beyond recognition," he muttered as he viewed the marred finish. "But that sure beats the hell out of it being me," he half-chuckled at himself. Suddenly, a man in camouflage appeared. He seemed to spring up from the path itself, his left hand stretched palm out toward Lincoln.

"Halt!" A combat rifle was slung around his right arm in such a position that he could fire if necessary.

Lincoln's vehicle was only rolling along at less than five miles per hour. So stopping immediately was easy to do.

"Lincoln Black?" the camouflage figure shouted at him. "Are you Lincoln Black?"

He nodded. Then, he answered verbally. "Yes. I am Lincoln Black."

A woman Major stepped from behind the guard. "What hunts within the walls of your office as if it were in a dark wood?"

"Owls." Before the word was out of his mouth completely, he realized that he had said it wrong. "I'm so sorry. The proper response is: What hunts within the walls of your office as if it were the dark woods? Great Horned Owls." Theo and his obsession with special security went back as far as they all did together, back to Vietnam where he had been the travel agent for their team. That was where he met up with Gwynn Camsron for the second time— through Theo. "That's the response. Great Horned Owls."

"Mr. Black. Please exit your vehicle and come with me, sir. Your vehicle will be repaired and secured until you are ready to depart."

"Oh, you have a Cadillac repair facility here?"

"Welcome to Theo's Hideaway, sir. And you might like to know that we have just about everything here that we could ever need in a motor pool, thanks to Gwynn's treasure and to your hard work. I am Major Magdalena Averroes, at your service. We met briefly once before. It is an honor, sir."

Theo's Hideaway, as all those who were a part of The Nine called it, was a series of interconnected caves that had been reinforced and designed to house the major leaders of the country. While researching a book on the subject of an attack on America, Theo had discovered the super top secret abandoned and little known-about underground facility that had been originally designed to house top government and private officials in case of an attack on the US. The only ones who knew about it were the people who built it and those few inside Secret Service who had a need to know along with appropriate State Department and Defense Department officials. Most of them only knew that facilities existed. Few, if any, knew where any of them were actually located.

Major Averroes ushered Linc through an opening in the mountain that closed behind them immediately. "I'll try to brief you as well as I can between here and Command Central where they are expecting you."

"Thank you Major. The only other time I was here, I was blindfolded. I had absolutely no idea where I was until I was sitting at the stainless steel triangle table in the center of Command Central." He snapped his fingers. "That's where we met!"

"Yes, sir. So, then, you already know that the facility name is The Caverns of Woe. What you may not have been told during your blindfolded tour before is that the word Woe is actually an acronym for We Overcome the Enemy. As you can readily see, it is buried deep inside the earth. It is a virtual underground city and was designed to also serve as the hub of the FEMA subterranean network and its underground facilities which exist beneath several major airport terminals throughout the country.

"It was originally designed as a Last Chance Facility or Continuity Of Government facility. COG for short. This secret network was to work as a political control center for our backup government.

"The facility consists of many different levels. I've been here since the Nine first came here, and I still don't know how many.

"There are tunnels to quite a few major cities around the country. Sorry, I can't be more specific on that, but that's strictly need to know. Only a select few would know those kinds of details.

"We are, for all practical security purposes, invisible. Unless someone accidentally stumbled upon something or someone exposing the subterranean system, no one could ever detect it through technology. At least, not in our life times. Betsy Ross pretty much has that under control for sure, sir.

"The facility can comfortably support at least 5000 people but can be massaged into support for as many as ten to fifteen thousand peak capacity. In order to be able to support such a large population on a continuing basis, the infrastructure of The Caverns of Woe provides for a self-sustaining environment. It includes: microwave communications systems; a small spring-fed lake, a pair of 250,000 gallon water tanks and several ponds (both salt water and fresh water) supporting a variety of water-based protein growth such as fish, shrimp, and oysters; streets, sidewalks, and parks; a nuclear powered generating plant that drives a complete municipal infrastructure from sewage treatment and creation of water to electricity and transportation (electric cars); a hospital; cafeterias; private living quarters and dormitories; office building space; closed circuit TV and radio as well as radio and TV studio; massive supercomputing facilities with war game simulators and personal information on millions of Americans. Well, somebody's got to maintain and repair all that stuff."

"And that would be you?"

"Yes, sir. That would be my responsibility."

"Damn big job Major Averroes."

The Major smiled broadly as she drew his attention to the meeting complex behind the transparent double doors in front of them with her outstretched hands. "This is the heart and soul of the complex. You've been inside there once before." As she continued, he could not help but note the increased sense of pride imparted with every breath of her presentation.

"The Caverns of Woe is the self-sustaining underground nationwide command center for approximately 100 other Federal Relocation Centers around the country. There are several COG facilities within a three hundred mile radius of Washington D.C. In the event of nuclear war, declaration of martial law, or other national emergency, the President, his cabinet and the rest of the Executive Branch would be 'relocated' here."

"Guess that didn't work out too well this last time, huh?"

Despite herself, the Major had to stifle a belly laugh. "That's very good, sir. But, allow me to provide you with a little numismatist style humor while we're waiting for the signal to enter. I was informed that you are an avid coin collector. Is that correct, sir?"

"Yes, Major, I am guilty as charged."

"This numismatic joke is, actually, a riddle of sorts, I imagine."

"All right, Major. Let's hear it, then."

"You have two coins that equal eleven cents. One is not a penny. What two coins are you holding?"

"I presume that the one that is not a penny is a dime. The remaining one that is not a dime is a penny. That approach also works for a number of other coin options, Major. You know, like two coins totaling thirty-five cents but one is not a dime, or two coins totaling thirty cents and one is not a nickel."

"You really are as clever as rumored, sir."

"Why thank you, Major, I think."

"You're most welcome, sir. Looks like they're ready to open the doors for us, sir."

The glass doors slid open generating practically no noise and seemingly little or no friction. That was how the Caliphate had done it, and The Nine didn't have much time to change it back before it became set like a great coconut custard pie. "But, Major, did you ever think about this seldom-considered facet of the humor diamond? No matter how you cut it, if you subtract that penny from that dime, you end up with nine cents. And, that's how much I paid to see the first film I ever saw in a movie theater, George Pal's original film version of 'War of the Worlds.'"

Nine Circles
Of Salt

21
Gauguin Twilight

**"Red sky in morning sailor take warning;
red sky at night, sailors' delight."**
[Music: "Gauguin Twilight"]

From far out past the farthest horizon, various shades of magenta twilight spread above the earth in Gauguin brush strokes. In that light, torrential rain spattered like blood on the waves that roared and frothed onto the vanishing island beach in front of him for what could actually be the last time for him or for anyone else from his Clan or from any other. By this time tomorrow they might all be dead. What was visible of the islands around him were dark holms in the sea like humps of the spine of some gargantuan monster lurking in the deepening twilight.

The wind swirled in twister-like gusts, spraying him with the blood rain and the tops of the waves from what seemed to be Homer's wine-dark sea. Greek for "wine-dark" was *oinos*. The word actually translated to something like "sunset-red," as best he could recall. Homer "coined" the phrase in the *Iliad* when Achilles, after the funeral of his beloved Patroclus' who had been killed in battle, looked out over a "wine-dark sea" as the sun went down. And, that was what this night was like under this simmer dim, this midnight twilight with its brush stroke sky. It was as if nature had been turned upside down.

In his right hand Gwynn clutched a rolled plastic bag that held his boarding pass for the jet charter to Charlottesville. This was like his sword. He had been staring at it for what seemed to be hours before the storm raged in from the west. The flight was scheduled for noon tomorrow. Then, by rental jeep, on to The Caverns of Woe. His left hand curled around the handles of Theo's *Neo Geo* athletic bag. This held his armor.

For the ninth time since he had uncovered the vault, he would have to slip back into the skin of Chace Durante. Those were his requisite circles of salt. Yet, each time he assumed the role became more precarious than the time before. He did not know how much longer he would be able to continue the ruse without being caught, or how much longer he could hold out from actually transforming into Chace Durante—a man who, actually, only existed electronically. Hopefully, the alternative identity would soon not be necessary at all. Gauguin painted it better and said it better than anyone he could think of: "Life being what it is, one dreams of revenge."

His revenge would be *on* the murderers of Senator Abigail Keayrn. His revenge would be *for* all those people who had placed stones on his cairn over the years. Each village he helped save in Vietnam. Each young person he helped graduate in St. Thomas. His revenge would be the people's revenge. His revenge would restore truth and beauty to a world gone false and ugly. His revenge would be *on* the murderers of America. His revenge would be a July Fourth Ragnarök.

This island had been his garden during these trying times because he knew he was completely alone with himself and his past. He had not seen the Custodian of Eynhallow Kirk, Flagg, since their first encounter when he discovered the vault. He had searched the small island several times for the least sign that anyone lived there, but he could find none. Although somewhat puzzling, it was also strangely liberating to know with some certainty that he was the only person on the island. And, somehow, the compulsion for revenge cooled for moments at a time. Then, he could just be himself when he was visiting the vanishing holy island without having to assume any role as Chace Durante or Gwynn Camsron or Gwynn VII or anyone else real or imagined for that matter.

Glasgow had instructions to wait for Chace Durante if he did not arrive on time. But, the Thorodale would be off at first light, Captain Flett had assured him. And, he had promised to take him all the way to Scrabster Harbour, "at full speed ahead as soon as it is light enough to travel. That'll be about three am this time of year," Flett teased. They had become like old friends over nine trips. Sadly, their timing would not be right for dinner at The Captain's Galley this trip. He had to make a noon deadline to Glasgow, but, at least, it looked like he would make that on time. So, if, per chance, his only hope was this one last opportunity to restore what had been lost.

And, if by some dumb chance, he could only choose one thing to restore. What would that one thing be?

Fiery slashes of color still painted the sky. The pigments permeated everything. The sea was wine-dark. His clothes were wine red. His skin seemed to bleed wine-dark from its pores. Then, almost ruthlessly, the seemingly endless twilight was, suddenly and finally, absorbed by the darkness. Even then, the darkness was not complete. It was more like a thin piece of black paper with a pernicious red light shining behind it threatening, at any moment, to shred the paper with its intensity. Until such time, no longer did the late night sky burn with the bright beacons that romance and adventure bring when doing what is right simply because it is the right thing to do.

The rains gradually transformed into an almost calming mist. The winds abated to occasional light gusts. Yet, once nature's art work had vanished and the silence had been assaulted by the Harbor Seals that remained from their haul-out earlier in the day, he did not hear the persistent Adhan that permeated America. Here in the midst of the Orkney Islands, he had come to appreciate that absence more than he could ever express, more than anyone could know or understand. That absence was nearly meditation in itself.

In the summer of sixty-two, his meditation had been defined by a fifty-seven Chevy and the first true and pure wisdom that ever possessed him. It seemed to have always taken him over when he was behind the wheel, but, for the life of him, he could not quite recall exactly what that appropriate epiphany had been. He only remembered that he actually experienced it that evening for the first time and every time afterwards when it manifest itself the epiphany was always the same like a recurring dream or nightmare depending on point of view.

The initial feeling had begun with an inner glow that he thought would be like the internal version of heat balm heating him up from the inside out as he shoved the turquoise-over-white fifty-seven Chevy Coupe full-throttle into the outskirts of Blue Field, West Virginia, gateway to the West Virginia Turnpike. The innermost streets of the mountain village lay in wait for him as the outlying carnelian swatches of the evening dissolved around the buildings and houses, wafting their way into his past before he even realized it was his past.

He only felt the searing gush from his medulla oblongata through each tingling chakra of his spine. That was the same lighting that struck his second chakra every time a female of such delight, reeking of Dr. Bronner's peppermint soap and freshly harvested, home-dried dope, sucked and suckled him. Her legs spread like divergent paths. Her back arched to embrace the universe with her thighs and him as one small and seemingly insignificant part of it. The musty musk darkness between her taut tits after all those years still stirred the cooling coals that occasionally served as his loins.

Memories of his first sincerely received and perceived brush with epistemological death by epiphany smoldered but did not yet flame. Wreckage and carnage already ordered the universe for many others back then. Not yet, for him. All that was no more than a Faustian surprise yet to come.

He lifted his bearded face toward the memory. The foam on the waves that roared upon the shore as night began to etch its inevitable way into the true and pure darkness that really was the center of all things conceivable and inconceivable was the color of what was left when there was only his selfness to ejaculate into the space and time warps of her herbal pink and black.

Even as memory, the surges and regurgitations cauterized his very soul, sometimes with pleasure, sometimes with pain. It depended on the situation, the Special Forces Staff Sergeant would instruct him just a few years later in life, only months before he somehow wandered voluntarily from Princeton into Vietnam. The answer to every question, the Staff Sergeant emphasized every day in special intelligence training, was enemy, weather, terrain, or it depends on the situation. Somewhere within the framework of those options and whatever craft the trade had to offer him, all truth lurked.

But, Staff Sergeant didn't have an answer for Abigail Keayrn. He still mourned her as if she had died yesterday. The video of her being stoned to death in the Grenadines on the beach at Whale Island continued to haunt him both awake and asleep. He remembered having a new kind of epiphany while he was also being held captive on that small Caribbean island by his former teammate in Vietnam. He called it the epiphany of helplessness.

Never in his life since the passing of his father had he felt really helpless. In fact, most of his life he had considered himself to be pretty much in control. By the time Abbie's husband, Sal, had segregated them so that he had no idea not only where he was but also where she might be, he was beginning to understand the word and the depth of its true meaning. With all his training, with all his skills, with all his knowledge, with all his physical capabilities, he was incapable of doing anything to save the only woman he had loved since that summer of sixty-two. And, he did not expect to love another regardless of whether he died or lived tomorrow.

The soft undulation of the Caribbean Sea would have normally lulled them to sleep after a long day of sailing. That night, anchored in a sheltered cove off a very small island just south of Guadeloupe, their senses were keen and edgy, heightened by the sea air and the mission. When they accidentally touched or bumped up against one another, the electricity that surged through them both was more than palpable. It was practically visible and clearly unavoidable.

The television was muted. The stereo was off. The only sounds other than their voices and the occasional creaking and cracking of the Brown Pelican were the low, soft swells lapping against its hull. He recalled how enthralled she seemed to be with his story of the Medallion.

"So, you just walked away from that incredibly rich family heritage?"

"Yeah, I guess I did at that. Right into a rice paddy."

He had slowed the Chevrolet to what seemed to him to be practically a stand-still in order to navigate the slumbering mountain community of Blue Field without drawing any undue attention to him or his nineteen fifty-seven force of nature. He turned the volume down on Del Shannon's *Runaway* as he lowered the volume on the stereo radio with speakers in the back. That was an innovation by his friend's friend that she had accepted graciously and passed on to him for a short time.

"Drive my customized cherry fifty-seven Chevy to Milwaukee for me. I'll pay all expenses and, say, twenty-five a day. Put you up in Milwaukee over the Fourth, and give you all the Milwaukee beer you can drink and a free train ride or flight home," Francesca offered. "Your choice."

Even ten years his senior and married to some humpbacked millionaire drug salesman who looked like he came straight from the pages of a Terry Southern or Victor Hugo novel, she was the hottest woman he had experienced in his, still, 45 rpm life.

"Their fireworks are some of the coolest anywhere!" She knew. She grew up with them down on the lake shore where they honored the living and the dead, the rapture and the dread, the unspoken and the said. "And, my fireworks aren't too bad either." She had paused, smiling quickly as though she were concerned about being caught smiling at him in that way at that moment.

"So, you will be there in Milwaukee with me?"

And, she answered, "Yes. I'll be there in the hotel that overlooks the park beside the lake. Yes." There, she explained, the fireworks display would light up the sky with colors enough to scramble the message and the mind receiving it. It would be the ultimate McLuen-esk moment, she promised. Her breath stuck in her throat. She trembled. He recalled the hard-on expanding in his pants.

"This is the deal, sweetie pie. I'll be available when you need me. And, I'll do what you request whether it be dictation or dick tasting. Do you get my drift?"

"I do," he had mumbled. "But what about him?"

"The old humpback bastard is selling insurance to some big company in LA. He'll be gone for two weeks. He wouldn't be in Milwaukee anyway. I'll just be there for the summer with my family like I am every summer."

"That's a long time just to close an insurance deal, isn't it?"

"I don't know. I never ask. I'm just happy when he's gone."

It was a time when he still saw all things as possible, even Francesca in the hotel suite overlooking the lake and the fireworks that made Gerty McDowell's look like a paltry pageant at best. And, Francesca did not have a game leg. She actually walked incredibly on two very beautiful divergent paths, paths that in his mind seemed to reach the ceiling when she was on her back. The ultimate promise of that actually happening was what he had known would get him through Blue Field without a hitch. That was what he had known would carry him along the West Virginia Turnpike without a ticket, along the Ohio River without drowning, and ultimately to the land of beers and she in the hotel by the lake.

Should he plant those seeds or not? He knew instinctively that was at least a part of why she wanted him. The old humpback hubby didn't have enough of those microscopic, swizzle-tailed spermatozoa to make a baby, but he had plenty. And, there was nothing like a baby to serve as a constant excuse for lack of intimacy. That, Shakespeare and Samuel Clemens notwithstanding, was the real question. He had fantasized it enough times. But, he didn't even know if the seeds would germinate or if he wanted them to. After all, they were ancient seeds with deep roots so he'd been told all his life. He didn't know how many years, not really. But they were many generations old, he was sure of that. He also didn't know what might grow from them if the seeds actually sprouted.

These were things humans were not programmed to think about. These were things best left unspoken and unthought. These were things to be done, not to be analyzed. These were the realities that reside between the thighs of love and hate, between the thighs of give and take, between the thighs of dark and light, between the thighs of wrong and right, between the thighs of ice and fire, between the thighs of dispassion and desire. How often did the potential roads not taken look so damned good?

And, to be sure, he understood how accepting certain realities could be difficult. He knew that all too well. He recalled a conversation he and Linc had in The Caverns of Woe mess just after he arrived, fleeing from the Caliphate authorities.

"Yes, Linc. I know I used to think that the pitches slowed down for everybody."

"Yeah, I knew when we met that evening on the baseball diamond in Greensboro that you were one of those guys who was real special but was absolutely convinced that he was like everybody else."

"I guess I must have been in high school or, maybe, early college before I really came to understand that the baseball slowing down for you as it approaches the plate is not a standard tool of perception for everyone else. Betsy Ross, now she picked up on that right away because her Father was a pro ball player.

"And, one of my coaches—I think it was like my senior year at Wilmington High. The hitting coach—I just can't place his name right now. He was just taking a look at my swing in the batter's cage.

"'You wait awfully late before you pull the trigger. You know, commit your wrists.'"

"'Well, coach, Gabriel.' That was his name. Coach Gabriel. I said 'the ball comes at me like it's in slow motion or something, so I feel like I've got all the time in the world to finish off my swing.'"

"'Oh really? Do you know how rare that is?'"

"'I don't know. It's like being in a zone or something.'"

"'Yes, I know.'"

"'But, it's not just sometimes. It's every pitch.'"

"'So, you hold off until the very last because you know you can?'"

"'Basically, yeah, I guess'"

"'That's how you get so much wrist into it every time. Well, I'll just be damned.'"

How, then, is one life plucked out like that from all the rest to be able to see the pitch in slow motion, to be able to lead the revolution? Is there truly no other way? Had he simply been doomed to hit .400 or programmed to resist? Was he blinded by his own prejudices and preferences, by his own fears? Now, in this moment of his perfection, was he, in fact, too imperfect? Was he the warrior legend had promised? The warrior who could lead his people back to the safety of the comfortable tragedy they called their lives before the new and uncomfortable tragedy of the Caliphate trumped it hands down, well, hands *and* foreheads down?

On the night of July Fourth, nineteen sixty-two, Francesca was there, as she had promised, at the hotel next to the lake. The fireworks exploded as they did, too, in rapturous sex of every kind in every position of the *Kama Sutra*. He gave her enough of himself to populate Milwaukee, and she was so thankful she asked for more.

Then there was the epiphany.

He realized now that it was not actually something that continually came to him when he found himself behind the wheel of a car. It was, instead, what came into that suite on the lake illuminated by the last of the fireworks every time Francesca's humpback husband burst through the door. He foamed at the mouth and screamed like a wild man as he waved two forty-four's in front of him. Without a word, he began to spray the room with rounds from the old west display pistols Francesca had given him as a birthday gift two years before. The air reeked of burned gunpowder.

Gwynn dragged a nearly paralyzed Francesca onto the floor and pushed her under the protection of the bed. He blocked her with his body as shots continued to ring out until the revolvers ran out of bullets. Yet, despite all evidence to the contrary, Gwynn felt that he was in control of the situation, that he would, somehow, make this all turn out okay. He listened carefully. The husband was not reloading. Gwynn edged his way from underneath the bed toward the husband. His two pistols lay smoking on the royal blue carpet of the bedroom, one by each hand, in the suite by the lake in Milwaukee. Sirens screamed in the night. Security was pounding on the door. And, the humpback cuckold wept. Gwynn was confident that he could master the moment.

That was his epiphany.

In the end, the longing for the Chevrolet or the lust for the girl was still what it all came down to. Each had been his inspiration at one time or another, but he refused to be limited to either the girl or the car. To him, they were, somehow, inseparable.

Now he had to fight so that both could survive. The new day was just beginning to seep up from the horizon as if the light behind the black paper had finally burned its way through, and in only a short, too-few hours. He was just happy that he would be able to sleep on the plane. Maybe, depending on how rough the seas would be this morning, he could even catch a snooze on the Thorodale. He could see lights, just now, popping on in the boat's portals. Probably the young one, Galen, in the galley already fixing breakfast. His father, Captain Flett, would soon be sending the other two older brothers for him in the dingy.

He had barely completed his thought when he heard the high whine of the dingy's engine off in the distance. He strained to see the Thorodale through the pre-dawn mists accumulating along the shoreline. As the pitch of the engine rose, he saw what looked like a couple of rockets strapped together coming around the bow of the boat and making straight for the beach and, consequently, for him. He placed the boarding pass inside the *Neo Geo* gym bag. The bag was a good bit heavier than on previous trips because he had taken out so much paper before. And, this was the ninth trip, the last trip to complete the metaphorical spell first cast by Thorodale in the ancient days. He had been very careful not to ever take more with him than he could carry in the bag. He did not want to draw undue attention to himself. That was why it had taken so many trips. This would be the last trip. The bag's final load was mostly the last of the coins and the pages of some biography notebooks that seemed to be an on-going record of the Clan of Gwynn. Most of the documents he had not even had an opportunity to look at yet.

Tomorrow he would die with honor or The Nine would be victorious and return the government of the people, for the people, and by the people to the people. Either way, there was no one to inherit the Medallion, and, in a sense, that was fitting. After all, this was the time of great need that the Vault of the Unnamed Knight had been built for. This was the time of great need that those who held the Unnamed Knight trust knew would come and gave of their possessions to prepare for even though they would not live to see it themselves. Another time, another crisis of cultures and religions would require a new mythos and its progeny built upon another thousand years of history.

Just like that evening in 1962 when he eased Francesca's fifty-seven Chevy so quietly through Blue Field, West Virginia, he planned to quietly carry Theo's gym bag right onto the private jet in Glasgow and, without notice, walk off the plane with it in hand after landing in Charlottesville just as he had done successfully eight times before.

22
"Live Free or Die!"
[Music: "Gauguin Twilight"]

Allahu Akbar, Allahu Akbar.
Allahu Akbar, Allahu Akbar.

The amplified Adhan ricocheted off the surrounding mountain ridges, battering its way into Theo Theodora's thoughts like thunder. The Caliphate army was preparing for Salat Ul Asr completely unaware of what the real thunder said with regard to the dying and the dead.

Ash-hadu alla ilaha illa-llah.
Ash-hadu alla ilaha illa-llah.

Damn, Gwynn would be proud of him for that thought, now wouldn't he? Theo laughed quietly to himself. He had even made it rhyme.

Ash-hadu anna
Muhammadar-Rasulullah.
Ash-hadu anna
Muhammadar-Rasulullah.
Hayya 'ala-s-Salah, Hayya 'ala-s-Salah.
Hayya 'ala-l-falah, Hayya 'ala-l-falah.
Allahu Akbar, Allahu Akbar.
La ilaha illa-llah

Datta. Dayadhvam. Damyata. Give, sympathize, control. That was what Eliot wrote as what the thunder said. His cell phone pulsed in the lower left pocket of his ghillie. Give him the Damyata, Damyata, Damyata. To hell with that Datta and Dayadhvam stuff. They simply provided convenient diversions from the goal. Finally, without prejudice, those two little devils were all about confusion and delusion designed specifically to keep everyone from the prize except those few who knew what the words and their progeny really meant.

Shantih shantih shantih. "The Peace which passeth understanding." A formal ending to this abbreviated Upanishad, he chuckled into his hands.

Even though it made practically no sound, to Theo, under these circumstances, his cell phone's pulse reverberated also like claps of thunder every bit as loud as the muezzin's words even though he knew that no one would ever be able to hear the pulse anyway, especially with the Adhan ringing in one's ears. It was about time he called. He fished the phone from the belt slot on his left hip and glanced at the display. It was not him. Instead, the phone showed a text message from Văn. Food would be ready within the hour. If no mission action was taking place, then the soldiers could eat one unit at a time.

He remembered vividly Văn's reaction when he had first seen the sign painted in red letters over the entrance to The Caverns of Woe: "Lasciate ogne speranza, voi ch'intrate."

"Abandon all hope, ye who enter here?" Văn had looked at him quizzically. "Not what I would call a great recruiting slogan, Theo."

"Caverns of Woe here. City of Woe in the *Inferno*. Strictly an ironic reference to Dante's famous lines, my dear Văn. We don't ask that you abandon all hope. We only ask that you live free or die." He laughed, but Văn knew he was "dead" serious about that part of it.

He had told Văn many times since then that he was their real secret weapon, because the troops, to a person, would kill for his cuisine. As long as Văn was cooking, the enemy was in very deep trouble. With his uncanny ability to impart his knowledge, skills, and values to others, he had quickly trained enough chefs so that sometimes even he did not know whether he had personally cooked something or one of his protégés.

The words of Islam were to be in Arabic only, yet the muezzin chanted in English, something that puzzled Theo. Such actions did not seem consistent with leaders who seemed to believe that all an infidel had to do to desecrate the *Qur'an* was to touch it, even by accident, and that the holy book could only be read by submitters. Such sinners are to be executed.

Allah is the Greatest, Allah is the Greatest.

Allah is the Greatest, Allah is the Greatest.
I bear witness that there is none worthy of worship
but Allah.
I bear witness that there is none worthy of worship
but Allah.

He could only conclude that the Caliphate was using the Adhan to call the people of the USI to prayer in Arabic and in English. Then, whether they wanted to pray or not, none could use the excuse that they did not understand the call. Theo laughed to himself. He had found himself doing that a good deal lately. For that to actually work, the muezzin would have to say the words in Spanish, French, Italian, German, Hindi, Japanese, Chinese, Vietnamese and a few dozen more. It would take until the next prayer time just to utter the Adhan. The muezzin's voice from the improvised minaret atop a tank echoed up from the valley below, where the intersection at Rockfish Gap of I-64 and USI 250 created the crosshairs for the conflict that had been building ever since the Caliphate takeover.

I bear witness that Muhammad is the Messenger of
Allah
I bear witness that Muhammad is the Messenger of
Allah
Hasten to the Prayer, hasten to the Prayer.
Hasten to real success, hasten to real success
Allah is the Greatest, Allah is the Greatest.
There is none worthy of worship but Allah.

Theo understood that this opportunity today was basically their one chance for real success. They were poised to hit DC and retake control there and in all of the state capitols across the country the moment this deed was done. He sensed that this would be their one big chance to unseat the Caliphate once and for all. If they failed here in these valleys, on this day, then the Caliphate would be forewarned as to their potential power as a revolutionary force. And, regardless of the newfound wealth from the Vault of the Unnamed Knight, The Nine would not be able to prevail, because the Caliphate would never be so lax again. From now on, they would truly be ready for them.

The phone pulsed again. This time a new caller number displayed, one he didn't know. This had to be him then, didn't it? He answered the call. "About damned time, LT. I mean, what the hell, it's just the most important mission in the entire world—probably ever. So, don't worry about not getting here on time or anything like that, okay?"

"Hey, hold on a minute, Theo. I *am* sorry, but the goddamned plane was delayed in Glasgow."

"Why?"

"I really don't know."

"Were you late?"

"No. I definitely was not late. Something technical—with one of the engines I think. That's what the Captain told us anyway. And, it didn't seem to be suspicious, you know political or anything like that."

"Or like maybe somebody realized you weren't Chace Durante or recognized you for who you really are and maybe wanted to turn you in for the reward?"

"Not that I could tell. Anyway, if that had been the reason, then they would never have allowed us to leave."

"Probably true, LT. Probably true. So, where are you now?"

"In a rental jeep about fifteen minutes away."

"Okay, LT. Be careful driving in. Charlie has already arrived. Looks like there's going to be a big bivouac here tonight."

"Charlie? Charlie? Theo, they are not the Viet Cong. That was forty whatever years ago."

"Aw, come on, LT. I know that. But, it's just too convenient to fall back on old habits, you know?"

"Yeah, I do. And, no matter who the information is on, it never hurts to have reliable intelligence on the enemy. Right?"

"All joking aside, right. Especially from a trusted friend in the news media like Worth."

"Especially." Gwynn paused. "So, you realize, then, that the fact that the plane was delayed and that I was late for your Ragnarök party means your whole big deal about leasing a jet because you can control what happens and you can't control a commercial flight has now been blown out of the proverbial water, so to speak."

"I know that you could have sent me a text message, LT." Theo feigned irritation. "I sort of have my plate a little full here."

"And, I'll bet it's filled with Văn's food."

"You really could've sent me that text message, LT," he sputtered.

"I know, Theo, but I really needed a good, close-range dose of your abuse."

"Glad to oblige, I'm sure. But, seriously, LT, we have to shake this malaise, this limbo that sets in when you're waiting to strike. You know what I'm talking about. So, we need you here ASAP. Get your ass here fast, LT, so you can give them one of your 'give your right ventricle for your country' speeches you're so damned good at. Convince our warriors that we can take these guys out and set things right again before they get too sugared up on Văn's chow to care and go to sleep on us."

Gwynn belly-laughed. "Right."

"I mean it, LT. Damn, we don't want to be chasing this same banner for the rest of our lives."

"Short as that may be."

"Yes, short as that may be."

"See you in ten."

* * * * *

"Allahu Akbar!"

The human bomb's sandy white robe gleamed in what remained of the moonlight that drenched the Ellipse and the Washington Monument where he stood. He reached inside his robe with his left hand and pulled out an electronic detonator.

"Allahu Akbar!"

He raised the detonator above his head as he opened his robe with his right hand exposing a bomb of C4 slabs strapped around his upper body. A red light blinked rapidly where his heart should be. Even with his robe opened he did not expose his 'awrah. After all, within a matter of moments, he would become a martyr for Jihad.

"Allahu Akbar!"

His left hand thumb pressed the detonator button. The red light froze. The moon was instantly blotted out as if it had been eclipsed by the sun. A raging thunder filled the air around the memorial as it shattered into thousands of chunks and crumbled into what seemed to be a huge fiery pit in the grass of the Ellipse.

Saladin Keayrn's screams still rang in Gwynn Camsron's head, even though the Caliphate was now nearly a year old. He was sure that Sal's screams would be one of the last things he would ever hear before he died. Gwynn peered through his binoculars at the bivouacked caravan of vehicles down in the valley just off of I-64. Each truck, each jeep, each APC, each tank bore the green crescent and star that had rapidly replaced the stars-and-stripes, the cross, the Star of David, and every other religious and government symbol that was not Muslim. Hell, if he was in their sandals, that's what he would've done.

This operation had been designed over the past ten months as the culmination of all their efforts. It would be the shining symbol of rebellion for future generations to remember and revere. A strike as devastating to the new Muslim Caliphate as Sal Keayrn's destruction of the Washington Monument had been to America just a year ago. It would be their final and lasting commitment to freedom. There would be no turning back once this attack began. No second chances if it did not succeed. In the vernacular of Las Vegas, they were—one and all—"all in."

Gwynn could see banners sporting the likeness of Lars Hansen with the words "Lars Hansen President for Life" printed in two lines under it in green flanked by green crescents and stars. Similar banners with a picture of Saladin Keayrn and the words "Our Martyr" or "The Immortal Leader Lives Forever" flew beside them.

"Well, Hansen certainly got his reward for betraying his country, didn't he?" Gwynn spat his question at the figure crouched next to him behind their natural ditch-and-tree blind about a thousand yards away from the Caliphate bivouac area. They had been surprised earlier when they probed the perimeter of the Caliphate forces and discovered that there seemed to be no security beyond a few hundred yards out from the camp perimeter. "Not so sure about Sal though," he sniggered. "I haven't heard from him yet as to whether he received his forty virgins or not."

Also covered by a sniper's ghillie, Theo Theodora responded with a muffled grunt. "Is it forty or seventy-two? I never could keep that straight, you know. Either way it certainly looks to me like those folks out there think that the Immortal Leader is not ready to collect on those virgins in paradise—no matter how many—LT. At least, not just yet."

"Yeah. For some reason, the people seem to believe that he's still alive and kicking."

"The people have every reason to believe he is still alive and kicking, LT. His picture is everywhere. His voice is everywhere. You've heard the speeches, the pronouncements of faith, the fatwah against The Nine. They show video. They play his recorded voice over loudspeakers, on radio stations. Everywhere. Thus, no longer The Leader, he is now the Immortal Leader because he somehow survived that suicide bombing of the monument."

Gwynn shook his head vigorously. "But, that voice of the Immortal Leader sounds so fake to me, like he is always speaking in a minaret or an echo chamber. It sounds more like one of those digitally manufactured voices than the real human thing. And, don't forget. I saw it happen up close and very personal, Theo. And, believe me, there's no way anyone survived that blast. No way in hell."

"I remember it well, LT. Hell was exactly what it looked like when I found you there on the mall in front of where the Washington Monument used to be. Smoke and fire were all around you."

"Yes, that was too real for words, Theo."

"Yes, way too real."

"It was worse, even, than Vietnam."

Theo nodded. "So, I guess, on the home front here, we're not just plotting to blow up golf courses anymore, are we, LT."

Gwynn stifled a chuckle. "No, I guess we're not, Theo. It's definitely not the sixties and we're definitely not in college, and Rockfish Gap, Virginia at the junction of Interstate 64 and USI Highway 250, is definitely not the local country club golf course where we're planning to detonate a few fireworks."

"If so, this golf course has the worse damned roughs I've ever seen," Lincoln chimed in from inside his ghillie with a coarse whisper and muffled laugh. He knew their story well. More than once they had told him how when they were in college they plotted to blow up a golf course at a local country club near Princeton just to show that they were committed to the sixties revolution, that they were committed to action not just talk. Of course, they also had assured him, they never actually implemented the plan.

However, they did just the opposite of what would have been expected of so-called radical intellectuals of the day. Upon graduation, they joined the Army and helped to forge a major counterinsurgency special unit that operated for more than three years before they had to be shut down. It still amazed him how so many of those he had come to know as comrades in arms in Vietnam were so directly involved in this fight to the death. It was almost as if Vietnam had been their basic training.

In the beginning, just after Sal blew up the Washington Monument and himself, there were just nine of them. "The Nine" was how INN's Ellworth Hayes had dubbed them. "Just some interesting background for you. Nine is a symbolic number, obviously. There were nine original Knights Templar when they were formed during the First Crusade. The year: 1118. The place: The Kingdom of Jerusalem. The new order's sworn purpose: to provide protection for pilgrims from Europe who visited the Holy Land."

Ellworth had beamed the world-wide audience as he continued that night nearly ten months ago. "Another possibility. Since the leader and only identified member of The Nine—USI's most wanted, Gwynn Camsron—is of Scottish extraction, the number nine may refer to the nine circles of salt it takes to make the invisible become visible according to Norse and Scottish legends. Some rumors suggest that because this terrorist is a former hippie from the nineteen sixties, the number may refer to the Beatles song, 'Revolution Nine,' and the phrase 'Number nine,' that is repeated often in that song—a song that is, of course, banned by the Caliphate as is most so-called American and European music because the Caliphate has determined that they perpetuate moral depravity. These are just several of the many reasons why there might be nine of these demented revolutionaries out there somewhere plotting the overthrow of the Caliphate. Keep tuned in. We will keep you informed. For now, I'm Ellworth Hayes for ICN and its Appears Global International affiliates world-wide. Good night."

The reference was used so often that they soon came to call themselves "The Nine" and continued to do so even after the nine became thousands, then tens of thousands and hundreds of thousands spread out all over the country in abandoned military facilities, mostly underground, but all well hidden and secret even to the new Caliphate. Others simply lived and worked day to day as though everything was just fine now that the Caliphate had set everything right in the world. They would continue that existence patiently as good little Dhimini until the time came for them to act.

"Caliphate authorities would not comment on camera about yesterday's attacks. However, the Caliphate Central Command Commander, Mullah Quagmyr, told us, and I quote: 'It does not matter if there is nine of the infidel dogs or nine million of them. The United States of Islam's superior legions support the President for Life and the Immortal Leader and will stand as the mighty Army of Allah against any such pitiful enemy that would have the temerity to attack them.'

"I asked Commander Mullah Quagmyr why, then, have his legions not been able to stop sneak attack after sneak attack by the terrorists over the past nine months. The Mullah responded by demanding we cut off the recording session. His cadre of body guards confiscated all of our notes and recordings and we were forced to sign non-disclosure agreements which, I guess, I am close to violating at this point. Suffice it to say, the supreme Commander of Caliphate forces refused to answer any further questions.

"The President for Life's office has released a statement supporting the—and I quote—'tough, direct, and justified questioning by ICN's news anchor Ellworth Hayes. He knows that we want him and the network to always pursue the truth.'"

Those first nine began with Gwynn and Theo. That was how The Nine had begun to form. That Theo and Gwynn had somehow ended up almost unwittingly starting this same small band of fugitives from the occupying Muslims was nothing short of stupefying to both of them. It seemed like a replay of them being the ones who originated their special intelligence team in Vietnam right out of Princeton. Now, they had taken it upon themselves to re-declare the independence of the United States of America and to organize the resistance to the occupiers until the time came when they would become vulnerable to being overthrown.

The Nine HQ location in the Virginia mountains was a secure

and self-contained "safe" location developed just a few years earlier to house the government should a nuclear attack or a terrorist invasion take place. It was comprised of a series of tunnels and caves hidden in the side of a mountain. No one occupied it or had even discovered it after the takeover.

The invaders knew nothing of such secret off-the-books locations. However, Theo knew because of some work he had been doing on a new book about off-book operations. He knew that this location near Rockfish Gap was the primary command central for a network of such secret operations centers throughout the country that was interconnected by a closed one-way fiber optic communications system. They could contact outside the system provided certain protocols, but no one from outside could penetrate the system. Cell phone messages were the alternative for those in the field to contact inside. Then the one contacted would communicate from inside the system to the outside. Nothing was fool proof, but that was about as close as it got.

Ellworth remembered vividly the day they officially committed themselves to each other and to the cause. It had been a couple of months into the effort before they could arrange a time when each of them could meet at Central Command at the same day and time without arousing any suspicion.

"We pledge our lives, our fortunes, and our sacred honor," The Nine had sworn that night to each other just as their forefathers had sworn nearly 250 years before.

Gwynn Camsron, the Commander of the Nine had looked at those seated around the triangle stainless steel table that occupied the exact center of Command Central, as if he were tallying attendance. Three people sat along each of the triangle's sides. To Gwynn's right, Theo Theodora, his second in command. To his left, Lincoln "Walks Alone" Black, Chief Financial Officer and Operations Planning; along the side to their right sat Betsy Ross Smith, Operations Development, Planning, and Training; himself as media insider and undercover agent; and Chef de Cuisine Conrad Văn Lý. Ellworth often joked that he was seated at the table between truth and beauty. He was just never quite sure which one was which. Along the left side of the triangle was Elle Darby, Civic Action, Propaganda, Surreptitious Hill Liaison; Antonio Garcia, Corpsman in Afghanistan, Medical Intern and resident; and Magdalena Averroës, Maintenance & Services/Motor Pool.

"There are nine of us united in this limbo. We are not all of one faith or one creed or one race. We do not all share the same political philosophies. But, we are all patriots, and we do share one overwhelmingly important value, my friends. We must live free or die!"

"Perhaps, then, that should be our motto?"

"That's a good idea, Văn. If you put that in the form of a motion, then we could discuss it."

"I move that 'Live free or die!' serve as the official motto for The Nine."

"Second?"

"Second," Betsy Ross Smith responded, a little too loudly, and quickly covered her mouth with her hands.

"Okay, the floor is open for discussion. What do we know about the phrase? What does everyone think?"

Before anyone could respond, Lincoln leaped to his feet. "Excuse me, Gwynn, for interrupting here. But, this couldn't be more perfect! According to you, Gwynn, one of your ancestors, the Son of the Scholar of Inverness, deposited thousands of these coins in the vault you discovered in the Orkney Islands." Lincoln held up a gold coin.

"The value of things is important. The location of this facility is, for example, so valuable that those of us who don't know where it is were blindfolded when we were brought here today.

"But the value of these coins is not what matters here, although they are probably worth somewhere between two hundred and sixty-five to five hundred Euros each. The current exchange rate is two point nine five eight five eight USI dollars to one Euro. That is twice the rate that it was before the Caliphate. Then it was one point four seven nine two nine. Now, that would be somewhere between seven hundred and eighty-four dollars and fourteen hundred and seventy-nine dollars each.

"The coin has on its obverse the motto *Vivre libres ou mourir*, French for 'Live free or die.' When Gwynn showed me these coins after his return from that first historic trip to the vault, I suggested that each of the founding members of The Nine should have one. He agreed, and we also agreed that we would award them to new members as they earn our trust and demonstrate their leadership and other capabilities and, most of all, their loyalty.

"I have here a coin for each of you, the original Nine. 'Medals of confidence' my friends and fellow patriots—the French Revolutionary tokens of the Monneron Brothers. As I present you with your coin, please tell us what you know or think is important about the phrase and what your opinion is about it serving as our motto."

Lincoln approached them clockwise around the table, beginning with Elle Darby to his left. He handed her one of the Monneron de 5 sols au serment 1792 coins struck at Matthew Boulton's Soho Mint as tokens of exchange for The Paris firm of Monneron Freres. "You were blindfolded like me, weren't you, Elle?"

"Well, Linc." Elle paused. She still felt a little out of place here even though she had come to see The Caverns of Woe as something like a second home, a retreat from DC and all its trials and tribulations. "Yes, I was." Running a Senate office with the Senator *in absentia* was like nothing she had ever experienced. "And, I will do it whenever necessary to protect this location. If I don't know where this location is, then I can't tell anyone, no matter what they might promise me or do to me."

"Yes, Elle. I totally agree."

"Thank you, Linc, for this totem, this symbol of our struggle. Most of us probably know that 'Live Free or Die' was the official motto of the state of New Hampshire. What you might not know is that it remains the state's motto, despite all that has happened. Hard to believe, isn't it?"

Because the Caliphate froze everything in place when the Immortal Leader and the President for Life took over, there had been no elections at any level. In fact, as the Tears of Allah induced heroin haze gradually lifted in the days following the take over when the water of truth returned to normal, everything else seemed to return to normal too, continuing as it always had like nothing had changed. Maybe everyone experienced a collective bad dream. But, of course, things had changed. The active policy meant, however, that absent people like Senator Abigail Keayrn had not yet been replaced.

"It is also probably the best-known of all our state mottos." She clasped the coin to her chest. "And, I don't know about anyone else, but it totally expresses my feelings and my beliefs."

Next to her stood Antonio Garcia. Everyone called him "Ant" not only for the first three letters of his given name but because he scurried around all the time like an ant and worked tirelessly like an ant. An anchor baby at birth, he had grown up to be a decorated corpsman in Afghanistan, then a star medical student, Intern, and Resident at Johns Hopkins before the Caliphate came into power. Because he had fought against Muslims before, he was considered suspect by the Caliphate. He was watched continually.

Ant was a man of much action and few words. So, one day he simply did not appear for his rounds as Resident. He also did not appear that evening for a dinner with colleagues that had been scheduled weeks before. He disappeared from the view of the Caliphate. He vanished without a trace. Now he lived full time at The Caverns of Woe and ran medical operations for The Nine.

"During the Siege of Barcelona in seventeen thirteen and seventeen fourteen, the Barcelona defenders flew black flags with the motto 'Live free or die.' If it was good enough for my ancestors, then it's good enough for me."

Magdalena Averroës was next. "I know all of you are used to talking to me about how your jeep is running or when vehicles will be ready for a mission or something like that. But, my hobby is, has been for years, American Revolution history. And, I would like to suggest that another possible source for the phrase is Patrick Henry's famous March twenty-third, seventeen seventy-five speech to The Virginia House of Burgesses. It contained the legendary quote: 'Is life so dear, or peace so sweet, as to be purchased at the price of chains and slavery? Forbid it, Almighty God! I know not what course others may take; but as for me, give me liberty or give me death!'

"I vote yea."

"There are all kinds of contemporary culture references that would support the idea that, quote, the people, close quote, would find the motto appealing," Chef de Cuisine Conrad Văn Lý began as he accepted his coin from Linc with a slight bowing of his head. "For example, Bill Morrissey wrote a song entitled "Live Free or

Die" that appeared on his first album The song focused on the irony of a prisoner serving time in the State of New Hampshire's jails and hand-stamping license plates with the motto 'Live Free or Die.'

"Also, there have been some pretty bizarre ones like at the Kabul, Afghanistan airfield where 'Live free or die' was spray painted onto the back of a crashed rusted-out Soviet tank.

"History makes it clear that this phrase was created over these centuries just for this time and this place." He suppressed a chuckle. At the same time, he kissed the coin almost reverently. "Leave it to the inscrutable Vietnamese guy to blend humor and seriousness together in the same Phở. So, even if the phrase was not chiseled out of history just for us, in all seriousness, the words do apply."

"The phrase really incorporates a lot of history." Ellworth's eyes were moist as his trembling fingers reached out for the coin Linc proffered.

"Another of the blindfolded ones."

"Yes." At this moment, he could not avoid Dee Dee's eyes in his mind any more than he could avoid Linc's eyes in the reality facing him. Her voice rattled through his memory. "Believe it or not, I actually did a special several years ago about this very subject of 'Live free or die' as used in national mottos. I was really quite surprised to discover how many different places and philosophies it has represented.

"'Liberty or Death' is the national motto of Greece.

"'Freedom or Death' is the national motto of the Republic of Macedonia.

"'Liberty or Death' is the national motto of Uruguay.

"'Better dead than a slave' 'Rise up, Free,' was a Frisian oath at annual parliament style meetings at the Upstalsboom tree in the early first millennium." Elloworth paused. "Want more? I got more!" No one responded, so he proceeded.

"The phrase may also be connected to a speech of Camille Desmoulins titled *Better to Die than not Live Free* delivered early in the French Revolution.

"And, to bring it all back home, on January 1, 1804, Jean-Jacques Dessalines proclaimed Ayiti or, as we know her, Haiti—then a French slave colony—to be free and independent. Dessalines is said to have torn the white section from the French tricolor flag while shouting, 'Vivre libre ou mourir!' which means 'live free or die' just like what appears on this coin.

Ellworth grasped the coin with his left hand and hugged Linc with his right arm. "Thank you, brother. Thank you for your help in Vietnam. Thank you for this." He turned back to the triangle table. "I also vote yes."

"I agree with Văn," Betsy Ross Smith opined. "The people will love it because it is already such a major part of our daily culture. And it's not going away because of some Caliphate. It's too imbedded in our pop culture, books, TV shows, and movies. Appropriately, a book by New Hampshire writer Ernest Hebert is entitled *Live Free or Die*. TV, films. I know there are a number but . . . Bruce Willis' two thousand and seven movie *Live Free or Die Hard*, was the fourth in the Die Hard series. This kind of continued use of the phrase really speaks to the fact that it is truly a part of our American psyche."

"The phrase, as we use it today," Theo picked up just as Betsy Ross stopped, "actually originated in a toast written by General John Stark on July 31, 1809 for an anniversary reunion of the Battle of Bennington. Poor health forced Stark, New Hampshire's most famous soldier of the American Revolutionary War, to decline an invitation to speak. Instead, he sent his toast by letter. In it he wrote, and I quote." Theo paused for effect. "'Live free or die: Death is not the worst of evils.'"

"The first Convention of the Delegates of the Scottish Friends of the People in Edinburgh in December seventeen ninety-two used the phrase 'live free or die' and referred to it as a 'French oath.' That's the same year as this coin was minted."

"Thank you, Gwynn. Thank you all." Lincoln "Walks Alone" Black stood once again behind his own chair at the table. He had made a circle out of a triangle. "It is unanimous!"

"The Nine!" Gwynn shouted, holding up his new medal.

"The Nine!" they all stood and responded. Their coins gleamed in that dull kind of way that raw gold reflects artificial light.

"Live free or die?"

"Yes! Live free or die!"

Gwynn clenched his eyes shut, now, against the tears of memory. Such lights we maintain against the darkness. The sun was set.

Twilight was upon them. Soon they would attack. He spoke softly but with resolution into the mouthpiece that distributed his words across the country to all The Nine forces and volunteers poised and waiting. "Good evening, everyone. This is Gwynn Camsron. Each and every one of us faces a moment like the one that is upon us a little differently, my friends. Each of us will have to find his or her separate peace with the killing and the sacrifice. Both are difficult. Both can be criminal. Both can be honorable. Fight well this evening. Fight with honor, but live to tell of our victory." He paused. He felt a tremor run through his throat as he prepared to speak the words. This was it, the most important four words he would ever utter: "Live free or die!"

These fragments they had shored against their ruins . . . .

Shantih Shantih Shantih.

23
Chef de Cuisine
Conrad Văn Lý prepares to serve his troops
[Music: "Chef de Cuisine"]

At the head of the chow line, *Chef de Cuisine* Conrad Văn Lý started from his recurring nightmare that was now happening for the first time during the day. In it, he has no eye lids and is invisibly suspended over an endless mixture of acid, oil slicks, and sewage pounded by perpetual rains of filth and excrement. The stench pollutes the air to a point that makes it painful to breathe. Those caught up in the tides and swells of that vile sea seem to be always almost, but never quite, drowning. They are sort of, but not quite, in a perpetual state of going down for the third time in the garbage of their individual and collective lives. Every time, the same booming trio of voices surrounds him. Barking like Cerberus in broken harmonies, they accuse him: "You see what you have made them become?" And, he always responds: "An ocean full of Ciaccos doesn't make me the creator of hogs." And, he doesn't even speak Italian.

Then, without warning, he plummets toward the slushy sea and jolts to a stop just before he splashes down in it. Only inches away, barely submerged in the sea of lost souls, his Father's black eyes stare blankly upward. His rosary dangles about his neck next to his necklace with the golden Buddha. His mouth opens as if he is trying to speak. Instead of words, however, viscous bubbles pop to the bewildering surface. He wakes up with a gasp, sweating profusely yet shivering at the same time.

This day mare version had been no different except that when he awoke he was actually standing at ease in front of the entrance to the mess chow line rather than cold sweating in his bed in his quarters in The Caverns of Woe. He glanced about. No one seemed to have noticed.

He, then, officiously scoured the open expanse of the meadow The Nine had chosen as the primary mess and service area. The four mobile units that comprised Field Command Headquarters were parked just a few hundred yards away behind the mess tent. A number of things had to be considered. Proximity to The Caverns of Woe was major from a logistics point of view. They could not risk too much traffic movement on public highways that could easily be monitored. Instead, they opted for breaking new pathways through the wild areas in order to avoid detection. Security and invisibility were nearly equal in importance. Enough open relatively flat area to set up his cooking tents and the main mess tent for the troops but with sufficient cover. The crab grass carpet of this small valley was definitely no sea of garbage filled with bodies, at least not yet.

"Chef? Chef Văn?"

The voice he heard calling his name was not the bark of Cerberus. It was the voice of the Lead Team One commander asking where he should have his troops line up for chow.

Lý Văn Conrad stood erect, his tall white chef's hat perfectly positioned on his head. He clasped still-damp hands behind his back, smelling now more of hand soap than of the garlic scalloped potatoes he had helped one of his chef's get ready for the final meal, their last supper before the attack. He eyed this first unit to enter the mess area. They waited patiently for his direction. But, they needed to eat now. They always messed first for a reason. They had to be ready to go at any time. They were the point of the spear head.

Yet, they were not just the point of the spear. They were the tip of the point of the spear. The special few among the elite of the elite. That was what Gwynn had in mind when he designed a special combat unit patch for Lead Team One—a white round shield with a single black icon in the center, the *Eihwaz* rune.

"They are almost like knights of old," he had opined, "so they should have their own special coat of arms." Gwynn had confirmed that the icon was actually one of twenty-four icons or markings in the runic alphabet.

"Captain. Please have your men start the line over here," he shouted to the commander, waving them to his side where the food line began.

"Thanks, Chef Văn." The young commander of the elite Lead Team One smiled as he approached, his company of men in toe. "Okay, men. Move out to the chow line."

"I checked it out on the Internet," Gwynn had explained. "It is the symbol of the Yew tree and all of its strength, reliability, dependability, and trustworthiness. Above all else it represents an honest man who can be relied upon." Gwynn had paused as if reflecting. "And, I do firmly believe that the people you most want leading you into a conflict are, above all else, honest people who can be relied upon."

As Gwynn told the story, he had seen other runes on walls of the church leading up to the Vault of the Unnamed Knight. But, the *Eihwaz* rune was the only rune on the wall *inside* the vault itself. It was positioned underneath a verse, which had been etched into the sandstone, like a signature. He believed that it was, somehow, symbolic of their cause, and, as he put it, "It looks sort of like a one, you know, for Lead Team One."

"You are more than welcome, Captain Achilles. Take your team along this food line into the main mess tent. You'll find seating throughout the tent."

"Do you recognize me, Chef?"

"You mean other than from our staff meetings at The Caverns of Woe, Captain? Should I?"

"No, probably not." He wagged his head. "It's just that I have eaten in Văn's often enough that I somehow felt like we knew each other. Know what I mean?"

"Actually, Captain. Yes, I think I do. There really is some kind of very personal connection between the one who cooks the food and the one who eats it."

"Exactly."

"Come with me Captain Achilles. Let's sit at my table and have a bite to eat. I haven't had time myself. I'll have one of my staff serve us."

"No need, sir. Thank you kindly, but I can get my own chow, just like my men. I *would* like to sit and eat with you though."

"Perhaps you could tell me what you think is going to happen today when you and your troops will lead our attack."

Everyone called him Chef Văn, but Lý Văn Conrad was actually how his name would have been ordered in the Vietnamese naming convention. The family name was passed on by the patronymic naming system, so his Father's family name was positioned first. For Conrad, that name was Lý. The Lý's were among the least used names of about one hundred common family names. The top names were so popular because, in the past, people often took a king's family name to show their loyalty and respect. Over many generations, such family names would become permanent.

His Father, *Chef de Cuisine* Lý Duc Gia, had been the personal chef for one of the most influential generals in the Army of the Republic of Vietnam, General Nguyen Huu Nam. He had learned the skills of his profession through working in the restaurant kitchens under the apprenticeship of a number of French chefs. He and his wife, Kim Hoa, barely escaped with their lives when the Americans finally left because General Nam took them as part of his "family" when the U.S. evacuated him. As they had so many times told Conrad and his brothers and sisters, their food, culture, and conventions traveled with them on that C-47 out of Tan San Nhut Airbase. The General was confident that his money combined with his chef would be their ticket. In America, Gia became known to all as "Excellent" or "the Excellent One" because his first name translated as "excellent" in English and his restaurant was also excellent. Five star and five diamond ratings every year since the restaurant had been rated by the Mobile Travel Guide and AAA respectively.

"Believe me, Chef Văn, I have heard all of the jokes about my name."

Văn smiled. "Oh you mean like 'How's your heel doing?' or 'Get shot in the heel lately?'"

Captain Achilles nodded, fighting with a grin. "That's the idea."

"Well, I certainly would not want to be accused of relying on stale humor."

The young Captain had not been dipped into the river Styx at birth, but he had deserted the army when it became the USI Army. He had been a Special Operations commander with particular skills and abilities in the area of insurgency and counterinsurgency operations. He heard through the intelligence officer's grape vine that there was some kind of military being formed to fight the

Caliphate, but no one seemed to know anything about it beyond the rumors.

Achilles, after his brother, Pat's, funeral, looked out over sunset on the Pacific Ocean, knowing his brother would never see another sunset or sunrise over a wine-dark sea or anywhere else. The Caliphate guards prevented *even* him from ever actually seeing Pat in the casket close up so he could touch him. Only at a distance with guards in between. There was not much to touch.

Pat had been the one who needed watching out for. He was the baby brother and he knew it. Achilles very well understood that Pat had manipulated him all his life with that baby brother game, and he just did not care. He had truly felt that he was responsible for Pat especially since their parents had died within days of each other after they witnessed the American Flag burned from the flag pole at their capitol building in Raleigh. Pat, impetuous to a fault, finally could be restrained no longer. He publicly vowed to exact revenge on someone in some way, but before he could do anything he was "accidentally" cut down and crushed almost literally to a pulp by a Caliphate Central Command vehicle.

The motorized "thing" that splattered his young Pat all over the road was reported to be "the size of a building on wheels." Whatever it was, his brother's body was about as close to obliterated as any human body he had ever seen. And, he had seen more than just a few, some of which he had obliterated himself.

What was left of Pat was in the coffin. That was why he now stared out over the Pacific instead of into the dead eyes of his dead younger brother, because there was little left in that coffin to stare at or to touch. He knew that day as he prepared to bury what was left of his brother he would have to do something. He could no longer, regardless of the costs, remain complacent.

He knew Worth Hayes from some news coverage on him and his unit before the Caliphate takeover, and he knew that he had done a lot of reporting on The Nine and that his reporting had also been the source of some of these rumors. So, Achilles contacted him on the pretex of a follow-up story on his unit after the changes.

When they met, Worth, in response to his questions, told him that he had many reports of such a vehicle as the one reported to have killed his brother. "Nobody gets home video stuff anymore with the government clamping down so much on all that. So by the time ICN or a local news team can respond to any reports, the huge behemoth, whatever it was, would be long gone," he explained to Achilles at their first meeting. "And, the descriptions one gets are like those blind people in the Chinese story who are trying to describe an elephant by the part each of them is touching."

After a couple of meetings, he felt he knew enough. More importantly, he felt safe. He knew as a warrior that he could never feel completely safe. There was always risk. But, he felt safe enough. So, a few days later, with Worth's assistance, he went on a three-day pass and simply disappeared without a trace into The Caverns of Woe. There he was assigned to work with Betsy Ross Smith, Lincoln Black, and directly with Rob Roy Brown on developing a military force that theoretically resembled more conventional field commands yet practically speaking was more like Special Forces teams. He was particularly partial to the concept of having every unit, regardless of mission specialty, equipped with all of the tools necessary for its mission under the team commander.

The unit Rob Roy Brown had designated as Lead Team One was the point of the tip of the spear, so to speak. Achilles advocated that the unit should have the most elite Special Forces-capable personnel, scout vehicles, armored personnel carriers, light tanks, artillery, helicopters, and whatever else they might need to perform the mission of Lead Team One.

There would be Lead Teams throughout the country at various command locations. Each Lead Team would be the point of the spear for that area force. In Achilles' structure, there would be no infantry, artillery, armor types of specialty units of any size. All of those resources would be assigned to specific standard teams tailored to particular mission specialties: Lead Teams, Engagement Teams, Reinforcement Teams, and Support Teams. His idea was eagerly embraced, massaged, and implemented as LERS—Lead in. Engagement follow-up. Reinforcement to finish. Support for all three. Simple, lean, and mean. That was what insurgency was all about. And, they were the insurgents now.

Conrad's middle name was the same for him and all of his siblings—three older sisters and two younger brothers although it was unusual for males and females to have the same middle name.

But, his parents decided that they wanted a middle name that reflected the first generation of Americans in their family. So, it represented their generation, and it was also the name of their family's restaurant, the same one his Father and General Nam had opened together in Georgetown in September, 1975. It also was the same name whether he used the American or the Vietnamese ordering conventions. That name was Văn.

Văn's given name was Conrad because his immigrant parents wanted to honor his birthplace with a more American type name as they had with the girls before him—Amy, Lynn, and Joyce. By the Vietnamese convention, that name would appear last. In America, Lý Văn Amy, Lý Văn Lynn, Lý Văn Joyce, or Lý Văn Conrad would have been too peculiar and drawn too much attention. So, in order to blend in better with their new neighbors in their new country, it was Amy Văn Lý, Lynn Văn Lý, Joyce Văn Lý, or Conrad Văn Lý instead. His two younger brothers completely abandoned the family heritage choosing to totally Americanize their names: Eddie Lee and Jack Lee. Even though their high school diplomas bore the Americanized versions of their names, as soon as they were old enough, they legally changed their names over the strenuous objections of both Mother and Father Lý. They believed in adaptation to survive and succeed. They did not believe in abdication of their culture.

By the time he was born, Conrad's parents were determined that the first boy born to them in their adopted country would be groomed to run the family business. So, Conrad graduated from Harvard's MBA program and returned home to run what had become Văn's Enterprises, a collection of several extremely high-end eateries along the east coast and a relatively new Internet Café and Supply.Com web site where they supplied prepared foods as well as herbs, spices, dried foods, cooking supplies, and a lot more all with an "Asian Fusion" kind of slant from a strong Vietnamese French base.

As a good son, he did what he had to do. The Internet business had been his first innovation within months after he took control. But, Conrad's first love was the kitchen, so he was in the kitchen every chance he got. He was an artist with food and quickly became celebrated for his surprise fusion specials one day a week. And, it was due to this artistry that he met Theo Theodora who had become a regular at the restaurant during Conrad's time in Cambridge.

On that one evening a week, while the Adhan resounded over Georgetown announcing the time for the Maghrib prayers, he walked along the line of diners that built up while they awaited the opportunity to grab one of his fusion specials. This happened every week, even though they never publicized it and the days it happened were purely random as a result of Conrad having to find time in his busy CEO schedule to do what he most wanted to do—create with food.

One Thursday, the sun had set sometime earlier but the last of the red light had not yet left the sky in the west. He had been amazed at how the customers returned so quickly after that maniac blew up the Washington Monument and initiated the whole Caliphate overthrow. Now, only a couple of months after the Caliphate take-over, life in Georgetown seemed to be more or less back to normal, except for the five times a day that a call to prayer echoed throughout the city in both Arabic and English.

He was just about to return to the kitchen where his sous chefs were all, no doubt, in near cardiac arrest because of his disappearance from the kitchen even though it was always very predictable that at some point he would go out and check the line. As he opened the restaurant door to return to the kitchen, he spotted a face in the line near the entrance that seemed familiar. He paused, searched his memory banks, and quickly recalled that the man he was looking at had lectured about terrorism and its threat to the United States in modern times at Harvard when he was a freshman. His name was Theo Theodora. With his published views, Conrad was surprised to see him running around loose. He let the door slide closed and walked toward him. "Mr. Theodora?"

"Why, yes, I am he."

"Conrad Văn Lý, sir." As usual, he inverted the order of the name to track the more American order of first, middle, and last. "I attended your Terrorism in Contemporary Society lecture series at Harvard several years ago. All eight lectures, in fact. Fascinating. Absolutely fascinating. Even more so since your last couple of books. And now, all that's happened."

"Yes. With all that has happened." He paused, a bit taken aback by the situation. "That would actually be four years ago I believe."

"I believe you're right."

"So, you are the chef here, and you went to Harvard?"

Conrad nodded.

"I didn't realize that Harvard had a culinary college."

"It doesn't, Mr. Theodora," he chuckled a little self-consciously. "I was in the MBA program." He extended his hand. They shook.

"My goodness. An MBA Chef with an interest in terrorist politics. Now that's not a combination one runs across very often. Like being Buddhist and Catholic."

"And, as you probably suspected, I am both." He bowed slightly. "Please allow me to usher you in personally and seat you at the Chef's table."

"Well, thank you. I know your Father slightly from eating here so often over the past several years. I just sort of discovered this place one day while walking around."

"I will personally prepare your special this evening. It is an honor to have you with us Mr. Theodora."

"Once Pat died so ignominiously," Achilles was saying. "I realized that I had a duty to my parents and my brother, not so much to avenge their deaths, although, truth be told, that would have to be part of the telling. The duty was more to do the right thing no matter what it takes. To honorably defend what I believe in. I knew, then, that nothing could honor them more than that. So, as a result of doing that, here I sit with you, sharing our last meal before the great battle that will probably decide the fate of this world for generations to come. And, I want to say to you, my friend, on behalf of myself and my men, thank you for this incredible meal. You have made this, in the words of the great Chief Sitting Bull, 'A good day to die.'"

"And, will we die this night, Captain Achilles, or won't we?"

"Many of us will die, no doubt. But, history will not allow us to lose this evening, Chef Văn, no matter how many of us must die to make that so," Achilles concluded.

Văn specifically avoided a response to the Captain's prediction. He wanted to be that sure, himself, but he was not. Yet, he did not want to betray even the slightest hint of insecurity, the least wavering of confidence to this brave young Captain Achilles, commander of HQ Lead Team One—the *Eihwaz* knights, as they were very affectionately referred to by everyone in the movement.

"How was your fusion special, Mr. Theodora?" Văn had asked.

"Very special, Chef . . . ?"

"Văn. My first name is Conrad, but my friends and everyone here at the restaurant call me by my middle name, Văn." He shrugged. "One man. Two names. At the corporate offices, they call me Conrad as CEO. Here, they call me Văn for Chef."

"Chef Văn. Would it be improper for me to invite you to share a bottle of Vang Dalat with me to show my appreciation for such an awesome meal?"

"Not at all, Mr. Theodora. It would be my honor." With a wave of his hand toward the *maître d'hôtel*, Conrad Văn Lý took the chair offered next to Theo rather than across from him.

Nearly two hours later, the remaining bus boy who had responsibility for closing the restaurant for the night timidly approached with their third bottle of Vietnamese wine.

"Go home, young man. I think I can still close up a restaurant," Văn kidded. "Don't you?"

"Yes, Chef." He pulled his hands together below his chin and bowed his head slightly. "Good night Chef. Good night, sir."

"Good night." Văn did the same.

"Good night, and thank you for your service tonight." Theo bowed to the young man. Then he turned to Văn. "This has to be it for me, Văn. To terribly paraphrase Robert Frost, I still have miles to go before I can pass out."

"Your food is all ready. You could feed a small army with that much food. I had the kitchen staff pack it so that it will travel well with you. Just about everything should last up to at least a week if you refrigerate it in an industrial cooler." He shrugged. "If all you've got is a regular refrigerator, still up to four days, no problem."

"You are too kind, Văn."

"You could stay with us tonight."

"No, I am expected somewhere before morning."

"Where are you heading with such resolve?"

"Toward a revolution I think."

"Hey, Theo!" Văn glanced around the restaurant as if he suspected they were being watched. "Where the hell did that come from?"

"Look, you seem like a young man who knows his way around a kitchen and you have an MBA from Harvard. So, I would guess that you are reasonably smart, well informed, and socially concerned. And, you told me here tonight at this very table that you wish you could do more to right the ship. Didn't you?"

"Yes."

"Well, we really need somebody who knows about cooking for lots of people."

"We? We who?"

Theo leaned to his left, his face nearly touching the young Chef's. "I'm really taking a chance here." He inhaled deeply. "You know that small army you just referred to feeding? Well . . . ." Then the words exhaled with his breath. "You ever hear on the news about a group called The Nine?"

"You mean those terrorists who are trying to overthrow the Caliphate?"

"That's us."

"My god!" He slugged down a full glass and poured another almost in a single motion. "My god!"

Theo tried to laugh. "Well, hell. They have to be somebody, don't they."

"Perhaps you're right. I just thought it was something the Caliphate made up, you know, to give us a dangerous enemy within to unify us in a fight against them."

"Well, Văn, we are not fictional characters, and we are not terrorists. We're also not actually The Nine. We're one short in that respect, but we're still looking for number nine. We're patriots. This new Caliphate is not our America, the one you or I was born in, the one our parents believed in whether born here or somewhere else."

They sipped wine for several minutes in complete silence. Only the diminishing clanks, clinks, and tinkles of a kitchen closing down disturbed the vacuum of soundlessness.

"You're right, Theo."

"You would not be able to live a split existence the way I do. The person in charge of administration, logistical support, and most importantly food has to be on the scene full time."

"Okay. But, if I were interested, how soon?"

You could come with me tonight."

"I could leave a note."

"No. You just disappear."

"Disappear?"

"Yes."

"But, what about my family? They rely on me?"

"That's how it has to be. No trace."

"I need to think this through."

"That's fine. I understand. But, you cannot talk it out with anyone. I cannot emphasize this enough. You can talk about this with absolutely no one. Do you understand? If you ever mention even one word to one person you will not only jeopardize me and my position as court jester and intellectual pin cushion. You will imperil the entire movement."

"I understand. When will you be back?"

"I can't say. But, when I do come back, I will be expecting your answer. One night soon I will line up for one of your surprise fusion specials. You will see me when you check the line. And, if you plan to join us you'll have to leave with me that night immediately after closing the restaurant. No good byes. No looking back. Okay?"

"Okay."

As he looked out over the lines of troops being given the best food possible to keep their morale high, he joked with himself that no one had ever fought a revolution on gourmet foods before. To the best of his knowledge, this would be a first. And, if Captain Achilles was any indication, they were all ready and willing to die today if that was to be the cost. His cell phone buzzed. The number was Theo's.

"Văn here."

24
Worth Hayes
[Music: "Chef de Cuisine"]

Buck Sergeant Ellworth Hayes had been low man on the totem pole in their four-man unit. He had always assumed that was because he was not a real field agent or combat type. He was the man of words, the propaganda expert. The "com & con" man was what they called him. He killed with words. But, when it came to killing the enemy with bullets or bayonets or bombs or bare hands, he had simply not been as accomplished as his three teammates.

He was also the last one recruited. Gwynn, or LT, had been recruited first. He was the hot shot out of Princeton that had it all they said—guts, glory, everything. "A warrior poet" was how one officer's Top Secret appraisal report had put it. He brought his Princeton roommate Theo Theodora along with him as number two. That was a deal breaking condition. He and Theo were on their own kind of 'Buddy System.' Sal Keayrn was third because they needed a Seal. And, he was fourth because they needed a "com & con" specialist.

Of course, he could not discount Lieutenant Lincoln Black, MACV Personnel, as sort of a fifth team member. He was, after all, their "Travel Agent" the entire time. Linc took care of them all. Even at the end, when the unit was dissolved—as if it never existed. All of a sudden, he had medals on his record that his personnel file could not account for. He had nearly four years in but no one anywhere ever knew him or worked with him or remembered ever serving in the same unit with him. Linc worked it all out on paper for him, for all of them. Ellworth came to understand later on that he was really like a beam of light. Everyone saw it and no one saw it. In a way, that became his motto for life. Everyone sees me and no one sees me.

"Your beam count was a record today, Worth," Pyl Trumbo whispered in his earpiece. Ellworth could sense the devilment in his voice.

"I thought that the Caliphate had forbidden the viewers from reporting a "beam" from my glowing head and the network from counting them," he responded.

"Yeah, well, I think it probably had something to do with the fact that it's the nine eleven anniversary. The first one since, you know, the new Caliphate. So we all sort of broke the law a little today for Dee Dee."

"Well, thanks, Pyl. Thanks to everybody, please. I know Dee Dee would thank you too if she could."

Since that time months ago, Worth had made it a part of his daily routine to take a walk, after his morning telecast. This morning seemed no different, yet it was. It was *the* morning of *the* day. He left his office in L'Enfant Plaza as usual to walk along the Potomac Tidal Basin and reflect on the coming day. Only, today, he contemplated the impending Battle of Rockfish Gap and what it might mean to the world and to them. He still was not sure how he accomplished it, but ICN was on alert in case some kind of surprise attack were to occur on the eve of the Washington Monument being blown up. He had given them just enough to hook them but not enough for anyone to be able to figure out if, when, or where. Only, it could be. It clearly made sense, even to the most ardent skeptic, that this would be when any disgruntled bunch would try to make a symbolic gesture of protest, of revolt—on the eve of the first anniversary of the Caliphate takeover.

Walking from the ICN offices toward the river on Independence Avenue, Worth passed the Ellipse. There was no tall tower now, only the blackened crater where the Washington Monument used to be, where he witnessed from his offices hell breaking through the crust of the earth and bleeding fire onto the chunks of granite that had once been the monument to their first president. The grass underneath them had blazed up, then smoldered.

The cherry trees given to the United States in friendship from a former foe, the Japanese, were not in bloom this time of year, but that really did not matter much anymore. The Caliphate had cut down all the cherry trees in DC within days after the take over. None had been allowed to stand. If there was a reporting of a cherry tree, Caliphate police would immediately respond. If the culprit was, indeed, a cherry tree, the police would cut it down, pour lye on the stump remains, and haul the tree away.

But, the people were there, still, as if the cherry trees had never been chopped down, as if they would, still, bloom again in the spring. Snatches from their lives invaded him as he passed the John Paul Jones Memorial on Maine Avenue that hugged the Tidal Basin while Independence Avenue crossed over it. "I have not yet begun to fight!" He was a Scot like Gwynn. Those were his words in the face of threatened defeat. And, that was why the people chose to recognize that boy from Kirkbean, Kirkcudbrightshire, Scotland who had a compulsion to go to sea. Because he was defiant, even in the face of defeat.

John Paul spent more time at the small port of Carsethorn on the Solway Firth than at Kirkbean school. He talked to the sailors and studied the ships. When at school, he taught his classmates what he had learned from the old salts like how to maneuver their little boats to mimic a naval battle. Taking his stand on the tiny cliff overlooking the road, he shouted shrill commands at his imaginary fleet.

At the age of 13, he signed up for a seven year seaman's apprenticeship. His first voyage on the *Friendship* of Whitehaven as a ship's boy took him to Barbados and Fredericksburg, Virginia. The ship was in port for several months there, so he stayed with his older brother William, a tailor, who had emigrated there and flourished. Young John Paul spent his time learning navigation.

Years later, when Captain Richard Pearson of the *Serapis* asked Jones if he was prepared to surrender his ship, Jones, according to most historical accounts, replied, "I have not yet begun to fight." Most accounts written immediately after the battle, however, record Jones' words as something more like, "I may sink, but I'm damned if I'll strike." Such words according to one student of the battle are a "simple direct answer, to a simple direct question." While observers do not agree on Jones' exact words, all recall Jones' determination to continue the struggle and the iron will he demonstrated at this crisis in the battle.

These people wandering these streets of shattered visions faced that kind of decision every day. Most did not demonstrate the same zeal for honor and duty, the same blind determination in the face of seemingly insurmountable odds. Most of the poor souls crouched on the Tidal Basin bank, covered in the mud of the day, striking and biting each other as if one were the other's last meal. They just lost their job. They just lost their best client. Their best friend slept with their wife or their husband. Someone beat them to the tickets for the Redskins game. The Capitol Hill Restaurant wouldn't give them a reservation for tomorrow lunch—not even dinner, mind you—but l-u -n- c- h- e- o-n.

They were the wrathful, the spiteful, those who were so consumed with anger that they could not truly live themselves. Worth believed, with all sincerity, that he had become one of those people since his sister's death. He expected, at any moment, to see his own face gurgling and choking and gasping for breath in the black muck of the swampy river Styx better known in these parts as the Potomac.

Would he betray The Nine? Would he betray his team oath? If to do so would give him the ability to destroy all those responsible for Dee Dee's death? He honestly did not know the answer to that ultimate question. What he did know was that his best realistic option to exact any revenge at all was to make damn sure that The Nine won and to make damn sure that their battle was covered for the world to see at the quintessential video game—Ragnarök at Rockfish Gap.

He knew that for every person he saw wandering this path there were hundreds if not thousands of equally disillusioned, dispassioned souls invisible to him and to others who had absolutely no idea what was going on and what was more did not really care much anyway as long as they knew enough to remain politically correct and continued to collect their paychecks. He took a left on West Basin Drive through West Potomac Park to Ohio Avenue. Then, right to the FDR Monument. A handlettered sign read: Phlegs' Tidal Basin Paddle Boats and Water Taxi. That was where he would certainly find a boatman to get him to his noon rendezvous with his staff and equipment in the network's Alexandria field operations offices. He was officially on stand-by today, and he had absolutely no intention of returning to his office. He wanted to be with his field team when word came of the attack. Then, they would chopper in.

Ellworth remembered all too vividly every detail of what went on the day the twin towers crumbled. Pyl Trumbo, was also his producer at that time. He barged into the holding room where he was taking a breather during the long on-the-half-hour commercial break. "Dee

Dee's on the phone for you Worth."

"Hey, Pyl, I'm on the air here, just taking a commercial break. Get it?"

"I think you're gonna want to take this, Worth. She's at the Twin Towers."

"What? What the hell is she doing there?"

Pyl waved for a phone to be brought in. "Don't worry. We've still got two minutes before you're back on live. And, I've got somebody lined up to sub for you if need be for a few minutes."

Ellworth snatched the portable phone from a new associate producer intern—Marlee Something-or-other—niece of one of the sponsors' CEO's. He didn't remember which one. "Dee Dee?"

"Oh, God help us, Worth. It's like being in hell here. Oh, God help us, Worth. It's like being in hell here." Her voice continued in a loop. It did not sound hysterical the way you might expect when a commercial airliner has just crashed into the building next to you. It just sounded broken.

"But, you're okay, Dee Dee? Right?"

"It can't be! No, my God, it can't be again!"

The voice coming through the ceiling speakers announced to the world, however, that it could be. "The second tower has just been hit. Here is some of the footage we were able to capture."

"No! Nooooo! My God, Worth. They just hit us, too. The walls are dissolving."

Simultaneously Worth heard the voice that blared from the speakers and the one that blared from the telephone. The first voice was his substitute while he was on the telephone with his sister who was trapped in a burning, collapsing building. She was the second voice. The one that seemed to be coming from inside his head.

"We're all gonna die here, Worth," she repeated over and over again. It was automaton-like. "We're all gonna die here."

"Dee Dee? Are you still there? Are you okay? My God, sis. Say something."

"We're all gonna die, here, Worth. We're all gonna die."

"No! Dee Dee. Listen to me. We will get to you somehow. Just hold on there. Okay?"

"This entire wall is just gone. I can look out and see down thirty-three floors. Fire is raging behind me, now, and above me and beside me and . . . ."

"Dee Dee. Please. Focus on finding a way out of that office."

"I have, Worth. I have found a way out. Good bye, brother. I love you so much."

He could hear something over the phone that sounded like rushing wind. But there was no other sound until the signal went dead. It was later reported to him by a number of people who had been in other parts of the second tower that she had not thrashed about in the air as she fell. She had not screamed. In fact, she had not even seemed to be conscious as she tumbled beside her cell phone until they both hit the pavement below.

25
Betsy Ross Smith
[Music: "Chef de Cuisine"]

"Honey, I'm sorry that I don't know much of anything about all that girl stuff. I only know basketball and baseball and such. You know, me, honey. Anything with a ball and I can do it. Surprisingly, that also seems to mean the mouse "ball." So, I can promise you that you will also know computers. Sports and computers. That's about as good as I will ever be able to get it for you, honey. I guess it could be worse. If only your mama was still here. Poor darling. She'd be able to help you with all that girl stuff. But I do promise you that you'll be the best damned computer whiz and ball player anywhere around—boy or girl."

As she stared out towards the convoy, Betsy Ross Smith knew she would remember her Father's words for as long as she lived, whether she died today in battle or lived to be a hundred, because he had more than kept his promise to his six-year-old daughter on the day of his wife's and her mother's funeral. Filburt "Fil" Smith retired very early as the all-star second baseman for the Boston Red Sox and took a job with a new company called Microsoft to pursue his second favorite career, computer programming and design. That way, he could put down some roots and do his best to replace the loss of Miriam Smith, beloved wife and mother, to breast cancer.

He was confident that he could provide for his daughter very well with this new computer direction, and he would be able to come home every evening and be there for her on weekends. Filburt even found a way to persuade his employer to let him be the baseball coach for a little league baseball team because his star power would help him develop contacts through the parents. He coached. Betsy Ross was the star from the time she was old enough to play. And, the company got client after client to buy their computer software through Fil's contacts to major corporate executives through the kids who played on his teams as well as the teams of his opponents.

Except for that one huge loss, some might say BR had led a rather charmed life. High school place kicking phenomenon, although to her mind she should have been a wide receiver phenomenon, but the coaches would not allow her to play a position that required so much contact. Star point guard and .350 hitting right fielder also on the high school boys' teams. She may have been the very first female high school athlete to ever letter in three heretofore "male" sports.

When she decided on her higher education direction, however, she opted for an academic scholarship to Harvard where she planned to major in the computer sciences. All the universities that recruited her for sports scholarships were only interested in her playing "girls" sports, and she saw absolutely no future at all for women like her in professional sports. But, she couldn't help herself. When spring football practices were announced, she walked on as a place kicker and not only made the squad but became the number one kicker for three seasons and leading scorer her junior and senior years. She was the flavor of the year, as the sports press put it, for her entire college career because she was a young woman forcing her way into the world of young men and not only getting away with it but excelling at it.

Right out of Harvard, she shocked everyone by joining the Army because the pros, in spite of her proving herself at the college level, still would not let her play with the men. And, she shocked everyone who knew her even more when she quietly and quickly maneuvered herself into position to be the first female in black ops, serving three tours in Iraq and Afghanistan and becoming the first woman ever to win a Silver Star for gallantry. Yet, even that honor was more than slightly tainted, since it was well-accepted among her peers that she should have been awarded a Medal of Honor and was not, basically because she was a female.

Now here she was. A war hero five years out of Iraq and Afghanistan. She had already been in and out of two Internet companies with several million in the bank that was frozen by the Caliphate because of their suspicions about her political opinions and activities. However, up until now they had not been able to prove anything, so they allowed her to remain free and to go about what seemed to be her daily business of providing security systems and personnel at the highest levels of security in business and government. No other organization could provide the depth and texture of security on all levels, so despite the Caliphate's concerns about her, the United States of Islam was one of her consulting company's richest contracts. This put her in the bizarre position of the Caliphate government paying her company big bucks while that same government froze her personal accounts.

"The terrorist attack on another Green Crescent City, this time just outside of Butte, Montana, reportedly took the lives of thousands who were being held there waiting to be released back into the community and brotherhood of the great Caliphate." Ellworth Hayes hesitated. What he was about to do next was tricky to say the least. "The authorities are still not entirely sure that the center—basically a Quonset hut city to house the culturally estranged among us—was actually still occupied. We'll have more on that later on in the show tonight. The unknown terrorists are thought to be members of The Nine underground."

"That's my guys, guys," BR gushed in her most girlish manner to all those working in the computer and control complex that occupied the inner sanctum of The Caverns of Woe, better known by those who called it home as Theo's Hideaway. "Of course, Mr. Hayes helps out some, too, by indicating that the report of so many deaths might be erroneous. That's not much, but, what the hell? Any little bit helps when it comes to trying to wake the people of this country up. Green Crescent Cities are a big time symbol of the domination by these Caliphate bastards. So, these guys from Montana wanted this to be their first mission after they completed their training at Theo's Hideaway."

"Aha! Am I to understand that you know the terrorists who conducted this raid of destruction?" Lincoln teased from behind the flat screen in front of him.

"Like, I say, hell yes. I not only know them, I trained them, baby!"

"And," Lincoln chimed in, "in case all of you haven't noticed, this kind of activity has increased exponentially over the past six months."

"The same thing happens every time. Our guys hit. The news guys report it as a terrorist attack."

"But the people know the truth. They know it's The Nine."

"They do. But, I doubt if most people realize that we conduct about a dozen or so attacks for every one that is reported. And, that's even with having somebody on the inside like Worth who can influence what gets coverage and what does not.

"The person responsible for making these things happen is . . . ." She turned slightly to her right and motioned toward the man standing beside her. "Rob Roy MacGregor Brown. He was my Team Leader in Afghanistan. When I became a member of The Nine, he was the very first person I thought of to give me the best possible strategic and tactical advice as well as act as my Field Leader of Operations. That's why most of you never see him around. He's so often out in the field."

Rob Roy MacGregor Brown was named for Robert Roy MacGregor or Red Robert—usually known simply as Rob Roy. He was a famous Scottish folk hero and outlaw of the late 17th and early 18th century, who is sometimes known as the Scottish Robin Hood. Rob Roy is from the Scottish Gaelic Raibeart Ruadh, or Red Robert. According to his Mother, the name of his ancestor was a result of the fact that Rob Roy had red or auburn hair.

Rob Roy MacGregor Brown was born to Margaret MacGregor, wife of Donald Brown, with the assistance of the resident Spae-wife. He also had red hair when he was born in the two room cabin in the mountains of Colorado near Glengale-At-The-Head-of-Lake-Catherine. It was a community that had always been, and remained, isolated from the rest of the world by refusing to allow roads to be built to their town. The only ways in or out were the lake to a small but navigable stream and, then, to the Colorado River or goat paths and wagon trails to the main road back to civilization which abruptly ended four point two miles away.

The day Rob Roy turned sixteen, an actual shooting war began over that road project. The citizens of Glengale-At-The-Head-of-Lake-Catherine began a guerilla style campaign against the state of Colorado and the United States Federal Government led by his Father when they tried to force a connector highway through the dense Aspen stands to their small town. It would be great for their tourism, they had been told. But, their response was that they had no tourism trade, nor did they want any. They simply wanted to be left alone.

Although, as their leader, Donald made them all vow never to purposely kill anyone, he also led them on daring raids when they sniped from the cover of the trees at those who attempted to push the road through. On one such raid, Rob Roy led a small team of high school friends. They all played on the town's school football team. Rob Roy was their quarterback, their leader on the field, so it seemed natural for his Father to put him in charge of the "young folks" as he put it. Their mission was to disrupt the operation of the road graders who were trying to punch another quarter mile into the Aspens and that much closer to their homes. A ricochet from a Rob Roy round hit a driver in the throat. Even from a distance, he could see the blood spurting from the man's aorta.

Abruptly, after completing barely a quarter of a mile of the spur at a cost of millions of tax payer dollars and the life of one road grader driver, the governments capitulated.

"As President of all the people of these United States, I would first like to express our deepest regrets and most profound sorrow for the unfortunate death of Sprauge Jones, a road grader driver first class for the state of Colorado, who was unintentionally shot by one of the protestors from Glengale-At-The-Head-of-Lake-Catherine.

"To every citizen of Glengale-At-The-Head-of-Lake-Catherine, I want to say that if you truly wish to remain isolated in the manner you are today, then neither the state of Colorado nor the United States government has the right to force it upon you.

"Instead," the President had continued, "we offer another approach to allow the fine citizens of principal in Glengale-At-The-Head-of-Lake-Catherine options to their isolation without intruding on their space and privacy. We offer wireless technology."

Grudgingly the small population of American Revolutionary Purists or ARP'ers, taken unawares by this new gambit, allowed the intrusion of modern wireless communications. Rob Roy was, probably to the shame of his Father, one of those who wanted cell phones and satellite television and access to the World Wide Web. He argued that they could allow these things because the wireless infrastructure could be developed without the need for roads or any other actual physical intrusions on their way of life.

In order to avoid prosecution, his Father and Mother signed permission for him to go into the military of the enemy, the United States Army. "Look at this as a God-send, son. You don't go to jail for killing that driver."

"But, I didn't mean to . . . ."

Donald put up his hands in defense. "I know, son. I know. But, now you have learned that what you mean to do and what you do are not always the same. And, son, you can also learn all that the enemy knows and bring it back here to us."

What he actually learned was that Glengale-At-The-Head-of-Lake-Catherine was probably only able to exist *because* of that Army, not in spite of it.

Betsy Ross Smith, prone in a Ghillie overlooking a convoy of the United States of Islam, knew very well that less than a year ago, the vehicles that made up this convoy had been the property of the Army of the United States of America. Now, what was left of them after the battle would soon become her responsibility. "Don't you guys be messing up my vehicles when you start shooting your wads, okay?" She poked Theo in the ribs. "They'll be my responsibility soon as you guys take them back."

26
Theo Theodora
[Music: "Theo"]

In the early hours of the previous July Fourth, Theo had found Gwynn on his knees near the edge of the smoldering crater opening into hell that had once been the Washington Monument. Gwynn's ears still bled from the intensity of the explosion ignited by their former teammate in Vietnam, and he was muttering "Allahu akbar?" over and over again as if it were some kind of question that needed, no required, an answer.

"That was the only time I can ever remember perceiving you as helpless, LT. Even when Quetel and I rescued you from Whale Island, you almost seemed as if you were staying there of your own volition, not because you couldn't escape on your own but because you weren't ready to yet." Theo whispered behind his hand to an anxious Gwynn and Lincoln as the three lay in their spots overlooking Rockfish Gap like Harbor seals during a haul-out.

Theo recalled those moments, not as if they had happened recently rather than nearly a year ago but as if those moments were actually happening right now as he recalled them even though the reality was obvious, even relentless, that much had already happened as they watched the Caliphate convoy preparing to settle in for the night. The plan was, according to their sources, to continue on to DC in the morning arriving in time for the combined July Fourth celebrations in DC and New York.

First, he remembered, he had to get them out of DC. Escape was not going to be all that easy either. He made that assumption based upon what he was already observing regarding the security and policing of the situation. The explosion site just behind where Gwynn knelt was already cordoned off by an abundance of yellow crime scene tape and being actively guarded. Others pretending to conduct a crime scene investigation seemed to be more interested in managing and sanitizing the scene than in investigating it forensically. Most of those in uniform already wore white armbands stamped with green crescents and stars and it was less than an hour since the explosion. He had been delayed by the chores attendant to landing a seaplane in the Potomac, a pretty good feat for a guy who hadn't flown an aircraft of any sort for years while Gwynn dashed off in a taxi to save the day. He simultaneously had become increasingly concerned to preserve his "innocence." The sequence of events unfolded in a time frame that reinforced the perception that he was not connected to this tragedy in any way even though he knew both men who clashed there.

It was crucial that he be convincing to the investigating authorities. His "innocence" must be preserved at all costs. If necessary, he knew he might have to denounce Gwynn, and Gwynn would understand. It had seemed like Sal had snapped his fingers with a very big, very loud bang and immediately the new Caliphate of the United States of Islam appeared—alakazam!—like magic. Of course he had not realized that at the time. He only sensed danger, and if there was one thing he had learned long ago while serving with LT in Vietnam, when you sense danger you are obliged to act accordingly.

He had assured Gwynn that he knew of a place that would be safe until they could figure out what was happening and plan what to do and how to do it. "It'll be okay, LT," he remembered saying. "Somehow we'll all be okay." He piled the stunned man he had known so well all those years ago as unstunnable into his metallic silver BMW 48i SAV like he was bones in a sack of flesh and pointed the machine in the direction of Francis Scott Key Bridge and US 29. He would take that route over the bridge named after the man who wrote "The Star-Spangled Banner," then south to Charlottesville. Then hang a right heading west to Rockfish Gap and a very secret place he knew as The Caverns of Woe. The name was somewhat of a double entendre. It meant a place where no one would be unless the country was in deep trouble from some type of invader. That was one kind of woe. The second kind of woe was an acronym for We Overcome the Enemy. And, according to all that research he had done several years ago, the facility hidden inside the mountains along Rockfish gap was designed and equipped to do just that—hold out and ultimately win against any invading enemy—human, microbial, nuclear, or extra-terrestrial.

He recalled how they talked after Gwynn had somewhat

recovered his senses as they crossed the Potomac. They both knew instinctively that America had been stolen, and it would be up to them and others like them to take it back.

"Now that we're out of DC, we'll probably be okay. Even a virus doesn't spread that fast, does it, Theo?"

"Hey! LT! You're back!"

"Yes? I think, therefore I am back."

"Humor is good."

"Wow, what a plan Sal pulled together, huh, Theo."

"Yeah. Even better than ones we all pulled off together back in the day."

"This is probably going to be very serious, right?"

"I'm thinking this is extreme prejudice kind of serious, LT. Very bad. I'm thinking we're gonna need the team, LT, at least what's left of it. You are the best one of us to be the fugitive, the outlaw, the man on the run. You always were. You cared the least for creature comforts. You could survive with practically no resources under just about any conditions. And, I mean, my God, by breakfast you'll be Public Enemy Number One anyway. So, we might as well exploit that. We'll get you some kind of cover real quick. No more shaving from now on though. You'll need the beard as well as your mustache. And, let the hair grow shaggy. You know, Buffalo Springfield style. Soon you'll look like you probably time-warped from the sixties except for the gray."

"Screw you. You don't have anything left to get gray. But, of course, *you* are the perfect one for the insider. Or, perhaps Worth? He's bald, too. Anyway, you've made it clear that I wouldn't do simply because I will soon be Public Enemy Number One," he laughed. "And, we can use Worth as the perfect press secretary because nobody will know he is one of us either."

"Maybe he can use that shiny noggin of his to beam out some Morse Code messages for us or something."

"So, I guess it's for real, huh?"

"What's that, LT?"

"Our old team has definitely received its invitation to a reprise."

Theo shook his head and clucked his tongue in mock bewildered agreement.

"This is WETA, Washington's Classical Music Radio with John

Chester Midnight. All night every night from midnight to six am. We're being told to suspend our programming momentarily for this breaking news from the Ellipse. Ladies and gentlemen. A mad suicide bomber blew up himself and the nation's most sacred monument, the Washington Monument, just as the clock struck midnight and it became July Fourth. According to Associated Press reports, this may have been the beginning of a massive attack . . . ."

"Allahu akbar!" a new voice snarled from the radio speakers interrupting the newscaster. "This station now belongs to the new Caliphate, the United States of Islam. All praise to Allah and to the Immortal Leader. Allahu akbar!" Then the radio station went silent.

"Immortal Leader? What the hell is he talking about, Theo? Their Leader is dead."

"Put yourself in their place, LT. What would you do?"

"I'd tell everyone that our Leader miraculously survived a blast that no mere mortal could have survived."

"So, Sal becomes the Immortal Leader."

"Brilliant."

"Yeah. Dead and he's still beating us up."

It was past dusk as Theo steered his 48i toward Yancey Mills. The engine continued what seemed to be its sporadic loss of compression. It had been back and forth ever since they hit that huge pot hole just this side of Charlottesville. The good out of the situation had been a completely resurrected Gwynn, trying to help him puzzle out what was wrong and where the next place might be that would have a mechanic equipped to deal with a BMW.

"Allahu akbar!" another voice shouted through a lot of piercing feedback from the radio speakers. "WBZS now belongs to the new Caliphate, the United States of Islam. All praise to Allah and to the Immortal Leader. Allahu akbar!" Then another radio station went silent.

"Try AM, LT."

"Okay."

"This is WDCT, 1310 on your AM dial. You're very own Arlington, Virginia Asian-American place for music, news, and sports."

"Allahu akbar! This station now belongs to the new Caliphate, the United States of Islam. All praise to Allah and to the Immortal

Leader. Allahu akbar!"

"I guess it's both bans, LT. We better find someplace to get this toy of mine looked at and maybe find out what exactly is going on."

"Yeah, that thing on the radio makes me think that we're right. I mean, what would you or I do if we wanted to take over a government?"

"We'd rely directly on our old training that tells us communications is one of the most basic assets that must be seized and controlled from the outset."

"And, that's what they are doing right now—the YUNUS Apparatus and their followers. So, it looks like we may not have much choice in the matter. They're taking over and we're gonna have to take it back."

"Look in the Virginia Guide, LT, for a garage. It's in the glove compartment. I'll check the radio." As he flipped the stations, one after another was either off the air or was broadcasting in a mixture of Arabic and English, informing everyone within earshot that a new power was in town, the new Caliphate, the United States of Islam.

"You have a Virginia Guide in your glove compartment, Theo?"

"Well, yes. Hell, I live here most of the time, don't I?"

Gwynn smirked good-naturedly as he skimmed the pages. "Here we go. Coming up on a berg in Albemarle County called Yancey Mills. Unincorporated community named after Charles Yancey, a businessman who ran a tavern, store, mill, and distillery in the area, which became known as Yancey's Mill. The original mill still stands, under the name of R.A. Yancey Lumber Corporation.

"Today, Yancey Mills is the site of the intersection of U.S. Route 250 and U.S. Route 64, which you are coming up on as I speak. Otherwise Yancey Mills is little more than an education oasis—the location of Western Albemarle High School, Henley Middle School, and Brownsville Elementary School. Also, by the way, a pair of gas stations." He paused and looked out the window for a moment. "Hey, take a look, Theo. The station on the right hand side of the road looks like it might still be open. It's Mag's Maintenance and Services, one of the two listed here."

As Theo pulled into the station, Gwynn dog-eared the page and closed the guide, then continued along the radio dial trying to find some kind of information as to what was happening.

"Allahu akbar! WHUR now belongs to the new Caliphate, the United States of Islam. All praise to Allah and to the Immortal Leader. Allahu akbar!" Just like all the others, that station also ceased broadcasting.

"Jesus, this radio blackout is happening so fast, it's getting pretty scary, Theo."

"Yes, but at least there's a light on in that garage, and we've got to do something about this damned vehicle, no matter what's going on around us, LT. A freaking BMW for Christ sake!" Suddenly laughter began to erupt from deep in Theo's throat. "Are you listening to me, LT?"

"I don't have any choice, Theo. I'm encapsulated in this pod with you at speeds up to one hundred miles per hour—in spurts of course. But, at least, you are pretty damned funny. Ranting and raving about problems with your BMW toy while radio station after radio station is being taken over by the new Caliphate, and the world is falling down around us."

He assumed a grin as he pulled up in front of the garage section of the gas station and tapped his horn once. "Yes. You have to admit, I've still got it."

"Still got what, Theo?"

"I've still got what it takes," he spluttered and tapped the horn twice more.

"What it takes for what?"

"What it takes to embrace the absurd, LT. What it takes to embrace the absurd."

"That's so true, Theo. I mean look at us now. I'm sure Samuel Becket would be proud."

"Allahu akbar! Station WMZO now belongs to the new Caliphate, the United States of Islam. All praise to Allah and to the Immortal Leader. Allahu akbar!"

"Be there in a sec!" came from inside the garage as Magdalena Averroës peeked out from the yellowish light inside the building, a wilted Washington Nationals baseball cap tilted slightly sideways on her thick black hair that was pulled back in a ponytail. Mag's Maintenance and Services was how the tag read on the left breast pocket of her coveralls when the door opened wider framing her in a wedge of yellowish light as she approached. Theo lowered the driver's window as if her appearance had triggered some kind of hypnotic state.

"Magdalena Averroës." She proffered her hand. Theo shook it firmly, all the time eyeing her name tag sewn on her coveralls. "Oh, my name tag. Mag. Oh, it's Mag. Short for Magdalena, you get it? Nobody wants to think of me as a girl. Plus, nobody around me wants to think about me being Spanish or, worse, a Moor. Actually my family's from Mexico DF. Districo Federal."

"Yes, I've been there many times," he murmured.

"My ancestors actually are from Spain. We go back to Averroës, a Spanish-Arab philosopher in the twelfth century, He lived from eleven twenty-six to eleven ninety-eight and was best known in the Arab world as Ibn Rushd. He was far more important and influential in Jewish and Christian thought than in Islam, however. So half my family's Catholic and half my family's Muslim." She shrugged. "And, as a woman, I'm not much better off with either bunch. Go figure."

"Well." Theo seemed to suddenly remember why they had stopped. "This damned machine of mine is Protestant. It is protesting being driven. It suffers from some mechanical malady."

Magdalena smiled. It was a genuine, warm kind of smile. "That's pretty funny for somebody who's from the city with no sense of humor. Anyway, Ibn Rushd was a learned man in medicine. Unfortunately I am not. But, fortunately, I am a learned woman in auto mechanics, especially BMW mechanics."

"And clairvoyance. How do you know where we're from?"

Her smile transformed into a full-lipped grin as she pointed at the license plate on the car. "Dah! You came from DC, right?" Magdalena Averroës asked as she openly eyed the license plate again for emphasis. "That's why you can't see the obvious?"

"Yes," Theo responded as he and Gwynn fidgeted while this female modern day grease monkey was trying to figure out why he was losing control of his steering. "Guilty as charged. We are from the city with no sense of humor and incapable of seeing the obvious. It has just been attacked by radical Muslim forces, embarrassingly, led by a former Vietnam war comrade of ours who blew up the Washington Monument . . . ."

"And himself with it." Gwynn interrupted and prepared to

introduce himself and Theo, but Theo caught his eye first and indicated, with a glance, not to give names yet. He could read the guy's mind still, after all these years. He understood Theo's concern as to whom Magdalena Averroës might be. Obviously, this takeover was coming from the most grass roots levels. Just about anyone could be a YUNUS Apparatus sleeper warrior or supporter just waiting for that signal.

"Allahu akbar!" suddenly blared from a small portable on the tool bench inside the garage. "Station WKDV now belongs to the new caliphate, the United States of Islam. All praise to Allah and to the Immortal Leader. Allahu akbar!" Then the radio station went dead.

"That's some of your Muslim guys, Mag," Theo tried to kid but realized before the words were even totally out of his mouth that he had made a mistake by the frown that immediately covered their new-found mechanic's rather lovely face.

"They're not *my* Muslims, DC. You don't see me out there taking over radio stations, do you? No! Why? Because, as a woman, I get absolutely no freedom and no respect from those seventh century hooligans." She forced herself to stop. "I'm sorry. Just pull your car inside the garage here, and we'll take a look."

"Hey, I'm the one who is sorry. I didn't mean. I was just . . . ."

Once under the bright yellow lights inside the garage, Theo parked the car and jumped out. "You got a TV here?"

"Yes, DC. I do. Over there by the water bottle cooler."

Gwynn spotted it and turned it on.

"We get cable here. Great reception."

The screen was blank. Gwynn flipped channels with the remote from the shelf below. A digital display appeared on every channel over a looped video of the Washington Monument exploding. The message included the call letters of the channel and the same message as the one they heard on the radio.

"They're all the same. Just like the radio stations. I guess I'm not surprised."

"Me neither, LT. Me neither."

"Pretty damned smart, you know."

"What, LT?"

"The Washington Monument footage they're playing behind the

message."

"Yeah. A real psyche out."

"Oh, this is not good is it guys from DC? I had heard something on the radio earlier about a coup or something. I guess that's why you made your stupid joke, DC. This shit's for real, huh?"

"Yes, Mag. I'm afraid it is very much for real."

"An organization called the YUNUS Apparatus has taken over the United States of America and is, as we speak, transforming it into the United States of Islam."

Almost as if to avoid the next part of the conversation, Mag returned her focus to the car. "Don't see a lot of BMW's of any sort out this way, but I don't think I've ever seen a 48i even though Sport Activity Vehicles of all shapes and types roll through here headed for Skyline Drive and the Blue Ridge Parkway."

"Can you figure out what's wrong?"

"I can hook it up to my analyzer."

"Oh, will it hurt?"

"Funny guy, DC."

As Mag opened the hood to begin the analyzer hook up, she continued. "Don't I know you from somewhere, though, DC? On the news or something?"

"I'm a writer. At least I was. I don't know what I'll be by tomorrow. Maybe you saw me on an interview show or a book jacket."

She snapped her fingers. "You're that *Ethics for the New Age of Extremism* guy with the repeating kind of name." She snapped her fingers again. "Theo . . . ." She slapped her forehead. "That's it! Theo Theodora. Oh, my god! I saw you on INN with that Ellworth Hayes guy. The one that beams everybody with his shiny bald head." She grinned impishly. "It was sort of hard to tell the two of you apart."

"Oh, now that hurts a lot worse than being hooked up to your analyzer, I'm sure."

"That's just because it isn't you hooked up to the analyzer. It is your BMW. You are just trying to get hooked up with me."

"Well, I've got to admit I don't recall ever seeing a grease monkey that looked so good in their coveralls."

"You do go on, now don't you?" She turned to his companion.

"He does go on, now doesn't he?"

"Forever and forever and forever." Gwynn sighed.

"Don't listen to him. He's Gwynn Camsron, and he tried to stop the guy from blowing up the monument. Talk about being crazy. Now, I'm helping him escape the authorities who will obviously want to prosecute him for attempting to stop someone from becoming a martyr or something like that." He grinned. "You're half Muslim, so you say. Maybe you can figure that out, huh?"

She made a face of mock displeasure that was transformed almost instantly into a real face of discovery and illumination. "I don't know about the Muslim part, but . . . ."

"Can you fix the vehicle so it'll make it at least another forty or fifty miles or so?"

"Yes, DC. I think I can take care of it in about five minutes."

"But, you haven't even finished hooking that incredibly invasive machine of yours up to my car yet. How can you know what's wrong?"

"Because it's just a loose connection here. See?"

He moved close to her. Her coveralls smelled slightly from the oil and gas odors she worked with all day. But the warm natural fragrance of her overwhelmed him. "This connection to the distributor cap."

"Oh, then get on with it my good grease monkey," he chuckled, stepping back from the fragrance and the heat. "Get on with it."

"Go grab a coke or whatever out of the machine and cool off DC," she quipped. "It doesn't take coins. It takes kicks to the bottom left side. Of course you take your chances with what comes out."

"Sort of like political upheaval," Gwynn muttered half-aloud.

"Yes," Theo agreed. "Like political upheaval. Will it be Coke, Pepsi, or Dr. Pepper?"

Mag finished tightening the connection. She reached into the driver's side and flipped the ignition. The engine started immediately, purring like the proverbial kitten. She motioned to Theo to take the driver's seat. "Now, what am I going to do, DC? A half-Muslim half-Catholic Moor female mechanical engineering drop out auto mechanic? What *am* I going to do, now? Those Jihadists will never allow me, a woman, to continue running my own gas station and garage."

"For starters, you're going to give me a bill."

She waved him off with both hands. "No charge! No charge! Just meeting you two characters has been payment enough," she chuckled.

Theo glanced over his shoulder at Gwynn who was approaching with a Coke in one hand, a Pepsi in the other, and a Dr. Pepper trapped under his left arm pit. "Something for everybody," he grinned. "And, now we can all di di mau out of here. I got shotgun!"

Theo looked over at Mag and shrugged. "What can I tell you? He has been a continual source of surprise and bewilderment to me since our days at Princeton way back in the sixties. If you are confused, just take it as an invitation. Mechanics and maintenance will be of key importance to the struggle. *We* can use you, Magdalena Averroës."

Prior to the rise of the Caliphate, Theo's books had always sold moderately well, but it was his last couple of books on terrorism that had made him into some kind of writer superstar. He had been celebrated as an instant terrorism expert after he published his book, *Whatever Happened to Peace, Love, & Understanding (Ethics for the New Age of Extremism)*. Within a couple of weeks it was number one on the bestseller list and stayed there for several months. He appeared on just about all the major news and talk shows on radio, satellite, network and cable television, as well as being featured on web sites, chat rooms, and blogs of various religious and political leanings. He explained that his work was based on two premises. His first premise was that when one takes activism to the extreme, it results in the annihilation of everyone else. His second was that passivism taken to its own logical extreme culminates in the annihilation of self. He had even been interviewed by his old war buddy from Vietnam, the INN News Anchor, Ellworth Hayes. "So, you see, Worth. Every human being ever born is programmed to kill everybody else or kill himself. One way or the other. Now, there may be a few truly confused souls who are programmed to do both as well as significant disagreement and confusion regarding which acts constitute killing others and which are acts of killing themselves."

"Allahu akbar! "Station WAGG now belongs to the new

Caliphate, the United States of Islam. All praise to Allah and to the Immortal Leader. Allahu akbar!" Then the radio station went silent as the BMW flew along the blacktop toward the Caverns of Woe.

Theo knew he could best serve by leading a true double life. He would be, first and foremost, LT's number two once again. But, he also would become the volunteer foil for Islamist debate. He had the perfect kind of reputation to be the target of all the scholars and Imams and Mullahs and the hatred of practically every Muslim on the face of the earth. And, his known relationship with Worth could be played as well to help keep them both above serious suspicion. Worth would be the finger pointer that made the Caliphate seem open and legitimate. He would be the fool that made the Caliphate seem right.

As he put it to Gwynn, "You will play the outlaw. Worth will be the cultured curmudgeon, and I will play the fool. My model will be the fool in *King Lear*. I will simply convince the powers that be that I will be most useful to them as a person whose opinions could be pilloried by their Islamic scholars in public, on television, whatever and where ever. After all, I was the lone voice raised in alarm at what might happen. And, it did. That makes me a true 'love to hate' target."

The same TV type appearances he used to wallow in with the greatest of pleasure were now converted into performances where he allowed those who could not best him to best him and to use him as the target for their misfiring. Should they miss their target, he would immediately jump into the line of fire and take the metaphorical bullet of his own volition. He saw it as taking one for the team—again and again and again.

From the beginning, both he and Gwynn had realized that insiders were going to be essential to their success. Keeping in the Caliphate loop as much as possible gave both him and Worth many opportunities to use their skills to make themselves very well informed. They also enjoyed a certain freedom of movement that they could never have experienced on a daily basis as fugitives, like Gwynn, or even as suspicious persons. Theo also was able to hire a feature reporter for *Neo Geo* as a special consultant, a man named Chace Durante.

27
How Am I Not Dead?
[Music: "Recorder of Jihad"]

Eight expertly shod hooves thudded along the old Damascus Highway, kicking up sand and water behind as they pounded the soaked, packed-sand road at a gallop. The hooves of the white and the oil-colored Arabian stallions sounded like the muffled thuds of polo ponies on thick turf. Approaching the outskirts of the city, an unseasonable torrential downpour still pelted the two riders relentlessly.

Ibrahim suddenly reigned in his white to a canter, shouting like a tourist guide at his guest, Saladin Keayrn. His Father, Saladin Muhammad, had been a student of his good friend Hassan al-Banna many years ago. Ibrahim was not a tourist guide, however. He was still Chief of the local tribe and the one who kept the stories of the great Salah-ad-Din just as he had been all those years ago when he had ridden this same road with the young man's Father.

Almost as if by Ibrahim's command, the rain stopped.

"It has been more than seven hundred and fifty years since that fatal February rain fell on this very road and soaked the unprotected Salah-ad-Din, peace be upon him, as he greeted Hajj pilgrims upon their return from Mecca.

"The people of Damascus came out in full force that day. They were strung out along this very highway to honor their exalted Jihad leader."

The equine brothers slowed to a walk.

"After all, Salah-ad-Din alone, peace be upon him, had united the tribes. He alone had taken Jerusalem back from the kafir Crusaders. He alone had also finally repelled the English King Richard of the Lion Heart and his Templars. No amount of rain could put out that fire.

"Just like today, young Saladin. This July Fourth, nineteen hundred and sixty-five is Independence Day for your adopted America. Yet, here you are, returned from your Hajj, a journey your namesake was never able to make, on the very date of the Battle of the Horns of Hattin when Salah-ad-Din, may Allah be pleased with him, and his united Muslim armies defeated the Crusaders and took back Jerusalem.

"And, now refreshed and renewed in Allah, no amount of fear or intimidation will stop you from completing your mission for the New Brotherhood, the mission of your Father, Saladin Muhammad, may Allah be pleased with him."

Ibrahim leaned forward in his saddle. "It takes time, and the time is now, son of my brother. Just as it was for your namesake and his."

"Salah-ad-Din Yusuf Ibn Ayyub or Righteousness of Faith Joseph, Son of Job, may Allah be pleased with him, was born in Tikrit, Iraq in the year five hundred and thirty-two AH. That means *anno Hegirae* or in the year of the Hijra. It equates to eleven thirty-eight AD, the way infidel calendars count it. This has been our way since Umar declared—more than five hundred years earlier—that the year the prophet and his followers, peace be upon him and them, migrated to Medina would be the first year of the Islamic calendar. On the very night he was born, Salah-ad-Din's Father and Mother had to flee their home and high position in Baghdad because the brother of his Father had killed a man.

"In five hundred and forty-seven AH or eleven hundred and fifty-two AD, that same uncle, Shirkuh, brought him to the court of the great Nur-ad Din. Although he was only fourteen, he was already *Adab*, a student of the *Qur'an* and of poetry. With Shirkuh as his mentor, Salah-ad-Din also became very glib and capable both within the military and court society. Very quickly he became very *Zarf*.

"Just four years later, he was already the king's personal liaison officer. He was never far from Nur-ad Din's side on the march or at court in Damascus. It is said that sometime that year the king invited him to join his team in a polo match—a sign of very high favor.

"Soon he became the leader of a united Muslim Caliphate. At the Battle of the Horns of Hattin in five hundred and eighty-three AH, eleven hundred and eighty-seven AD, he and his united armies of Islam routed the Crusaders on the plains between two extinct volcanoes, the Horns of Hattin, and the Sea of Galilee, reclaiming Jerusalem for Islam.

"So the story goes, his son Al-Afdal cried out as the Crusaders retreated further and further into the trap of the Horns: 'We have beaten them, Father!' Salah-ad-Din, may Allah be pleased with him, turned in his saddle to face his son who was witnessing his very first battle. 'Be silent, my son. We shall not have defeated them until the royal tent of King Guy falls.'

"Now, at the exact moment Salah-ad-Din, may Allah be pleased with him, spoke, the King's red tent collapsed to the ground. He leaped from his mount and prostrated himself. 'Glory be to Allah and thanks to Him for this great victory for Islam.'

"'What, then, do we do with the Templars and the Hospitallers,' al-Afdal asked his Father, 'now that you are letting King Guy and the other leaders go free?'

"'Remember what they did to us at the Battle of Ramla?' Salah-ad-Din, may Allah be pleased with him, replied. 'They killed off half my army. They almost killed me! They are too dangerous to set free. Kill them. Kill them all!'

"That night, seated on a dais before his entire army of Allah, Salah-ad-Din, may Allah be pleased with him, watched as the scholars and ascetics that had so strongly supported his Jihad efforts behead each one of the seventy-five Templars and thirty-seven Hospitallers they had captured that day in battle, impaling each head upon a pike.

"The next morning as the bodiless heads of the Templars and Hospitallers looked on, the remaining Crusader prisoners were marched the 400 miles to Cairo where they would be forced to work extending the city's fortifications and building Salah-ad-Din's dream place for learning and worship, the Citadel.

"So, that is how we must treat the infidels—no mercy, no honor, no respect. It worked for Salah-ad-Din, may Allah be pleased with him. It will work for us."

"Yes, Ibrahim, it will work for us."

"Your Mother, Seanad, she has been a good teacher, it seems, in spite of the fact that she is a woman and not truly one of us."

"Yes, she has." Sal smiled. "On the verge of seeming heretical, she has been as good as any Father or person of middle eastern birth. Even when the New Brotherhood's plan forced her to give up her only child so that I could leave Dublin when I was twelve and become a citizen of America, she not only allowed me to leave but she also encouraged me to leave. Over the years, she has discreetly kept in very close touch."

His best characteristic was also his worst. He fervently believed that he could do anything. Seanad had repeatedly told him that was true, because he was the son of an Irish mother and an Egyptian father who was executed as a true martyr for the old Brotherhood just before he was born. He was to be one of its revivalists. Seanad had told him over and over how his Father and her husband, Saladin Muhammad, made sure that she learned everything he could teach her about Islam so that she could someday pass that on to their son. She told him how the black-and-tans—disguised in their new Irish police uniforms—came for his Father and dragged him from their small cottage like a wild dog, to hang soon after in Eqypt while he was still in her belly. She told him that, when the time was right, he would carry on for his Father.

When Saladin sailed on that ship for England and then America, the future of the entire Muslim Nation rested on his twelve-year-old shoulders. He would make the necessary transition to his new support family in the United States, become a citizen, and await instructions. But, he would keep Seanad's name as he had for all these years. No one was to know that his Father's last name was Muhammad.

"Saladin," he remembered his Mother saying time and again, "you must never let anyone know who you are, that you are the son of Saladin Muhammad, may Allah be pleased with him, and that you are destined for greatness as the Leader and ultimate martyr for Allah."

"But, mother, is it not wrong to mislead and deceive people? To lie?"

"To be sure, Saladin, my son. Islam forbids lying. The *Qur'an*, Surah 40:28 says: 'Truly Allah guides not one who transgresses and lies.'

"That simply means that Allah does not approve of lying. But, in His service, Saladin." The smile on her round face became almost rapturous. "That's a different story."

She paused and brushed her long thick raven hair back from her face almost as if to give herself a better view of things. "The Arabic word *Takeyya* means to prevent, or guard against. The principle of *Al-Takeyya* tells us that Muslims can lie to prevent harm to themselves, to fellow Muslims, or to Islam itself. You can even deny the faith, Saladin, if you do not mean it in your heart. *Al-Takeyya* is based on *Surah 3:28*. Can you recite it for me, my son?"

"Let not the believers take for friends or helpers Unbelievers rather than believers: if any do that, in nothing will there be help from Allah: except by way of precaution, that ye may prevent them from harming you. But Allah cautions you to remember Himself; for the final goal is to Allah."

"Yes, that's very good. Now, according to the verse you just recited, a Muslim can pretend to befriend infidels. He can act as though he believes as they do until the time is right.

"So, Saladin, my son, it is permitted for you to do things contrary to the faith like drinking, not praying or fasting as required, uttering insincere oaths, kneeling to a deity other than Allah, and even renouncing belief in Allah if you must.

"A good story about when it is permitted to lie, my son, is the story of the assassination of Kaab Ibn al-Ashrf, a member of the Hebrew tribe, Banu al-Nudair. It had been reported that Kaab had shown support for Muhammad's enemy, may Allah bless him and grant him peace, and that he had recited amorous poetry to Muslim women.

"'This Kaab has harmed Allah and His Apostle,' Muhammad, may Allah bless him and grant him peace, proclaimed as he asked for volunteers to rid him of Kaab Ibn al-Ashraf.

"'I will volunteer on the condition that you allow me to lie, because that is the only way I will be able to convince his tribe that I am against you,' Ibn Muslima explained. With Muhammad's consent, may Allah bless him and grant him peace, Ibn Muslima went to Kaab and made up stories that showed his unhappiness with Muhammad's leadership, may Allah bless him and grant him peace. Once he had gained Kaab's trust, he lured him away from his house one night and assassinated him in a remote area under the cover of darkness.

"Even denying your faith can be forgiven, my son, according to *Surah 16:106*. It says: 'Any one who, after accepting faith in Allah, utters Unbelief, except under compulsion, his heart remaining firm in Faith—but such as open their breast to Unbelief, on them is Wrath from Allah, and theirs will be a dreadful Penalty.'

"This verse was revealed to the Prophet after he learned that Ammar Ibn Yasser was forced to deny his faith when kidnapped by the Banu Moghera tribe. Muhammad, may Allah bless him and grant him peace, consoled Ammar by telling him, 'If they turned, you turn.'"

"What does that mean, Mother?"

"Simply this, my son. If they captured him again, he would be allowed to deny The Prophet, may Allah bless him and grant him peace, again.

"These and similar passages from the *Qur'an* and the Hadiths clearly reveal that Muslims' unintentional lies are forgivable and that even our intentional lies can be absolved. It is also clear that if forced to do so, Muslims can even deny faith in Allah, as long as they maintain the profession of faith in their hearts

"Faith is inseparable from community in Islam, Saladin. As you know, the *Qur'an* almost always addresses the Believers and not the Believer. All acts of worship that are declared pillars of Islam have a group form in one way or another. The five daily prayers are best performed in congregation. The special Friday prayer cannot even be offered individually. Zakat is obviously aimed at making the rich of the community take care of the needs of its poor. Fasting, a basically individual act, is done by all during the same times. Hajj is unified by bringing the believers together at the same time in the plains of Arafat in their remembrance of Allah.

"Those who join in the worship of Allah produce a Brotherhood, a community that goes beyond the borders of countries and embodies the best moral values of the faith: Mercy, compassion, fear of Allah, piety, and justice. It is a tremendous force in the service of Right and against Wrong. *Al-Maida* 5:2 tells the members of the Brotherhood, the community, to help each other in righteousness and piety but not in sin and rancor. They are to be 'strong against Unbelievers but compassionate amongst each other,' according to *Al-Fat-h* 48:29. 'They do not do injustice to others nor do they tolerate any injustice to themselves.'

"The *Sahih Muslim* hadith tells us that in their love and concern for each other, all members of this Brotherhood are one body: 'When any part of the body suffers, the whole body feels the pain.'

"The new Brotherhood will someday be a force for good, a

purveyor of peace and justice for everyone. It will provide stability in an unstable world. To the downtrodden and oppressed everywhere, it will provide freedom. And, you will be their Leader.

"And, remember this, Saladin. When giving commands regarding the Islamic Brotherhood, the *Qur'an* underscores the community or group aspect of Islam. In *An-Nur 24:61*, instead of saying 'greet each other,' it says, 'greet yourself.' Instead of saying 'do not defame each other,' *Al-Hujurat 49:11* says 'do not defame yourself.' Instead of saying 'do not kill each other,' *An-Nisaa 4:29* says, 'do not kill yourself.'

"If you were truthful with the kuffar, my son, and you told them that your name was Saladin Muhammad, not Sal Keayrn, then the infidels would misunderstand you. They would resist you. They would attempt to destroy you. But you will be the Great Messenger, The Leader. When the time is right, they will have to follow or die!

"Until that time, you must keep your purpose hidden from them. You must keep who you are hidden from them. Remember all this, my son, as you embark on your great journey to America to a new family who will support and sustain you in your mission. For it is up to you to live that life you are destined for—the life of the son of the creator of the 'secret apparatus'.

"Allah's message is clear, my son. You must stop us from continuing to kill ourselves. That is worth all the lies you could ever tell."

"This is what you came to see and hear, son of my brother. Is it not? This is what Hassan al-Banna, may Allah be pleased with him, wanted me to show your Father . . . and, now, you. Is it not, Saladin Keayrn, son of Saladin Muhammad, may Allah be pleased with him?

"Now you can return to America and to your new wife. Congratulations, by the way."

"Thank you, Ibrahim."

"You will serve in the Army where you will learn all you can in Vietnam about fighting. Then you will disappear and continue with the New Brotherhood's work just as your Father, may Allah be pleased with him, did before you with the old Brotherhood."

"Speaking of the old Brotherhood, is that a copy of the old *Al-Manar* there in your saddle bag, Ibrahim? A little dated don't you think? Like thirty or forty years old?"

"Yes. But it was your Father's teacher and my good friend, Hassan's, favorite magazine, may Allah be pleased with him. The Syrian, Rashid Rida, may Allah be pleased with him, published it for many years out of Cairo. Hassan, may Allah be pleased with him, shared Rida's primary belief, may Allah be pleased with him, that the decline of Islamic civilization relative to the West could only be reversed by returning to an unadulterated form of Islam, free from all that diluted its original message."

"Yes. I know, and I concur completely."

"Yes. And are you clear on what your responsibilities really are, son of my brother?"

The left haunch of Saladin Keayrn's stallion twitched as large drops of rain began to splash off of its shiny black skin once more "Yes, Ibrahim. Even now, I can hear my Mother reminding me that my Father established and commanded the old Brotherhood's first military wing—the 'secret apparatus'. And, because I am his son, what my responsibilities are to Allah. She learned well from my Father, and she has taught me well for my Father.

"I know that it is up to me to recreate the 'secret apparatus' in a new form to invade the United States and ultimately establish a World Caliphate there.

"As The Leader, I will be required to prepare for and ignite the final invasion, very likely at the sacrifice of my own life."

"Yes, Saladin Keayrn, son of Saladin Muhammad, may Allah be pleased with him. It is like we have been riding from the past to the future along this road today just as I did with your Father so many years ago. And, that future awaits you now in America as his did for him back then in Isma'iliyya."

Ibrahim turned in his saddle looking back down the road they had traveled during the bitter rain. It was, indeed, like looking back in time. "How could we have known then what sacrifice your Father would have to make." He shook his head saddened for the moment by the ghosts he saw behind him. "Dying, as he did, hanged in that Egyptian prison. How can we know, now, what sacrifices you may have to make?" He glanced skyward, shielding his eyes from the rain with his left hand. "Or, when you may have to make them."

Observing only dark storm clouds and more rain coming from the other side of Damascus, Ibrahim nodded to his new protégé.

"Salaam Alaykum. May Allah be pleased with you, son of my brother." Ibrahim touched the reins lightly and turned the white stallion south. He waved for Sal to follow.

"Ensha'allah, Saladin Keayrn! Ensha'allah!" He tapped his horse's right flank, and the white stallion galloped away from Damascus seeming to dissolve in the thick pelting drops.

Saladin Keayrn felt as though he were awakening from some kind of vision or dream, a recollection of what had happened so long ago on the road to Damascus. Yes, he had been and done a lot of things in his life, but he didn't know if anything he had ever been or done was actually "for real." He became a husband after his junior year at Columbia. It was necessary. A part of the plan. Then he was an NROTC college graduate. Also part of the plan. Then he became a Navy Seal who was never assigned to a Seal Team but was assigned to a new, very secret special operations combined-services team in Vietnam. Not exactly part of the plan. More like fortunate coincidence.

From far off and close at hand simultaneously—something only memory could do—the gunfire was still as clear and terrifying as it always was back then. He used to call it "clearifying." For the first time in nearly three years together, they hadn't known, on that day, what hit them. No one from any direction had ever caught them unawares before.

Once he realized what was actually happening in the ambush, he went down. Worth had seen him fall. He had made sure of that. He knew that they would search the area compulsively for as much as a couple of weeks to completely satisfy everyone all the way up to the President that he was actually missing. No body. No trace of him. In fact, no trace of the NVA scout unit either. He was officially MIA after an ambush by unknown forces. Part of the plan.

* * * * *

"It is time, Saladin, for you to truly begin your own war for Allah. You have learned what you can from them, have you not?"

"I have, sir."

"But, being extracted from Vietnam by our elite Muslim secret forces is only the first step, only the beginning," the Mullah continued.

"We must provide you with a new identity and a new direction far removed from whatever your former comrades-in-arms might expect. Allah has a day for you, my son. It will come in its own time. Until then, you must become others in order to survive. But, you must always continue to pass on the fire of our Jihad to those you encounter along the way. Be patient and vigilant, my son. Soon, you will be with me here in Afghanistan once again. Then, you will be able to finally emerge as your true self."

* * * * *

"Come with us, sir."
"Who are you?"
"We are from the Mullah."
"The Mullah?"
"Yes. He says your time making pizzas here in Milano is finished. You must come to him now in Damascus. Your day has come at last."

* * * * *

"You will pose as a carpenter here in Damascus while you work with the Mother of Doves—a female contact, unfortunately. Beware of her, Saladin. She is a true seductress of the highest order. She can make you think you have already attained paradise. Her code-name is, aptly, Semiramis taken from a mythical Assyrian queen who founded the city of Babylon and ruled in the 6th century BC. She was renowned for her beauty and wisdom. Legend says that her celestial mother abandoned her at birth. She was discovered and reared by a flock of doves.

"You see, Saladin, this first Semiramis conquered many lands and built Damascus. Then, after a long and prosperous reign, she vanished from earth in the shape of a dove. Thereafter, she was worshiped as a deity, acquiring many of the characteristics of the goddess Ishtar. But, there is no God but Allah."

"There is no God but Allah."

"The dove was her sacred bird. So, she was known under the names of Semiramis, Priestess of Doves, as well as Semirna,

Mother of Doves.

"Our present-day Semiramis prefers Mother of Doves." The Mullah's thick lips curled into a very carefully orchestrated smirk. "These modern females. They think that Allah has somehow given them genitals like a man's." He smothered a chuckle, shaking his head. "It must be the fault of infidel science. Islamic science would never permit such thinking. I just do not know what to make of these modern females."

"They are, indeed, a puzzle, sir."

"However, together, you will destroy the golden doves of Damascus—that symbol of god when there is no god but Allah—and blame it on the Christians and the Jews," the Mullah explained.

"It is well known that doves and pigeons are very abundant in Damascus because they enjoy such a special status as a result of the legend of Semiramis. The Golden Doves are the most special. Your plan, once executed, will send the city into upheaval and despair because of the sacred nature of those birds.

"Just think of the symbolic quality of your act, Saladin. In Genesis in the *Bible*, Noah sends out a dove after the flood. In the New Testament a dove is the symbol of the Holy Spirit. In Islam, doves and pigeons are respected and favored because they are believed to have assisted the Prophet, may Allah bless him and grant him peace, in distracting his enemies outside the cave of Thaw'r in the great Hijra.

"What a blow for Allah!"

* * * * *

"Welcome our newest warrior leader, the son of Saladin Muhammad, may Allah be pleased with him, the founder of the original secret apparatus. Before you is the man who engineered the destruction of all the golden doves in Damascus and successfully blamed it on the Christians and the Jews." The Mullah addressed the Taliban leadership from across Afghanistan assembled in the Bamyan valley that day to witness the destruction of another culture. "The warrior who will someday be The Leader. Today, as his first official act with us, he will command the destruction of these abominations behind us. They are un-Islamic and idols forbidden under Sharia law. They cannot be permitted to exist!" The Mullah nodded toward Saladin.

"He has come home in a manner of speaking. Salaam Alaykum, Saladin Keayrn Muhammad. Peace be upon you."

"Salaam Alaykum. Peace be upon you. And, all of you." Saladin immediately turned toward the battery the Mullah had assembled. "Artillery commander! Commence firing at will!"

"Fire!" Fire at will!"

A barrage of anti-aircraft and artillery fire followed. Then another. Both with little effect. That first day, the assault did not seem to do much damage. So each day, Saladin assembled his artillery firing squad and tried again. After several days, the statues finally began to show some signs of damage, but the targets were far from obliterated. It was as if they refused to be erased.

After seven days of shelling, Saladin ordered anti-tank mines placed at the bottom of the niches that had developed from the shelling. In that way when fragments of rock broke off from artillery fire, they might set off the mines, giving the statues a double dose of explosive destruction.

Finally, after nearly a month, Saladin ordered his soldiers to be lowered down the cliff face. They located holes in the statues and placed explosives in them. These "hot spots" provided additional destructive power when shells hit near them and detonated them.

"There is only one way to control the Dhimmi until we can convert or eliminate them," Saladin responded when news correspondents prodded him about the wonton destruction by the Taliban in Bamyan. "We will destroy everything they have made in every way possible just as we smashed the two idols in the side of a cliff in the Bamyan valley.

"They hewed the main bodies of the two statues directly from the sandstone cliffs. The artisans created details in mud mixed with straw coated with stucco and painted them to enhance the expressions of the faces, hands, and folds of the robes. They constructed lower parts of the statues' arms from the same mud-straw mix.

"And, the Taliban destroyed them on orders from our great leader Mullah Mohammed Omar.

"I, The Leader, was there when we destroyed them. Why did we destroy them? Because they were built by that people and they represented that people and their culture, both which we could not allow."

* * * * *

"Today marks the anniversary of the day our Immortal Leader destroyed the Buddhas of Bamyan, the day he believes was the day he actually ascended to the position of The Leader who would lead us to the new Caliphate we now enjoy, the United States of Islam." Ellworth continued speaking into the camera lens just off to his right. "On Six March Two Thousand and one, Mullah Mohammed Omar declared that Muslims 'should be proud of smashing idols. It has given praise to God that we have destroyed them.'

"The new spokesperson at the time, simply referred to as The Leader, explained that the Taliban had destroyed the Buddha statues in accordance with Islamic law. 'It was purely a religious issue,' he said. "We, of course, know now that The Leader was one in the same as our Immortal Leader.

"Just today, a release from the Immortal Leader's office announced that in celebration of the first anniversary of the new Caliphate on July Fourth, President for Life Lars Hansen and The Immortal Leader will command the destruction of the Statue of Liberty just as the Immortal Leader commanded the destruction of the Buddhas of Bamyan."

After the killing of the golden doves and the destruction of the Buddhas, others finally began to call him The Leader, and he easily assumed that role, the one his Mother had prepared him for so fastidiously. Now, when he was Sal, was he Sal? What was being Sal? Being The Leader? Was being The Leader what it meant to be Sal? Was being Sal what it meant to be The Leader? Or were these also just roles, other parts in the play? Was there really such a thing in this plane of existence as some objective, baseline reality that we can all agree is "for real"? Or is it exactly like that poor infidel bastard Camsron always said it was?

"No one reality is more real than any other," Lieutenant Gwynn Camsron had emphasized many times during what he used to refer to as "training sessions" for the members of his team. "Your very life depends upon that fact, because it is you who are the manipulator of the moment. And, as long as you can keep that up successfully, you can stay alive."

Saladin Keayrn was shocked by the similarity between what the Lieutenant or LT had said to him and what his very own Mother had told him at least once every day he could remember until, at twelve years of age, his destiny forced him to leave her for America and his new role in the Nation. "You are destined to be The Leader, my son. All roles, all realities are real, but among competing realities yours is supreme. Islam is supreme, my son. That is Allah's will."

The big distinction between what the two had told him was that Gwynn's version was behaviorist observation whereas his Mother's view was a metaphysical and ethical conclusion. And, that conclusion had simmered in his synapses from birth. How could anyone expect that he would take on any other part but the one he had assumed?

This situation he found himself in now was, however, the most surrealistic reality he had ever encountered. His nearly black eyes darted about in their sockets looking for some cue card, some clue as to what was going on here. His eyes found what seemed to be the arm of a person. Another human being trapped in this reality along with him. By the type of sleeve, the person was probably a Doctor. Suddenly his eyes froze as Saladin realized that he somehow knew the probable Doctor was suddenly staring at him.

"Praise Allah. I am Doctor Zenith Nadir, Immortal Leader."

As he bent forward over the bed, Saladin could see a blurry face, dark creased skin more suited to a Bedouin than to a physician. His deep brown eyes had tears in them.

"How am I not dead?"

"It is a miracle of Allah the merciful and compassionate."

"Compassionate?" The last thing he remembered was a feeling of being blown to bits by the biggest flash bang in history. His head was still pounding and his ears were still ringing from the explosion he had detonated. Somehow his vest bomb did not explode.

"Where am I?"

"A super top secret mobile hospital bus complex where you are absolutely safe and protected. The security is—I don't know how else to say it—ferocious. The exterior—skin I believe they call it—is retooled every few weeks to look like something different. A small army occupies a portion of the bus and several lead and follow vehicles. I mean when we drive by, people know that it is somebody special, probably high up in government or super rich. They just don't know it's their Immortal Leader."

"How long have I been . . . ." His dark eyes continued to flick and dart about still trying to see something that would make real sense to him, but he was far too confined to see much of anything. . . . "Like this?"

"Oh, sir, you have been in a coma now for nearly a year."

Saladin tried to reach out to the young doctor, to touch his arm, anything to ground himself more securely in this version of reality that it seemed had gone on pretty well without him for nearly a year. But he realized that what he thought was his left hand did not respond when he desired to move it toward the doctor. "Doctor, I am reaching out to touch you, but my hand is not moving."

"You are fortunate to be alive at all, Immortal Leader."

"Fortunate, indeed, Doctor." His eyes thrashed about in their sockets even more frenetically. "Is there anything I can move other than my mouth?"

"No, Immortal Leader. Strange isn't it? Nothing seems to function in your entire body except your mouth, which of course means that certain muscles, your tongue, certain arteries, and your brain seem to function properly. You are breathing, eating, drinking, and defecating mechanically."

How could he have put together all the sins of violence so perfectly into one act? Violence toward others. Violence toward Allah and nature. Violence toward self. Sounds almost like a Faulkner Noble Prize speech. Man against man. Man against nature. Man against himself. Something his old friend, Gwynn, could probably appreciate.

"Let me get this straight, Doctor. What you are saying, Doctor, is that, for all practical purposes, I am a consciousness without a body, a disembodied spirit?"

28
President for Life

[Music: "Recorder of Jihad"]

1
26 Ramadan 1403. July 6, 1983.

Salaam Alaykum. Peace be upon you.
In the name of The Leader, may Allah guide him.
In the name of The Prophet,
May Allah bless him and grant him peace.
In the name of Allah, the merciful and compassionate.
Islam is superior to all human conditions and earthly religions.

My name is Lazarus Ibn Hassin. I am Recorder of Jihad. You will only know of me as I reveal myself within these pages which I shall scribe each day, preserving the tales of our holy Jihad as it unfolds for the sake of history and the followers of Allah. Every action of the new Brotherhood, every movement of the YUNUS Apparatus, every word from The Leader somehow, through the will of Allah, becomes a part of my record of the events that lead to the final cleansing. Allah chose me of all those who could have been chosen to become this recorder of our growth and our victory for Allah and for all of Islam.

This night, I preserve my first formal memory as Recorder of Jihad.

This day is 26 Ramadan 1403. Each year, the Night of Determination is the night when, the *Qur'an* says Allah determines the course of the world for the following year. In the case of this night, the charted course went far beyond any single year.

The Pu`u `O`o Eruption was just beginning in the Kilauea volcano on the Big Island when I, as Lars Hansen, approached the railing that separated humans from the spews of sparks and lava oozes of the current spasm of mini eruptions that only began after I already had made my way to the lava field's edge. Nearly imperceptible explosions continued to make the earth tremble around me ever so slightly and darkness began to settle over the craters of the creators of new land.

I realized that I needed to be careful. After all, Kilauea was one of the most active volcanoes on Earth. It could really blow at any time, and it seemed like it was getting ready to truly let off some steam. The volcano predominantly released basaltic lava in effusive eruptions, although occasionally it experienced explosive eruptions as well similar to what was happening at that time.

I wanted to leave this hell-like place and the sooner the better. But, I had to wait for The Leader. In order to distract myself while I waited for him to arrive, I recalled everything I could about Kilauea. It stands just under 4200 feet tall on the flanks of the larger volcano Manua Loa on the southeastern side of the Big Island. Legend tells us that Kilauea is home to Pele, the volcano goddess of ancient Hawaii.

Flakes of fire were falling so close to me that I could almost feel their sting on my skin. The dense air sizzled as if the hydrogen atoms in it were burning. Then, suddenly, I recognized The Leader's face as he strode toward me although I had never seen him or a likeness of him before. He radiated as he seemed to emerge from Kilauea's fire itself.

"Salaam Alaykum. Peace be upon you, Recorder of Jihad." He held out his hands to me in greeting.

"Salaam Alaykum. Peace be upon you, Leader." I reached out for his hands as we moved closer together, flashes and sparks dancing in the air just beyond us like a Tesla coil symphony.

"It is told to me that I am The Leader and you are The Recorder for what is yet to come."

"I am told the same as you." I grasped his right hand in a handshake and lightly touched his upper right arm with my left hand.

"Then we must forge our pact here and now, in the presence of this humbling force of Allah's will, to take over the USA and establish a great new Caliphate, the United States of Islam. "

"As is our destiny."

"As is our destiny. Let the record begin with today's meeting, Lazarus . . . ah, Lars.

"It is at hand."

What is at hand?

The final cleansing is at hand!

To the glory of the great Caliphate, the United States of Islam.
In the name of Allah, the merciful and compassionate.
Salaam Alaykum. May Allah be pleased with you.

2

27 Ramadan 1403. July 7, 1983.

Salaam Alaykum. Peace be upon you.
In the name of The Leader, may Allah guide him.
In the name of The Prophet,
May Allah bless him and grant him peace.
In the name of Allah, the merciful and compassionate.
Islam is superior to all human conditions and earthly religions.

Today is 27 Ramadan 1403, the second day of my recording of the history of our Jihad. In order for you to understand the history I write down, you must understand the eyes through which you are seeing that history.

I was born Lazarus Hassin and Lars Hansen, son and only child of Ishmael and Rebecca Hassin. They changed their name to Hansen when they immigrated to the United States just moments before my birth. That way I would be native-born American Lars Hansen, not alien Lazarus Hassin. That way I could legally become President. It was all part of the plan, they assured me many times during my early years.

Growing up, I had one of the most peculiar and rare qualities. I never threw up. My parents both swore that I never threw up as a baby. So the story goes I never even belched up my Mother's milk when she burped me just after feeding. Not when I had too much pizza or too much beer at my high school graduation picnic. Not even when I had the flu. So I have been somewhat culturally deprived in that regard or protected, depending upon how one may view it. Therefore, when a person describes something as "bad enough to make me want to barf," I sincerely do not know what that person means.

My family settled in Phoenix. Mel and Becky Hansen, as they were known in America, established their own house and office cleaning services business out of their own home and office off Black Canyon Road. Becky ran the business out of her basement office. Mel provided the customer relations as well as the muscle and skills to get the jobs done. Their business was one of the first of its type in the area. As the business grew, my Father was able to secure a contract with the city to provide maintenance services to the sewage disposal system.

My parents instilled in me a fanatical, blind belief in our mission, the mission of Jihad, the mission of the new Caliphate, the mission of the United States of Islam. It was all part of the plan.

At first, I did not understand what a Caliphate was or why it was important. I did not comprehend why I had to pretend to be Catholic in public—and even in our home as far as decorating it with religious symbols, photographs, or art—when I was actually a Muslim. My parents explained to me again and again until I either began to understand or became so numbed by the repetition that I took it on as my own. I was, as they told it to me, destined to become the Recorder of Jihad. Together with The Leader, who will emerge, we are destined by Allah's will to establish a new Muslim Caliphate in America—the United States of Islam. Then I will become President for Life.

I did not stray far from my purpose or my place to obtain my higher education. Once I graduated high school, I took a job as a proof reader for the *Arizona Republic* and drove my VW bug to Tempe just about every day to attend classes at Arizona State University, until I had accumulated enough credits and enough mileage to graduate with a Bachelors in Business Management. Next, I continued at the ASU Law School and became an editor for the *Arizona Republic's* legal publication where I proofed and edited items such as notices of bankruptcy and foreclosure and announcements of incorporation.

On my first day at Arizona State University Law School, I met the woman who would allow me to achieve the first two things that the plan required me to accomplish, that was to find a proper wife—not, unfortunately, by Islamic standards but rather by the inferior standards of what was required for the job and to establish a powerful and influential position in society.

The plan was based on the idea that it would be much better to blend in than to call attention to myself. That meant I would have to seriously deceive Medea Angelo, the woman I targeted for my wife, because she could never know of my true destiny. Not even if she were loyal to the cause. Not even if she were Muslim. No outsider could be trusted with the power that knowledge could create.

The first major research assignment in ASU One L was specifically designed so that there was only a single reference volume in the entire library that held the information required. I caught Medea with the volume. As far as she knew, no one else had yet found it. I enticed her into a deal. It would be us against them—the two of us versus the rest of the entire One L class. We would get the information and hide or destroy the book, claiming when asked that we never used it, because when we came to find it, the volume was not there. Not knowing how long it might be before we could ever hope to grab the book for a few minutes, we decided to go immediately to the Supreme Court library and use the copy there. And, being good fledgling law students, we of course actually laid the foundation for our alibi. We actually went to the Supreme Court library and made a big deal out of telling the librarian that we were from the law school and were there checking out references for a first year research project. With that strategy, we won the competition and began our law school careers together as successes when everyone else had failed. The missing volume magically reappeared the following week on the bottom shelf of one of the book bins on wheels that the librarians used to move books about.

After that escapade, we were joined at the hip for three years. The day after graduation from law school we got married. A month and one honeymoon later we hung up our shingle as lobbyists/lawyers. We focused on representing clients to the legislative and the executive branches of federal, state, and local government.

The plan was to ingratiate ourselves with top level business executives and politicians, building a base of potential future support from very satisfied clients and wait for further instructions. When the plan dictated, I would position myself for political office. If I could become the Chief Executive by election rather than invasion, Islamic takeover would be a clean and simple matter.

3
17 Safar 1409. September 28, 1988.

Salaam Alaykum. Peace be upon you.
In the name of The Leader, may Allah guide him.
In the name of The prophet,
May Allah bless him and grant him peace.
In the name of Allah, the merciful and compassionate.
Islam is superior to all human conditions and earthly religions.
My name is Lazarus ibn Hassin. I am Recorder of Jihad. Today
is 17 Safar 1409. This was a great day and night for Allah, for Islam,
and for all Muslims over the entire world.

Through our team efforts over the past five years, my wife,
Medea, and I have bought and sold political offices with regularity,
with skill, and with impunity. We have basically used Medea as a
concubine to wangle our way into positions of power and control
over CEO's as well as Governors and Senators.

I grew to like it, watching her seduce others. We engineered
videos from multiple angles that we later watched together.
Sometimes, I even viewed her work live, secluded away from her
and her prey. She was such a natural. And, the power she gave me
over these men, and sometimes women, because of what I saw and
recorded was mind-boggling. We gained control between the legs of
major forces in both business and politics in short order with our
second winning strategy together. The first, in law school, had been
"deprive the enemy of what is necessary." The second, in life after
law school, was "control the enemy's desire."

Then, today, The Leader finally called me personally and told me
about the available CEO position at the Whale Institute. He hurriedly
explained that the success of the plan hinges upon me securing the
Whale Institute CEO position. It is where they need me now, so that
I can cover up the gradual disappearance of large numbers of
humpback whales that will be occurring over the next several years.
If I am able to pull this off, The Leader promised me that I will not
only continue as Recorder of Jihad but, when we establish our new
Caliphate, I will also assume the position my parents had predicted
for me, President for Life.

"You will be the only other person on this earth who knows

everything I know, Lazarus ibn Hassin."

I told Medea that our lives would be in danger if I did not get the job because certain nefarious people expected me to take that job and do certain things for them. "I can tell you no more," I said. "But, if you do not do this thing with the Secretary, then we are both doomed."

It was not as if Medea was especially surprised by the assignment. She had seduced many a man and woman for the sake of our future. Never knowing whether I was watching or not did, she had admitted to me more than once, put a special, unnamable kind of edge on the acts every time. With the Secretary of the Interior of the United States, however, who was eighty-one and in failing health, no amount of kinky was going to put any edge on that. Instead, Medea had to marshal all of her skills and discipline in order to secure the Whale Institute CEO position for me, a position that would finally lead to my own Golden Fleece—President for Life—just as Mel and Becky predicted. That was the plan.

Tomorrow, that plan will move yet another step further along with the Secretary of the Interior appointing me to the position of CEO of the Whale Institute in Maui, Hawaii. Exactly what The Leader wanted me to accomplish.

Medea is already looking forward to being away from the desert and the dry air. She is ready for some humidity and ocean spray and ukulele music and some Don Ho instead of Navajo. She most certainly has earned every bit of it.

Salaam Alaykum. May Allah be pleased with you.

4
26 Ramadan 1427. October 18, 2006.

Salaam Alaykum. Peace be upon you.
In the name of The Leader, may Allah guide him.
In the name of The Prophet,
May Allah bless him and grant him peace.
In the name of Allah, the merciful and compassionate.
Islam is superior to all human conditions and earthly religions.
.

My name is Lazarus ibn Hassin. I am Recorder of Jihad. Today is 26 Ramadan 1427.

Another Night of Determination is upon us, yet we have no new direction. Nearly eighteen years have passed here at the Whale Institute. I have noted and appropriately hidden reports of diminishing humpback populations in the Caribbean of major proportions, yet no further activation word has come. I have not heard from The Leader in all those years until today when I received a phone call at the Whale Institute from someone who identified himself simply as "The Leader." The voice sounded like the man I had met at Kilauea, but the person with that voice was not acting or sounding as if he knew me, which seemed rather strange.

The Leader explained that due to a number of things beyond their control, they needed to speed up the plan. He told me that the Jihad needed me to begin making blatant negative political moves against one Senator Abigail Keayrn who was making far too much noise and way too much progress in closing off illegal alien access to the United States. "This kind of movement means we must, ourselves, move faster and more aggressively. And, we must be more creative. So, we have devised a new plan."

"A new plan?"

"Yes. You will soon begin receiving contributions from Submission Whale Research—SWR —and many other global non-profit organizations dedicated to world betterment. You should use these funds as much as possible to further your own political efforts."

"And, what do I do after receiving these contributions?"

"You can finally begin to make your political moves, Recorder of Jihad. Everything is beginning to fall into place as we discussed and hoped for that day at Kilauea. Now, all that remains is for you to stake your claim and extinguish your nemesis in one fell swoop."

The voice from Kilauea hesitated. "And, because you'll be going after this woman senator who will automatically have the public's sympathy, you will have to be very, very sympathetic yourself. I would say you have to become as pitiable a figure as a man can be. And, you need to make that happen as soon as you can."

"Oh, that's all?"

"No need to be testy about it, Recorder of Jihad. You do understand what I mean by being as 'sympathetic as a man can be,' don't you?"

"Unfortunately, I believe I do." He bit his lower lip before he spoke again. "But, if it wasn't for her, Leader, we would not be where we are now."

"And, Allah will know her as an unwitting martyr to our cause." The voice in the phone paused. "Put simply, if you plan to be President for Life of the new Caliphate, the United States of Islam, then you will have to do whatever it takes to get there, now won't you? Otherwise you'll always be looking back in time to what you might have done."

Salaam Alaykum. May Allah be pleased with you.

5
26 Ramadan 1429. September 26, 2008.

Salaam Alaykum. Peace be upon you.
In the name of The Leader, may Allah guide him.
In the name of The prophet,
May Allah bless him and grant him peace.
In the name of Allah, the merciful and compassionate.
Islam is superior to all human conditions and earthly religions.
My name is Lazarus Ibn Hassin. I am Recorder of Jihad. Today is 26 Ramadan 1429, a spectacularly important Night of Determination. The Leader has invited me to attend the next session of his YUNUS Apparatus Warrior Training School in the Tobago Quays. My assistant is already arranging a two-week Caribbean vacation as my cover for this most awaited and anticipated opportunity to finally study at the feet of The Leader.

How did The Leader put it?

"You are not yet a sympathetic enough figure, Recorder of Jihad. You must come to comprehend in more depth what you are required to be willing and able to do in order to accomplish your mission."

In the name of Allah, the merciful and compassionate

Salaam Alaykum. May Allah be pleased with you.

6

19 Rabi' Al-Awwal 1430. March 15, 2009.

Salaam Alaykum. Peace be upon you.

In the name of The Leader, may Allah guide him.

In the name of The Prophet,

May Allah bless him and grant him peace.

In the name of Allah, the merciful and compassionate.

Islam is superior to all human conditions and earthly religions.

My name is Lazarus Ibn Hassin. I am Recorder of Jihad. Today is 19 Rabi' Al-Awwal 1430.

The television screen is glaring at me with two large red blinking words that are almost like blood shot eyes: "Breaking News" as I sit on the couch we had made love on so many times while watching our tapes. Otherwise, the great room is nearly dark.

"Good evening. This is Ellworth Hayes with breaking news for INN."

The television intrusions have not allowed me to establish any separation between myself and the encroaching realities that surround me. Those intrusions are insistent on being noticed even though I already know what the "Breaking News" is. As I slug down my fifth Courvoisier, I already know what Ellworth Hayes is going to say. After all, I made it happen.

"Medea Angelo Hansen, the wife of Lars Hansen, CEO of the Whale Institute in Maui, Hawaii and a front-runner for the vice presidential nomination at the Democratic Convention in August, died this morning in a tragic helicopter crash while she was shooting photographs of humpback whales off the coast of Maui."

I must write this in the past tense. I need the distance. I cannot face it in the present tense. May Allah forgive me for my cowardice.

He cursed God with an obscene gesture as twilight capitulated to a sudden and astounding darkness that wrapped his mind in a hijab made with the threads of fear and security tightly entwined into the same yarn. It absorbed everything in its path. That contradiction percolated in his mind like his father's waste pits, like the memories of his many deeds for Allah including this latest one.

He had finally been able to understand the need for this act he had put off for so long. The epiphany came during their study of the Ninth Lesson of the *YUNUS Apparatus Manual for Warriors* at The

Leader's Warrior Training Camp. It simply and bluntly instructed them: "Most of all know that if all else fails, the warrior must be willing to martyr his fellow warrior who has been captured and knows too much. That is what it requires to be a YUNUS warrior, a part of Allah's Spear."

The Leader explained carefully to them, all the time looking specifically at him, how this did not limit itself to fellow warriors. They also had to be ready to kill not only their entire cell but even their families if necessary for the sake of the mission.

Salaam Alaykum. May Allah be pleased with you.

7
24 Jumada Al-Akhirah 1430. June 17, 2009.

Salaam Alaykum. Peace be upon you.
In the name of The Leader, may Allah guide him.
In the name of The Prophet,
May Allah bless him and grant him peace.
In the name of Allah, the merciful and compassionate.
Islam is superior to all human conditions and earthly religions.

My name is Lazarus ibn Hassin. I am Recorder of Jihad. Today is 24 Jumada Al-Akhirah 1430.

I threw off the barely gray 1200 thread count Egyptian cotton sateen sheet and two hand-made quilts. They were smothering me. I sprang straight up in the bed gasping for air. Even in my bed in the White House—covered and protected by body guards and my quilts, one green with white crescents and stars and the other white with green crescents and stars—I still awaken often in the middle of the night thinking that I smell my father coming in from work even though he has been dead for nearly ten years. My Father's sewer maintenance contract with the city had been a first for the city and for their business, and Mel had brought home the stench of success with him every evening in his hair, on his skin, in his clothes ever since.

The Aaron Silver death and Bridget—what's her name?—Yow, the green peace spy. Becoming a bringer of death feels powerful. It becomes easier each time to let the necessary blood. Both deaths are being blamed on Senator Abagail Keayrn. She is the perfect target because of her blatant political agenda against me and my work to preserve and protect our environment. But for her obsession with me, the young man and woman would not have come to such a tragic end.

That was the spin. That was the plan. That was the stench in the bedroom.

In the name of Allah, the merciful and compassionate

Salaam Alaykum. May Allah be pleased with you.

8
12 Rajab 1430. July 4, 2009.

Salaam Alaykum. Peace be upon you.
In the name of The Leader, may Allah guide him.
In the name of The prophet,
May Allah bless him and grant him peace.
In the name of Allah, the merciful and compassionate.
Islam is superior to all human conditions and earthly religions.

My name is Lazarus ibn Hassin. I am Recorder of Jihad. Today is 12 Rajab 1430. At one minute past midnight, The Leader became the Immortal Leader when he survived his destruction of the Washington Monument. His explosion shook the world to its very core and transformed forever the United States of America into the great new Caliphate for Allah, the United States of Islam.

At last, it is truly at hand.
What is at hand?
The new Horns of Hattin is at hand!
What is at hand?
The final cleansing is at hand!
To the glory of the great Caliphate, the United States of Islam.
In the name of Allah, the merciful and compassionate

Salaam Alaykum. May Allah be pleased with you.

9
23 Rajab 1431. July 4, 2010.

Salaam Alaykum. Peace be upon you.
In the name of The Leader, may Allah guide him.
In the name of The Prophet,
May Allah bless him and grant him peace.
In the name of Allah, the merciful and compassionate.
Islam is superior to all human conditions and earthly religions.
My name is Lazarus ibn Hassin. I am Recorder of Jihad. Today is 23 Rajab 1431 or the American 4 July 2010.

The Prophet, Muhammad, may Allah bless him and grant him peace, came to me in a vision during Salat Ul Fajr. The ruby red appearing at the rim of the earth under the white predawn eastern sky seemed to morph into a fuzzy kind of profile of the Prophet, may Allah bless him and grant him peace. His voice, like the rumbling of a volcano, said to me:
"At last, Messenger, Recorder of Jihad, it is truly at hand."
And, my voice asked him:
"What is at hand?"
"The final cleansing is at hand!"
To the glory of the great Caliphate, the United States of Islam.
In the name of Allah, the merciful and compassionate

Salaam Alaykum. May Allah be pleased with you.

10
23 Rajab 1431. July 4, 2010.

Zero Seven Hundred Hours

Salaam Alaykum. Peace be upon you.
In the name of The Leader, may Allah guide him.
In the name of The prophet,
May Allah bless him and grant him peace.
In the name of Allah, the merciful and compassionate.
Islam is superior to all human conditions and earthly religions.

My name is Lazarus ibn Hassin. I am Recorder of Jihad. Today is 23 Rajab 1431.

Although I am President for Life Lars Hansen, I know only that this meeting was arranged by my Chief of Staff who, it seems, has a finely honed sense of humor in that he has scheduled the meeting with a dead person. I know little about the meeting except that it is scheduled for Camp David. It has something to do with governance policies particularly relating to my views on the "Falsifiers of Words Act" now before Congress. It basically states that anyone who is not a Muslim and makes any type of false statement to a Muslim or another infidel will be punished by hard labor or having his or her tongue cut out or both. What else I actually do know is that I could not be meeting with the person listed on the schedule, Senator Abigail Keayrn, mainly because she is the "late" Senator Abigail Keayrn—"late" meaning that she is dead, not delayed. The Immortal Leader had her stoned to death in the Tobago Quays before the take-over. Maybe it is that pesky Darby girl, Keayrn's go-for girl. She has been trying to set up a meeting with me using various guises since the Senator was reported as being killed in the Tobago Quays. However, no body had ever been found. That fact alone seems to keep Elle Darby alive.

As Caliphate Forces Marine One sets down on the Camp David heli-pad, I, President for Life Lars Hansen, do not know what to expect, and I really do not like that.

Zero Nine Hundred Hours

This is still 23 Rajab 1431. I am, once again, aboard Caliphate Forces Marine One. This time on my way from Camp David back to the White House. I have just witnessed something that I never thought I would see in my entire life. Tonight, I will give a world-wide July 4th address intertwining the July 4th that represents American Independence from the British and July 4th that represents Salah-ad-Din's victory over the Crusaders at the Horns of Hattin. The Immortal Leader and I are to be the honored guests at the New York celebration where we will blow up the Statue of Liberty. However, after what I have just witnessed in a meeting at Camp David, I am no longer sure about what I should say or do tonight.

At last, it is truly at hand.
What is at hand?
The final cleansing is at hand!
To the glory of the great Caliphate, the United States of Islam.
 In the name of Allah, the merciful and compassionate

Salaam Alaykum. May Allah be pleased with you.

29
Ragnarök at Rockfish Gap
(The Realm of Traitors)
[Music: "Ragnarök"]

Operation Ragnarök was Theo's term. He was the Scandinavian one of the bunch, although Gwynn had discovered more than a passing kinship with the Norse from his own Orkney Island connections. Ragnarök also served as their command password.

In Old Norse mythology, the word referred to a series of major "cleansing" events that would occur at some point in the future, including various natural disasters, a great battle, and the subsequent submersion of the world in water. Afterwards, the world would resurface, renewed and fertile.

"Live free or die, my friends," Gwynn whispered into the cell phone that connected to all The Nine forces across the country. "Live free or die!"

As those words launched the operation, the future became the present with nothing further to separate them.

* * * * *

Lars Hansen President for Life was clearly shaken to the core after the meeting at Camp David. In fact, he threw up just before he boarded Caliphate Forces Marine One. Finally, in one retching epiphany, he understood what was meant by something making you want to puke. Airborne and heading toward Washington, the helicopter disintegrated into a particle storm of fire, flesh, and bone that scattered President for Life Lars Hansen, his pilot and co-pilot, and two Caliphate secret service agents over a major portion of Catoctin Mountain Park at zero nine ten hours.

* * * * *

"Ellworth Hayes, here, atop a captured APC that's leading the victorious Nine troops in their mop up of the Battle of Rockfish Gap.

As you can see, their call to arms "Live free or die!" is popping and snapping in the evening breeze inscribed by fifty white stars in a blue field and shaped like the coiled snake on the "Don't Tread on Me" Gadsden flag. Otherwise, the battle flag is a replica of the flag of the United States of America.

"Reports from across the country are already coming in detailing victory after victory for the forces of The Nine.

"My former comrades-in-arms Gwynn Camsron, Theo Theodora, and Lincoln 'Walks Alone' Black are walking point for the mop up operation. They are searching, based on my intel, for the most likely location of the Immortal Leader's bus. We all want desperately to capture Saladin Keayrn, no matter what. He is, after all, our problem. He was once one of us."

They were all pledged to always protect a team member's back, no matter what. They were also pledged because of that to hold every team member accountable. That was what they were doing now to Sal. They were going to hold him accountable for his many betrayals.

Scouring the valleys near Rockfish Gap in their search for Caliphate Central Control was like journeying toward the center of the Ninth Circle of Hell. Everywhere, bodies bled and smoldered in heaps and piles like burning refuse. Some who still lived cried out in pain and horror, many begging for death. Wrecked jeeps, APC's, and tanks were strewn across the area for miles in all directions like twisted, charred, smoking sculptures.

Gwynn was beginning to wonder where all of them came from when he suddenly became aware of a great shape in the distance, mostly hidden by the smog of battle that still clung close to the ground. "Look at that! Can you see that?" The vague shape evoked prehistoric monsters, dragons, giants of the earth.

"What is it?"

"Can't make it out through this damned haze, Theo. Can you Gwynn?"

"No, Linc. I can't get a good enough look as yet."

"Whatever it is, LT, it's really big."

"We need to check it out before we move everyone forward much further."

"Yeah, Linc. Could be a trap."

"Okay, Theo. Get Captain Achilles on the com and tell him to close recon that area and report back to us ASAP."

Gwynn, Theo, and Lincoln continued to lead the advance toward the giant, smog-shrouded shape. For a brief moment, Gwynn thought he heard Flagg's voice guiding him through the island mists, and he idly wondered how Eynhallow Kirk could have suddenly been transported to the Virginia mountains. It was astounding how much the fog-cloaked form evoked those Scottish ruins.

As they led their troops through the nearly opaque air, they gradually saw the form for what it truly was. "Ladies and gentlemen, what seemed like some kind of prehistoric beast or dragon from a distance seems to actually be Saladin Keayrn's complex of connected buses that have served as the center of the Caliphate's power—Caliphate Central Command—and as the permanent home of the so-called Immortal Leader, Saladin Keayrn.

"The entire command center complex seems to be made up of five double-wide, double-deck buses attached like train cars, giving it the appearance of a monstrous centipede. The current skin on the bus depicts an epic battle that shows Armageddon for The Nine at the hands of the holy armies of the United States of Islam. I guess the bus art folks got that one wrong." Ellworth stifled a chuckle.

The sight of near-cartoon warriors of Islam annihilating The Nine army unnerved Gwynn, for a moment. Was that the reality and, they, the bus skin? Was he really still alive? Or had he been struck down, dead in battle but he did not yet realize it?

He remembered earlier screaming at Doctor Zenith Nadir who had been captured during the early stages of the battle of Rockfish Gap and quickly became a source of insider information no one expected. "You're telling me that Saladin Keayrn—the man you call The Leader . . . ."

"The Immortal Leader," Doctor Nadir corrected immediately almost as if he feared retribution if he did not. "Now, he is the Immortal Leader."

"You're saying that this man who blew himself and the Washington Monument all to hell last July Fourth, opening up the Inferno itself onto this earth, really is still alive?"

"That is exactly what I am saying," Doctor Zenith Nadir affirmed. "Exactly."

"And, how do you know this, Doctor Nadir?"

"I am one of only a very small handful of people who even know of his condition. Not even our esteemed President for Life knows. Everyone else believes the Immortal Leader is simply a recluse for religious and security reasons, but I treat him on a daily basis. Well, treating him may not be exactly the correct description of what I do, but I see him daily and minister to his living remains as best I can, having so little to work with." He contorted his face into a mask of great distaste.

"Living remains? What do you mean by that, Doctor?"

"Even being a doctor, it is difficult for me to look at him. I don't know what he will do without me or someone to give him constant care and attention."

"Where, Doctor? Where do you work?"

"Everywhere. Anywhere."

"What do you mean by that?"

"The Immortal Leader lives in a huge self-sufficient complex of double-decker buses that travel continually, changing veneer every few weeks as if that would somehow hide the fact that it is five connected buses. We were traveling with this convoy as part of a war games effort being conducted by Central Caliphate Command, ironically, to gain the protection of the troops so near to the old July Fourth. They were to escort us to Washington tomorrow.

"I'm sure that you will find the buses very well-protected by what is left of the convoy troops. Where they retreated to is where you will find the buses, and where you find the buses is where you will find the Immortal Leader. He cannot exist without them, and they believe they cannot exist without him."

∗ ∗ ∗ ∗ ∗

"Theo! Sal's alive!"

"What do you mean, Sal's alive? That's not possible!"

"I have a POW here at The Caverns of Woe interrogation center who says he's a doctor who, as he puts it, ministers to his living remains as best he can."

"I don't see how that's possible, LT."

"Believe me, Theo, I was there almost at ground zero, and I

don't see how he could have possibly survived either."

"So, does this doctor know where Sal might be?"

"Yes. It's a large complex of double-decker buses. He thinks five. He and several others live in one of the buses. When some of Rob Roy Brown's elite forces assaulted it, they thought they were going after a command center because of all the electronic and power hits they were getting with their equipment. The doctor had just stepped out for a smoke break when they hit. The buses buttoned up and sped away, leaving the doctor behind."

"Don't tell me. The buses got away."

"Yes LT. I hate to report it but the buses got away."

"I think we put some people on finding these buses that hold the living remains of Saladin Keayrn. What do you think?"

"I agree with you, LT. Let me get it moving. I'll put Achilles on it. The story was that his younger brother was smashed literally to bits by the same monster."

"Time is critical, Theo. We actually have the bastards on the run. Well, I guess partly because they don't know what it is they're running from."

"A couple of hours, tops?"

"Okay, Theo. That would be great. Let me know when it's located. I want to be in on the capture. As you well know, I have a personal thing or two to settle with the living remains of Saladin Kearyn."

* * * * *

"Ellworth Hayes again, still reporting from the front lines of this historic Battle of Rockfish Gap. Only a few fanatics remain to protect the Immortal Leader according to Captain Achilles' report over the com. They are still facing random small arms fire as Lead Team One continues to attack the bus complex, for the second time. Right now it's difficult to see any of the enemy combatants anywhere as our guys take control of the buses.

"We can still hear sporadic gunfire as our troops enter the middle bus area where the Immortal Leader is reportedly located."

Gwynn saw what he thought, at first, was an apparition leaning over some lumps in a hospital bed. The lumps appeared to be the living remains of Saladin Keayrn. Linc followed him inside and closed the door. The apparition turned toward them, its head and body covered in a radiant white robe. When it seemed to realize that they were not who it was expecting, the apparition raised a 9mm with both hands from the shadows of light created by the robe, pointing it at Gwynn.

Gwynn could not see the face, but he could see the eyes. The same hazel eyes that had enticed and seduced him aboard the Brown Pelican, the same hazel eyes that had stared out at him in seeming desperation from the video disk on Whale Island. Those were Abigail Keayrn's eyes. But, how could that be?

"But, you're dead. I saw you stoned to death on that video."

"Of course you did. You saw what we wanted you to see once the Immortal Leader, peace be upon him, showed me the way of Allah and I said the words.

"Look upon your Immortal Leader. When I finally witnessed for myself the power of his Allah, I realized that you can never prevail! There is no god other than Allah and Muhammad is His messenger. We will always win because you are weak," she shrieked at him, "even those of you who claim to be like us. Just ask what happened to Caliphate Forces Marine One earlier today with the President for Life on board." The 9mm trembled in her adrenaline-riddled hands.

"Death to all infidels! Death to all who oppose the Immortal Leader. Death to you, Gwynn Camsron! Allahu akbar!"

Gwynn remained frozen. He wanted to move. His instincts told him to move. But, he could not.

She pulled the trigger.

He was sure he could actually see the bullet coming at him while he stood there unable to do anything but watch the bullet coming at him.

"No!" Linc screamed and simultaneously shoved Gwynn out of the line of fire and onto the linoleum floor. The bullet hit Linc almost directly in the heart, taking out a small chunk of his shoulder blade as it exited his body due to the close range.

Gwynn clawed his way back across the floor to his fallen brother's side. Blood gushed from his heart through the wound in his chest with every pump. Gwynn grabbed his waterproof and tried to seal off the bleeding by applying it with pressure to the wound. It was something he remembered from basic training. "You stay with me, Walks Alone. You hear me? Medic! Stay with me, man. Stay with me! Somebody get a fucking medic!"

Linc looked up at him as best he could with his eyes nearly rolled back into the top of his head. "Remember how we put it to those suckers in Greensboro, brother? I guess we should've known even then that it was bound to end up like this—one of us dying in the other's arms."

"Medic!" There was a distant part of him that expected to hear the thumping rotors of hueys coming in to take them out of the jungle. Medic!

"Live free or die, brother." He gurgled blood as he repeated each word. "Live free or die." Then without further explanation or delay, Lincoln Walks Alone Black breathed his last, a partial smile frozen on his lips. Gwynn cradled him in his arms and wept like Francesca's humpback husband, without reservation or consideration of the circumstances or of the gun still pointed at him by Senator Abigail Keayrn. Although she still had him covered, the pistol now shook in her hands as she struggled to regain her control and her aim.

Theo approached Abbie from the side as he circled in from the previous bus. His pistol aimed directly at her head. "If you even look like you're *thinking* about pulling that trigger, ma'am, then I will be obliged to blow your skull into more pieces than your Immortal Leader."

She glanced toward him for a millisecond out of her periforal vision then refocused on the man on his knees in front of her with his dead friend in his arms. She did not see them as pitiable. She saw them as no better than cockroaches that deserved to be squashed, exterminated because they did not accept the way of Allah.

"And, I can assure you that I do not, under any circumstances, miss."

The Glock steadied as her hands calmed down and ceased to shake. She prepared to squeeze the trigger.

"Damn it, Abbie, I mean it! Put down the gun!"

At the last fraction of a second before her finger could complete the pull on the trigger, Theo fired three rounds into her head so fast it almost sounded like one round being fired. Her skull exploded. He just followed his training from all those years ago. Head shots kill. Multiple head shots kill instantly.

"Are you satisfied now, Sal?" Gwynn struggled to gain his feet as he slithered about in the blood of his friend. "Look at what you've done to Abbie, to Linc, to our country, Sal, and to yourself. You look worse than that character in Dalton Trumbo's movie *Johnnie Got His Gun*." He pretended to laugh.

"Just look around you. See who's lying dead on the floor around you. All former friends and lovers." He paused. "Oh, that's right." Then, he almost did laugh. "You can't look around, can you? Your mouth, like the Devil's, is all you can move, and you still talk out of all sides of it at the same time. Fortunes of war, Jihad, and all of that forty or seventy-two virgins and paradise stuff, you think?"

Gwynn trembled for control. Even with Lincoln and Abbie lying in pools of their own blood, his rage did not diminish. His desire for revenge did not abate. He could hardly believe that, once he had seen this pile of what was left of a human being, he still wanted to bash in his already bashed-in head. He still wanted to torture his already tortured body without mercy just to hear him scream. But could Sal even feel enough to scream. Could he feel anymore at all? Could he ever?

"Tell me, Sal. When you presided over the destruction of the Buddhas of Bamyan, did you ever, in your wildest dreams, think that your destruction of art and symbol would uncover fifty caves behind them, crammed full of even more art and symbols. Did you ever bother to find out that researchers believe the wall paintings at Bamyan were painted between the fifth and the ninth centuries by artists travelling on the Silk Road, the trade route between China and the West. They are some of the oldest oil paintings we know of on earth. And you who despise such things unearthed them.

"Well, that's sort of what has happened here, Mister Immortal Leader. You blew up our monument and discovered an army behind it that you did not expect."

"But none of that really matters much anymore, now does it, my old friend. Life and death have been simplified and reduced to a single red button, that one there, the one illuminating from the console of the portable life support unit beside you. It even has its own backup generator in case of power failure. Real state of the art stuff, that red button of life and death."

"So what do you want from me, Sal? Forgiveness? For there is none. Affirmation? Your affirmation is based on the troops who follow you willingly or unwillingly. And, they are all being hauled off to processing and rehab centers as we speak. Soon there will be none . . . .

"Or death? And, there is, by definition, none for the Immortal Leader."

"Just press the button," he interrupted. "That's all I want from you, my old friend." His voice broke. "Please, Gwynn. Just press the button. Let me go in peace."

"Forgiveness. Affirmation. Death. And, the greatest of these is death. These three to end your misery. Why should I?"

"By Allah, I let you go. I let you go twice."

"You did not let me go, Sal. You betrayed and abandoned me."

"So? What? So, now, you betray and abandon me?"

Gwynn reached out his right hand toward the red button. His fingers trembled still, but only slightly. Saladin Keayrn, son of Saladin Muhammad, flinched mentally at the expectation of being shut down by a button on a machine at any moment and finally knowing what it meant to be dead. "Do it, Gwynn! Push the button!"

The lights flickered then went out. The room became pitch black except for the green light on the backup generator showing that it was now operating and the red button on the life support console still glowing. They could no longer see one another.

"I choose to not kill every day of my life," Gwynn continued, his words seeming to lose their power as they swam through the darkness trying to reach that thing lying on that bed that he used to know as a friend, as a comrade in arms, as part of a team whose members would never betray one another.

"That's something most people never even consider, you know, never even think about. They don't consider the possibility that they have a conscious choice about it at all. It's their basic operating system, their modus operandi not to make any such choice. From birth, they are programmed *not* to even consider killing as an option except when the proper authorities tell them to kill. So, most people when they get pissed at somebody at work might think or say, 'I'd really like to kill that guy.' But they don't actually mean it. It's just an expression of extreme emotion. What they may do, however, is destroy the guy at the next staff meeting or the next intra-office basketball game. Me? I don't like being so directly accountable all that much, but I know that I always have a choice whether I like the choice I may have or not. The programming in me has been modified, so I do think about it. I do make a conscious choice not to kill or to kill depending on what the needs of the moment might dictate."

"Yes, but not today. Today, you killed and enjoyed it."

"I did kill today, out of choice, because of what I consider to be necessity. And, if you call that metallic taste of the enemy's blood in my mouth enjoyment because I know that taste means the enemy is vanquished, then, yes, I enjoyed it, also by choice. It is all about choices, Immortal Leader. Yours and mine."

"But I had no choice, my old friend."

"Oh, but you did! You chose not to kill me on Whale Island because of your team oath. Right?"

"Yes," he responded grudgingly.

"That makes it doubly hard for me to choose, you understand. Not only did you not kill me, but I am equally obligated by our team oath not to kill you as well."

"That's not the kind of choice we're talking about, my old friend. I was destined to be the Immortal Leader from the time I appeared in my mother's womb. I had no say in that. My mother and my father, even in death and martyrdom, made sure of that.

"When I was snatched in Vietnam during that staged ambush that you thought was an NVA scout unit, it was the New Brotherhood's elite come to rescue their future Leader and provide him with a new life, a secret life, so that he could prepare for what was to come. I thought that moment was the Washington Monument last July Fourth, but it seems that today was really the moment that was to come. Either way, how could I stop it from happening? I had no voice. I had no choice. I only obeyed the will of Allah."

"It is a truly convenient way to avoid accountability for your actions to think you have no choice, to be guided by some divine voice that you cannot produce yet claim you cannot ignore. It's like a Son of Sam defense: 'I was just following orders' or 'The dog made me do it?' That never worked for homework, and it certainly doesn't work for mayhem and murder.

"For me, I know my destiny brought me to this fight, but my choices brought me to this place and to you, Immortal Leader. And, I must say, the ninth circle of hell seems to suit you. It is the appropriate place for one who abandons and betrays those who loved him and nurtured him and kept him alive all of his life. Living in captivity forever as a pile of bones encased in what remains of your flesh—and to be conscious of that state—I believe is still not hell enough for you, Saladin Keayrn Muhammad."

Gwynn groped for the exit in the absorbing darkness, touching things as he went so that he would not slip on the blood covering much of the floor. He felt like he needed to get out of the bus before the darkness soaked him up too, like the spray of red light from the console. Once it was free of the bulb on the console the light was absorbed into blackness within a matter of inches. "Be careful coming out, Theo. The blood has made it very slippery over here."

He and Theo would return for Lincoln's body once power was restored. But, now, he definitely did not want to take Lincoln out in the darkness and inadvertently unplug or disconnect any of the systems essential to the continued survival of the Immortal Leader. Sal would be getting off way too easy if he disconnected him from that emergency generator.

Gwynn's fingertips touched, then grasped the metal handle of the exit door. It was like a rod of dry ice burning his hand with its Kelvin-like cold. "Have a great life, Sal." He had always believed that dry ice was some kind of perfect metaphor for the opposites of our existence. Robert Frost's fire and ice all rolled up into a single rod that was, now, the lever to the outside world. He pushed down on that lever and flung the door open. A red flare sputtered to life like a midnight sun over what was left of the Caliphate's troops being herded single file into truck after truck by The Nine forces. The prisoners would be taken to holding stations where they could be processed and, hopefully, released. Most of the Caliphate's military was forced service anyway. They were controlled primarily by drugs and fear, so they would probably need more drug rehab and psychological counseling than anything else.

"I'll contact the various teams and see how we stand with capitol takeovers, LT," Theo whispered from behind. "Sorry about Abbie. I had no choice."

"There's always a choice, Theo. I'm just glad you made the one you did. Thanks. You saved my ass."

"My pleasure, as usual, LT." From behind, he put his arms around Gwynn's neck for just a moment. "My God, it's a beautiful night, isn't it, LT?"

Gwynn watched the last flare fizzle and fade back into the Rockfish Gap darkness like the Caliphate was already fizzling and fading into the night of history, revealing a heaven full of other glittering interstellar histories, a sky full of stars.

"Now it is, Theo. Now it . . . ."

Cradled in the arms of his second in command, Gwynn Camsron's neck snapped much too easily. The clasp on the golden necklace broke. The Medallion of Bannockburn fell noiselessly onto the soft grass. He had always been so vulnerable to attack from the rear.

"Sorry LT. I had no choice."

THE END

[Music: "When in the Course of Human Events"]

About the Author

Timothy Brannan was born and raised in Raleigh, North Carolina. He holds a Bachelor of Arts in English and Philosophy and a Master of Arts in Literature and Writing from NC State University. Both as an undergraduate and a graduate student he was mentored by the late Dr. Guy Owen (*Ballad of the Flim-Flam Man*, *Season of Fear*) and submitted the first creative writing Masters thesis ever accepted at NC State University. Timothy later earned a Juris Doctor from Florida State University.

After serving in Viet-Nam in Army Military Intelligence and Psychological Operations and traveling around the country and Mexico, he met his life soul mate while working for a publisher in New York. They left the city and traveled all over the US in a yellow International Travel-All -- their own version of the Merry Pranksters bus. After marrying in 1972, they pursued Masters Degrees and then moved to the mountains of NC where Timothy taught GED in a youthful offender prison. In 1978 they moved to St. Thomas, USVI where Timothy served as the Chief of Staff for the USVI Senate Democratic Caucus. In that position, he was instrumental in the Virgin Islands being included in President Reagan's initial Caribbean Basin Initiative and in developing legislation that rescued the Virgin Islands economy. He has since served as Chief of Staff, Legal Counsel, and political consultant for a range of lawmakers, politicians and interest groups.

Timothy's fiction and poetry have been published in a variety of magazines and small press publications over the years. In 2008, they established Gemini Publishing and Gemini Studios in 2012 as projects to assure publication and production of his creative works.